Praise for Donna Grant
The Dark King series

"Loaded with subtle emotions, sizzling chemistry, and some provocative thoughts on the real choices [Grant's] characters are forced to make as they choose their loves for eternity." —*RT Book Reviews* (**4 stars**)

"Vivid images, intense details, and enchanting characters grab the reader's attention and [don't] let go."
—*Night Owl Reviews* (**Top Pick**)

The Dark Warrior series

"The world of the Immortal Warriors is a thoroughly engaging one, blending powerful ancient gods, fiery desire, and touchingly human love, which readers will surely want to revisit." —*RT Book Reviews*

"[Grant] blends ancient gods, love, desire, and evil-doers into a world you will want to revisit over and over again." —*Night Owl Reviews*

"Sizzling love scenes and engaging characters."
—*Publishers Weekly*

"Ms. Grant mixes adventure, magic and sweet love to create the perfect romance[s]." —*Single Title Reviews*

The Dark Sword series

"Grant creates a vivid picture of Britain centuries after the Celts and Druids tried to expel the Romans, deftly merging magic and history. The result is a wonderfully dark, delightfully well-written [series]. Readers will eagerly await the next Dark Sword book."

—RT Book Reviews

"Another fantastic series that melds the paranormal with the historical life of the Scottish highlander in this arousing and exciting adventure." *—Bitten By Books*

"These are some of the hottest brothers around in paranormal fiction." *—Nocturne Romance Reads*

"Will keep readers spellbound."

—Romance Reviews Today

TORCHED

DONNA GRANT

St. Martin's Paperbacks

This is a work of fiction. All of the characters, organizations, and events portrayed in this novel are either products of the author's imagination or are used fictitiously.

TORCHED

Copyright © 2018 by Donna Grant.

For information address St. Martin's Press, 175 Fifth Avenue, New York, NY 10010.

ISBN: 978-1-250-10959-0

Printed in the United States of America

Our books may be purchased in bulk for promotional, educational, or business use. Please contact your local bookseller or the Macmillan Corporate and Premium Sales Department at 1-800-221-7945, ext. 5442, or by e-mail at MacmillanSpecialMarkets@macmillan.com.

St. Martin's Paperbacks edition / June 2018

St. Martin's Paperbacks are published by St. Martin's Press, 175 Fifth Avenue, New York, NY 10010.

10 9 8 7 6 5 4 3 2 1

Sometimes we're blessed to have special people enter our lives, and I've been privileged to have such a person. Liz Berry isn't just a beautiful soul, she is one of those people who truly touches someone with her warmth and generosity.

Liz, this one is for you. Not only because you love the Dragon Kings, but because you had a thing for Ulrik from the beginning. Now you have your own Dragon King.

ACKNOWLEDGMENTS

Writing is a singular process, but it takes a special group of people to get a book ready to go out into the wild. A special shout out to everyone at SMP for getting this book ready, including the amazing art department for such a stunning cover that matches the character to perfection. Much thanks and appreciation goes to my exceptional editor, Monique Patterson.

To my amazing agent, Natanya Wheeler, who is on this dragon train with me.

A special thanks to my children, Gillian and Connor, as well as my family for the never-ending support.

Hats off to my incredible readers and those in the DG Groupies FB group for keeping the love of the Dragon Kings alive. Words can't say how much I adore y'all.

Dear Reader—

You have come on this journey with me through numerous books—some of you even from the very beginning with the Dark Sword *series. I've received so many emails over the years about Ulrik. And honestly, at the beginning, I wasn't sure if he could be redeemed. He has taken me on a merry ride of ups and downs, and his book nearly did me in while writing it. I don't think I've ever had such an emotional story where every word was like giving birth. Yet, how could I expect anything less from the King of Silvers?*

We writers put our hearts and souls into our stories, and I can't begin to tell you what an absolute thrill it is when readers become so caught up in a series that they come dressed as a character to a signing or create files of their thoughts on who Rhi's Dragon King is.

I wouldn't be here without all of you. This is my "Thank You" to each and every one of you for buying the books, for posting reviews, for sending me emails, and for keeping the love of the Dragon Kings going.

I love hearing you, so don't hesitate to reach out to me in the links below. Follow the magic, my lovelies!

xoxox,
DG

Website → www.DonnaGrant.com
DK Website → www.MotherofDragonsBooks.com
Newsletter → tinyurl.com/DonnaGrantNews
Text Alerts → text DRAGONKING to 24587
Facebook → facebook.com/AuthorDonnaGrant
FB Group → http://bit.ly/DGGroupies
Twitter → twitter.com/donna_grant
Instagram → Instagram.com/DGAuthor
Pinterest → Pinterest.com/DonnaGrant1
Bookbub → http://bit.ly/2siVQKK
Amazon → http://amzn.to/2f8xeP0
Goodreads → http://bit.ly/2vinVCD
Spotify Playlists → http://bit.ly/donnagrant_author

PART ONE

Fate will chew you up and spit you out many times, taking you away from those you love and dumping you into places you never wanted to be. It's up to each of us where we choose to belong. We can either fight everything, or accept what we're given and make the most of it.

—ULRIK

PROLOGUE

When it all changed...

Revenge was a powerful motivator. It was the only thing that kept Ulrik putting one foot in front of the other as he walked away from Dreagan.

It wasn't enough for Con to take away his magic. No, the King of Dragon Kings had also banished Ulrik from his home and friends. It was a cruel blow that turned Ulrik's hate and anger into one fiery need—vengeance.

After all he'd done for the Dragon Kings. Not only had he carved most of the dragons in the mountain caves, but he'd set the foundation stone of the home they would build, as well. Didn't that mean anything?

So what if he'd killed a few thousand humans? They had turned against all Dragon Kings despite the Kings allowing them to remain on the realm. Never mind that the mortals had betrayed him or slaughtered entire clans of the smaller dragons.

It was all Ulrik could do not to rush back to Dreagan and his mountain, to four of his Silvers that had been captured and lay sleeping. But that wasn't to be.

Don't look back.

Without thinking, he tried to shift so he could fly away. He stumbled down a hill when nothing happened.

He fell to his knees, his head lifted skyward. His chest clutched painfully as a bellow rose up within him. The clouds drifted lazily past, unknowing and uncaring that he craved to fly among them.

Not being able to shift was the most malicious, spiteful thing Con could've done to him. Constantine, the King of Dragon Kings, who was like a brother. His betrayal cut nearly as deep as Nala's.

"Nay," Ulrik stated through clenched teeth.

He wouldn't think of the human he'd given his love to who had deceived him. She was dead, and he'd made sure her soul was destroyed so she could never be reincarnated.

Ulrik lowered his head and climbed to his feet. He needed to get as far from Dreagan as he could. He'd flown around the entire world, so he knew exactly where he wanted to go. First, though, he had to get off the island.

He walked for days until he came to the coast. All around him, humans celebrated the defeat of the Dragon Kings, stupidly believing that all the dragons had departed the realm. How he wanted to kill them. His hatred grew for the beings without magic that he had once sheltered, cared for, and helped. He wanted them wiped away, ground into dust and forgotten.

Instead, he walked into the sea and began swimming. Even without his powers or the ability to shift, he was still immortal. And he was still a Dragon King. Not even Con could take that away from him.

But his old friend had made a grave mistake. The King of Kings should've killed him because Ulrik would go after Con. It was simply a matter of time before Ulrik acquired his magic again. After that, there was nothing that could stop him from challenging Con and taking over as King of Dragon Kings.

Then his fury would turn to the humans once more.

After Ulrik had reached land again, he walked. He lost count of the days as one bled into another, the sun rising and setting and rising again. His thoughts alternated between rage at not being able to shift, and loathing for Con turning against him.

But always, his disgust and revulsion for the humans was there.

He hiked through heat, wind, rain, sandstorms, and snow. He didn't eat, drink, rest. Or sleep. He shied away from anyplace there were mortals because he knew if he were close to them, he'd kill them all. Yet the humans seemed to be everywhere he turned.

Being banished from Dreagan, besieged by humans, and unable to shift was too much. He had nothing to hold onto, nothing that rooted him. And each day he couldn't take to the skies, he felt his mind cracking.

Where once he'd had an idyllic life surrounded by friends and family, knowing only peace and love, now he was living in Hell. With new demons clawing their way up his body and taking root in his mind—and his very soul.

The last thing he wanted was to be found by the mortals, so he ran to the highest mountain. He climbed to the top where the air was thin and freezing, and no human could survive. There, he found a cave that he staggered into before falling to his knees.

He clutched his head and screamed at the pain, the anguish, and the hatred inside him. The dragon within him clawed and roared to be released. The need consumed him until it was all he could think about.

Ulrik staggered to his feet and ran to the entrance before jumping into the air. He kept trying to shift as he fell thousands of feet before landing in an agonizing pile of shredded skin and broken bones.

Tears he couldn't hold back flowed as his body lay shattered among the rocks. If he couldn't shift, he wanted to die. But even that had been taken from him. His body mended itself, and he began the climb back to the cave.

He welcomed the cold and the hunger that pierced his stomach. He traveled so far back in the cave that he couldn't see the sky that made him ache to fly. There, he tried to slumber, but there was no way for him to take to the dragon sleep that would allow hundreds of thousands of years to pass.

Depression took him. He didn't move for days, staring at the cave walls as images of the life he had taken for granted blurred with the betrayal and banishment. He had no idea how much time passed before he finally rose and picked up a rock. With each dragon he drew, the more he yearned to shift and fly. The madness he'd felt after leaving Dreagan returned with a vengeance.

Ulrik could feel his mind slipping away piece by piece, and there was nothing he could do about it. He raged against Con, against the humans—against everything.

His hate devoured him.

And he welcomed it with open arms.

Hate was all he had. And in that loathing, he thought of various ways he could kill the humans and Con. Oh, the scenarios he imagined! They were the only things that gave him even a shred of satisfaction.

During his madness, there were fleeting moments of clarity that brought the ache of all he'd lost forward, slamming into him like waves crashing against the cliffs during a winter storm. Fortunately, the saneness never lasted long. So he continued to plot his revenge against Con and the mortals down to the last detail. The plans were elaborate and far-reaching, but in the end, he'd get the retribution he sought.

It felt amazing, rewarding even, to come up with such a scheme.

Then he'd remember that he was a Dragon King locked in a human's body.

Ulrik didn't know what prompted him to stop drawing one day and walk to the cave entrance. As he stood at the opening, he looked out over the world below and saw that the human settlements had grown.

It was a reminder of everything he'd lost when the Dragon Kings roamed freely, ruling the realm that was rightfully theirs since the dawn of time.

He returned to his drawing, but the next day, he went to the entrance once more. That continued for days, and then weeks.

Somehow through that, his mind began to clear, and the insanity started to recede. Yet one thing remained— revenge. It drove him, bringing to mind all the scenarios he'd concocted to bring down Con and the mortals.

Time to an immortal meant nothing. Ulrik didn't notice the rise and fall of the sun or moon. He didn't know when one day ended and the next began. What he lived with was the knowledge that he was utterly alone and trapped within a body he detested.

Perhaps it was the loneliness that prompted him to walk out of the cave. Whatever the reason, he traveled halfway down the mountain and stopped at a lake. Since he couldn't remember the last time he'd tasted water, he knelt at the edge and dipped his hand into the crystal blue depths.

The icy cold was the first thing he noticed. He brought a handful to his mouth and swallowed. It rushed down to his stomach like frozen fingers, but the taste was sublime. He drank until he could drink no more. As he leaned over the water, gazing out at the beauty, he realized he was hungry. Insatiably so. He looked down then and saw a face reflected back at him.

For a moment, he didn't recognize himself. His hair was well past his hips, and his face was covered in a long, thick beard. He held up his hands before him and saw that they were covered in dirt and muck. A glance at his naked body showed the same.

Ulrik rose and looked back up the mountain to where his cave was located. He could return and remain there. Or he could travel farther down and see what he discovered. For all he knew, the Dragon Kings were still sleeping and hiding.

He decided to continue down the mountain, though he kept hidden. When he reached the valley, he followed the river to where he'd seen the distant settlement. Except when he got there, he found a city.

It came as no surprise that the mortals laughed at his nudity, pointing their fingers and calling out crude comments. Not one offered him food, clothing, or shelter. He'd expected nothing different though.

He quickly hid and waited until nightfall before he stole clothes and shoes as well as a dagger. Then he returned to the lake. The moment Ulrik immersed himself to wash, it seemed as if the frigid water jolted the last vestiges of madness from him. Almost as if it jarred him from a long sleep.

He took his time bathing and swimming before he finally emerged. That evening, he hunted and ate his first meal in . . . well, a long time. He spent the night staring at the stars, recalling how it had felt to have the wind rush over his scales as he looked down upon the land, the trees nothing more than small dots.

And he promised himself that, however long it might take, he would fly once more.

The next morning, he used the dagger to shave and cut his hair. So when he looked at his reflection in the lake again, he could see traces of the man he'd once been.

But the trusting fool was long gone. He'd seen the horror that was humanity, and the disgust that was his fellow Dragon Kings. He recognized where he stood among them—alone.

And that was perfectly fine with him. He needed no one.

For to trust was to be betrayed.

Yet, he'd get close to the humans. He had a use for them that would lead him right to his goal of becoming the King of Dragon Kings. And his plan began that day.

Ulrik returned to the city. This time, the mortals either ignored him or gave friendly waves. For days, Ulrik wandered, observing people and mentally taking notes. It didn't take long to determine who the main players were. He wasted no time introducing himself and making the first move of many in his ultimate plan.

He also discovered that he'd been in his cave for over a thousand years.

For the next month, Ulrik continued to build on those key relationships. With just the right word, he was able to get the mortals to do whatever he wanted.

Soon, with everything in place, he set out for Scotland. Along the route, he repeated the steps he'd taken at the first city, finding the influential and important people. By the time he stepped off the boat onto Scottish soil hundreds of years later, he had a network of humans willing to do whatever he wanted.

Though he longed to return to Dreagan, he remained on the east coast of Scotland and traveled southward.

It did his heart good to be back on the soil of his home-land.

He began finding discarded items that intrigued him. At one settlement, he traded a vase for a bag of coin. In turn, he used that money to buy items to build lodging on a piece of land. He kept that parcel, changing it through the centuries until it became The Silver Dragon.

What had started as a place for him to store the items he found and a spot to sleep, eventually became his antique shop. It didn't take long for him to learn that he had an eye for finding things that others would pay handsomely for.

In a matter of months, he'd built up considerable wealth. Since he cared nothing for coin, he used it to strengthen and solidify the network he was creating.

He began loaning money to powerful individuals who had fallen on hard times, indebting them to him. Ulrik was shrewd and cunning—even devious—but when the future was at stake, he'd stop at nothing.

Two years later, he found himself near Dreagan. He'd been unable to stay away. Seeing the beauty of the land and feeling the magic that pulsed like a heartbeat made him recall that horrible day he'd lost everything.

He'd been stripped bare and left to rot. Somehow, through it all, he'd found his way back to sanity. The dragons he'd once considered his family, his brothers, no longer meant anything to him.

It wasn't just Con who'd turned against him. All the Kings had.

And every last one of them would pay.

CHAPTER ONE

February
Dreagan

Revenge could make you do things you swore you'd never do. At least that's what Ulrik told himself as he stood in the massive cavern that held his sleeping Silvers and faced off against Con.

"I'd say this is a surprise, but I'd be lying," the King of Dragon Kings said.

Ulrik looked over the man he'd once considered his brother. Con's blond waves were tousled. His black eyes were as impassive as his face. He wore an impeccable black suit. The white dress shirt beneath was free of wrinkles. Ulrik noticed the gold that flashed at Con's wrists. The gold dragon head cufflinks that he was never without.

"Is this where you challenge me?" Con asked.

Ulrik had fully expected to do just that. Taking over as King of Kings had been his goal from the moment Con banished him from Dreagan all those thousands of years before.

"No' this time."

Con raised a brow. "If you're no' here to challenge me, then why are you here?"

"To warn you." Though Ulrik had begun to wonder if he was losing his sanity again. Why the hell was he there?

There was a long pause before Con asked, "About?"

"Mikkel."

"Ah, Mikkel," Con said and put his hands into his pants' pockets. "Your uncle. How is it I doona remember him?"

Ulrik shrugged, not wanting to talk about family history. "He kept to himself mostly. He was a loner."

"How is Mikkel here?"

Ulrik turned and walked to the four caged Silver dragons. They slept peacefully, but it would only take one word from him to wake them. How he missed seeing the sun reflect off their silver scales.

"The simple answer is that he didna go over the dragon bridge with the others," Ulrik replied. "The complicated answer is that because he remained, there were a few seconds after you bound my magic that he became a Dragon King."

Concern lined Con's face, and his eyes briefly closed. Finally, Ulrik found something that could shake Con's cool exterior. But his joy was short-lived because Ulrik knew the ramifications of his uncle remaining behind.

"That doesna make sense," Con said with a shake of his head.

Ulrik put his hand through the bars and laid it upon the silver scales of the dragon closest to him. He softly stroked down the beast's long neck. "You know as well as I that no clan can be without a King. When one dies, or is unable to continue his duties, another is found."

"There were four Silvers within the mountain, but they were sleeping, so the duty couldna fall to them," Con said as he faced Ulrik.

"So it fell to the only one left—Mikkel." Ulrik scratched his brow and began to slowly walk around the huge cage. "He spied on me for . . . well, I doona know how long. He watched me, and he watched Dreagan."

Con's gaze narrowed. "He must have been verra good at hiding when he shifted."

Ulrik smiled and chuckled softly. "That's the only amusing part of this story. You didna just bind my magic, you bound the power of any Silver who might become King. As my abilities left me, Mikkel became a King and shifted into his human shape. Then he was left unable to return to his true form."

"Bloody hell," Con murmured.

Ulrik stopped and squatted beside the cage next to one of the dragon's heads. "While your attention has been on me, Mikkel has carved out a spot for himself."

"How long have you known he was here?"

"A few years. He showed up at my store. At the time, his plans aligned with mine, so we joined forces."

Con walked to stand beside Ulrik and leaned against the metal bars. "And now?"

"I realized immediately that Mikkel was using me. If he'd been strong enough to become a Dragon King, he'd have taken over when my father was killed in battle. Instead, the honor came to me." Ulrik straightened and looked Con in the eye. "Mikkel tried to control me these last years. I allowed him to believe he was."

"But you used Darcy's Druid magic to unbind what we'd done."

"Aye."

"How many Druids died trying to touch dragon magic before you found Darcy?" Con demanded.

Ulrik shrugged. "That's of no consequence right now."

"I beg to differ. Just as Darcy did when you tried to kill her."

"If I hadna, Mikkel would have. I timed it perfectly so the Druids could find her."

Con's face contorted with disbelief. "I'm supposed to believe you?"

"Do or doona. I've no reason to lie."

"You only have one reason. One agenda. To kill me."

Ulrik didn't bother to confirm or deny Con's claim. Why state what each knew was truth? It was a waste of time.

"Watch out for Mikkel. He's a devious bastard who intends to take your place," Ulrik said as he pivoted on his heel and began to walk away.

But Con's voice stopped him. "That's why he has Eilish."

Ulrik turned back to Con. "Eilish has power we've never seen in a Druid before. She could verra well kill a Dragon King for all we know. Right now, Mikkel has her focused on you, but I'm also on her radar."

"She helped Esther and Nikolai. Perhaps I can dissuade her from working with Mikkel."

"He has information she wants. Until you learn what that is, she'll remain under Mikkel's thumb." Ulrik glanced at his Silvers. "I'm leaving them here for the time being, but make no mistake. I *will* wake them."

Con's face was unreadable as he regained his composure. It had always been a handy trick. Something Con had learned when he was a youngling. It kept people guessing about what he was thinking.

"Will Eilish unbind Mikkel's magic so he can shift?" Con asked.

Ulrik gave a single shake of his head. "I doubt it, but I hope she does. She's a smart one. She knows all about the Dragon Kings, so I'm sure she has figured out what has obviously escaped Mikkel. If she unbinds his magic, he'll return to his true form—that of a dragon."

"Because he isna a King, he can no' shift back and forth."

"Precisely. He may listen to her, but if he doesna, he'll be easy to track and . . . detain."

Con gave him a flat look. "You mean kill."

"Your point?"

"He's in your path. You want me to be up in arms over the chaos he's caused, when in fact, you've caused some of it yourself. You wouldna be here now if Mikkel were no' in the picture. He messed up your plans."

Ulrik took a deep breath and glanced at the ceiling as he nodded. "That he did. I've been forced to reevaluate things."

"So you came here out of the goodness of your heart? To warn me?"

"Something like that." Ulrik then clasped his hands behind his back and touched the silver bracelet that allowed him to teleport out of the cavern.

But he didn't leave Dreagan. Instead, he went to Con's mountain, far below the surface where Con kept a weapon that the Dark coveted. It was the only instrument on the realm that could wipe out the impervious Dragon Kings.

Which meant Ulrik could use it against Mikkel.

He walked a few feet in front of the weapon and stared. It was bathed in a soft light that hovered above the wall. Hidden for eons, the King of Kings obviously knew of the weapon, as did Kellan, the Keeper of History, but Ulrik had discovered it about eight hundred years earlier when he was hiding in the mountains.

He knew next to nothing about it. Not how to use it or even if he could. Yet it was a risk he was willing to take if it came down to it. There was no way he was going to allow Mikkel to take everything he'd come back from madness to obtain. He'd wallowed in his insanity for centuries, but it was his need for revenge that slowly brought him back.

And Mikkel was now standing in the way of that.

Ulrik wasn't exactly keen on removing a member of his family, but Mikkel had given him no choice. Now that the two of them were at war, Ulrik would have to move up some of his plans and once more alter a few of them.

While staring at the weapon, he thought of Eilish. The Druid's power made her a formidable enemy. It was too bad he couldn't convince her to join him. She would be an amazing asset. And he wouldn't ask her to kill Mikkel.

Because he wanted to do it himself.

Ulrik walked closer and raised his hand. Right before he touched the weapon, he felt dragon magic. He smiled and dropped his arm. Of course, Con had surrounded the area with magic to alert him if anyone ever tried to take his prize.

"You win, old friend," Ulrik murmured to himself. "For now. But don't expect that to last much longer."

He turned on his heel and began walking back through the tunnels of the mountain. Ulrik wasn't sure why he didn't teleport out. Perhaps it was because he wasn't anxious to leave.

No matter what, Dreagan would always be the home he'd chosen, the place he'd helped to discover and mark as the Dragon Kings'.

He walked for several minutes in the darkened tunnels before he stopped. Being a Dragon King gave him the ability to see as well in the dark as the light, and his gaze had snagged on something along the wall next to him.

It was an outline of two dragons that had been chiseled into the rock. Ulrik put his hand on the one nearest him and looked at the second.

A long forgotten memory surged of he and Con laughing and teasing each other about Ulrik's upcoming vows with Nala. Con had had reservations because she was mortal, but he completely backed Ulrik's decision.

"When are you going to find your own woman?" Ulrik asked.

Con shook his head. "Doona concern yourself with me."

"You're my friend, my brother. Of course, I'm going to worry about you."

"It's a waste of time."

Ulrik laughed. "Come. I've a surprise for you."

They walked deeper into the mountain and stopped before the long wall. Ulrik watched as Con ran his hands over the lines of the dragons.

"You and me," Ulrik said. "No friendship has ever been stronger, and there's nothing that will ever tear apart our bond."

Con looked at him, a wide smile in place. "Brothers."

"Brothers."

CHAPTER TWO

Ireland

It was too bad Eilish had discovered that the price for information was more than she wanted to pay. Though she should've known the cost would be steep. Especially when dealing with a man like Mikkel.

Except he wasn't a man. He was a dragon, who was now locked in human form.

She'd taken an instant dislike to Mikkel from the first moment he walked into Graves. The others in the bar had glared at him with hate or gave him a wide berth. The fool actually thought the occupants had feared and respected him.

In fact, the Fae—both Dark and Light—and the Druids who recognized Mikkel, detested him for various reasons. The mortals had enough sense to stay away from him.

Eilish drummed the fingers of her left hand on the black wood of the bar. Her claw-tipped finger rings clicked softly while the lights twirled, music blared, and bodies swayed. She heard and saw none of it. Her mind was occupied with . . . other things.

The deal she'd made with Mikkel was contingent on the information he possessed about her mother. While Eilish had been raised in Boston, her father and stepmother never spoke of her birth mother. Even when Eilish asked specific questions, they always turned the conversation away. The more secretive they were, the more determined she became to find out details on her own.

She'd begun digging for information about her mother but found nothing. It wasn't until she overheard her father mentioning something about her mother's family in Ireland that she had a destination.

The next week, she'd bought a ticket and boarded a plan to the Emerald Isle after leaving her father a note. The moment her feet touched Irish soil, she'd felt the magic within. This was where she belonged.

Coming to Ireland hadn't gotten her any closer to finding her mother, though. It was difficult without a name. But that didn't stop her. She was a Druid, after all.

And she had the finger rings.

The day she received them was the only time her Dad had spoken of her mother. He'd handed her the small box on her eighteenth birthday and said, "These belonged to your mum. Don't ask me any more than that."

The magic within the finger rings was astounding. As soon as she'd put them on, the magic seeped through her skin and made her one with the jewelry.

After that, she'd rarely removed them. Once in Ireland, they stayed on her fingers, even in sleep. They were her connection to her mother. Somehow, she knew they would lead her to the answers she sought.

A glass of whisky was slid in front of her. Eilish lifted her gaze to Cody, her lead bartender. His blue eyes crinkled at the corners before he winked at her. Then he turned away, running a hand through his blond curls as he spoke with a customer.

Eilish drained the whisky and slowly set down the empty glass. Mikkel had found her at Graves, though she had yet to learn how he knew of her, or discovered that the bar was hers. Most likely, it was through his network of spies.

Graves was her sanctuary. When she came to the small village, she'd fallen in love with the old building as soon as she saw it. Eilish also noted the number of Fae who walked the streets, some in disguise, some not. The idea of opening a pub where she could keep an eye on the Fae took root. It wasn't long before she began testing out her magic against any who dared to even think of harming anyone in the village.

Somehow, the people within the small community became hers to look after. It took only one encounter against the Fae for them to realize she would stand by the rules she set and carry out the punishment—death— to any who preyed upon those in the village.

Despite that, Druids and Fae flocked to Graves, a place where they could be themselves. Even the mortals who entered the building were aware that the bar was far from normal. Yet not one human died within its walls, and no one had been killed—or disappeared—because of a Fae.

Eilish looked at the dance floor before her gaze moved to the curving stairs that led to the upper level. When her eyes locked on the man standing on the landing staring at her, her heart actually skipped a beat.

Until she realized it wasn't Ulrik. Though the two were nearly identical with their impressive physiques, shoulder-length black hair, and gold eyes, it was the gray hair at Mikkel's temples that gave him away. That and the deadness of his eyes.

Her disappointment was so great that she had to keep herself from showing her disgust. The last time she and Mikkel had spoken, it hadn't gone well at all.

He gave her a nod and made his way down the stairs. As usual, the sea of people parted around him. He took the stool beside her and motioned for the bartender.

Cody looked her way. She gave him a nod to pour the drinks.

"I hear my nephew paid you a visit."

She stared into Mikkel's golden eyes and noted the fake British accent. She had no idea why he pretended, but it was easy to draw out the Scottish brogue. She just needed to make him angry.

For a moment, Eilish could almost pretend it was Ulrik sitting next to her. But Mikkel had spoiled that by speaking. "He came to see me, yes," she answered.

"How did he know of you?"

"You know. I hate spies. More than that, I hate people spying on me."

His smile was cold and calculating as he took the glass Cody set before him and drank down one and then the other whisky. Then he met her gaze. "We had a deal, you and I. You carry out my orders, and when I'm finished with you, I'll give you the information you covet."

"No."

There was a pause before he chuckled. "You promised to kill Ulrik and Con."

"I said I'd kill Ulrik in exchange for the information. You added Con later," she stated.

"Which you agreed to."

She felt magic pulse through her left hand from the finger rings in response to the anger that rose within her. Instead of blasting him with her magic, she took a deep breath and released it. "I did, but I didn't agree to be at your beck and call. What happened in Venice with Sebastian? Don't do that again."

"Or what?" Mikkel asked with a smile that didn't reach his eyes.

"Or I won't help you."

He shook his head, giving her a look as if she were a wayward child. "Oh, my dear, but you will. Because you want to know who your mother is."

She'd had enough of him holding that over her. "The only new knowledge you've shared is that her name is Eireen."

"I have her surname. That would make it easy to find her."

"I don't believe you."

Instead of becoming angry, Mikkel smiled. "You want it, you'll have to kill Ulrik."

Eilish swallowed at the news and kept her face impassive. "Now?"

"Yes."

She bowed her head. "Once he's dead, you'll tell me my mother's last name?"

"Of course. I always keep my word."

It was on the tip of her tongue to call him the lying bastard she knew him to be, but she kept her mouth shut.

Mikkel leaned closer, studying her. "What did you and Ulrik speak about when he visited?"

She almost asked him which time but decided to see how much his spies knew. Ulrik's first visit had been inside Graves. The second had been out back. That would make it easy to determine where Mikkel's spies were.

"Not much. He saw us in The Silver Dragon. Apparently, the store has some magic you didn't know about." Neither had she, but then again, she hadn't cared about being seen.

Maybe that should become more of a concern.

Mikkel's gaze narrowed briefly. "So he knew we were both there?"

"Yes."

"And?"

She fought not to roll her eyes. "He said he wanted to meet the Druid working for you."

"Is that all?"

"Yes."

"He did nothing else? Said nothing else?" Mikkel pressed.

It was Eilish's turn to narrow her gaze. "We threatened each other and had a drink. That was it."

"Good. Keep it that way."

"You say that as if you think something will happen between Ulrik and me."

His hand came to rest atop hers. It was everything Eilish could do not to yank away from him. By sheer will alone, she kept still, watching him intently.

"If you ever do find yourself . . . attracted . . . to him, call me."

Even though she knew better, she still asked, "Why?"

"In case you missed it, Ulrik and I could be twins."

Perhaps in looks, but that's where it ended. Eilish kept that bit to herself. There was no need to tell Mikkel that she thought Ulrik was a better man in all ways.

"I'll be seeing you soon, my dear," Mikkel said before he slid off the stool and walked away.

Eilish didn't release her breath until Mikkel had walked out the door. By then, she'd had enough of the crush and noise of Graves. Odd since she'd sought out exactly that to help drown out the thoughts in her head about Ulrik.

She pushed off the stool and walked to the stairs

behind the bar that led up to the third floor, which was her private residence. The door was locked to her magic only so no one else could get in.

Eilish hurried inside and halted. "So Mikkel's spy is within Graves."

Since he hadn't said anything about Nikolai or Esther being with Ulrik on his second visit, it was easy to deduce. Mikkel's spy could be anyone—a patron or even an employee.

Wonderful. She'd never worried about being spied on before, but now she'd be driven to look for the person. Or people.

Damn Mikkel.

Damn Ulrik.

Damn her father.

Damn her mother.

If only Eilish didn't have this drive to learn of her mother. If only she could put the past behind her and never let it intrude upon her again. But the questions nagged her. Questions she desperately needed answers to.

That need had led her to work with Mikkel. She wasn't a murderer. In fact, the only person she'd ever killed was the Dark Fae who accosted her when she first arrived in Ireland, the one who went against her rules and attacked a member of the village.

Yet she'd agreed to kill not one, but *two* Dragon Kings. All to have Mikkel pass on the full name of her mother. God. What was she becoming?

She wasn't sure she could look at herself in the mirror. And she hadn't even killed anyone yet. But she had done horrible, horrible things. She'd crossed a line long ago.

And she was just now realizing that.

What did that tell her about her life?

"I'm fucked. Totally."

She had two choices. Either she could embrace who she was becoming and do everything Mikkel asked so she could finally get the answers she sought about her mother.

Or . . . she could shake off the hold the past had on her and tell Mikkel to kiss off.

Her thoughts went to the man Nikolai and Esther claimed was her real father—Donal Cleary. A man who had loved her mother. Someone who now resided in London.

Not long ago, Eilish had stood outside The Porterhouse pub for an hour, debating whether to confront Donal. In the end, she had chickened out.

Donal was a link to her mother. At least Eilish hoped he was. She believed Nikolai and Esther. She wasn't sure she could take it if they had lied to her. The knowledge of Donal had given her a small thread of hope, and she was clinging to it with everything she was. He could be what allowed her to sever her link to Mikkel.

She felt as if she were coming unhinged. As if she no longer knew what was right and what was wrong. As if she were spinning in circles and letting chance throw her off the crazy ride she was on.

And, dammit, why did she have to keep thinking about Ulrik?

He surprised her again and again. First, by coming to see her. Then by helping his fellow Dragon King, Nikolai. Eilish had sensed there was a deep friendship there, one Ulrik was trying to ignore.

But he'd done a poor job of it because the next thing she knew, Ulrik was helping Nikolai fight a group of Dark.

That's when she'd gotten to see Ulrik in his true form. Silver, sleek, powerful. He was insanely beautiful. And terrifying.

CHAPTER THREE

Dark Fae Palace

The malicious intent of the Dark fairly seeped from the gray stones of the palace to soak the air and everything around it. And Ulrik could care less.

Before he'd been banished from Dreagan, he would've fought the Dark with everything he was. He would've laid waste to them, happily ripping them apart.

Now, he was aligned with one.

And not just any Dark. The new king, Balladyn.

Ulrik moved through the arched corridors of the palace, walking past many red-eyed, black-and-silver-haired Fae on his way to see the new leader. He'd known it was only a matter of time before Balladyn killed Taraeth and took over.

It would be a shock for a lot of the Dark who had only known Taraeth as king. He'd reigned longer than any other Dark king before him, but Ulrik suspected that Balladyn might last even longer than Taraeth.

A lot of that had to do with Balladyn himself. Once the commander of the Light Army and captain of the Queen's Guard, he had been revered and respected by the Light Fae. But all that had changed when Usaeil, the Light Queen, learned that Balladyn was in love with Rhi.

Petty, demanding Usaeil hadn't been able to accept that. Not because she loved Balladyn but because she was jealous of everything Rhi was—and Usaeil wasn't.

It wasn't until quite recently that anyone learned how the queen had approached Taraeth and asked him to kill Balladyn. Except, instead of killing him, Taraeth turned Balladyn Dark.

Now, the new king was after his own revenge—against Usaeil.

And where did that leave Rhi?

The first female of the Queen's Guard, Rhi had loved—and lost—a Dragon King. After millennia apart, Balladyn's and Rhi's paths crossed again. It still amazed Ulrik that despite everything, Balladyn's love for Rhi had trumped his hate.

Balladyn had also managed to convince Rhi of his feelings, and the two were now lovers. But for how long? Whether Balladyn wanted to admit it or not, Rhi was still very much in love with her Dragon King.

But that was one relationship Ulrik wouldn't get in the middle of. Rhi was more than capable of handling things herself.

At the last minute, Ulrik detoured from his path and turned left to the stairs. He went up two levels and made his way through the maze of hallways until he stood before a door. For long minutes, he silently stared at it before pushing it open.

He remained in the doorway, refusing to go inside. All the blood had been cleaned, and the body removed. But nothing would erase the memory of Muriel viciously killed by Mikkel. It was just one more reason Ulrik wanted to take out his uncle.

Muriel had been Taraeth's slave and forced to spy

upon Ulrik. But she had risked everything by coming to Ulrik with a proposition. She would give him information if he helped her get revenge.

It seemed that everything always came back to retribution. It didn't matter what species, it was a driving force.

"I figured you'd come here," said a deep, Irish voice.

Ulrik turned his head to the side as Balladyn walked up beside him. Balladyn nodded his head of long, black-and-silver hair in greeting.

Ulrik returned the nod. "Muriel didn't deserve such a death."

"Some would disagree with you. She was Dark, after all."

Ulrik frowned. "And you are King of the Dark."

Balladyn's face broke into a smile. He crossed his arms over his chest, his black shirt stretching tightly across his shoulders. "That I am. And it's fekking fantastic."

"I take it the transition went smoothly?"

"It has."

Ulrik closed the door to Muriel's room, saying his final farewell. Together, he and Balladyn walked. After the group of Dark Fae that attacked Nikolai and Esther, Ulrik wondered if Balladyn had heard he joined the fight. "Have you spoken to Rhi?"

Balladyn gave a half-hearted shrug. "I've not."

"I hear anger in your words."

Balladyn halted and turned to him. His face contorted with such fury that it surprised Ulrik. "I thought she was on my side."

"Rhi is loyal to a fault. You know that."

"Aye. Loyal to the Dragon Kings," Balladyn spat.

This was growing stranger by the second. "What happened?"

Without a word, Balladyn grabbed Ulrik's arm and

transported them to his private chambers at the top of the palace. There, Ulrik watched as Balladyn paced away, letting the full force of his rage show in his clenched fists and contorted face.

"You said I could trust you. That we were to trust each other."

Ulrik nodded. "That's right. It's no' something either of us does lightly."

"No. We don't." Balladyn stopped and whirled to face him, his chest rising and falling rapidly as he stared at Ulrik for a long, silent minute. "When I attacked Taraeth, the bastard managed to get me with a blade. I killed him, but I was also dying."

Ulrik could guess what happened next. "You called out to Rhi."

"I wanted her with me when I went. Instead, she brought Con."

Now Ulrik was truly shocked. Con, who could heal anything but death, was one who never went against his moral standards—and Con had a particular hatred for the Dark. As all Dragon Kings did. Well, all but him. Ulrik would've bet his entire, sizable fortune that Con would've refused to heal Balladyn.

But the truth stood before him now.

"Aye," Balladyn said with a nod, his red eyes burning with hate. "That's right. The fekker healed me."

"Did he ask for something in return?"

"He left without a word."

Now, that was truly odd. Ulrik glanced out the window to see it raining heavily, preventing him from seeing the pretty Irish countryside the Dark claimed as theirs. A magical barrier stopped anyone from viewing the palace, and any mortal who was stupid enough to get close lost his or her life to one of the thousands of Dark who called the palace home.

Ulrik watched Balladyn carefully. The Dark had changed, and it wasn't all because he was now king. Though they were getting to the root of the problem. "But you were healed and able to take your new position."

"Aye." Balladyn stalked to stand in front of Ulrik. "When I mentioned to Rhi that I didn't like being beholden to Con, she said that I could wipe the slate clean by stopping the attacks on Dragon Kings."

"And your response?"

"We exchanged a few more words, and then I came here to take my rightful place," Balladyn stated.

Now Ulrik had his answer. Balladyn was changed because Rhi asked Con to heal him, and Con did. Rhi had wanted to save her friend and lover. It had never entered her mind that Balladyn would think he owed Con.

But that's not how Balladyn saw it. And he'd never see Rhi's side.

Ulrik could only imagine how Rhi must be hurting. Whether she'd meant to or not, she'd become a dear friend to the Dragon Kings, and not just because she loved one. Because she was loyal and true.

While nothing but pain and heartache had been dealt to her time and again.

In many ways, Rhi fascinated Ulrik. How she could get beaten down so many times and manage to find her feet again without being consumed by the need for vengeance intrigued him. But the light within Rhi shone brighter than in any other being in the universe.

It made her stand out. It made everyone flock to Rhi. It made her a friend—and an enemy no one wanted. It made her special and unique.

And with just a few words, Balladyn had lost her forever.

The bastard didn't even know it yet. He was too caught up in his anger to see it, but it was obvious to Ulrik. And when Balladyn finally realized it, the fallout would be immense.

"I hear you released a new edict to the Dark," Ulrik said.

One side of Balladyn's lips lifted in a smile. "Open season on humans."

"Just so you know, a group of Dark attacked a mortal a few nights ago. That human happened to be the mate of a Dragon King. One I took into my home as a youngling and raised."

Balladyn was quiet for a heartbeat. Then he asked softly, "You fought alongside a King?"

"I am a Dragon King. And aye, to answer your question, I did. I willna have any King lose his mate."

"Even if that King is Con?"

Ulrik held Balladyn's gaze for a long minute, refusing to answer.

"How many of my Dark were killed?" Balladyn asked.

"All seven."

Balladyn turned away at the news. "Have your objectives changed?"

"They've no'. I still intend to kill Mikkel, and I will challenge Con."

"Mikkel was scheduled for a meeting with Taraeth an hour ago. He was a no-show."

Ulrik wasn't surprised. "It looks as if a Dark is spying in the palace for my uncle."

"I'll find the culprit. I was looking forward to that meeting so I could kill Mikkel."

"He willna go down that easily. It will take someone with a more cunning and devious mind than he has. Me."

Balladyn turned back to Ulrik and chuckled. "I'd like to be there to see it."

"It'll happen soon. I'm expecting a visit from the Druid."

The Dark's forehead furrowed. "The one Mikkel believes can kill Dragon Kings?"

"The verra one."

"You don't sound fearful. Is it because you know she can't hurt you?"

Ulrik lifted one shoulder in a shrug. "I've no doubt she can. If it's meant for her to end me, then she will. The power within her is palpable. She's strong, and she knows it. Mikkel was smart to get her to align with him."

"Where is this Druid?"

"In Ireland. She owns Graves."

Balladyn nodded his head in recognition. "I've heard some Dark speak of the pub. I didn't realize she was the Druid running it. I hear she's put that village under her protection. Even humans go to the bar, and none of the Fae harm them."

"It's true. I've seen it for myself."

"I might need to pay her a visit."

Ulrik felt a wave of protectiveness rise within him, but he hastily shoved it aside. Eilish needed safeguarding from no one, especially him.

In his mind's eye, he kept seeing her standing in the shadows, watching him and Nikolai fight the Dark. He'd even briefly contemplated going to her and talking again, but that was a foolish move.

After all, soon, she'd come to kill him.

Or rather *try* to kill him. He wasn't going to allow that to happen.

"By the way," Balladyn said. "Did you ever hear of a Dark Fae named Fintan?"

Ulrik gave a shake of his head. "Who is he?"

"A white-haired Dark."

"Ah. The most feared assassin Taraeth had. I saw him once, but never knew his name." Ulrik cocked his head to the side. "I heard Taraeth had him killed."

Balladyn ran a hand down his face. "If he did, then I talked to another white-haired Fae recently."

"Oh? Where was this?"

"Galway. He said there's a Fae named Bran who is building an army."

This was the first Ulrik had heard anything about this. "Is he right? Is this Bran gathering troops?"

"I continue to have Dark go missing. This white-haired Fae says Bran is the cause. Somehow, this fekker is getting to my people without me knowing."

Ulrik tugged the cuff of his dress shirt and shifted his shoulders in his suit jacket. "Doona divide your attention. Focus on one problem at a time. We take care of Mikkel, and then I'll challenge Con."

"I am focused, but I'm not going to let this problem continue."

Ulrik knew it was pointless to keep talking to Balladyn about it. "Watch your back."

"Same to you."

With a nod, Ulrik pivoted and exited the room. Unfortunately, no matter how hard he tried, he couldn't stop thinking about the Druid.

So, when he touched the silver cuff on his wrist, it was no surprise that he found himself at Graves.

CHAPTER FOUR

He needed to find her. Ulrik didn't know why he searched for Eilish, only that the demand consumed him.

Thinking of her thick, dark hair had him searching everywhere for a glimpse of her inside the pub. He explored both floors to no avail. His gaze lifted to the ceiling above him. The building had another floor, and Ulrik suspected that it was her private space. Which meant there was a way to get to it from inside. He just needed to find it.

If it were him, he'd hide the door and stairs so the entrance was difficult to find. Since she'd want it fairly protected, Eilish wouldn't put the access where anyone could stumble upon it. Which meant it would be somewhere semi-protected.

His eyes slid to the bar. For the next thirty minutes, he studied every angle of it until he found the hidden doorway. He slipped unnoticed through it and then began to ascend the stairs.

When he reached the top and found the doorway barred with several layers of Druid magic, he smiled.

"Clever," he murmured.

Her magic was strong enough to keep other Druids and even Fae out. But there was nothing stronger than dragon magic. He was able to get through her spells and open the door without any trouble.

He came to a halt as he looked around the wide space. Closing the door softly, he leaned back against it and saw two other doors, most likely her bedroom and the bathroom. In all the millennia he'd dealt with antiques, he discovered much about a person simply by how they decorated their space.

A lack of adornment could mean the person was a minimalist who enjoyed clean lines. The eccentrics loved anything and everything, never deciding on one type of style.

While there was a myriad of varieties between the two polar opposites, Ulrik's favorite type of designer was the one who knew what they liked and felt comfortable surrounding themselves with it.

Eilish was exactly that.

The Druid tilted more toward the minimalist side in that there were few decorations about. But there were two things in abundance—books, and plants.

There were a few paintings on the walls, and each was of an Irish landscape, varying in colors and depictions, but they had the common element linking them. One long wall was taken up by floor-to-ceiling bookshelves. And each shelf was filled with books.

In fact, there were volumes stacked in other places about the room, as well. He grinned when his gaze slid to the end table beside the sofa that had three titles stacked, with a lamp resting on top.

There was a small table with two chairs close to the kitchen. The only other place to sit was the Chesterfield sofa that had seen many years as evidenced by the creases in the dark brown leather.

There was a book lying on one of the cushions with what looked like a torn piece of paper between the pages marking her spot. Draped on the back of the sofa was a crocheted blanket with ten-inch-long chevrons in a mix of gray, rustic brown, cream, and navy stripes.

Somehow, he wasn't surprised to find an antique, wool, Tabriz rug. Persian rugs were known for their masterful weave, with each piece having a meaning.

Ulrik walked to the floor covering for a closer look. The allover pattern consisted of many recognizable Oriental motifs such as the lotus flower, palmettes, and even Persian roses called *gül* in a tonal brown palette with shades of beige and taupe.

He bent and touched the tasteful floral design outer border that completed the glamorous composition. This was a rare rug, and one for connoisseurs. Ulrik would've paid any price to have it himself if he'd known it was for sale. The fact that Eilish had such an eye for beauty only revealed another layer to the exceptional woman.

Because he knew the rug and the paintings weren't there by happenstance. Eilish knew art, or at least she knew what she liked.

He heard movement in one of the other rooms and slowly straightened. A heartbeat later, the door opened, and Eilish walked out with a watering can in hand. She went from plant to plant, stroking their leaves and talking to them as she watered.

It was another aspect of her that he hadn't expected. Most people had artificial plants in their homes because they wanted the green color without the responsibility.

But Eilish surprised him again.

Her dark locks were loose and tucked behind her ears. She wore a pair of black jeans and a wide-necked cream sweater that exposed a shoulder and her mocha skin. And she was barefoot.

Ulrik didn't know why that pleased him, but it did.

He studied her at his leisure. If he were honest, he'd admit that her oval face with her incredible high cheekbones, large eyes, and full lips captivated him. She was a beauty without compare. He could say that with honesty because he'd seen some truly gorgeous women. And not one rivaled Eilish.

It wasn't just her face or her amazing body that was trim and toned with long legs and mouthwatering curves. It was her mind, her astuteness, and her strength that entranced him.

She finished watering the ivy and was moving to a fern when she paused. Her head swiveled to him. If she was surprised to see him, she hid it well.

Too well, in fact.

Ulrik put his hands into his pants' pockets. "Doona let me interrupt you."

"How did you get in?" she demanded and moved to the next plant.

Her dismissive attitude amused him. "Dragon magic, lass. I did warn you that it's verra strong."

"When did you tell me?" she asked, glancing at him.

Ulrik thought about that a moment and shrugged. "Perhaps I didna, but you act as if you know everything about Dragon Kings. I'm betting you doona."

She shot him a withering look and continued around the room until all the plants were watered. After setting the can down on the spotless kitchen counter, she faced him. "Is that why you're here? To tell me what I don't know."

Since he wasn't sure why he was there, he smiled in response. "You have an eye for art."

"I've always liked it," she said with a shrug of her bare shoulder.

"And the rug?" he asked, jerking his chin toward it.

Her dark gaze moved to the rug, and she stared at it a moment. "It called to me. I saw it, and knew I had to have it."

"That is an antique that sells for over a hundred thousand pounds."

"I know." Her gaze lifted to him, daring him to question how she'd obtained it.

Ulrik bit back a grin. "If you ever want to sell it, let me know."

"You say that as if you believe we'll both be alive years from now."

"A nuclear bomb couldna kill me, Druid. I didna eat for over a thousand years and survived. What makes you think you can end me?"

She held his gaze, refusing to answer.

He took a step toward her. "You talk a good talk, I'll give you that. But have you actually killed a Dragon King? Since all of them besides me are on Dreagan, the answer is nay. I'm to be your first, then. You must be verra confident in your magic."

"What do you want?"

"Afraid to talk to me?"

She rolled her eyes and folded her arms across her chest. "I thought I was obvious before. We're enemies."

"Are we?"

She raised a dark brow. "You know we are."

"Because you agreed to my uncle's proposition? That was a poor decision since you didna get a chance to hear from anyone else."

"And you have such a proposal?" she asked.

He shrugged, twisting his lips. "Mikkel will die. Whether it's by my hand or another Dragon King's, the plans he has will never see the light of day."

"He's come a long way."

"I suppose he has, but he willna get much further. His alliance with the Dark Fae is finished since they have a new king. Mikkel made a mistake by alienating Balladyn. Then again, my uncle is asinine like that."

There was a ghost of a smile on her lips that she quickly hid. "He's obsessed with you."

"Only because I'm the King of Silvers. He ignored me before my father was killed. I knew there was discord between them, but I didna know it included me. Once Mikkel learned that my magic and power were greater than his and I'd be the next Dragon King, his dream of reigning over the Silvers was crushed."

She licked her lips and glanced at the floor. "He told me how he became King of the Silvers for a few minutes after you were banished."

"Ah." Ulrik chuckled. "He was a King long enough to shift into human form. I doona even know if he got the tattoo. But that taste of power has set him on a course that will end in his death."

"And yours? Your course is set on vengeance. You don't think it'll end in death, as well?"

He smiled slowly. "Victory or death. Those are my only two options. I'm prepared for either."

"Are you?"

"Aye."

She dropped her arms to her sides. "Do you want to die?"

"The life I've had for these countless millennia isna a life."

"But you have your magic returned. You can shift."

He frowned at her and cocked his head to the side. "Are you trying to convince me to change my mind?"

"From what Mikkel told me, you and Constantine were closer than brothers."

Ulrik looked away as memories of the past assaulted him. "That was before Con betrayed me and banished me from my home."

She grew quiet as her gaze lowered to the ground. He was suddenly insanely curious about what she was thinking. A dozen words popped into his mind that would get her talking and give him information.

But he said none of them.

It had become a habit of his to manipulate and use people, and, oddly, he discovered he didn't want to do that with Eilish. Nor did he know why.

"Why are you in Ireland?" he asked.

Her gaze lifted to his. For several seconds, she merely looked at him. "Answers."

"About?"

"Me."

He looked down at her left hand and saw that she wasn't wearing the silver finger rings. "And Mikkel told you he had those answers?"

She nodded slowly. "He knows what no one else does."

"Mikkel isna the only one with contacts."

"You want me to work with you, so you'll say anything," she said, but there was no heat to her words.

Maybe that's what he'd originally wanted. It was still what he wanted. Wasn't it? "Tell me what your questions are. I'll find the answers, and then you can decide if you want to continue helping Mikkel or no'."

Her gaze narrowed sharply as she looked at him warily. "Ulrik, King of Silvers, doing a good deed just because? That's not the man Mikkel told me you were."

"There is much my uncle doesna know about me."

"With Mikkel, I always know where I stand. I can't say the same about you. I know you want to use me against him, but I can't understand why you're taking this approach."

Ulrik scratched his chin. "I make no excuses for myself, Druid. I have a vast network of spies and employees worldwide. I have connections to both the Dark and Light Fae. I sway, manipulate, and maneuver mortals to do what I want. And I've killed." He took another step. "Mikkel told me to take the life of the last Druid who had the power to touch dragon magic."

Eilish asked, "Did you?"

"I knew if I didna, he would. Darcy wasna just any Druid. She was also a Dragon King's mate. The one thing I willna stand for is a King losing his mate. I made sure when I attacked Darcy that other Druids were near enough to save her."

"Then get her to help you."

"Her magic is gone."

CHAPTER FIVE

Light Castle, Northwestern Ireland

Usaeil was always one to make an entrance. And this time would be no exception.

She teleported to the tall, double doors of the castle and threw them open. The Light Fae milling about turned their heads her way and gasped before quickly sinking into bows and curtsies.

Usaeil kept her eyes straight ahead as she entered her castle. With her head held high, she strode through the corridors into the main area of the castle where the Fae congregated.

She smiled as the hall went quiet when she appeared. Without so much as a look, the crowd parted for her. She walked through them, not bothering to respond to those who spoke to her. When Usaeil reached the front of the hall, she climbed the steps and turned to face the crowd.

It would be grander if she called a meeting of all Light, but speaking in front of a few hundred was enough. Her command would spread quickly, with others adding to her words.

Which is what made it so fun.

She put her hands on her hips and glanced down at her long, white dress that molded to her like a glove. Her gaze moved across the Fae who stood just a few steps below her.

"There is a traitor among us," she declared.

Murmurs swept through the hall. She hastily quieted them by lifting her hand.

"I'm here to call out that person, so everyone knows her name. Rhi, is the traitor," she stated.

Someone from the back yelled, "What did Rhi do?"

Usaeil's blood boiled at anyone daring to ask her such a question. "Rhi is banished from this castle from this day forward. Any Light who helps or harbors her will suffer her fate, as well."

"We're so glad you've returned, my queen," someone said.

She turned her head and saw the Captain of the Queen's Guard, Inen, watching her. She smiled at her people before making her way to Inen.

"Banished?" he asked when she approached.

"Question me once more, and you'll find yourself there, as well," she announced as she walked to the throne room.

Inen fell into step beside her. "What did Rhi do?"

Usaeil came to a stop and faced him. "I'm Queen of the Light. My edicts are law. It doesn't matter what Rhi did or did not do. She's banished. Never again will she set foot in this castle. Rhi walked away from her responsibilities. Let her discover what it feels like out in the world without anyone to turn to."

"My queen," Inen said, shifting his feet. "Rhi is loved by our people."

"Not for much longer."

Usaeil continued on to the throne room. Right before Inen followed, she closed the door. Then she teleported back to Canada. The movie wasn't quite finished.

Besides, there was nothing better than having the humans fawn over her. Hollywood was where she belonged. She was adored and worshiped—as her people used to do. Odd that she'd found her place among the mortals.

Not that any of the Light would ever learn of her secret. They were too wrapped up in their own lives to pay attention to any human for more than sex.

Her visit to the castle was one of many moves she had planned to get rid of Rhi once and for all. All she had to do now was wait for Balladyn to kill Rhi. Since Taraeth had cocked up Balladyn's murder, Usaeil would be there to see Rhi's—and make sure the bitch was dead once and for all.

Usaeil couldn't think about Rhi without reflecting on all the ways she'd believed her nemesis was a friend and not just someone protecting her. So many times, Usaeil had gone out of her way to safeguard Rhi.

The Fae was reckless, wild, and impulsive. Despite that, Rhi had actually caught the eye of a Dragon King.

Usaeil shook her head. No. She wouldn't go down that road again. She had Con, the King of Dragon Kings. There was none mightier than he. Their love would be spoken about forever.

All she had to do was wait for him to realize that his concern about the Kings accepting her as their queen was of no importance. Con was the one in charge. He need only issue a command, and the others would follow.

She'd been determined to stay away from him until he came begging back to her, but she couldn't go another moment without having her arms around him. Usaeil thought of his office at Dreagan and waited for her magic to take her there. Nothing happened.

She tried teleporting to a dozen other places, and it worked fine. Why then couldn't she go to Dreagan?

"Rhi," she said through clenched teeth.

Another interference. And she was tired of it.

Usaeil teleported to a doorway that only a Fae could see. It would take her to Taraeth's throne room where she would demand action be taken immediately. She was done waiting for them to contact her. It was time Rhi died.

She walked to the portal and tried to go through it. But she was blocked.

What was going on?

"Taraeth," she said, knowing the Dark King would hear her. "Come to me, now!"

The seconds turned to minutes as she waited. And the longer she stood there alone, the more her fury grew. It wasn't as if she could walk into the Dark Palace. No one could know the Light Queen was talking to the Dark King. The ramification on both sides would be tremendous.

That's why she'd built the doorway. Yet someone had blocked her.

"It's almost too funny watching you."

She spun around at the male voice and glared at Balladyn, who stood behind her with his legs wide and his arms crossed over his chest. His black-and-silver hair was pulled away from his face to fall with the rest down his back.

"Why can't I get in to see Taraeth?" she demanded.

"Because I tore down the doorway in the throne room. And don't bother building another. I've made sure that can't happen."

She looked him up and down. "Who do you think you are doing such things? Once Taraeth hears about this. . . ."

Balladyn clapped slowly, his smug grin wide. "That performance is nearly good enough for a nomination for. . . ." He paused, frowning. "What's it called again? An Academy Award? I do wonder what the Light would think of your little *hobby*."

Usaeil opened her mouth to give him a piece of her mind, but he spoke over her.

"You can call for Taraeth for the next hundred years, but he won't hear you. He's dead." Balladyn's smile dropped as he scowled at her. "I killed him."

"That's not possible," she muttered in disbelief.

Balladyn held his arms out and smiled coldly. "Oh, but it is." His arms dropped to his sides. "None of the Dark will be hunting Rhi. If you want to kill her, then you'll have to face Rhi yourself. But I know you won't do that. You're too much of a coward."

"I can best Rhi with my eyes closed," she boasted.

Balladyn's brows shot up on his forehead. "Really? I'd like to see that. Call for Rhi now."

"I don't bow to your whims," she stated and lifted her chin for dramatic flair.

"You forget, Usaeil. I know your secrets. I know how you think. I know the movements of the Light Army because I trained them. If you think to attack me, I'll come for you with all the wrath of the Dark. And we will decimate the Light. So be very careful, *Queen*."

It wasn't until he was gone that Usaeil breathed easier. She'd always known Balladyn had the strength and power to do great things. He'd been a great asset as her Captain, but he'd had to go and admit that he was in love with Rhi.

Everything always came back to Rhi.

Con had recently asked Usaeil to join her army with the Dragon Kings to fight the Dark. Perhaps now was the time she would let that happen. It would give her a reason to seek Con out as well as show him how she wanted to fight for this realm. It would also put them together often, reminding him of the passion they shared.

Yes, that's exactly what she was going to do.

Balladyn didn't think he could hate as deeply as he did Usaeil. He'd given her his loyalty, his fighting skills, and his friendship.

What had she done in exchange? Asked Taraeth to kill him.

In some ways, that would've been better than enduring the endless torture until he finally gave in to the darkness and became a Dark Fae.

What Usaeil had done to him wasn't enough. She'd dared to repeat her offense, but this time, against Rhi.

No matter how angry Balladyn was at Rhi right now, he wasn't going to allow Usaeil to carry out her plans. Though Rhi knew about Usaeil going to Taraeth to kill her, she didn't know that he'd cancelled that order.

Balladyn considered calling for her, but he wasn't yet ready to see her. There was still too much anger. And Rhi was better than anyone in battle. She would know how to stay alert and be prepared for any sort of danger.

She would make an excellent ruler. And he still wanted her as his queen so they could unite the Fae. If only he were sure of her love for him.

His thoughts slid to a halt. He'd told her of his love, but had she actually said it back to him? Balladyn couldn't recall an instance.

He fisted his hands at his sides. No doubt she was still in love with her Dragon King. The bastard should be skinned for discarding Rhi so heartlessly. And it didn't help that she kept going to Dreagan and interacting with him constantly.

How could her love die when she continued returning to the source time and again?

Balladyn wasn't too worried. He had complete faith that Ulrik would become the next King of Dragon Kings. Ulrik's hate for his fellow Kings would come to light when he exacted his revenge on them.

Then Rhi would finally be free.

And Balladyn would be there for her. As he always was. Only then could the love between them truly blossom.

Until then, Balladyn would have to keep an eye on Usaeil. Her power was tremendous, and he wouldn't underestimate her. Too many had done that in the past, and she'd smote them from existence.

That wasn't his only problem, though. This Bran who kept taking Dark would have to be stopped. Balladyn had only done an initial investigation after speaking with the white-haired Dark in Galway.

Balladyn was positive the Fae was the infamous Fintan—the most feared and deadly assassin ever. If Fintan were alive, that meant either Taraeth didn't have him killed. Or . . . Fintan had become something more.

Like a Reaper.

Suddenly, all the research Balladyn had done for Rhi in regards to the Reapers sprang to mind. That's when he realized that Rhi had stopped asking about them.

Was that because she now knew one?

There was much more going on than Balladyn realized. Taraeth, the fool, had been oblivious to it all. But Balladyn wasn't going to make that same mistake.

Usaeil might want to pretend the Reapers weren't real, but his research had told him otherwise. The fact that Rhi had been adamant about finding out all she could about them was also another clue.

If the Reapers were real, then what were they doing on Earth?

More importantly, who were they after?

This Bran definitely had something to do with it. And if Balladyn could catch him, it would do wonders for building a relationship with the Reapers.

With his mind now set, Balladyn returned to the palace.

CHAPTER SIX

He was sin and seduction. In one smoking hot package of carnal sexiness that made her forget everything.

Eilish tried to ignore the thumping of her heart when she discovered Ulrik in her home. And that pounding had nothing to do with fear or dread.

When that hadn't worked, she tried magic. Much to her dismay, nothing could stem the tide of wanton havoc he wreaked upon her senses.

The King of Silvers stood tall and imposing, daunting and arresting before her with his light gray suit and black dress shirt. His tailor-made clothes only added to his mystique while hiding the power she knew was beneath the attire.

And how she'd love to see him.

Every delicious inch.

His striking gold eyes had seen and experienced much in his long life, and it was visible in the way he held himself, in how he looked at things, and most assuredly, in the manner he spoke.

With his black waves parted on the side and hanging just past his shoulders, Ulrik wore his dangerous look with ease. His strong jaw and chin were clean-shaven. Black brows arched ever so slightly over his thick-lashed eyes. He had wide lips that were full and decidedly tempting.

Yet her perusal was cut short by his declaration that Darcy no longer had her magic.

"How is that possible?"

"She's from the Isle of Skye. Those Druids vowed never to do or help evil," Ulrik explained.

Eilish blew out a breath as she understood. "And your plan was—*is*—evil."

"The Ancients seem to think so. Those long-dead Druids decided to take away Darcy's magic because she helped me."

"You knew she didn't have any powers when Mikkel told you to kill her, didn't you?"

Ulrik gave a single nod. "He wouldna have listened to me, so I didna bother telling him. Darcy is at Dreagan and mated to Warrick now. And Mikkel believes she's dead."

"How can you plot against your own kind while saving the mates? If you kill Con, you'll then turn to wiping out the rest, which will leave the mates without their Kings."

A black brow shot up on his forehead.

"Am I right?" she asked. "Or have you changed your mind about killing your brethren?"

His gaze slid away, and a small frown formed. "I found Nikolai shortly after he'd hatched. His parents had been killed. I took him in and raised him."

"So he was your son."

Ulrik's gaze snapped to her. "In many ways, yes. Then he became King of Ivories. He was one of my closest friends."

Eilish was more than shocked that Ulrik was sharing

such information. She wasn't sure Mikkel even knew any of this. "You helped Nikolai. You brought him to me, and then you fought alongside him. Do you still hate him?"

"I'm no' sure what I feel anymore."

"Because of Mikkel," she guessed. "He caused you to step in and protect your brethren. I'm sure it all changed when you decided not to kill Darcy."

"She wasna the first."

Eilish cleared her face of the frown that had begun to form. "I'm beginning to think Mikkel doesn't know you at all."

"He doesna," Ulrik affirmed, a hard edge to his words.

"Who was the first?"

Ulrik turned away and walked to the sofa where he picked up the book she'd been reading and glanced at the cover before replacing it. "Rhys's mate, Lily."

Eilish wasn't the kind of person who liked to be surrounded by people. She was perfectly content spending hours, days even, on her own. Even when she was younger, she hadn't been one to want to chat with friends.

So she was surprised when she pushed away from the counter, walked to the sofa, and sat in an apholstered corner. She looked up at Ulrik and motioned for him to sit, as well. There was a moment's hesitation before he lowered himself onto the cushion. He remained on the edge, as if he weren't sure he wanted to be there.

She wanted to know why he was there, but that was put on hold because of her curiosity. "What happened with Lily?"

Instead of answering her, he asked, "What has Mikkel told you about me?"

"Your story." She decided to sum up everything. "How you wanted to marry a mortal, but Con found out she was planning to kill you. Con and the others took her life, and you went into a rage and began the war on the humans.

The Dragon Kings sent the dragons to another realm and bound your magic before banishing you from Dreagan."

"That's what Mikkel told you?"

She lifted one shoulder in a shrug. "I condensed it."

He grunted, his gaze lowering to the rug. "You make it sound so . . . uncomplicated."

"I didn't mean to."

"It's no' your fault. You were no' there. Mikkel wasna either."

"Then how does he know so much?"

Ulrik turned his head to her. "Now, that is a good question."

She tucked one leg beneath her. "Yes. It is."

"Rhys has always loved women. All women. And they loved him."

Eilish listened intently, gaining new information about the Dragon Kings from someone other than Mikkel—someone who was actually a King.

Ulrik's lips pressed together for a moment. "Lily is nobility in the human world. She ran away from her family for a man. Unfortunately, he was abusive. She finally left him and began a new life, which included a job at Dreagan."

"I take it that's where Rhys and Lily met."

"Aye, though I doona know their story of how they fell in love. What I did see was Rhys's complete and total love for her. Mikkel, however, wanted to strike a blow against the Kings, and he was using Lily's estranged brother and her ex-boyfriend to do just that."

Eilish felt sick to her stomach. She'd known from the beginning that Mikkel wasn't a good guy. Then she'd gotten a taste of his depravity in Venice.

Ulrik looked at her. "They made Lily watch as they shot Rhys. Of course, he didna die, but she didna know that. Then Lily's brother killed her. I watched Rhys forget his promise to never harm a mortal and obliterate the two humans. The quickest way to break a King is to kill his mate before a mating ceremony is performed."

Immediately, Eilish thought about how Ulrik must have felt to discover that the woman he loved had been killed. He'd known exactly how Rhys felt.

"There was nothing Con could do to save Lily," Ulrik continued. "She was dead, her soul gone. But I could help."

Eilish frowned in confusion. "How? By bringing someone back from the dead?"

One side of his mouth lifted in a grin.

"That's . . . quite a gift."

"And one Mikkel doesna know about. Every Dragon King has a power. I can find the souls of the dead and return them to their bodies."

Eilish bit her bottom lip as she considered his words. "Mikkel is your uncle. How does he not know about that?"

"Because he doesna care to know. He thought he'd be the next King, but he wasna. It came to me. He tried to go off, and I stupidly pulled him back into the family, thinking he was upset over my father's death."

She made a face. "When really he was furious over you becoming King."

"Exactly. I never knew that until he came to me a few years ago. All this time, he was here, watching me, and I never knew it."

"You had no call to think anyone was around," she said.

His gave her a small smile. "Making excuses for me?"

"Mikkel doesn't know that you saved Lily then?"

"I doona know or care," Ulrik stated.

She hesitated before asking, "How did you save her? I mean, how did you find her soul if she was dead?"

Ulrik dropped his head down and leaned over, propping his forearms on his knees. "No one has ever asked me that before."

That comment made her heart ache for him. Whether she liked Ulrik or not, there was no denying that he'd suffered immeasurably, and for thousands of years. Some would say his actions prevented him from having friends.

She knew it was because he'd locked himself away to avoid interaction with mortals—and she was one.

Just as she was about to get up and end this . . . whatever it was they were having, he began talking again.

"All souls go to a place. I doona know what or where it is. But all I have to do is think of it, and I'm there. I can see them." He paused and swallowed before sitting up straight. "I might want to hurt the Kings, destroy them even. But something . . . happened . . . when I watched Rhys after Lily died. I had no choice. I had to bring her back." He glanced at Eilish. "I wiped Lily's memories of it."

Eilish gave him a shocked look. "Why?"

Ulrik rose and walked to the window where several of her plants sat on the sill. He touched a leaf and ran his thumb over it. He didn't bother to answer her question. "If you could have anything in the world, what would it be?"

"My mother," she replied without thinking.

He looked at her over his shoulder. "I believe you have a story to tell as well, Druid."

"Everyone has a story."

"So they do," he said as he faced the window.

Eilish pursed her lips, internally debating what—if anything—she should tell Ulrik. She wasn't a bad person, yet she had agreed to do terrible things for Mikkel.

"I get the feeling you were no' raised by Druids," Ulrik said.

She blew out a breath. "I wasn't."

"Then perhaps you doona know that there are two types of Druids. *Mies*, who hold true to the magic they were born with. And *droughs,* who give their souls to the Devil in order to make themselves stronger with dark magic." He turned to face her then. "There is another way to become a *drough*, however. Continue to do immoral and criminal things, and the choice will be out of your hands."

His words frightened her. Mostly because she'd been thinking about what would happen to her if she killed as Mikkel wanted. But she wouldn't allow Ulrik to see any of that.

She lifted her chin. "You almost sound as if you're trying to save me."

"Perhaps, I am." He slowly walked to her. "I'm doomed, Eilish. So is Mikkel. You doona have to be."

Unable to hold his gaze, she looked down at the cushion.

"Nikolai found your father," Ulrik said. "Were you looking for him, as well?"

Eilish shook her head. She hadn't really allowed herself to deal with the new knowledge. Because that would mean the man who raised her, the person who claimed to be her father—wasn't. And she couldn't handle that at the moment.

Ulrik rubbed a hand over his chin. "If you want to find your mum, then you should talk to Donal. My offer to learn of her still stands."

"I hate Mikkel," she admitted.

"Then share what you need with me. I'll give you a reason to sever all ties with him."

She lifted her gaze to meet Ulrik's gold eyes. "Do you really think he'll allow me to go that easily?"

"Of course, no'. Then again, you are a verra powerful Druid."

Eilish licked her lips and nodded. "I'm looking for my mother. All I have is her first name—Eireen."

"That's all I need," he said and vanished.

For several minutes, Eilish didn't move from the sofa. Mostly because she'd discovered that she liked talking to Ulrik. And she actually . . . missed him.

CHAPTER SEVEN

It was damn hard not to celebrate, but Ulrik was keeping himself in check.

For the time being.

He returned to the cottage on the lake in Ireland and opened his laptop. A quick search of Eilish Flanagan gave him very little. This was one time he wished he could call upon Ryder and get him working on it.

Ryder was the Dragon King who could create, design, and work anything electronic. He also ran the security at Dreagan. There wasn't anything Ryder couldn't find with his computers.

But Ulrik couldn't call Ryder, which left him only a few other means. He checked his emails on the secure server and found four from various groups he had searching on anything related to Mikkel.

Opening the first message, Ulrik read it and then checked the document listing an estate that had been purchased through one of several dozen shell companies owned by Mikkel. The home was in Westport, Ireland.

Mikkel already had two other houses in Ireland that Ulrik knew of. But his uncle had kept this one a secret.

Why? Ulrik checked the other emails to discover two more houses—one in Sweden, and another in Switzerland.

Ulrik opened the top, middle drawer of his desk and drew out one of the several mobile phones inside and dialed a number. It was answered on the first ring.

"Good work. I've another job for you," Ulrik said. "I want to know about the parents of Eilish Flanagan, who was raised in Boston, Massachusetts, but came from Ireland. Then I want you to see what you can dig up on women named Eireen, no surname, in Ireland. When you find Eilish's date of birth, look for an Eireen who gave birth during that time. I need this immediately."

"Yes, sir," the female replied.

He placed several more identical calls. Then sat back and waited. The anticipation was insufferable. If he'd been able to go to Ryder, he'd already have information.

Then an idea struck. There was someone at Dreagan who just might help him. He rose from the chair and touched the silver cuff.

When he blinked, he was standing in a bedroom within Dreagan Manor. He'd never gotten to explore the house. In many ways, Ulrik felt like more of an outsider within the walls of the dwelling than he did in the mountains of Dreagan.

The door opened, and V walked inside. As soon as he saw Ulrik, he came to a stop. V released a long breath before closing the door behind him.

"Why am I no' surprised to find you here?"

Ulrik met V's blue eyes. "It's nice to see you, as well."

V raked a hand through his long, dark hair and strode farther into the room to the fireplace. "What do you want?"

"Have you thought more about my offer?"

"I have." V turned to face him, putting his back to the

hearth. "I told Con we spoke, and I'm telling you that I've talked with him. Each of you has told me your side of the story."

There were some things that never changed. V was one of them. He always liked to weigh every option.

"And?" Ulrik asked.

"I honestly doona know."

Ulrik took that as a good sign that V hadn't sided with Con outright. "Good. I've a favor to ask."

V snorted, wrinkling his nose. "You've got some balls coming here, knowing you're banished, and asking me for help."

"I spoke with Con in the cavern with my Silvers earlier," Ulrik stated.

In a blink, V's face went slack. "Did you challenge him?"

"It was merely a conversation."

V blew out a breath, annoyance and resignation in his bearing. "What's your fucking favor?"

"I know Ryder must be looking into Eilish already."

"The Druid?"

Ulrik gave a nod. "She's working with Mikkel because he has information she wants that he's dangling over her head."

"And you want to give it to her," V said with a shake of his head.

"I do. So she can decide if she wants to help him or no'."

V's gaze narrowed on Ulrik as he crossed his arms over his chest. "Are you that worried she can kill you?"

"Maybe. Or maybe I doona want to see her corrupted by Mikkel because she didna know how else to find the information she seeks."

V stared at him for a long, silent minute. Then he

dropped his arms to his sides. "What do you need to know?"

"Her mother."

"After Nikolai spoke to Donal Cleary in London, he had Ryder begin his search."

Ulrik raised his brows. "And?"

"I doona know any more."

After countless eons doing things on his own or commanding others, Ulrik found it hard to ask for anything. But he knew this was important. If he could give Eilish what she needed, it could change the tide of everything.

And then he could return to his original plan.

"Look into it for me. Please," Ulrik added.

V glowered at him. "Damn you."

"Thank you."

Ulrik teleported back to the cottage before he was tempted to go to Ryder himself. Now he really did have everyone capable of uncovering information working on things.

He turned around to walk into the bedroom when his gaze landed on Rhi standing before a window looking out over the lake. Shock went through him at the fact that he hadn't known someone was in his cottage.

"Rhi?" he called when she didn't move.

She was dressed in all white from her scooped-neck sweater that fell to her hips to her jeans to the ankle boots. The glint of something on her shoes caught his attention. He moved another step closer and discovered that there were rhinestones on them, beginning lightly over the top of her foot before covering the entire toe area.

Her black hair was hanging down her back as she stood, unmoving. Almost as if she were mesmerized by the view. More than that, she looked sad. He didn't have to ask if she knew of Balladyn's new orders declaring open season on humans because it was evident in her demeanor.

"How did you find me?" he asked.

She blinked, then said in a soft Irish brogue, "This is a very tranquil place. Somewhere you could lose yourself."

"I suppose."

"I don't want to be here. I don't want to be anywhere, actually," she said.

Ulrik closed the distance between them. "I'm sorry you're hurting."

Her head turned to him. "I suspected that you and Balladyn were working together. I dismissed it because I knew you'd never trust anyone. And yet, you just confirmed it."

"We have a mutual enemy in Mikkel."

"As well as the Dragon Kings."

"And a mutual friend," he said, nodding to her.

Her head swiveled back to the window. "I want to disappear, but I can't. I have friends who need me, who count on me. There is much going on, Ulrik. More than you know."

"Tell me," he urged. Before, he wouldn't have cared, but now, he needed to know.

And he wasn't sure why.

She sighed and shifted to face him. "You were once a good man. You can be again."

"What if I doona want that?"

"You want to be able to return to your home. The fact is, there are more enemies besides the Dark and Mikkel out there attacking the Dragon Kings."

That wasn't a complete shock to him. While he'd been secretly visiting his Silvers, he'd heard a few conversations about other enemies.

Ulrik looked into the Light Fae's silver eyes. "I'll no' put aside my revenge."

"No," she murmured, her gaze drifting to the floor. After a small hesitation, she looked at him and said, "I'm planning my own retribution."

This wasn't Rhi. What had happened to push her to such a degree? Was it Balladyn? Possibly.

"Against?"

Rhi took a deep breath. "Usaeil."

Ah. He'd briefly forgotten that the Light Queen had asked Taraeth to kill Rhi. "You doona have to worry about that now that Balladyn is King of the Dark."

"If you think that will stop Usaeil, you're wrong."

"What else can she do to you that willna make her look bad?"

Rhi shrugged, shaking her head. "It's Usaeil. I wouldn't put anything past her."

"You're really going after her?"

"She instigated the breakup of me and. . . ."

Ulrik put a hand on her arm when her words trailed off. "You're still alive. You have a wealth of power that I doona think you've completely tapped into yet. She made a mistake making you her enemy."

"How did you do it?" Rhi asked softly.

He didn't pretend that he didn't know she was asking about him losing Nala. His hand dropped to his side. "I believed she was my mate. I was prepared to give her immortality, but it wasna until she was dead that I saw who she truly was. If I really loved her, would I have been able to destroy her soul?"

"Did you really?" Rhi asked, shock in her voice and on her face.

"Oh, aye. And I'd do it again. I know what you ask, but I doona think I'm the right person to answer."

She momentarily closed her eyes.

He caught her gaze. "Several times, you said you stopped loving your King, but I've known it for the lie it is every time."

"I want to stop."

"I wish I knew a way to help. What are you going to do about Balladyn?"

She shoved her hair back from her face. "I don't know. I was happy with him."

"The kind of happiness you had with—"

"Don't you dare say his name," she stated. Rhi released a long breath. "I was happy and loved. I saw Balladyn's eyes turn silver."

"And you believed that you could help him become a Light again."

She nodded her head slowly. "I was a fool. He's Dark and will never be anything else."

"He loves you."

"He wants me to be his queen and unite the Fae under one ruler."

Ulrik had to admit that wasn't likely to happen. Then again, he'd always known the new Dark King had high aspirations. "Did you get Con to heal him so Balladyn would be beholden to Con?"

"Never," Rhi said with a roll of her eyes. "All I wanted to do was save Balladyn."

"It'll take him a while to cool down."

She turned her head away. "He's made his intentions clear. It won't matter what I say. Balladyn will always believe that I wanted him indebted to the Dragon Kings."

"Because you love one."

Her gaze slid back to him. "I'm numb right now. Completely. But I have to return to MacLeod Castle. . . ." Her voice trailed off as if she realized she'd said too much.

He studied her intently. "What do you no' want me to know?"

"I told you the Kings had other enemies. You claim to want to destroy them, but then you actually help on occasion."

"Doona paint me a good man, Rhi. Shall I remind you of all the bad? I did try to kill Darcy and Rachel."

The Fae made a sound in the back of her throat. "I don't need reminding, but ignoring who you are and what connects you won't stop the enemy that's coming."

"What enemy?"

"Druids and Fae united to deliver powerful magic aimed at bringing down the Dragon Kings. Any and all."

CHAPTER EIGHT

If there was one thing besides betrayal that Ulrik hated, it was being surprised. Rhi's words shocked him to his very core.

Perhaps he should've paid more attention when he was wandering the tunnels of the mountain connected to Dreagan Manor. He'd assumed he, Mikkel, and the Dark were the only ones the Kings had to worry about.

"Tell me more," Ulrik demanded.

Rhi hesitated before saying, "A dragon skeleton was found on Fair Isle."

"How? I heard Con issue the order for all the dead to be destroyed before the dragons crossed the dragon bridge."

"It seems that there was more going on than anyone realized," Rhi explained. "It appears the White wasn't destroyed. It was killed and then cloaked with magic so Dmitri wouldn't find it when he was removing traces of the other dead dragons."

Ulrik shook his head in disbelief. "And you believe Druids and Fae did this? Our magic is stronger than theirs."

"Unless they combine their powers. As in a *mie* and *drough* and a Light and Dark."

"Holy shite." Ulrik turned away as he let that information sink in. It was nearly impossible to wrap his head around the fact that such a union would happen now, much less so many centuries ago.

The Fae ignored the Druids for the most part. To discover that both sects of such powerful beings gathered and focused their intent on the Dragon Kings unsettled him to his very core.

He spun back to Rhi. "Are you sure?"

She nodded. "There was a small, wooden dragon found beneath the skeleton that was an exact replica of Con. Any King that comes into contact with it has an overwhelming urge to kill every mortal. It happened to Con, Dmitri, Kiril, and Rhys."

Ulrik swallowed hard as the news kept getting worse. "Did you touch it?"

"No, but Shara did. It seems to affect Fae differently. We see other people, places, and times."

"And the mortals? What about them?"

Concern flashed across Rhi's face. "Nothing good."

"What are you no' telling me?" he pressured.

She sighed dramatically. "You'll keep pushing until I tell you, so fine. But you aren't going to like it."

He glared at her. "Tell me."

Rhi glanced away. "Dmitri's mate, Faith, touched it. She fell unconscious, and when she woke, she ran from Dreagan."

"Why?" Ulrik asked, confused. Dreagan was a safe place.

Instead of answering, Rhi continued. "Of course, Dmitri found her in the Dragonwood. He confronted her, and she began screaming about ending the reign of Dragon Kings. Then she lifted the wooden dragon over her head and ran at him. Right before she reached Dmitri, a blade extended from the totem."

Ulrik shook his head incredulity. "No."

"She stabbed him, intending to kill him."

Ulrik had thought his days of thinking about Nala and her desire to see him dead were long gone, but it seemed that was far from true. Though Nala hadn't attempted to kill him, he could well imagine her saying the things Faith had.

"What happened after?" Ulrik asked.

"Faith fell unconscious again. When she woke, she had no memory of any of it. We realized the culprit was the wooden dragon, so I took it."

He shot her a look of scorn. "You touched it?"

"I'm not stupid," she said with a flat look. "Of course, I didn't touch it. But when I gathered it with my magic, I was able to discern the Druid and Fae magic within. And before you ask, I've never heard anything about this."

Ulrik ran a hand down his face. "Con sent you to MacLeod Castle."

"He did. He knew the Druids there might know something. It seems the Ancients have tasked Isla with a connection to this thing somehow. Right now, the dragon is hidden while everyone digs for more information."

He pivoted away to walk off some of the anger that began to boil within him. The killing of the White brought back all of Ulrik's hatred for the humans—except it was Druids and Fae who had done this. Why?

No matter what direction his thoughts went, he couldn't discern why any Druids—who had learned about magic from the Kings—or Fae would take such actions.

"If I'm going to tell you, then I'd better tell you everything."

Rhi's words stopped him in his tracks. He turned back to her. "What else is there?"

"Con was having an affair with Usaeil."

"Of all the idiotic things for him to do," Ulrik stated as he began to turn away, then stopped. "What was he thinking?"

Rhi shrugged. "She had someone take a photo of them, though you couldn't really see Con's face. Usaeil did it because he wouldn't tell the Kings about their relationship."

"And she thought that would force him."

"Well, she did plaster copies of the picture all over the Light Castle. She wants to be mated to Con. She has this idea that the Fae will be the ones to finally give the Kings children since mortals can't."

Ulrik stared at Rhi for a long moment. "Does this have anything to do with Usaeil wanting you dead?"

"Con called off their affair, and somehow, I was brought up. Usaeil immediately assumed I had changed his mind about her."

"Things with Usaeil could spiral out of control quickly," he warned.

"I know."

"Balladyn intends to kill her. And I'm going to help."

Rhi stalked to stand before him, her nostrils flaring as her eyes blazed with warning. "No. Usaeil is my problem. She's the one who ruined so much in my life."

"She's your vengeance."

Rhi nodded once.

Ulrik couldn't fault her for her thinking, because his need for retribution was the only thing that'd kept him going for many, many centuries. He would step aside and let Rhi handle Usaeil however she saw fit.

Rhi put her hand on his arm. "I'm telling you all of this because your brethren are going to need you."

"Con is doing what he's always done. He tries to carry on as usual while handling problems. That's how things get out of hand so easily. Then he decides to deal with whatever issue it might be, but it always counteracts his vow to protect the mortals. Meanwhile, other difficulties arise until he has no choice but to take the action he should've done in the first place."

"War," Rhi said.

Ulrik shot her a hard look. "No. Confronting things. I'm stringing him along, and so is Mikkel. I understand why Con is biding his time there. Same with the wooden dragon. But Usaeil? Has he gone to her and dealt with that?"

"Actually, he has. We have something in store for her."

"I'm impressed." But Ulrik wasn't that surprised.

When Con decided to take action, things were handled quickly. With so many enemies circling, at least one issue had to be dealt with since Con's thoughts were divided by so many problems.

Rhi raked her gaze over him. "What are you going to do?"

"None of this changes my plans. Con will pay for what he did to me."

"I figured you'd say as much. I'm disappointed, but not surprised."

He crossed his arms over his chest and chuckled. "What did you expect?"

"I thought you'd changed after helping Nikolai."

"Nikolai is. . . ." Ulrik wasn't sure he could find a word to describe his relationship with the King of Ivories.

Rhi wrinkled her nose before saying. "Different? Not included with your thoughts about the others? Excluded because you raised him?"

It amazed Ulrik how quickly Rhi's mind could flip from one thing to another. When he arrived, she'd looked lost and nearly defeated. Yet now, she stared at him as if she were ready to bring the entire world down around him.

"My fight is with Con," Ulrik said.

The anger went out of Rhi with her next breath. "What changed your mind about the other Kings?"

"I doona know. Does it matter?" he asked as he turned his back to her and walked to the window she had vacated.

He felt her come up behind him. "It doesn't matter to me, no. Though I believe Nikolai might have had something to do with it. I'd ask you to look deeper into why your plans have altered. Perhaps you're changing."

"The only thing that will bring me peace is ending Con."

"The man you considered your brother? The dragon you would've died for?"

He spun to face her. "Betrayal tends to wipe away any ties."

A small frown formed between her brows as she took a half-step back. "What a hypocrite I am, telling you to forget your vengeance when I'm planning my own with Usaeil."

"Let me and Balladyn take care of her," Ulrik urged.

Rhi's frown deepened while she looked at him with confusion. "Why would you do that?"

"Because the light inside you shines more brilliantly and vividly than any star. If you go after Usaeil, it will be dimmed—and possibly go out."

"You mean how it diminished after I was tortured at the Dark Palace?"

Ulrik nodded slowly. "My soul is black. So is Balladyn's. We can carry one more death."

"But I've killed many before."

"In battle. Usaeil will be different."

"Not if she comes after me."

Ulrik smiled sadly. "Rhi, you're one of the bravest and toughest Fae I know. And your skills in battle are mindboggling. But the light within you gives you a measure of innocence. Killing in battle isna the same as taking a life because you enjoy it or want revenge."

"I'll forget about going after Usaeil if you do the same with Con."

"I can no' do that."

Rhi flashed him a tight smile. "Neither can I. Watch your back, Ulrik. Mikkel will send the Druid soon."

With that, she vanished. Ulrik slowly walked back to his desk. Thanks to Rhi, his thoughts returned to Eilish. He wished he knew what it was about the Irish beauty that kept him enthralled.

She could've spellbound him so he wouldn't want to fight her. Because, well, he didn't. The smart thing to do would be to follow her and wait until her guard was down, as it had been at her flat.

Then, kill her.

He wouldn't have to worry about how much power she might actually have, and he'd strike a blow to Mikkel in the process. It was a win-win.

Yet, he was doing nothing. It baffled him. Completely perplexed him. If he didn't know better, he might think he actually liked Eilish. Despite the fact that she was a Druid, she was still mortal. And his hatred of them ran too deep.

He sank into the chair before the desk and checked his email. It was too soon for his employees to have found anything on Eilish, but he clicked again just to be sure.

Ulrik raked a hand through his hair. "Stop," he ordered himself.

The Druid was just another pawn in the game. She was meaningless, insignificant. Irrelevant.

There was also a lot at stake for her. The only reason

she was in this war was because Mikkel had the answers she sought. Or did he?

Ulrik sat back in the chair and tapped his index finger on the desk. Mikkel had given Eilish the first name of her mother. It could've been exactly as the Druid described it, a way to pacify her.

Or, it could be that it was the only thing Ulrik's uncle had obtained. Since Mikkel's people were just as good as his, whatever information Ulrik was given was likely the same as what Mikkel got.

Ulrik sent out texts to his network, urging them to hurry in their digging into Eilish's life. Then he stood and paced the small cottage. When that didn't help, he jerked off his suit jacket. The rest of his clothes soon followed before he walked from the house and dove into the lake.

If he weren't careful, Eilish could become an obsession.

And he didn't have time for that.

CHAPTER NINE

A sound could make your insides shrivel up, and your heart thump in dread. That's what happened to Eilish every time the cell phone Mikkel gave her rang. How she hated the ringtone. She'd changed it, but it didn't help. Because it wasn't really the phone she loathed but Mikkel.

She stood staring at the mobile on the kitchen counter as it vibrated, sending it moving across the surface. Finally, she picked it up.

Then, with a sigh, she said, "Hello?"

"It's about bloody time," Mikkel stated angrily through the phone.

Eilish closed her eyes, thankful Ulrik wasn't still there. "What do you want?"

"It's time for you to kill Ulrik."

Her eyes flew open as her stomach plummeted to her feet. "What?"

"If he's gone, you can then unbind my magic, and I'll be able to shift at will."

"Are you sure killing Ulrik now is wise?"

There was a long pause, which made her stomach

tighten with trepidation. As she waited for Mikkel to talk, she thought over the words and even her inflection to see if she'd let anything slip through the mask she wore around him.

"Why are you asking that?" he questioned in a soft voice.

Eilish turned and walked to her door where she began recasting the wards that Ulrik had broken through that would keep everyone out, including Mikkel.

She finished the spells and lowered her hand. "Right now, the Dragon Kings have their sights set on Ulrik. You take him out of the game, then the Kings will come after you."

The laughter on the other end of the line was maniacal. And it caused ice to run through her veins.

"The Kings know nothing of me," Mikkel said. "They'll be chasing their tails trying to figure out who their new enemy is."

Eilish was glad she'd left that message in Esther's mind about Mikkel when she returned her memories. Esther was smart. She'd figure it out and tell the Dragon Kings exactly who Mikkel was. But Eilish wasn't going to let Mikkel know that little tidbit.

"I want Ulrik dead within the next two days. Figure it out and do it," Mikkel ordered. "Or all the material I have on your mother will be burned."

The line disconnected.

Eilish slowly lowered the phone before dropping it onto the kitchen table. She pivoted and walked into her bedroom. She stood just inside the doorway, her mind a riot of thoughts.

Everything she knew about magic she'd learned on her own. It wasn't until she arrived in Ireland and met other Druids that she discovered there was an entire world she hadn't known existed.

Not just of Fae or Dragon Kings, but of Druids, as well. The history, the broken bonds that had once held them all together, and the fact that most Druids didn't know what they were because their magic was all but gone.

She was a rarity. Eilish knew that now, though she kept it to herself. None of the other Druids knew just how much magic she had, and she intended to keep it that way.

The fact that she made the village a safe haven for the mortals and supernatural alike had brought her attention, but mainly it was how she had defeated the Dark that gave her the notoriety. It also drew in others like her. They sought her out to talk—and most would speak to a rock if given the opportunity.

Eilish didn't even have to ask questions. All she had to do was sit and listen, and she learned so very much— it was also how she realized how far behind on her training she was. Despite that lack of knowledge, whenever she tried anything new, it came as easily as breathing, while other Druids worked years to gain even a smidgen of control.

Her ability to listen gained her insight into the supernatural. Like how Druids couldn't sense the power in each other, but the Fae, Warriors, and Dragon Kings could feel all magic.

That's what had led Mikkel to her. That and the fact that he'd heard what she'd done with Graves and the village. She'd never told him she could touch dragon magic, because she hadn't tried it yet. Not once had she displayed any kind of powers around him.

He'd assumed everything.

And the bastard had done his homework. He'd learned every tiny, mundane detail of her life—and what she searched for. So, he'd dangled the carrot of her mother before her, and Eilish hadn't hesitated. She'd accepted his offer, believing that she could handle whatever he wanted.

Besides, it was bringing her closer to the Dragon Kings. A species she was immensely interested in because of the recurring dream she'd had at least once a week for the past seven years. All she ever saw of the man was the dragon tattoo on his chest, but she knew he was coming for her—and not in a good way.

With all of that combined, it was no wonder she'd agreed to kill Ulrik. With every Dragon King she removed, it was one less that could come after her. Never mind that she'd never committed murder before.

Or battled a Dragon King.

That was before she'd learned that the Kings were truly immortal. The only being who could kill a Dragon King was another Dragon King. But Mikkel assured her she could do it with her magic. Then he dangled the information about her mum before her again.

Eilish was powerless to keep from responding exactly as he expected her to. And she hated it. Almost as much as she detested him.

Her head turned to the vanity table where the silver finger rings lay. The magic within them amplified her own. It was an advantage she didn't intend to ever let anyone know about. Even if they didn't have magic, she would still wear them because they were her mother's.

All she wanted was to know who her mother was. Eireen's likes and dislikes, who she loved. And why she had given Eilish up to be taken far from Ireland.

For seven years, Eilish had built up herself and her magic, searching everywhere for information on her mother. Seven long years with tiny grains of hope that were dashed before they could be realized. And Mikkel was willing to give her everything.

She just had to kill to gain it.

But murder would turn her *drough*.

That was another difference between Mikkel and Ul-rik. Mikkel must have assumed she was already *drough*, which was why he had no problem telling her to kill.

Ulrik had known she wasn't. Because he'd taken the time to study her, not just her background.

Mikkel already knew everything about her mother. Ulrik, however, was trying to find it. Sadly, Mikkel wouldn't give her the time she needed to allow Ulrik to uncover anything. Which meant, she had no choice but to continue her alliance with Mikkel.

She walked to the vanity and put each finger ring on her left hand. Then she tapped two of the claws together and thought of Ulrik. The next second, she was standing outside a cottage next to a lake. She was about to go to the door when she heard a splash.

She turned her head. The crescent moon allowed very little light, but it was enough that she could see someone in the water. And she knew it was Ulrik.

With her heart slamming against her ribs at the thought of seeing him shirtless, she slowly made her way to the water's edge. The closer she got, the faster her heart beat, which caused her breathing to increase. Her mouth went dry, and her hands grew clammy.

She saw the dark shape swimming far out into the lake before diving beneath. She skimmed the surface with her gaze, waiting for him to reappear. Shivering in the cool temps, she couldn't imagine putting one toe in the chilly water.

Minutes ticked by as she tried to figure out where she was. It could be Scotland, but she couldn't shake the feel-ing that it was Ireland. There was something about the land that she knew, recognized. It had been that way from the moment she stepped onto Irish soil. So what the hell was Ulrik doing in Ireland?

"What a surprise," came a deep, Scottish brogue behind her.

Her stomach fluttered before she turned to face Ulrik. It took everything she had to hide her disappointment when she discovered he was fully dressed in jeans and a black sweater with the sleeves pushed up to his elbows.

The only indication that he'd just been in the water was his wet hair and bare feet.

"I didn't mean to interrupt your swim," she said.

The fact that he'd discerned her presence meant that she would never be able to sneak up on him. So when she killed him, she would have to do it face-to-face.

His stance widened as he crossed his arms over his chest, completely unaffected by anything. "I didna expect to see you so soon. I'm going to need more than a few hours to get the information."

She was trying to find a way to reply to that when his brows shot up, and he grinned.

"Ah. I see," Ulrik murmured. "Mikkel sent you to kill me."

Well, there was no use lying to him. "Yes."

"Tonight?"

"Soon," she replied.

His lips twisted. "A pity. I could have saved you from turning *drough*."

"I'll only become evil if I commit murder. I know you'll fight me."

Ulrik's arms dropped to his sides. "It doesna work that way. You're planning to kill me. That means you're going to set the time and day. Aye, I will fight back, and if you do manage to take my life, you will forfeit all the good in your soul. Let that sink in. And when you're ready, come inside."

She watched as he turned on his heel and strode into the house. Eilish remained rooted to the spot, desperately trying to find a loophole in what he'd just told her.

The more she thought about it, the more she knew Ulrik was right. Was she prepared for the Devil to have her soul for information about her mother? And what if Ulrik could find the intel just as Mikkel had?

Her eyes slid to the open door where light flooded into the night. Ulrik waited for her. But why? Why not just kill her and remove his uncle's magical pawn? Why go to such measures to keep her from turning evil? Why offer to help?

He was presenting her with another way out. If she could trust him. For all she knew, Ulrik wanted to use her just as Mikkel did. But Ulrik wasn't asking her to kill.

She shoved her hair over her shoulder and walked to the door. When she reached it, she paused and peered inside to find Ulrik pouring two glasses of wine.

He looked up and motioned her inside. "Come in."

Eilish glanced down at the threshold. Then she lifted her foot and stepped over it. That step felt significant, as if she'd just made a decision.

Ulrik took his wine and drank, his gaze on her. He lowered his arm. "I would tell you of a group of Druids you should talk to, but since you attacked Esther and Kinsey, I doona think they'd be too keen on speaking with you."

"I take it these Druids are friends of the Dragon Kings," she said as she walked to the table and lifted the wine glass to her lips for a taste.

"They are. Immensely powerful Druids, too. They could fill in a lot of the holes you have."

She raised a brow. "You say that as if you don't think I know what it means to be a Druid."

"I think you're still learning. The fact that you didna know about *mies* and *droughs* says it all. Have you no' encountered many Druids at Graves?"

"Some," she said with a half-hearted shrug. "It's not as if we spoke of good and evil. Some I knew weren't exactly good people, but I thought it was like anything. There is good, and there is bad."

He swirled the red liquid in his glass. "Things are always different when you throw magic into the mix."

"Mikkel told me a lot of things about you and the Dragon Kings."

"Did he now?" Ulrik asked, amusement lifting the corners of his mouth.

Eilish glanced around at the small cottage. It was cozy, and—oddly—seemed to suit Ulrik. "At first, he only told me you weren't good enough to be a Dragon King. I pressured him for more, and he told me the tale."

Ulrik grunted, his gaze on his wine.

She swallowed and took a step toward him. "I've no right to ask, and I wouldn't be surprised if you said no. But . . . will you tell me your story?"

"Why do you want to know?" he asked, meeting her gaze.

She looked deeply into his gold eyes. "I want to hear it from your lips."

Because with him, she'd get the truth.

CHAPTER TEN

Sometimes, the past came barreling back without warning. This wasn't one of those times. This time, Ulrik had been asked to drudge it all up again.

"You know the facts," he said, unwilling to think about that horrible time—or what followed.

Eilish nodded. "I shouldn't have asked."

He watched as she turned her head away and blew out a breath. There was a forlorn look on her face that was like a kick to his stomach.

More than anything, he wanted to ignore her request, but he kept coming back to the fact that no one ever asked for his side of the story. This was someone who seemed genuinely interested, someone who hadn't been poisoned against him—though Mikkel had tried.

"I loved her," Ulrik said.

Eilish's head swung back to him. "How did you meet . . . ?"

"Nala," he said. "Her name was Nala."

He walked to the chair next to the fire and sat. A moment later, Eilish took the seat opposite him. His gaze was locked on the dancing flames.

Ulrik drank deeply from his glass before he said, "Some of the Kings shied away from the mortals. There was anger all around that we gave up land for the humans. I wasna exactly pleased with the prospect, but we vowed to protect the magicless species.

"I watched them for a wee bit. They struggled to get shelters built in time for the coming winter. I wondered how we could give the promise of protection and then do nothing to aid them. I made the decision right then to become involved."

Eilish's voice was soft when she asked, "So you helped them build homes?"

"I did," he replied without looking away from the fire. "I also gave the village my protection. I built a home there where I invited the humans inside and fed them. That's how I met Nala. She was so beautiful and gregarious. She was always laughing, always smiling. I think that's what drew me to her.

"It wasna long before she made it clear she was interested. After that, we were inseparable. I knew right away that I wanted her to be mine, but I didna say anything. For the next year, I allowed her time to become accustomed to everything I was. She never shied away, never turned her back on me. So, I asked her to be mine."

"What did the other Kings think?" Eilish asked.

Ulrik met her gaze and shrugged. "There were those we were shocked. Con told me I was making a mistake."

"Why?"

"No mortal had birthed a breathing bairn from a Dragon King—and still hasna. Most of the women miscarry early on in the pregnancy. Con knew I was giving up continuing my line."

Eilish's forehead frowned. "What prevents the babies from being born alive?"

"We doona know."

"I thought maybe the others believed Nala wanted to become immortal."

He drained the rest of his wine and set the empty glass on the floor. "I never told her. I planned to tell her after the ceremony. There were many Kings who believed we shouldna mix the blood of two species, and that's why none of the bairns were born. Perhaps they were right."

"There has to be another reason," Eilish said.

Ulrik shrugged. "Either way, it didna matter to me. All I wanted was Nala. You see, I didna want to become King. My father fell in battle, and before I realized it, I was a Dragon King. Yet, I accepted my role and carried on as I'd seen my father do. I had an amazing clan. The Silvers were fierce fighters, loyal beyond anything you could imagine."

"You were happy."

He twisted his lips ruefully. "Aye. I didna realize it was all about to come crashing down. But there was a time when family surrounded me. I had a strong clan, I had the woman who I wanted as my mate, and I had friends who meant everything to me. I was riding atop the world. When you fly that high, the fall is a mighty one."

"What happened next?"

His gaze swung back to the flames as he took a deep breath and slowly released it. "Con summoned me. He asked me to fly over an area where some humans had settled. He suspected their border dispute might come to war, and he wanted my take on it. I left immediately, un-knowing that while I was away, Con called all the Kings together and told them whatever it was he'd found out about Nala."

"So Con knows why she planned to betray you," Eilish interrupted.

Ulrik nodded without looking at her.

"Ask him then."

It was pride that kept Ulrik from doing exactly that. "Why would I ask my enemy anything? And why would I believe what he said?"

"You said Con was like a brother."

"He was," Ulrik replied. "Which is why his betrayal cut so deeply. It wasna his right to hunt Nala down and kill her. It was mine."

Eilish blew out a breath. "Maybe he was trying to save you from having to do that."

"That's exactly what he claimed when I confronted him. He said the decision to go after her was unanimous among the Kings."

"The very beings who had vowed to protect mortals? Those who gave up land for us? I'm beginning to think they did this for you, not *to* you."

Ulrik rapidly gained his feet and walked around his chair. He then stopped, one hand on the back of the seat as he fought for control of his anger. "I can no' describe the level of hatred that rose in me. I needed an outlet, somewhere to direct it. Why no' the very beings who had caused it."

"Humans," Eilish said.

He glanced at her. "It helped my cause that the mortals had hunted smaller dragons, wiping out entire clans to fill their bellies. And we did nothing. Yet when a dragon occasionally ate a human, it took weeks of negotiation with them to come to a truce, and that was only after we punished the dragon responsible. But the mortals never penalized their own. They never came to the table for discussions. Nay, the burden was always ours.

"I saw them then for what they really were. A curse, a blight. A nuisance that needed to be wiped away. So I intended to cleanse our realm of your kind."

Ulrik fisted his hand as the old, familiar rage bubbled within him. "I stated my intention. Con immediately tried to talk me out of it, but half of the Kings had already joined me. And we began that verra night."

He closed his eyes and fell into the memories of that long-ago time that seemed as fresh as if it had just happened. "Their screams were like music. We burned everything they owned so that the sky was darkened with black smoke. And we slew thousands. At first, they tried to fight back, but soon, they were running for their lives. We made headway, but the Kings who sided with Con worked against us."

"How?"

His eyes opened, and it took him a second to remember that he wasn't fighting the mortals. He turned toward Eilish. "Some of the Kings commanded their dragons to stand guard against the humans and to only fight other dragons. I came upon a village where Kellan's Bronze dragons were standing sentry, waiting for our attack. But the humans attacked them before we got there."

"I don't understand," Eilish said, her brow knitted deeply. "Didn't the dragons fight back?"

"Kellan had commanded them to protect the humans only."

"So the dragons . . . stood there and let themselves be killed?" she asked angrily, shock filling her features.

He gave a nod of his head. "When I saw the carnage and the dragons writhing upon the ground as they slowly died, I ordered my Silvers to make sure no' a single human from that village lived. No man, woman, or child."

When Eilish turned her head toward the fire, he continued. "Eventually, one by one, the Kings aligned with me returned to Con, each of them asking me to stop the war. I didna understand. This was our realm. We'd allowed the humans to remain. We welcomed them and gave them homes. In return, they had wiped out three different dragon clans, the smallest of our kind. We were dragons! We had magic. It would've been so easy to remove the mortals once and for all, and then we could've returned to normal."

She set her drink on the floor and clasped her hands in her lap before looking at him. "What was their reasoning for standing against you?"

"That we'd made a vow to protect the mortals, and that we couldn't punish all for the sins of a few. My argument was that we should've been watching over our own first and foremost. The dragon clans that were wiped out as food for the humans can never be replaced. They're gone. Forever."

Her throat bobbed as she swallowed. "I'm sorry."

He shook his head and turned his back to her to look out the window. "Even with only my Silvers, we made headway removing the mortals. Until Con and the others used their magic to create a dragon bridge."

"What's that?" Eilish asked.

"A way for dragons to travel from one realm to another. Con sent the dragons to another realm without visiting it first. He still has no idea if the dragons are alive, or if they were taken to a place where they were killed off. The bridge only goes one way, which is why none of the dragons have returned. They need the Kings' magic to recreate it, and Con couldna risk no' being able to return." Ulrik felt the band around his chest tighten and begin to suffocate him. "This was our home."

He cleared his throat, tamping down the tidal wave of emotion that threatened to choke him. "All but four of my Silvers obeyed Con. I watched in horror, first as the dragons disappeared over the bridge, and then as my Silvers were trapped and magic used to force them to sleep. Then Con turned his attention on me."

Ulrik heard the chair squeak as Eilish rose. Her shoes

clicked softly on the wooden floor until she reached the wall before him. She turned to lean back against it and met his gaze.

"You don't have to continue."

"But we're getting to the best part," Ulrik stated and met her gaze. "This is where Con, the man I thought of as my brother, the dragon I would've gladly died for, bound my magic. Oh, but he didna do it alone. The other Kings added their magic to his so that it overtook me, and I couldna fight it. I was condemned to walk this wretched place in a form I despised for eternity because Con wouldna reverse his ruling. But that wasna all. While I was still dealing with the fact that I couldna shift into a dragon, Con banished me from Dreagan."

Ulrik was thankful that it wasn't pity he saw in Eilish's green-gold eyes. He didn't think he could handle that. Instead, he caught a glimpse of anger and shock.

"Where did you go?" she asked softly.

If he didn't like to think about his banishment, he loathed remembering those centuries in the cave. But it was too late. His story had taken him there, and he couldn't shut off his memories now.

"I wandered," he said. "While the Kings found their mountains and slept, I walked until I found a place where I would never encounter a mortal."

She tilted her head to the side. "Where was that?"

"On a verra high mountain that was covered in snow. No human could handle the temperatures or the thin air. There was a cave, and that became my home for . . . a long time. It was also the place where I went mad."

CHAPTER ELEVEN

Letting Go

The magic that filled the stones and grounds of MacLeod Castle was a much-needed boost for Rhi. She'd taken Con's advice and took some time for herself after she learned of Balladyn's order for the Dark to target humans.

But what did she expect of the new King of the Dark? A lot, actually.

He'd been her brother's best friend, *her* friend, and eventually, her lover. She'd also foolishly believed she could turn Balladyn Light once more. That wasn't to be. The darkness had a firm hold of his soul.

Since Rhi's mind was still reeling from Balladyn's actions, learning that Usaeil plotted to kill her, and the queen being the one who'd instigated ending Rhi's affair with her Dragon King, it was no wonder Rhi felt pulled in multiple directions.

She wanted to stop Balladyn, mostly because she was hurt by his actions.

She also wanted to confront Usaeil about everything. The Light Queen was an absent monarch nowadays, but Usaeil no longer cared about the Light. Not to mention

Usaeil tricking Con, lying to her, and wanting both her and Balladyn killed.

Then there was the wooden dragon. The mix of both Druid and Fae magic worried Rhi. There was something at work here, something that spoke of a sinister, ominous threat.

Since Rhi had offered to look into the magic within the totem, she returned to MacLeod Castle to see if Isla knew anything else. Unfortunately, everyone was asleep.

Rhi contemplated waking the Druid, then decided against it. She walked into the room where the occupants of the castle usually gathered and found a laptop. She curled up in a chair and set the computer in her lap before opening it.

The screen brightened to a blog called *The (Mis)Adventures of a Dating Failure*. Since the mates at Dreagan had already introduced Rhi to the blog, she decided to read the most recent entry.

Loneliness Is A Cruel Bitch

All my life, I've truly believed that there is one person for each of us. From my earliest memories, I've longed to find the man meant for me.

Some might roll their eyes at such a statement, but it's true. You could ask my parents if you don't believe me. I knew he was out there somewhere. I just had to get old enough to be able to find him.

It's like a . . . missing piece of me. As if I searched in a life before and couldn't find him. And I'm looking again.

I fear I'll not find him this time either.

With my other posts, I retold tales of my horrible dates and how I keep putting myself back out there. This time, I'm going to write about something else. Being alone.

I'm in a melancholy mood today, so perhaps that's the reason. I probably shouldn't be writing this at all, but here I am, typing away.

I'm not glum because I had a bad date, but because I spent the evening with my best friend and the love of her life.

Seeing them together reaffirmed that there really is someone out there for each of us.

But it also amplified the fact that I am utterly alone.

While most of my other friends settled for whoever they were dating while in their twenties and married, every one of them is now divorced—most with children.

I feel like the culture dictates that when you're in your twenties, and you've dated someone for a bit, the next logical step is marriage. But neither one stops and wonders, "Are you The One for me?"

Instead, they get married, have a kid or two, and then divorce, fighting over bills, items they acquired before and during their marriage, and the kids.

Divorce is an epidemic. I don't want to be a part of that. In fact, I'd rather wait until—notice I didn't say if—I meet the man who is my other half. If that means I'm alone, then I'll deal with it.

It's not the greatest thing in the world. Sometimes, the loneliness eats at my very soul, but I refuse to settle for anything less than the man who will love me with his whole heart.

Meanwhile, I'll continue on my dates, as awful, embarrassing, and horrid as they might be. If nothing else, they're entertainment for you, and maybe even an example of what not to do.

But when you're feeling low and wondering

why not go out with the guy/girl who keeps flirt-ing, hoping you'll give in, just remember—your instinct has already put them in the No column for a reason. They aren't The One.

You're waiting for that individual because we all deserve to find our other half. Be patient and hopeful. It's what I tell myself every night when I crawl into bed, and every morning when I open my eyes to a new day.

Until next time!

Rhi softly closed the laptop, her mind drifting to a place she didn't want to go, but she couldn't seem to stop it. She understood the blogger perfectly, but her dilemma was different.

Because she'd already found the man—or rather, dragon—meant for her.

Events had torn them apart and kept them separated. Rhi used to hope that they would one day find themselves rekindling their love, but that hope had long since flared out for her.

She'd mistakenly believed she could find happiness with another. And she had, for a short time. As much as she cared for Balladyn, she wasn't in love with him. The fight that severed their relationship made her realize that if it hadn't been this argument, it would've been some-thing else.

They weren't meant to be together. Balladyn wanted her to rule beside him, and she wouldn't become Dark. He thought they could reign over both the Light and Dark, and she knew that was just wishful thinking.

She wanted him to become Light again, but it was very clear that was no longer a possibility.

They each wanted the other to be something they weren't. Relationships like that were doomed from the beginning. It was better that it ended now. She'd never wanted to hurt Balladyn, but by taking him as a lover, she'd done just that. She'd wanted some joy in her life, and in exchange, she'd caused a beloved friend pain.

If she couldn't have the Dragon King who she loved with every fiber of her being, then she would have to be alone. The pain of unrequited love was something she'd endured over the past several thousand years. She could continue to bear it because she knew what it was like to find true love.

Rhi set aside the laptop and rose to her feet. She'd chosen what to focus on, and it was time to move forward with that. With one last look around the room, she teleported to the Fairy Pools on the Isle of Skye.

She walked along the path that hundreds of hikers who came to see the spectacular waterfalls and crystal-clear water took every day. The sky was cloudless with millions of stars blinking in the night.

What none of them knew was that the Fairy Pools were actually a place the Fae used to communicate with the Druids. The breathtaking beauty of the water and the mountains surrounding it only added to the magic and mystery.

Rhi glanced down as she continued toward the mountains. In some places, the water settled into a calm, pristine area where it was so clear you thought the bottom was inches away when it was actually over twenty feet deep. Other places were almost like rapids with the water flowing quickly and violently. The numerous waterfalls enhanced the entire experience.

Just when you thought you had reached the source of the water, you realized it continued toward the mountains.

A figure came out from behind a large boulder with a staff in his hand. Rhi halted and stared into the wizened face of Corann, the leader of the Skye Druids. He had a long, gray beard that fell down his chest, and equally long, gray hair. And he never went anywhere without his walking staff. All he needed was a long robe to replace his khaki pants, plaid flannel shirt, and old boots, and he could've passed as Gandalf.

"Hello," Rhi said as she approached the powerful Druid.

"It's been many years since I last saw you, Rhiannon."

She winced at the use of her full name. "Yes, it has. How are you?"

"My bones hurt," he replied tartly before walking to a set of rocks that were perfect for use as a seat. He sat, said bones popping as he lowered himself. "But you doona want to know of such things. What has brought you here?"

Rhi took the other rock. "When did the Skye Druids begin to keep records?"

"When we learned to write." He frowned. "Why?"

"What about before then? When information was passed down through stories?"

He moved his staff between his legs and rested it against his shoulder. "We wrote down those stories later. What is this about?"

"I'm getting there," she told him. Rhi licked her lips. "I suppose you've read all the records of your people."

"Several times over, in fact. What do you wish to know?"

"When did the Druids settle on Skye?"

He stared at her a long while, stroking a hand down his beard. "No' long after the dragons left."

Her heart leapt in her chest. She'd always wondered if Corann knew about the Dragon Kings. Now, she had answer.

"Be at ease, Rhiannon. I bear them no ill will."

She lifted her gaze to the sky. "So you know everything?"

"I know my ancestors' side of things. They came here to escape the humans who began hunting anyone that defended the dragons—and especially the Dragon Kings. It didna help that my ancestors began to display magical abilities."

"Oh, hell."

His eyes crinkled at the corners as he grinned at her response. "Aye, lass. I had a verra similar reaction, though I do believe my words were much harsher. My ancestors eventually went back to the mainland in secret and traveled to Dreagan, where the Dragon Kings once gathered. The stories tell of a great magic that kept everyone out."

"Your ancestors figured out where the Kings went."

He bowed his head. "They knew it would only be a matter of time before they reemerged, but no one expected it to be thousands of years later."

She leaned forward so that her arms rested on her knees. "I need to know if any Fae ventured onto this realm when the dragons were leaving?"

"I never read of such an event during that time period," he replied with a growing frown. "Then again, my ancestors were just coming into their magic and learning the ways of such gifts."

"But they had already divided into *mies* and *droughs*, right?"

His mouth turned down in a frown. "Unfortunately, that happened almost as quickly as the magic appeared. It never takes long for those dark of heart to find evil."

She couldn't help but think of herself and the darkness that had been prominent within her since Balladyn tortured her when he thought her responsible for him becoming Dark.

"You seek a specific event," Corann said, bringing her thoughts back to the present.

Rhi nodded and tucked her hair behind her ears. "Recently, an archeologist found a dragon skeleton."

"That's no' possible," Corann said in surprise. "The Kings destroyed them. My ancestors wrote about it."

"It was on Fair Isle. A White dragon was trapped with magic."

Corann leaned forward, his shrewd, black eyes holding hers. "Lass, we all know there is nothing stronger than dragon magic. Even the lowest dragon is more powerful than you and me combined."

"But what if it was a Light and Dark Fae and a *mie* and *drough* who combined their magic?"

He slowly straightened, shock filling his face. "Depending on the magic each held, it could happen."

"It did. They killed the dragon and masked it for many millennia until Faith, whose family is descended from Fair, found it. But beneath the skeleton was a wooden dragon, an exact replica of Constantine."

Corann got to his feet with speed that belied his age. His face was lined with worry. "It's no coincidence that they carved the dragon in the image of the King of Dragon Kings."

"But what does it mean?"

He began to walk away. Over his shoulder, he asked, "Are you coming?"

As if she had anywhere else to go.

CHAPTER TWELVE

Nothing could ever quite prepare someone for being flabbergasted. And that's exactly what Eilish was after Ulrik's statement.

She blinked at him. There was no doubt in her mind that he was speaking the truth. This was no jest. He really had gone insane. And that . . . took her aback.

As far as she knew, once someone went mad, there was no coming back from it. Then again, she was discovering that she knew very little about the Dragon Kings.

"I've surprised you," Ulrik stated.

She lifted one shoulder in a shrug. "You wanted to do that."

"So I did."

"Why?"

His gold eyes slid away from her a moment. "I doona know."

"You're not insane now. That means you somehow got past it."

Long, slim fingers raked through his thick, onyx hair that hung to his shoulders. "Aye. All I thought about every day, all day was getting revenge. It's what made me lose my mind, and also how I found it again."

She'd known Ulrik was nothing like Mikkel painted him to be, but Eilish was discovering that Ulrik was much more than she had ever imagined.

He fascinated her, intrigued her.

Enthralled her.

And she had to know more about this man who enticed her so.

"You obviously left the cave," she said.

"I did and found more mortals than ever before. I was naked and filthy, and the people I encountered laughed at and scorned me. I stole clothes and bathed. The next day, I went back to the village and was amused at how differently they treated me. That very day, I put my plans of revenge into motion."

She frowned. "That was . . . eons ago."

"Aye," Ulrik said with a smile.

But it didn't reach his eyes. They were cold and calculating as they watched her. He was within reach, but she didn't dare touch him.

Not because she feared him, but because she was afraid she might like it. There was much about Ulrik that appealed to her, but there was a dark side to him, one that called to her in a way that made her eager and apprehensive at the same time.

"You've proven how strong you are," she said.

He merely stared at her.

Eilish realized that to remain any longer was folly. The more time she spent with him, the more she wanted to trust that he would find the information about her mother.

"I should go," she said and began to walk away.

Ulrik sidestepped in front of her. "Did my story entertain?"

There was a note of violence in his voice, a subtle

warning that she took to heart. "Mikkel skimmed over most of it, and I can tell you, there is much he doesn't know. Entertain? No. It did help to clarify some things, however."

"Is that so?" he asked with a raised brow. "Do you normally take the time to get to know those you're sent to kill?"

"No."

"Then why me?" he demanded and took a step closer.

She involuntarily retreated, coming up against the wall. "I don't know."

"For a moment, I believed you."

"What?" she asked in angry disbelief.

He put a hand next to her head and leaned close. "Do you know what I discovered, Druid? That to trust is to forfeit your life. It's made me question everything and everyone. Countless times, Mikkel has tried to put spies among my people. I always spot them."

For a second, she couldn't speak, she was so stunned. "You think I'm a spy?"

"A beautiful, clever one."

She didn't want to think about the warm feeling that filled her at him calling her pretty. "I'm not a spy."

"Did Mikkel actually think I'd fall for your beauty and vulnerability? You both played a daring game, but I'm on to you."

Without thinking, Eilish shoved against his chest, barely moving him. "I'm not a damn spy!"

Rage filled his face as he glared at her. "No Druid with your power would willingly submit to anyone, much less someone like Mikkel."

"You don't know me."

She tried to move around him, but he blocked her. She tried a second time with the same results. With no other recourse, she gathered her magic and shoved it into his chest. The force of it sent a small shockwave through the cottage, knocking over chairs and lamps.

But it did nothing to Ulrik.

He glanced down at his body and then up at her. "You'll have to do better than that, Druid."

"I'm not a fucking spy," she said and tried to punch his face.

He dodged her blow, his hand ensnaring her wrist easily. He then pinned it against the wall. Without blinking, he captured her other hand and restrained it.

She fought against him, using her magic as best she could. But nothing seemed to work. Ulrik was undeniably strong. Worse, he seemed to know exactly how she would use her magic and blocked it with his own.

"If you're going to kill me, you'll have to do better than this," he taunted.

She didn't want to kill him, just as she hadn't wanted to hurt Gianna in Venice. Eilish had been able to hide her failure to carry out Mikkel's order for Gianna, but she wouldn't be able to do that with Ulrik.

"Enough!" she shouted. "Let me go."

"No."

She lifted her knee, trying to connect with his body, but once more, he proved his quickness. Next, she tried kicking, but it was evident that she was powerless when it came to Ulrik holding her.

Dropping her head back against the wall, she tried to catch her breath as she eyed him. "What do you want?"

A brief frown flashed over his features. "There's nothing I told you this night that is secret. I do no' care who knows. Run back to Mikkel and retell the entire story."

"This was for me," she said through clenched teeth. "Why can't you understand that?"

"Because everyone betrays me!"

His outburst caused both of them to still. She became

all too conscious of how near he was. How much his power and strength were doing wonderful, crazy things to her body and mind.

How she felt the heat of him—and craved more.

His gaze dropped to her mouth, and her stomach fluttered with anticipation and a need so fierce and carnal that it caused her knees to go weak. She stared at him, anxiously waiting for him to do something.

His head lowered gradually, as if he debated with himself the entire time. The next thing she knew, his mouth was on hers. For a heartbeat, neither moved. Then his lips began to slide seductively, sensually over hers.

She responded without a second thought. The taste of him was sexy and exotic. His tongue swept into her mouth to dance with hers. He sought, he claimed. And she greedily returned the ravenous kiss. She felt his hunger, tasted his desire.

Shared his passion.

His body pressed hers against the wall, holding her as he plundered her mouth until she was breathless and shaking for more.

And just as quickly as it began, the kiss was over.

She blinked to focus her eyes while her chest rose and fell with labored breaths. Her gaze landed on Ulrik, who looked at her as if he weren't sure what to do. He released her and stepped back. Then, without a word, he vanished.

Eilish flattened her hands against the wall, her mind a whirl of desire and surprise. Her hand shook as she brought it to her mouth and touched her lips.

The kiss had been . . . epic.

It had bared her soul and showed her what she truly craved—Ulrik. Then the kiss had brought out a wanton, carnal side of her that she hadn't known existed.

The one thing she was certain of was that she couldn't—wouldn't—kill Ulrik. She'd known that for some time, but the kiss had exposed all the secrets and wishes she kept shoved into the dark corners of her heart.

She pushed away from the wall, but she couldn't make herself leave the cottage. There was nowhere she could go that Mikkel wouldn't find her. But she wasn't afraid of him.

No, she was terrified of the passion within her. It shoved aside anything else, even her need to find her mother. She'd never experienced anything close to it, nor did she know how to handle it.

It drummed inside her, beating a rhythm that was wild and lascivious. Ravenous. And that was just from a kiss! She couldn't image how she'd feel if she ever gave her body to Ulrik.

The mere thought of them lying in a bed, their limbs tangled, made her stomach flutter. She had to get control of herself. It took several tries before she was able to stop thinking about Ulrik and their kiss. It was another few minutes before her heart slowed and her breathing returned to normal. Then she straightened from the wall and went to click the claws of her finger rings together, but stopped.

Eilish walked from the cottage and made her way to the lake. She stood on the shore and watched the pale light of the fingernail moon glint along the water.

It was a peaceful place. Quiet and calming. The exact opposite of Ulrik. Not to mention, it was in Ireland. From what little Mikkel had told her about him, Ulrik was a master strategist.

Which meant, he wasn't in Ireland by chance. It was part of his revenge. But against who? Con and the Dragon Kings? Or Mikkel?

Or both?

As she stared at the water, her thoughts turned to the tale Ulrik had shared with her. Everyone had a story and suffered, but she'd been unprepared for the depths that Ulrik experienced.

It'd been hard to keep the sympathy from showing, but she managed it. Mostly because he'd have taken it as pity and become angry. But in truth, she did pity him. He'd loved hard and deeply, and was rewarded with betrayal the likes few ever endured.

Then to be cast out from the place he loved and belonged. . . . It was no wonder he'd gone mad. But Ulrik's strength wasn't just in his muscles and magic, it was in his mind as well as his determination.

He'd risen higher and faster because of his insanity. Not that she could tell him that. At the moment, he believed her a spy. And she couldn't blame him. He distrusted everyone, with good cause.

And just like with most people, he'd done terrible things. He'd also done amazing stuff. Did they balance out in the end? She wasn't sure, but the one thing she did know was that he belonged at Dreagan.

Eilish sighed loudly. She'd made her decision to stop working with Mikkel. He would respond by coming for her. In the meantime, she was going to prepare. Mikkel's attack could come from anyone. Because, like Ulrik, Mikkel had a network of people that spanned the globe.

The best thing for her to do would be to hide, but she'd made this mess for herself, so she'd face whatever came her way. Perhaps that would make up for tampering with the minds of Esther and Kinsey. She had already repaired Esther's mind, and she would do the same for Kinsey. If she ever got the chance.

Not that it would make up for the awful things she had done.

The first place Mikkel would attack would be Graves, as well as the village. She needed to make sure no one was hurt because of her. Eilish clicked her finger rings together and teleported back to her pub.

She began in her quarters and went to every window and door to reinforce the spells already in place that kept others out. Then she went down to Graves and began adding magical security that would protect the humans.

Next, she went outside and fortified the village. She didn't want any innocent deaths on her hands. There was enough she needed to pay for without adding that. But even she knew the spells were just the first line of defense.

Eventually, she'd have to face off against Mikkel. Frankly, she was looking forward to that. He wasn't a Dragon King, which meant they would be on much more even ground.

Perhaps she shouldn't wait for him. Maybe she should initiate the attack.

CHAPTER THIRTEEN

The kiss had been electrifying, exhilarating.

Utterly gripping.

Ulrik had needed to get away from Eilish before he continued kissing her. Or worse.

When he teleported away from the cottage, he'd gone to the only place he felt safe—his mountain on Dreagan. He knew no one would be there since each of the King's mountains was private. It was a place he went to often, a place where no one would ever think to look for him.

Being within its confines eased him, but not as much as he'd hoped or needed. He tried to sit but was soon back on his feet, pacing. When that didn't work, he walked the tunnels.

He knew what he needed. To fly. His skin was too tight, and the more he fought shifting, the more he ached for it until he could no longer hold back.

In his favorite cavern, he shifted without bothering to remove his clothes first. As soon as he was in his true form, he had an instant of relief from the desires that inflamed him. But the peace didn't last.

To his horror, they intensified.

He slammed his hand on the ground and felt his mountain shake. Then he raised his head to the opening high above him to the night sky. All he needed to do was jump and spread his wings. In seconds, he could be among the clouds.

Only, he couldn't. Not unless he wanted to challenge Con that night, and frankly, he wasn't up for it. His mind was too . . . troubled by the fact that he'd kissed Eilish.

And she'd returned that kiss.

He could still taste her on his tongue. Sweet and sexy. And he craved more.

Shaking his head, he tried to dislodge whatever had come over him, but it had a firm, unshakable hold. And the more he tried to forget the feeling of her silky skin, her softness, or the passion in her kiss, the more he thought about Eilish.

The more he hungered for her.

The more he ached.

Because he was so wrapped up in the Druid, it took him a moment to realize that someone was saying his name through the mental link shared by all Dragon Kings.

"Ulrik!"

The sound of V's voice pulled him back from the brink. *"Aye. I'm here."*

"I was beginning to wonder," V said tersely.

Ulrik blew out a breath. *"I was in the middle of something."*

"I got your information about the Druid. Do you want it or no'?"

"You know I do," Ulrik said.

V paused. *"Ryder found documents stating that Eilish Flanagan came to the US in October, twenty-five years ago. The papers said she was adopted by a man named*

Patrick Flanagan, who has dual citizenship in the US and Ireland."

"*Patrick must be the man who raised her. The one who told her he was her father.*"

"*Aye. Nowhere on the birth certificate does it state a mother.*"

If it were anyone other than Ryder looking, Ulrik would be worried about discovering the real mother. But he knew Ryder's affinity for locating information. "*What did Ryder find?*"

"*Nothing.*"

"*Nothing?*"

"*Aye,*" V replied. "*Ryder is unhappy at the moment. However, he's no' giving up looking. But there is nothing on the birth mother.*"

"*That can no' be right. Mikkel has the information.*"

"*Are you sure? He could be lying,*" V said.

That was always a possibility with his uncle, but Ulrik didn't think so. "*The birth mother's information is being hidden. I'm guessing Druids are involved. I know the woman's name was Eireen.*"

"*That will be helpful, but Ryder is going to want to know how I got it.*"

Ulrik stretched out his wings as he looked to the sky once more. "*You're right. Thank you, V. Say nothing more. I'll take it from here.*"

"*I hope you know what you're doing.*"

"*I always do.*"

That was a lie because ever since Eilish came into his life, Ulrik found himself focused on her when he should be thinking and planning other things.

"*Good luck,*" V said and severed the link.

Ulrik growled when he realized he hadn't learned anything more about Eilish. Knowing Ryder, he'd pulled up every picture, grade, and mention of Eilish from the moment she was born until the present day. And Ulrik had been too fixated on the mother to think about that until it was too late. Now, the other Kings would know everything about Eilish. She might have helped Nikolai and Esther, but they still wanted to find her.

The moment someone stepped within his domain, Ulrik knew it. Every mountain on Dreagan was linked with tunnels, just as each also had a hidden entrance for the Kings to enter and leave in dragon form.

He turned and faced the opening to the cavern. He didn't have long to wait before a tall form dressed in a black suit appeared.

Con.

The King of Kings halted just inside the cavern and raised his black eyes to Ulrik. "Should I take this to mean you're challenging me?"

Ulrik briefly thought about doing just that, but for some reason, he couldn't. Not because it didn't fall into his timeline that he'd plotted and planned for millennia, but because he honestly didn't feel like it.

He shifted, returning to his human form, and faced Con. "You'll know when that time comes."

"Then why are you here?"

"This is my mountain."

Con looked around. "I suspect you've been coming here for a while now."

Ulrik didn't bother to reply.

"As I thought," Con said. "I assumed when you caused the mountain to shake that it was time for us."

"No' everything is about you."

Con's brows shot up on his forehead. "How refreshing."

"Is this where you remind me that I'm banished?"

"I could."

Ulrik knew Con could enforce the banishment. As

King of Dragon Kings, he had the ultimate power. They stared at each other.

Then Con put his hands into his pants' pockets. "Ryder told me V is verra interested in the Druid he's been researching."

"I asked V to get me the information. My team doesna move as fast or as thoroughly as Ryder."

"We will stop the Druid," Con said. "One way or another."

Ulrik crossed his arms over his chest, undaunted that he was nude. "Her name is Eilish. As you know. I thought you wanted to persuade her to join you?"

"I'm prepared for either action," Con said. "She controlled Kinsey's and Esther's minds, forcing them to work with those at Kyvor against us. I should kill her for that alone."

"Some things never change, do they?" Ulrik replied.

Con made a sound of disgust. "You always did think you knew best in all things. Well, old friend, let me clue you in on something. If you think being a Dragon King is difficult, try my position."

"You wanted it. Wanted it so desperately, that you did anything to get it."

"I did nothing that you're no' doing now. Besides, you know how our kind works. If I wasna meant to hold this position, then I would've been defeated."

Con turned to the side and made his way to a rock formation. He took his hands out of his pockets and sat before returning his gaze to Ulrik.

Ulrik drew in a deep breath and released it. He was a bit taken aback that Con would lower his guard so, but more than that, Con's attitude caused Ulrik to think of them back in a time when they were still friends.

He missed those days. And he hated that he felt that way.

Con was the enemy. But so was Mikkel. And the enemy of his enemy was his friend.

For now.

Ulrik kicked aside his shredded clothes. "Talk to Eilish first."

"You act as if you doona want her to die."

"Magic is a precious commodity that is slowly being erased from this realm. Why kill one of the most powerful Druids around?" Ulrik asked.

Con's face was impassive. "I'm surprised you're no' trying to turn her to your side. Or have you, and she refused you?"

Ulrik was pretty sure the kiss was anything but a refusal, but he didn't bother saying that. "As I told you before, Eilish wants information. Mikkel has it and is using it to get her to do whatever he wants."

"And you know what information she's looking for."

"I do."

A small frown furrowed Con's brow. "Then why no' tell me?"

"And make it easy for you?" Ulrik asked, a brow raised.

"If I didna know better, I'd think you were willing to do anything to keep the Druid from Mikkel."

"There's much you doona know about me."

Con blinked, shock flashing over his face for a heartbeat before it was masked once more. "You want to save her."

For half a second, Ulrik almost told Con everything. Their conversation while in his mountain had harkened back to the days before he was banished, when he and Con shared everything, a time when there had been no secrets or animosity between them.

It would be so easy to fall back into that. But Ulrik had suffered too much, endured too much—and planned too long to allow that to happen.

Thankfully, Ulrik held his tongue. Their friendship was finished. It had been incinerated long, long ago when Con bound his magic and banished Ulrik.

Con rose to his feet. "You came to me the other day, remember?"

"I came to see my dragons. You happened to be there."

"You didna have to show yourself."

Ulrik dropped his arms to his sides. "It galls you to know I've been on Dreagan and within the mountains without your knowledge, does it no'?"

"If you want to save the Druid, you should tell me all you know."

That wasn't going to happen. Ulrik wanted Eilish away from Mikkel. If she didna want his help, then he'd nudge her in the direction of Dreagan. And Ulrik knew the perfect King to help her—Nikolai.

"Fine," Con stated. "But if you want more intel from Ryder's searches, you ask me. If your pride doesna get in the way."

"My pride?" Ulrik asked, taken aback.

Con turned on his heel and walked away. Over his shoulder, he said, "That's what I said."

Long after he was gone, Ulrik remained in the same spot. His mind was in turmoil. All his thoughts were in utter chaos. He wasn't sure when it had begun exactly, but he'd started to question some decisions and actions he'd made.

Even a hundred years before, he would never have helped Nikolai. It wouldn't have mattered whether he raised him or not. Ulrik's hatred had encompassed all the Dragon Kings.

When had that changed to be directed only at Con? Constantine was the root of it all, yes, but the others had made their decisions to bind Ulrik's magic, as well. Not a single one of them—not Nikolai, not Sebastian, not Anson—had stood with him.

To have the dragons who were his brethren turn against him was a blow that went deep, leaving a vicious scar. The Ulrik who had given so much of himself to not just his clan but all dragons was left with nothing.

He'd been stripped of who he was, forced to live out his days as a mortal. The Kings had stood behind Constantine, watching Ulrik with cold detachment.

Friends he had always been there for, the dragons he'd helped and known for thousands of years. He'd learned just how little any of that meant.

The Ulrik who had looked at life as a gift had withered and died that day.

And the Ulrik who took his place was one who thought of no one but himself.

It was that Ulrik who would survive.

It was that Ulrik who would get his revenge.

It was that Ulrik who would live on.

CHAPTER FOURTEEN

Westport, Ireland

Manipulation was entirely too easy. Mikkel almost wished it were a little harder, but mortals were selfish, needy beings that would do anything for the right price.

Oddly enough, many accepted a very low price.

Harriet Smythe was just such a human. Then again, it was her malicious nature that worked to his advantage. It didn't hurt that she believed any association with him would save her. She'd discover soon enough that there was nothing that could prevent her death.

But for the moment, she was an asset. A lovely one at that. He watched her pour tea in his study before rising from the chair and bringing him a cup.

She smiled, her blond hair pulled back in an intricate, twisted bun. The navy, A-line skirt showed off her pretty legs while the red-and-navy print, silk shirt hung becomingly over her breasts.

"Thank you," he told her as he accepted the cup.

She turned and sauntered her way back to the chair, swinging her hips so that it drew his gaze. She sat, crossing one ankle over the other before pouring her own tea. Then, in her British accent, said, "I've been thinking that Eilish's magic could still be within Kinsey and Esther. We could use that to our advantage."

"The two have already managed to break the Druid's hold."

Harriet shrugged, her blue eyes twinkling with glee. "The Dragon Kings might've broken Eilish's hold over them, but I doubt they were able to erase all of the magic. Not after how deeply Eilish went into their minds. What would it hurt to try?"

He took a drink of the tea, thinking about the steps he'd put into play at Kyvor with Harriett and her boss, Stanley Upton. Harriett had gotten away from the Kings, but Stanley hadn't been so fortunate. "None, I suppose. But why?"

"To remind the Dragon Kings that their time here is coming to an end. Why not scare them?"

He set the teacup down on his desk. "You believe this will frighten the Dragon Kings? My dear, it's going to take much more than that."

"It'll terrify Kinsey and Esther." Harriet's smile grew. "And when the Kings are unable to help the mates, then they'll feel fear."

Mikkel drummed his fingers on his desk, considering her words. "You may have a point."

"They took Stanley. I want them to give him back."

"And you believe that by having Eilish scare those two mates, that the Kings will come to us, Upton in hand, and hand him over to stop whatever the Druid is doing?"

Harriet sat back, her lips pinched as she grumpily turned her gaze away. "You make it sound childish that way."

"Because it is. I've been working against the Dragon Kings for thousands of years. Patience is the key."

"Stanley and I don't have thousands of years," she

snapped, setting down her teacup angrily. "We're not immortal."

He shrugged, uncaring of her dilemma.

She surged to her feet and actually stamped a foot as she fisted her hands at her sides. "Then why am I bloody here?" she yelled.

"I'd think twice about talking to me in such a way," he said in a cold tone. "You're the inferior being. If there was one thing my nephew got right, it was killing mortals."

Harriet's face paled, her blue eyes filling with fear as she slowly sank back onto the chair. "You said I'd be safe with you," she replied in a whisper.

"And so you are. Just remember your place."

"Of course."

He didn't bother to hide his smile when she picked up her cup, her hand shaking enough that it rattled in the saucer.

"What do we do now?" she asked before taking a sip of tea.

"I've given Eilish two days to kill Ulrik. My nephew has outlived his usefulness."

"The Dragon Kings will discover you once Ulrik is dead."

Mikkel smiled. "Yes, they will."

"I don't understand," Harriett said, confusion marring her face.

"You're not meant to. Now, run along. I've a meeting with Taraeth."

Harriet licked her lips and looked at him eagerly. "May I please meet the King of the Dark? I've heard you talk about him so much, and I've never met a Fae."

It was actually an easy way to be rid of Harriett when the time came, Mikkel realized. Taraeth would be happy for the gift, and Harriett would experience untold pleasure as Taraeth slowly drained away her soul.

"Not this time. Now, go," he commanded.

Mikkel then summoned the Dark Fae who was always near to take him to the Dark Palace. Despite all the magic the dragons had, they couldn't teleport as the Fae did. That was the one advantage the Fae had over the Dragon Kings.

When the Dark appeared, a silent, brooding male with close-cropped, black-and-silver hair, Mikkel demanded he be brought to the palace. The Dark touched his arm, and in the next second, Mikkel was standing outside the throne room.

The two guards on either side of the double doors opened them to allow Mikkel access. He strode inside, eager to get the meeting with Taraeth underway.

"Ulrik will be dead by tomorrow so we sh—" He trailed off when he found only Balladyn within.

The Dark raised a brow and grinned. "Oh, please do go on."

"I'll wait for Taraeth."

Mikkel had never liked Balladyn, and he loathed the Irish accents all Fae had. Balladyn wasn't a natural-born Dark, and he had once been high-ranking within the Light. Mikkel wasn't entirely sure Balladyn had relinquished his ties to them.

"Of course," Balladyn said.

Mikkel turned toward the red velvet sofas, but they were gone. Two sleek, black leather chairs were now in their place. He hesitated only a second before sinking onto one of them.

Balladyn, dressed in all black, walked slowly around the room. His black-and-silver hair fell midway down his back. Mikkel wanted to tell him that he looked ridiculous with the braids at his temples, pulling back the top half of his hair, but then again, the Dark knew nothing of fashion.

"You know," Balladyn said, scratching his nose. "You're not supposed to sit until the King gives you permission."

"Taraeth doesn't mind." Mikkel held Balladyn's gaze, daring him to do something.

Balladyn's lips curved into a smile before he pivoted and walked to the throne. He stood before it and turned to face Mikkel. And then he sat.

Just as Mikkel was about to tell him to get out of Taraeth's chair, the implication of Balladyn's actions hit him.

"It finally sinks in," Balladyn said with a soft chuckle. "Ah, the look on your face. The total astonishment and alarm, not to mention the disbelief, is priceless. I've waited for this moment since the first time you walked into this palace."

"When did you become king?"

Balladyn's smile disappeared. His red eyes stared threateningly at Mikkel. "That doesn't fekking concern you. No longer will the Dark be at your beck and call. Whatever alliance you had with Taraeth died when he did."

"Perhaps I misstepped." It grated on Mikkel's nerves to say such a thing, but he needed the Dark. So he would do what he had to in order to pacify Balladyn, but all that would change when Mikkel was King of Dragon Kings.

"You've done nothing *but* misstep," Balladyn stated as he rose to his feet and walked to Mikkel. "You walk around as if you own the Dark and this wretched realm. You come to Taraeth asking for his aid, and you shove it down the Fae's throat."

Mikkel scooted to the edge of the chair. "The arrangement Taraeth and I had was beneficial to us both. He would help me get onto Dreagan, and I'd give him the weapon."

"I know the deal you made." Balladyn's nostrils flared, his hate evident in his gaze. "Tell me, what is the weapon?"

Mikkel thought quickly. He didn't know what the damn weapon was. It was simply by chance that he even knew of its existence, and only because Taraeth had told him how Ulrik shared that bit of news. "You have to see it to fully appreciate it."

"Just as I figured, you don't know what it is."

"I can get it for you." Mikkel knew he was fast losing what little leverage he had.

Balladyn chuckled. "It really is too bad Ulrik isn't here."

Mikkel realized his intention right before the blade appeared in Balladyn's hand. He sent out a wave of magic that acted as a shield right before Balladyn's arm swung around and the sword slammed against it.

"You can't kill me," Mikkel said as he got to his feet.

Balladyn grinned. "Are you sure about that? You're not a Dragon King. You're nothing but a dragon stuck in human form."

Mikkel began to doubt himself. Maybe Balladyn could kill him. He wasn't going to wait around to find out. He ran from the room to where he knew a Fae doorway was. Since he couldn't see it, he had to hope that it was there.

Behind him, he heard Balladyn's laughter. "Run, Mikkel," Balladyn shouted. "Your time is drawing to a close."

Mikkel jumped through where he thought the Fae doorway was and found himself in an alley behind a building and immediately drenched from the rain. He straightened, ignoring the cold, and looked around at everything. He heard people talking and realized he was still in Ireland.

After a glance back, he began to walk quickly. He pulled out his phone and hit the app for his location. Anger ripped through him when he realized he was two hours from his estate in Ireland.

He walked down the alley to the sidewalk and located a pub. Then he called for his car. The time he had to wait for a ride would allow him to cool his irritation and see how this new complication affected his plans.

Mikkel yanked open the door to the establishment and walked inside, taking a booth toward the back. He might have lost the support of the Dark, but at least Ulrik would be dead and gone soon. He had felt the intensity of Eilish's powers. If there was ever a Druid who could do damage to a Dragon King, it was her. And she wanted the information he had on her mum badly enough to kill Ulrik.

Once he was King of Silvers, Mikkel would go after Balladyn. They'd see how confident and cocky the new Dark King was then.

Mikkel could hardly wait until that time. He hoped Ulrik died within the next couple of hours as he waited for his car. Then Mikkel could shift in front of all the mindless mortals drinking and stuffing their faces with food.

Their screams of terror would be music to his ears.

And he wouldn't wait long to challenge Con. That's where Eilish would come in handy again—assuming Mikkel couldn't kill him outright. Mikkel knew how powerful Con was. It had been a long time since anyone made Con battle in such a way. Yet Mikkel had been training for this in his mind from the moment he became a Dragon King, and the power was taken from him again.

Though, he should thank Con. Had the King of Dragon

Kings not taken action against Ulrik, Mikkel wouldn't have tasted what it felt like to have the power of a Dragon King surge through him.

It had been amazing. He'd waited an eternity for his brother to die. Mikkel had even challenged him at one point, but Ualan had simply laughed it off.

Even when Mikkel attacked him, Ualan had bested him in a few moves and told him to go home. That's when Mikkel had really begun to hate him. It was also when he began plotting Ualan's death.

It had taken just a few whispered words to the King of Ivories for a battle to brew over territory. Ualan had died, but Mikkel hadn't become King. The honor had gone to Ulrik. It had been unbearable to watch his young nephew take the reins of such a responsibility.

However, Mikkel couldn't repeat what he'd done with Ualan. Ulrik was shrewd, even more so than his father. As soon as Ulrik was King, he'd gone to the King of Ivories, and they'd come to an agreement.

It was hundreds of years later as Mikkel stewed in his fury that the answer for how to get rid of Ulrik came to him. It was in the form of a beautiful human woman who Ulrik had fallen in love with. Nala had been so easy to manipulate and frighten.

It had only taken a few words, and she'd done the rest. In all his planning, Mikkel never imagined the divide between the Kings, or that Ulrik would have his magic bound and be banished from Dreagan.

But it all had a silver lining. Because shortly, the title of King of Silvers would finally be Mikkel's.

CHAPTER FIFTEEN

Why did one kiss make her think of nothing else? Eilish found herself touching her lips constantly. Worse, she couldn't stop thinking about Ulrik.

She hadn't tried to sleep. She'd known better. Instead, she stood at her window and watched the sun come up. A shower and a change of clothes later, and her mind was still locked on the King of Silvers.

"Damn him," she muttered.

She made her way down to the pub. There was something about walking into Graves when it was empty and silent that appealed to her. She did it every day. It was a reminder of what she had created.

Though if some of her clientele had their way, Graves would remain open twenty-four hours a day. Eilish liked the way things were now. If only they would stay the same, but nothing ever remained stagnant.

Change was par for the course, and she knew it was coming.

She'd sensed it for over a year. Right about the time Mikkel had walked into Graves. If only she'd known then what she knew now. But hindsight was 20/20. She'd always hated that saying, but it was never more appropriate than at this moment.

Her cell phone vibrated in her hand. She lifted it to see a text from her father. If Patrick was her father. She still didn't know the truth of that. And maybe now was the time. Not that she wanted to hurt Patrick. He had been an amazing dad, but she had to know the truth.

About everything.

Eilish clicked her finger rings together while thinking of The Porterhouse in London. In a blink, she was standing on the sidewalk before the pub.

"Oy," a man said as he slammed into her. "Watch where yer going," he grumbled.

"Sorry," she said as he mumbled under his breath and walked around her.

Eilish had stood at the front of the pub just a few days earlier. She had so many questions about her past. Those inquiries had taken her to Ireland, and now London. She'd searched and visited numerous places and people, looking to find some clues.

Yet the idea that the man inside might very well be her biological father terrified her. Partly because if he were her father, then she'd been lied to by Patrick her entire life. Why? What was Patrick hiding from her? Or was he hiding from someone else?

There was no denying the anger within her as more and more truths came to light. She wanted to give her dad—Patrick—the benefit of the doubt, but she didn't think she could talk to him. She'd been dodging his calls for months because he kept telling her to come home. Now, she didn't answer because if she did, she would demand to know everything. And she'd rather see his face for that conversation.

She felt someone staring at her and turned her head to find a tall man with short, thick, white hair and a close-cropped beard staring at her as if he were looking at a ghost. Despite his startling white hair, he wasn't elderly. She'd imagine him to be in his mid to late fifties.

He took a tentative step toward her. There were tears in his blue eyes as he cleared his throat. "For just a moment, I thought you were Eireen. By the saints, you look so much like her."

At the sound of his Irish brogue, she knew she was talking to Donal Cleary.

He gave her a sad smile. "You must be Eilish. I was hoping you'd visit. Come in so we can talk."

She watched as he walked to the door of The Porterhouse and unlocked it. He looked over his shoulder and waved her forward. Eilish inhaled deeply and followed him. He held the door open for her. After she entered, he closed and locked it.

"It's too early for whisky," he said. "Shall I get us coffee?"

Eilish shook her head. She wasn't sure her stomach would be able to handle anything. She was a ball of nerves. It had been one thing to come to Europe to search for her mother. It was quite another to discover that the man you thought was your father really wasn't.

"Aye." Donal ran a hand through his hair. "Forgive me. I don't remember ever being so nervous except for the first time I met Eireen."

At the mention of her mother, Eilish said, "Tell me about her."

Donal's face brightened before he guided her to a booth. Once they were seated, he said, "I could talk about Eireen for days." He chuckled. "I keep expecting to hear you speak with an Irish accent."

His smile relaxed her. She leaned back against the cushion. "So much has been hidden from me about my mother. Then I learned about you."

"And you want to know the truth," he said with a nod. "Eireen was the love of my life. I think I fell in love with her the moment I laid eyes on her. It was like she shook my soul awake, and I hadn't even known it was sleeping. She brightened . . . everything."

Eilish's heart swelled at the knowledge that her mother had been loved so fiercely. She waited with bated breath for Donal to continue.

"Eireen came from a very strict family. She was a Druid, but her line had been diluted so many times that many were born without magic. But not her," Donal said proudly.

Eilish blinked and found herself returning his smile. "You know about Druids?"

"Of course," he replied with a smile.

She gave a short bark of laughter and glanced down at the table. This was a part of herself she wouldn't have to hide as she did with Patrick. Eilish could barely contain herself she was so happy. Then question after question filled her head. "How did you meet?"

"She was looking for other Druids and found her way to my pub. Eireen quickly discovered that there weren't just other Druids hanging about my place, but Fae, as well. Once she realized that, she was there almost every day. Because within the walls of my establishment, she could let her magic show and be herself. And it was a glorious sight."

Eilish wished she could've seen it. "So what happened? Did she have a run-in with another Druid or Fae?"

Donal shook his head, a small frown forming at her words. "Not at all. She began to learn and develop her magic with the help of the other Druids. Eireen could grasp any spell, no matter how difficult, with ease."

"So she was powerful?"

"Aye. And for six months, we had an amazingly beautiful life. We'd fallen in love and were making plans to marry. She wanted to leave Dublin and get as far from her family as she could. Then one day, her two sisters followed her to my pub."

Eilish sat forward and rested her arms on the table. Donal's gaze lowered to the finger rings and his gaze took on a faraway look. She removed the ring from her index finger and placed it in his hand.

Donal held the jewelry, lovingly stroking it. "Eireen used magic to conceal so much from her controlling family, but somehow, they discovered what she was doing. Her eldest sister whispered something in Eireen's ear. While I waited for her to tell them to go away, she rose and told them to wait outside."

"I don't understand. Why go with them at all?"

"She tried to explain it to me, but I was furious and wouldn't listen. I remember her saying that she had one last promise to her family to fulfill, but I couldn't see reason. She was a grown woman with her own place, yet she continued to fear her family. People who didn't have magic."

There was something more going on with that. Of that, Eilish was sure. No Druid would fear someone like that—family or not—unless there was good reason. And that usually meant magic.

"That was the last day I saw her," Donal continued. He set the finger ring near Eilish's hand and raised his gaze to her. "When she didn't return in a few days, I began searching for her. I even got the authorities involved, but nothing came of it. Not even the various private investigators I hired found anything. It was like Eireen disappeared off the face of the Earth."

Eilish returned the ring to her finger. "I was born in Ireland but brought to Boston. There, a man named

Patrick Flanagan told me he was my father, and he and his wife, my stepmother, raised me. I was never allowed to speak about my mum or ask any questions."

Donal jerked his chin to the finger rings. "Those were Eilish's. How did you come to have them?"

"My fa—Patrick gave them to me on my eighteenth birthday and told me they belonged to her."

Donal squeezed his eyes closed. "You are her daughter then. I knew it as soon as Nikolai and Esther showed me a picture of you." He opened his eyes and looked at her. "Eireen wanted a family. There was no way she would've willingly given you up."

"Then where is she? I know nothing about her other than that her name is Eireen."

"Eireen Duffy. She was from Dublin. But it won't do you any good to look. I've searched that city every few years."

Eilish felt buoyed now that she had pertinent information that could help in locating her mother. "But you didn't have a Druid helping you."

Donal hesitated before he sighed. "Multiple Druids have helped, as has a Light Fae. None of them have been able to locate Eireen."

"Oh." Thoroughly deflated now, Eilish didn't know what she was going to do. Then she remembered that there was someone who could search souls and see if her mother was dead. It wouldn't be the answer she was hoping for, but it would bring her and Donal closure.

"What does Patrick think of you being in Ireland?"

Donal's question jerked her out of her thoughts. She blinked, shrugging. "I didn't tell him for over a year. He thought I was traveling in Australia. But as soon as I told him, he tried to make me return home."

"Hmm," Donal said. "He didn't care that you left to

go off to Australia, but he reacts about Ireland. Is he Irish?"

"He is."

Donal nodded. "That explains the tinge of Irish brogue I hear in your words. But it's strange he would have such a reaction."

"I didn't think about it until you brought it up. I just assumed he thought my time having fun was over and he wanted me home."

"Does he still ask you to come back?"

She nodded slowly. "Every week."

"But he hasn't come to get you?"

"No. But I am a grown woman."

Donal smiled. "That you are, my dear. You're determined, just as she was."

She wanted to ask Donal if he was bold and daring, but all she had to do was look at The Porterhouse to see that he was that and more. Could she have gotten that from him? Could he really be her father?

"Is this your only pub?" she asked.

He looked around with pride in his eyes. "I own bars all over England and Ireland. Your mother wanted to buy this place. It was to be her wedding present. I remain here, hoping that she will one day walk through those doors."

Eilish looked at the door and found herself hoping for the same thing.

"What do you do in Ireland?" he asked.

She turned her head back to him. "I own a pub called Graves. It caters strictly to the paranormal, but I have rules in place that no Fae can harm any humans. I extended that to the entire village."

"Really?" he asked with wide eyes. "That is amazing. I use markings my family learned from the Fae long ago to keep everyone in check. They're on every building I own."

They shared a smile, and Eilish realized there was much the two of them had in common.

She glanced at the table. "Was my mother pregnant before she disappeared?"

"If she was, she didn't tell me. But I do know she wasn't seeing anyone else."

"But . . . there's always a chance she got pregnant with me right after she left with her sisters."

Donal scratched his chin as he considered her words. "Aye, I suppose there is. When were you born?"

"You mean, when did Patrick tell me I was born? I can't believe anyone."

"I've never given up hope of finding Eireen. I'll keep looking until the day I die. She's the only one I've ever loved. I know that you'll keep searching, as well. I'll help you in any way possible. I've money and resources."

Eilish swallowed, hating the mistrust she found swelling within her. "Are you offering because I could be your daughter?"

"I'm offering because you're Eireen's daughter. Whether you're mine or someone else's doesn't matter. Locating Eireen and finding answers to questions we both have is the priority." He paused. "But I would be happy to call you daughter."

Eilish felt a rush of emotion fill her. This was the most information she had ever learned about her mother. The fact that it came from a man who might be her biological father only made it all the sweeter. She found that she very much wanted to be the product of such a man and her mother—and their love.

She scooted from the booth and found a paper napkin

and a pen next to the register. There, she wrote down her number and brought it to Donal.

He accepted it with a grin. "Thank you."

"We'll find her," Eilish said, then clicked the finger rings together.

CHAPTER SIXTEEN

Hunger. It thrummed relentlessly through Ulrik. And there was only one person who could ease him—Eilish.

He'd never experienced desire that raged within him with such ruthless insistence before. While he knew full well the needs of the flesh, this was something altogether different.

Something palpable, something so profound he couldn't give it a name.

Or maybe he didn't want to name it.

Either way, it consumed him to such a degree that it was all he thought about. And all he wanted.

He'd left Dreagan and returned to the cottage in Ireland in the hopes the Druid might still be there. But only her scent of lavender lingered.

When he could stand it no more, he swam in the lake, but that only made him crave her more since she'd come to him there. Only one option remained.

Ulrik would go to her.

It was a risk. If she were playing the damsel for Mikkel, then he could be walking right into a trap. Since a female had planned to betray him before, he wasn't too keen on allowing another the opportunity.

At least with Nala, he hadn't known what she planned. He knew full well there was a good chance Eilish was playing him for a fool. How could he recognize that and still let his desires rule him?

Because he'd been an idiot and kissed her. Now that he knew her taste, he needed more. Hungered for more.

Craved more.

He strode from the water to the cottage. Once inside, his head turned to where he'd had her against the wall. The intoxicating taste of her had overwhelmed him, seduced him. He'd been so wrapped up in the pleasure that he'd barely heard her soft gasp—or felt her body soften.

Either she'd wanted the kiss as much as he, or she was a truly expert actress.

Ulrik usually had a nose for such things, but this time, he couldn't seem to work through the problem. He knew better than to trust her, yet he still wanted to go to her, wanted to kiss her once more.

And to his dismay, the thought of her giving in to him without any lies or promises was something he very much desired.

He squeezed his eyes closed and grabbed his head with both hands as he struggled to push her from his mind. He'd gone millennia without encountering anyone who pushed him to the brink as she did.

Why now?

Why *her*?

If he weren't careful, she could be the end of him. Eilish might well finish what Nala began.

And it was time he found out exactly where the Druid stood in all of this.

Without thought of clothes or drying off, he turned his

mind to Eilish and Graves before touching his silver cuff. He teleported to the third floor of the pub.

He smiled as he stood outside her door in the dim lighting and put his hand against the spells that were meant to keep him out. She'd added several more layers, but it wasn't enough. Not for him. It would, however, take a Fae and even Mikkel some time to get through the barriers.

Part of Ulrik wanted to bust through them as he had before to prove to her that nothing could keep him out. But a calmer part of him realized that if there were even a smidgen of a chance that Eilish might want to stop working with Mikkel, then he needed to leave the spells intact.

He knew she was in the pub. He could feel her. Though he wasn't sure how. There was magic everywhere, from Druids and Fae, but even without seeing her, he knew she was there.

Turning, he looked at the stairs, contemplating going down and finding her. Others would see him, which meant it would get back to Mikkel. No, he didn't want anyone to see him. But he did want Eilish.

And there was one surefire way to get her up there.

Ulrik faced her door once more and pushed hard against her barrier. She was smart enough to have added a spell that would alert her when anyone attempted to get into her home, and she'd come to find out who it was.

The stairway was wide enough for two people to walk side by side, and the landing to her flat was only slightly bigger. There was nowhere to hide, but then again, he wasn't interested in hiding.

Eilish was in a foul mood. She'd been elated after talking to Donal, and had even begun a new search now that she had her mother's full name. She'd learned so much from Donal, and she doubted Mikkel had anything else to add. It was just another reason to tell the asshole to kiss off. But he'd figure that out soon enough when Ulrik didn't die.

Once she returned to her flat, the exhaustion had overtaken her. She made the mistake of taking a hot bath, and she'd fallen asleep in the water.

The dream had begun harmlessly enough, but as always, it quickly turned. She was in the dark, but she wasn't alone. Just like a hundred times before, she gathered her magic, ready to use it. Why? She didn't know. Instinct told her to be wary. Suddenly, there was a dark shape looming before her. Right before he struck, she saw the dragon tattoo on his chest.

She woke with a jerk, sloshing water all over the floor. The dream was one she'd had for more than seven years. Usually, she could shake it off. But not this time.

It lingered, constantly popping into her head. The menacing feeling of the dream, as well as the knowledge that whoever the Dragon King was, he was going to kill her, haunted her.

She desperately wanted to know which of the Kings it would be, but it wasn't as if she could ask them to take off their shirts so she could see their tats.

Actually, if it hadn't been for Mikkel telling her that all the Dragon Kings had tattoos of the special blend of red and black ink, she'd never have known they were the ones who would be behind her death.

Of course, she hadn't helped her cause by working against them with Mikkel. She'd harmed two of their mates, and despite helping Esther, she wasn't so sure that either she or Nikolai would lend their aid if Eilish asked.

Fuck. She'd messed up big time.

She walked to the railing on the main level, looking down at the dance floor below. Her gaze went to the bar,

hoping she'd spot Ulrik. Just thinking about him made
her want to kick herself. What the hell was she doing? A
Dragon King was going to kill her. Why would she get
involved with one?

She inwardly snorted at that thought. There wouldn't
be any *getting involved* with Ulrik. He might have kissed
her as if he were a dying man and she the essence of life,
but the look on his face afterward had said it all.

And lest she forget, he'd also accused her of lying—
about everything.

Ulrik was too distrustful of everything and everyone
to ever have any sort of relationship. While he'd told her
his story, she'd briefly thought he might be able to be
saved. After all, he had come back from madness.

But the truth was, Ulrik was broken. Completely and
utterly. There was nothing that could heal him, mostly
because he didn't want it. He liked the course he was on,
and he'd remain there until either he killed Con or was
killed himself.

The dream of her death, along with Ulrik's breath-
stealing kiss, and her decision not to work with Mikkel
anymore was giving her a raging headache.

She couldn't even fix it with magic since she had yet
to learn to heal herself, but in some ways, she felt she deserved the pain. Especially since she was the one to
blame for her current situation. If only she'd heeded her
instincts and refused Mikkel to begin with. But the need
to learn about her mum consumed her.

Eilish ran her hand along the railing as she made her
way to the stairs. She was nearly to them when a rush of
heat stole over her right before her magic warned her that
someone was trying to break through her spells on the
upper level.

"Oh, I don't think so," she mumbled and strode to the
stairs. She rushed down them, people getting out of her

way as she approached. Eilish didn't slow until she got to the bar area. After a quick look around, she disappeared through the hidden doorway and started up the stairs.

She was halfway up when she raised her gaze and spotted Ulrik. Naked. Before she could begin to appreciate the sight of his chiseled body that fairly vibrated with barely leashed power, her gaze landed on the tattoo that covered his chest.

The dragon had its head resting on Ulrik's shoulder, his front arms looking as if it were hugging him while its back legs appeared to dig into Ulrik's stomach. The dragon's wings were spread, and the long tail wrapped around Ulrik's waist.

Her mind blanked, her heart skipped a beat, and she tripped on the stairs. Catching herself with her hands, Eilish straightened and returned her gaze to Ulrik.

He was frowning down at her. "What's wrong?" he demanded.

As if she were going to tell him that he was the one she'd seen take her life in her dreams. It was just her luck to find someone that made her blood heat only for him to be her killer.

She took a deep breath and tried to calm her now racing heart before she continued up the stairs. "Should I be happy you couldn't get through my spells?"

He waited until she reached him. Then he gazed at her with his golden eyes and said, "I chose no' to breach your wards and leave you defenseless."

"Why, thank you," she said sarcastically. "If you wanted to talk, you could've come into the pub."

She glanced at his body, noting the hard sinew, his broad shoulders, and the power that was usually deceptively hidden by his clothes. She'd known he had a nice body, but she'd never expected this. My God, he was breathtaking. Totally hot and mouthwatering.

"I want the truth," he stated.

It was going to be a long night. Eilish sighed and disengaged the wards enough for him to follow her through the door into her flat. Once inside, she replaced the spells and closed the door then leaned back against the wall.

She bit her lip as she gazed at his impeccable ass and muscular legs. His back was superb, but then she'd always been a sucker for a man with a great back.

He turned to face her. "You're no' demanding to know what I'm talking about?"

"What's the point?" she asked with a shrug. "You won't believe anything I say."

"Try me."

She gave him a flat look and pushed away from the wall. "I'm not going to waste my time. You can't trust, so you'll never believe anyone. Especially me."

"Try me," he repeated.

This time she heard the urging in his voice. Almost as if he wanted her to convince him to trust her.

She stared into his gorgeous eyes for a long time while he stood still as stone. Only when she looked away did he rake a hand through his coal black hair.

Here she was being a fool again. What was it about Ulrik that kept her on this same path? She knew she should get off and forget him, just as she planned to do with Mikkel. But she knew the answer.

It was that amazing kiss.

Damn him. Damnhimdamnhimdamnhim.

She blew out a breath and put her hands on her hips. "Fine. I'll play along even though it's pointless. Ask what you want, but know whatever I tell you is the truth."

"Is all of this an act so I'll offer to help and you can betray me?"

CHAPTER SEVENTEEN

This was the first time in his very long life that Ulrik wanted to be wrong. Yet as he stood and watched Eilish, he wasn't sure he could believe anything she said.

"Again with thinking I'm some spy for Mikkel," Eilish said.

But there was no heat in her words. It was as if she expected it. Was he that predictable? Well, when it came to trusting people, he certainly was.

The Druid sighed. "I'm not a spy. I'm not trying to betray you."

"Mikkel wants me dead."

"You're stronger than he is. You can best him."

"You forget. I saw your talk with him in my antique shop. I know that he wants you to kill me. I heard you say you could kill Con, as well. You didna even hesitate when he asked."

Eilish didn't deny any of it. She held his gaze and said, "Have you ever wanted something so badly that you did questionable, unethical, and horrible things to others to achieve it? That's me. I want to find my mum. Mikkel said he knew how to do that, and he'd only give me that information if I helped him. So, I became who he thought I was."

"A killer," Ulrik replied.

She nodded. "Yes."

"He felt the strength of your magic."

"Not once did he ask me if I'd ever touched dragon magic before."

"He didna need to," Ulrik said. "He's encountered such magic before. Mikkel only had to give you an incentive to get you to do what he wanted."

She walked to him, stopping a foot away. "I'm not spying for him. Nor am I setting you up for betrayal. I know you can't believe me. And sadly, it's your inability to trust that will cost you everything you've gained since your banishment."

Ulrik was about to tell her that it was because he didn't trust that he had gotten where he was, but she kept talking.

"Look at what you've achieved! You went mad. And you came back from it. You started with nothing, and have amassed an empire you care nothing about. You built it and use it simply to bring down your brethren."

"Con," he corrected.

Her head tilted to the side, a slight smile pulling at her lips. "You should rejoice in what you've done. More than that, you and the Dragon Kings have a common enemy. You should join forces. But you won't. You'll continue to believe you can do it all on your own. Hell, maybe you can."

She turned to walk away, but he reached out and grabbed her wrist. Eilish looked from his hold to his face. Ulrik told himself to let her go, to forget everything about her. He didn't need her help or the worry that she might be a spy. He was better off alone as he had been for so many centuries.

And yet, he couldn't release her.

The desire he'd mistakenly believed he could control erupted with the force of a volcano. His shaft hardened. The Druid's gaze lowered, her eyes rounding as his cock grew. And the longer she watched, the harder he got.

Even with her magic, she was still a mortal. He despised them.

But he didn't hate her.

He knew he should keep fighting the attraction, but he couldn't. Ulrik yanked her against him and slanted his mouth over hers. The taste of her made him moan. She was kissing him back, her tongue sliding against his.

At the moment, he didn't care if she was with him or against him. All he cared about was that she wasn't pushing him away.

He wrapped both arms around her, holding her leather-clad body tightly against him. But it wasn't enough. He needed her bare, skin-to-skin. Ulrik tore the leather tank top down the middle and tossed it aside. Her bra was next. While he unbuttoned her pants, her nails raked down his back.

"Boots," she said between kisses.

He leaned back to look at her with a frown.

Breathing heavily, she pointed to her feet. "My boots."

They both bent and hastily removed the footwear, but by that time, his impatience had reached its limit. He ripped her pants and yanked them from her. After, she held his gaze and slipped her black lace panties over her hips and down her legs before kicking them away.

His eyes raked over her amazing body. Tall with mocha-colored skin begging to be touched, Eilish was stunning. Her breasts were full without being too large. She was lean and had curves in all the right places.

He went to touch her, but couldn't decide if he wanted

to caress the swell of her hips, the indent of her waist, or cup her breasts.

Then she put her hand on his chest atop his tattoo. He felt something shift within him, almost as if his tat had moved. It made his breath catch. His eyes met hers. He saw the desire in her green-gold depths.

They came together in a tangle of limbs as they touched each other, the kiss wild and feverish. A groan tore from him as her hands roved over his shoulders and down his back. Her caress was light and sensual, as if her desire seeped like magic from her fingertips into his skin everywhere she touched.

He kissed across her jaw to her neck. His hand slid into the thick strands of her deep brunette locks as her head leaned to the side before falling back.

The taste of her skin was almost as heady as her kisses. Tracing his tongue down the slim column of her throat, he bent her backward over his arm so he could reach her breasts. The globes swelled, her nipples puckered beneath his gaze. And it made his balls tighten.

"I can't wait," she mumbled. "I need you inside me."

He wanted that too, but first, he planned to taste every inch of her. This wasn't going to be a hurried session. He was going to take his time.

Ulrik flicked a tongue over a nipple then blew on the peak. Eilish moaned and rocked her hips against him. He cupped the breast and massaged it. Then he wrapped his lips around the nipple and suckled.

The harder he sucked, the faster she rocked her hips against his cock. And he was just getting started. He moved to her other breast and teased the peak by holding it lightly between his teeth and moving his tongue rapidly back and forth.

When her knees gave out, he held her up with his

arms. He walked her backwards to the wall where he braced her. Then he knelt before her.

If she were going to die by Ulrik's hand, at least she'd go out experiencing true ecstasy. Eilish knew it was folly to give her body to him, but she couldn't seem to refuse him. Her body craved him. And that was that.

She looked down at Ulrik. My God, he was gorgeous. Sinfully so. With his gold eyes, midnight hair, and devil-may-care attitude, he appealed to her on a plane she couldn't name or find. There was no need to try and dissuade herself either because her body had made up its mind long before he kissed her.

That had only sealed her fate.

Those gold eyes darkened with the heat of his passion. He held her gaze as he lifted one of her legs and draped it over his shoulder. Her lips parted, her breath hitching as she waited for him to lean close.

As soon as his mouth touched her sex, her eyes slid shut, and her head fell back against the wall as pleasurable warmth spread through her. It settled low in her belly, tightening with each graze and flick of his tongue.

"Doona come," he ordered.

Was he crazy? As if she could hold that back, especially when she was so close. But she should've known he was going to help her do exactly that.

He pulled away, and she groaned in frustration. Her body pulsed with desire.

"Look at me."

She wanted to refuse him, yet she found herself opening her eyes. He moved her leg off his shoulder, but he didn't release it. Instead, he climbed to his feet.

He rested his other hand on her hip before caressing down her butt to the back of her thigh. With little effort, he lifted her, holding her legs wide as she reached for his shoulders.

"We come together," he told her.

She nodded, lost in a sea of gold. When she felt the head of him brush against her sensitive flesh, she gasped. And he smiled triumphantly.

Eilish twined his hair around her fingers as he pushed inside her. Ever since she'd spied his impressive length as he hardened, she couldn't wait to have him inside her. Inch by inch, he filled her, and her body stretched.

With one final thrust, he was fully seated. She waited for him to move, but he leaned in and kissed her. It wasn't like the frantic kisses from before. This one was sensual and unhurried.

And, somehow, it affected her even more.

Firmly in his hold, she was surprised when he stepped away from the wall. Then he began to walk toward her bedroom. And with every step, he moved inside her, sending pleasure shooting through her.

By the time they reached her bed, she was eager for more. And he didn't make her wait. He put a knee on the mattress and lowered her. She wrapped her legs around his waist once he released her.

He braced his hands on either side of her head and leaned over her before slowly pulling from her body. Then he drove back inside.

The slow, forceful thrusts tightened her desire, pushing her toward release. His command not to come repeated in her head. She tried to slow the tide, but it was gaining too much momentum.

Then he began to move faster, thrusting deep and hard. It threw her right to the edge of release, and she fought not to give in. The sight of his face tightened with desire as he pumped into her body, showed her that he too was fighting it.

She'd never gotten to the point of climax so quickly before. Yet, somehow, Ulrik knew just how to touch, just where to caress to make her yearn, to make her—burn.

"No' yet," he ground out.

She dug her nails into his arms as he continued to plunge into her. The sounds of their bodies joining, their flesh meeting, only added to the experience.

"I—ca . . . can't. I—"

"Now," he ordered.

With one word, pleasure exploded. Her body pulsed with such bliss that it was as if she were floating. And she felt his staff throb within her, felt his seed pour inside.

And still the climax continued.

Just when she thought she couldn't handle any more, the orgasm began to taper off. She opened her eyes to find Ulrik still over her—and still inside her.

"Once willna be enough," he murmured.

She knew exactly what he meant. He'd had his way with her, but she wasn't going to let that happen again until she had a chance to tease and torment him.

Perhaps this was how he would kill her. Death by sex. It was how the Fae did it. All in all, it was a pretty good way to go. In fact, if she had to choose, she'd pick dying in Ulrik's arms as he made love to her. It had been the best sex of her life, and she was sure he'd stolen some of her soul, just like the Fae did. Surprisingly, she didn't mind.

She found it impossible to keep her eyes open. The past few days had taken a toll on her, but the sheer force of her climax from Ulrik had wiped it all away, leaving her drowsy.

He withdrew from her slowly. The bed dipped as he stood. She wished he'd stay. She tried to tell him that, but she was already drifting off into the arms of sleep.

CHAPTER EIGHTEEN

Fucked. That's what he was.

Ulrik stood in the doorway of Eilish's bedroom, his gaze on her naked body lying with her head turned to the side and a hand by her face.

He'd watched her drift off to sleep, and for just a second, he'd almost curled up next to her. But he knew what lunacy that was. Already, he'd overstepped boundaries by making love to her. But damn, she'd been exquisite. Her body open and giving, her passion a magnificent thing to behold.

He'd thought to push her to her limits, when in fact, she was the one who drove him to his. No other had done that.

Ever.

Ulrik wasn't sure what to make of the Druid. She was gorgeous, passionate, thrilling, and dangerous. And he loved every layer he discovered. The more he uncovered, the more he wanted to know.

He ran a hand over his chest. It had taken him a while, but he finally realized what it was he felt. Relaxed. When was the last time he'd felt even remotely rested? He honestly couldn't remember.

That's how he knew that it was risky to remain around Eilish. He should've comprehended that when he wanted to help her. No. It went even further than that. It should've clicked when he didn't want to kill her.

She was a damn human. But, Heaven help him, he wanted to climb back onto the bed and make love to her again.

He turned away, raking his hand through his hair. He was so fucked.

After Nala, he'd sworn that no female would ever again get close enough to betray him. It was a vow he'd easily kept all these numerous, unending centuries. Right up until he walked into Graves and spoke with Eilish the first time.

He always had a plan, as well as numerous backup strategies for when things changed—because while most people were predictable, there were always occasions when the humans did something unusual.

Ulrik couldn't remember a time when he looked over his plots and didn't know what action to take. Every day, he went over the plans, changing and correcting things as needed to bring him closer to his end goal.

Why then was his mind completely blank? He didn't know what to do or where to go. He was a vacant screen, almost as if he'd been reset somehow.

He turned and looked over his shoulder at Eilish. Was she the cause? Surely, not.

"No," he murmured.

He wouldn't be put in such a position again. He'd been down that road once, and he didn't need to travel it ever again. No matter how wonderful she was in bed, no matter how much her courage and magic intrigued him, Ulrik was through with her.

His hand hovered over the silver cuff on his wrist that would take him back to the cottage. The fact that he didn't want to leave should've propelled him away instantly. So why wasn't he departing?

With every second he remained, he could feel himself spinning wildly. This wasn't who he was. He was controlled, calm. He was focused and driven. In short, he was obsessed with his vengeance.

He looked away from the Druid and took a deep breath. Then he teleported to the cottage to shower and put on clothes. Thirty minutes later, he was at his desk with his laptop open, reading emails.

His contacts had come through with information on Eilish, but there was nothing about her mother. A dark-haired, dark-eyed man pictured as her father, a Patrick Flanagan, caught his attention, though.

Nikolai and Esther had been sure Donal Cleary was her sire. If that were the case, then Patrick had either stolen Eilish as a baby, or he'd been told to take her. Neither option was good because that meant there was much more to the Druid and her past than Ulrik first realized.

The only way to get to the truth was to go to the source. He looked at the clock, calculating the time difference in Boston. After hiding the desk with his magic, Ulrik touched his cuff and thought of Patrick Flanagan and Boston.

A heartbeat later, he stood outside a brownstone. Ulrik glanced around to see if anyone had noticed his sudden appearance, but most everyone had their faces buried in their electronics.

Just as Ulrik was about to walk up the steps to the door, he noticed a man bundled in a coat with short, dark hair, striding toward him. Eilish's father—or kidnapper. The man spotted Ulrik and slowed to a halt.

"Patrick Flanagan?" Ulrik said. "I'm wondering if we could talk about Eilish."

"Who are you?" the man demanded, his Irish accent still thick after so many years in America.

"A friend."

Patrick raised a brow. "What's a Scot doing here?"

"Trying to find answers."

Patrick shook his head and sighed loudly. "She shouldn't be there."

"Why?"

"I keep hoping she'll come home."

"Why?" Ulrik asked again.

Patrick looked at him as if just remembering he was there. "I cannot tell you."

"If Eilish is in danger, then you should go to her."

"I can't."

Ulrik took a menacing step toward the mortal. His answer confirmed Ulrik's suspicions about the Druid. "Explain it to me. Now."

"Come inside," Patrick said as he pulled keys from his pocket.

Ulrik followed the human inside the brownstone and to the back where the kitchen was. Despite it being early morning, the man opened a cabinet and took out a bottle of whisky. Patrick downed two shots before offering some to Ulrik.

"I'll pass, and I'd rather you stay sober so you can talk."

"There isn't enough whisky in Boston to get me drunk," Patrick mumbled. Then he shoved away the glass and blew out a breath. "Is Eilish well?"

"She's thriving, actually."

"She lied to me," Patrick said. "I thought she was in Australia. I should've known she'd go to Ireland to look for Eireen."

Ulrik folded his arms over his chest. "Her mother."

"Aye." His face suddenly pinched with worry. "Eilish hasn't been in contact with the Duffys, has she?"

"I take it that's Eireen's surname. As far as I know, Eilish only knows her mother's first name."

Patrick put his face in his hand, his shoulders shaking. After a moment, he raised his tear-streaked face. "Eilish has magic, doesn't she?"

"A lot of it, actually."

"I looked for signs of it while she was growing up, but I saw nothing. And she so wanted to know about her mother. It was a mistake giving her Eireen's finger rings. But a child should know their mum, right?"

This puzzle Ulrik was trying to decipher was becoming more and more complicated. "You should've told Eilish things about her mother when she asked. Refusing to talk about her only made Eilish more keen to figure things out."

"I was trying to protect her."

"From who?" Ulrik demanded.

Patrick ran his arm over his eyes to wipe away the tears and sniffed loudly. "From her family."

"Why would she need to fear her family?"

"Because they want to kill her."

Ulrik's arms dropped to his sides. Of all the things Patrick could've said, Ulrik hadn't expected that. The need to protect that swelled within Ulrik nearly matched his anger. "Perhaps you should start from the beginning."

"If Eilish is using magic, they'll find her. I can't believe they haven't done it already."

"She wants to locate her mother, which means eventually, she'll find them. So tell me what's going on."

Patrick cleared his throat and leaned back against the counter. "I was a friend of Eireen's. We'd known each other since we were children. She would often come to my house to escape her family. They were so strict and cruel. It was during those times that Eireen showed me her magic. It was our secret, something we never discussed unless we were alone."

Ulrik remained silent, waiting for him to continue.

"We kept in touch long after we finished school. She told me she'd fallen in love with a man named Donal Cleary while she was looking for other Druids. She also showed me how much her magic had grown. I was going to help her leave with Donal so they could get married."

"Why was she keeping that from her family?" Ulrik asked.

Patrick lowered his chin to his chest for a moment. "That family was malicious. They kept Eireen bound to them in ways I can't even figure out after all these years. And after Eireen and Donal became engaged, I thought we'd celebrate. I was happy that she'd found someone who understood and accepted who she was, and I thought she was finally going to get away."

"You weren't in love with her?"

Patrick looked askance at him "Eireen was like a sister to me."

Ulrik inwardly shrugged. "Go on."

"She rang me, and I could hear that she was crying. She said she thought her parents knew about her magic. Her sisters had begun asking a lot of questions, and Eireen had to lie at every turn. I told her to leave that day with Donal. She cried harder, and I knew there had to be more that she wasn't telling me about her family. I never liked them. They were never unkind to me, but they weren't exactly likable people either. They never allowed anyone into their house, and hated that I was friends with Eireen."

Ulrik frowned. "Were you her only friend?"

"Aye. Up until she went looking for Druids. Those few

months after she met Donal, she was the happiest I'd ever seen her."

"So what happened?"

"I tried to get her to tell me why she feared her family. It was one of the few things she never spoke about. When she wouldn't, I told her to at least tell Donal. She said she was going to the next day. But then her sisters followed her to the pub."

Ulrik leaned back against the wall. "She told Donal she had one last promise to keep with her family. Do you know anything about that?"

"No," he said with a shake of his head.

"Do you know Donal?"

"I never met him. Eireen told me everything about him, though."

Ulrik narrowed his gaze on Patrick. "Donal never saw Eireen after that day, but I think you know exactly what happened."

His face paled as his expression crumbled. "Aye, I do, but I wish to God I didn't."

"Tell me," Ulrik demanded.

Patrick squeezed his eyes closed. "I'd been calling Eireen for nearly a week. It wasn't like her to not respond or return my calls. I was about to go to Donal when she rang me. There was such fear in her voice. She told me she was hiding by the port. She wanted me to come to her and make sure I wasn't watched or followed.

"It took me an hour to get to her once I realized I was being tailed by two different people. When I finally found her, I almost didn't recognize her. Eireen was filthy. Her clothes were dirty and torn, and her feet were bare and bloody."

"She escaped," Ulrik deduced.

Patrick nodded, swallowing hard. "I got her food, which she scarfed down. When I tried to get her to come with me, she refused. She said her family would know I helped her. But I wasn't going to leave her alone. Especially when she told me. . . ."

"Told you what?" Ulrik pressed when Patrick's voice trailed off.

"She was pregnant." The man wiped a hand down his face. "I tried to talk her into contacting Donal, but she said if she did, her family would kill him. I spent the next few hours convincing her that I wasn't going to leave her. If she wouldn't call Donal, then I would help her. We went on the run after that."

Ulrik pushed away from the wall. "Until she gave birth."

"Aye. Unfortunately, her family was closing in on us by then."

"Why did she fear them? She had magic."

"And it was that magic they wanted. Eireen put the babe in my arms after naming her. She told me to take her far from Ireland and make sure Eilish never returned. When I snuck out the of the building, I heard someone bust in the front door and bellow for Eireen."

CHAPTER NINETEEN

The Dragonwood on Dreagan

Where was the peace he used to find among the trees? How many times had Con walked the Dragonwood and found tranquility when his worries became too great? Why couldn't achieve it now?

He looked up at the trees towering high above him. The snow was melting as spring beckoned, showing yet another passage of time. There was much that weighed upon his mind, but the heaviest at the moment was Ulrik.

Con wasn't sure what to make of his old friend. He lowered his head and looked around him. The last time he'd seen Ulrik, he appeared visibly upset. There had also been a moment when Con thought Ulrik might tell him what bothered him, but it had passed quickly.

He wasn't sure if he should be happy Ulrik hadn't challenged him yet, or worried. Con was tired of waiting. More than that, he just wanted it over.

Ever since he'd banished Ulrik, he wondered at his decision. As the years went by, he told himself it had been the right thing to do. Over the last millennium, he'd begun to question himself again.

And now that Ulrik could apparently come and go on Dreagan as he pleased, it all seemed so silly. In having that information, Con had a decision to make. Did he continue to allow Ulrik to see his Silvers after so long of being without them? Or did Con make it so that Ulrik's banishment cut him off from Dreagan unless he killed Con?

The carefree, fun-loving, always smiling Ulrik had died the day his woman did. But the Ulrik Con spoke with recently seemed different from the last year or so. Ulrik showed hints of his old self.

No longer did Con see the hatred that had blazed so clearly in Ulrik's eyes when they fought in Edinburgh. That didn't mean Ulrik wasn't going to challenge him, however. The truth was, Ulrik was the most cunning individual Con had ever known.

Unfortunately, he wouldn't be able to deal with Ulrik right away. The one he would like to focus his efforts on was Mikkel, but so far, the snake had been so elusive that even Ryder couldn't locate him.

The sound of footsteps approaching had Con turning to look behind him. He spotted Vaughn walking his way. Each Dragon King had a specialty, and Vaughn's was anything to do with the humans' legal system.

"If you're walking the Dragonwood, then your troubles must be weighing heavily," Vaughn said as he reached him.

Con looked into Vaughn's Persian blue eyes and shrugged. "I've seen you out here on plenty of occasions."

"I might just like the trees," he replied.

They grinned at each other then.

Vaughn's faded quickly. "You doona have to carry it all, my friend."

"It comes with the position."

"Just in case, I've begun paperwork on all the various

companies and shell corporations Ryder has discovered that Mikkel owns under all his aliases. If he tries to come at us legally, I'll stop him."

Con gave a nod of appreciation. "It would be just like Mikkel to try something so devious. He doesna just want to be a Dragon King. He wants my position."

"We'd never follow him."

"You'd have to."

"We're all ready to find that prick, but I didna come out here to talk about Mikkel. Isla has arrived."

If the most powerful Druid from MacLeod Castle were at Dreagan, then it must be about the wooden dragon found on Fair Isle. "Did she say what she wanted?"

Vaughn shook his head as they turned and began the walk back to the manor. "She asked to speak with you and Rhi."

"Rhi isna here."

"I told Isla that. She wasna happy about it."

Con flattened his lips. "Have you called for Rhi?"

"Aye. She's no' been seen."

Con hoped that the Light Fae would be there by the time they got to the manor, but no sooner had he stepped inside the library than he realized Rhi wasn't there. Vaughn gave a nod before he proceeded down to his office.

With a sigh, Con turned to those in the library. Isla was pacing the room, muttering to herself. Standing off to the side was the Warrior, Hayden, her husband, who wouldn't take his worried gaze off her. Beside him was the leader of the Warriors, Fallon MacLeod.

As soon as Fallon spotted Con, he walked over. "Isla has been like this since she woke before dawn."

Con watched the Druid for a moment. "What's wrong?"

"She only said she needed to get here and see you

and Rhi. She's hasna said anything more. No' even to Hayden."

Which is why the tall, blond Warrior stood with such a concerned expression on his face.

Con gave a nod to Fallon. Then he said, "Rhi. I need you at Dreagan. Now."

The Light Fae would hear his call. Normally, she'd appear almost immediately. If she didn't, then something was wrong. Minutes ticked by with nothing. The longer Isla paced, the more troubled Hayden became.

"Rhi!" Con yelled.

There was a subtle shift in the air right before the Light Fae materialized in front of him. "What?" she asked irritably. "I was busy."

He pointed behind her. Rhi's silver eyes touched on Fallon before she turned around. As soon as she saw Isla, Rhi's attitude changed from irritation to alarm. She immediately walked to the Druid.

Isla halted when she saw Rhi. "Something is happening."

"What?" Rhi asked softly.

Con, Fallon, and Hayden all moved in closer to the duo.

Isla's ice blue eyes looked at Hayden before they landed on Con. "The Ancients keep screaming Ulrik's name."

The Ancients were long-dead Druids who chose to speak to other Druids, but it was always done in riddles. They had been the ones to choose Isla as the conduit regarding the wooden dragon when it was found—before the Kings even knew what it was.

"Ulrik?" Rhi asked and swung her gaze to Con. "Does this mean it's time for the battle?"

Isla shook her head of long, black hair, her ice blue eyes flashing. "They're saying nothing more than his name over and over. Along with the incoherent screams as they did when the wooden dragon was found." She swallowed and looked at each of them. "I can't decipher what they're trying to tell me, but their feelings are clear. They're scared."

"I'm sorry I didn't come sooner," Rhi said. She shoved her midnight locks over her shoulder. "I've been on the Isle of Skye with Corann."

Con perked up, hoping that meant she'd discovered something. "And?"

"We've been looking through the records of the Skye Druids."

It was the way she wouldn't quite meet his gaze that worried Con. "Spit out whatever it is you doona want to say."

Rhi glared at him before blowing out a breath. "Corann said that the Skye Druids were formed after the dragons were sent away. The original Druids saw the event. When they and other mortals tried to stand up for you, they were hunted."

"What?" Con asked with a frown. "We never knew."

"You wouldna," Fallon said. "You were saving the dragons and trying to stop a war."

Con slid his gaze back to Rhi. "Do they know who was there to put the magic into the wooden dragon?"

"That's what we were looking through the records for," Rhi explained. "The Skye Druids record everything. Much like you."

Isla walked to a chair and sank onto it. "So the culprits could be listed."

"If we're lucky," Rhi said with a nod.

Con saw the doubt in the way she held herself. "But you doona think so?"

"I don't," she admitted. "The Druids were hiding from those who chased them. They found Skye and used it as a means to keep anyone who wasn't a Druid out. The thought that any of them was on Fair Isle at the time—"

"Is slim," Con finished. So much for the glimmer of hope that had begun to shine.

Rhi shrugged, her lips twisting. "Corann is going to keep looking just the same."

"Whatever has the Ancients stirred up in regards to Ulrik has to do with the wooden dragon," Isla said. "I know it."

Hayden walked to stand behind his wife and laid his hands on her shoulders in comfort. "She's the only Druid at the castle the Ancients are talking to about this. Again."

Con moved to stand before Isla. He squatted down to look at her. "Is there a chance you are somehow connected to those Druids who created the wooden dragon?"

"Anything is possible," she said with a lift of her shoulders.

Con straightened and walked away, his mind jumbled with this new added development. Then he spun back to Isla. "In all the times Ulrik and Mikkel were attacking Druids, humans, and us, did the Ancients ever react as they are now?"

"Never," Isla replied.

Hayden's blond brows snapped together. "What are you getting at, Con?"

"That the Ancients could care less if Ulrik challenges me," Con said as he looked to Rhi. "Isla's right, this is about the wooden dragon."

Rhi visibly winced. "Well, I might've told Ulrik about it."

"And?" Con asked, curious as to his old friend's reaction.

Fallon looked at him in shock. "You're no' angry?"

"I don't have the energy to waste on that when, whether

Ulrik wants to admit it or not, the wooden dragon affects him because he's a Dragon King."

Rhi slowly nodded her head. "That's why I told him. I wanted him to know there were other things disturbing the Kings."

"What did he say?" Hayden asked.

"Not much," Rhi replied.

What had Con expected? That Ulrik would want to help? That wasn't going to happen. And unless they learned which Druids and Fae were involved, there might not be a way to figure out why they had targeted the Dragon Kings in the first place.

Or just what the group had planned for the Kings.

Isla reached up and grabbed one of Hayden's hands. "It doesn't matter what Ulrik wants or doesn't want. He's involved now, and by the way the Ancients continue to shout his name, I think he's closer to discovering something than any of us are."

"Or he could be involved," Fallon said.

Con gave a single shake of his head. "We've already ruled that out. Ulrik had his magic bound. There wouldna have been enough time for him to get from Dreagan to Fair Isle."

"If he isna helping them, then they could be targeting him," Hayden said.

Rhi's brow knitted. "You talk as if this group is still around. The Druids would be dead."

"Druids pass down their spells," Isla said. "They could've passed whatever intentions they had, as well."

Con clenched his fist. Something had to give soon. After all this time of protecting the realm and the mortals, why was everyone coming at the Kings?

The door to the library was suddenly thrown open. Thorn strode inside, his dark eyes locked on Con. "We've a visitor."

"Who?" Con demanded.

Thorn glanced at Rhi before he turned his dark head to Con. "A Light Fae."

"Here?" Rhi asked in surprise.

Con glanced at her before he asked Thorn, "Who is it?"

"Inen," said an Irish voice as he walked into the library.

Thorn spun around and glared at the intruder. "I told you to wait."

"This can't," Inen said with a frown.

Con met the Captain of the Queen's Guard's eyes. "Inen, what brings you to Dreagan?"

Inen blew out a breath and shoved a hand through the black hair all Light Fae were born with as he looked at Rhi. "I thought you should hear it from a friend."

"Hear what?" Rhi asked as she took a step toward him.

Inen sent a quick look to Con. "Usaeil has banished you."

Con immediately turned to Rhi to see the color drain from her face. Rhi was suffering blow after blow from Usaeil, and Con knew it wouldn't be long before the two clashed in a war that would devastate not just the Fae, but also the Dragon Kings and the mortals.

"I'm sorry," Inen murmured.

Rhi simply stood there, dazed.

Con looked at Inen. "Thank you for telling her."

"Usaeil . . . well, she's not the same," Inen said. Then he bowed his head to Con and disappeared.

For long minutes, Rhi stood silently. Then she looked at Con. "I think it's time for that confrontation with Usaeil."

CHAPTER TWENTY

It was a glorious feeling to wake with a smile. A contented, pleasure-filled smile. But it vanished when Eilish opened her eyes and found her bed empty.

She rose, walking naked through her flat, in hopes of finding Ulrik. The disappointment that filled her when he wasn't there was sharp, acute.

And centered right in her chest.

Looking out the window, she spotted the dark gray skies and rain that fell in buckets. Which matched her mood.

There was no use pretending she wasn't angry. Not when she hurt so deeply. How could he make such sweet love to her and then leave? Then she recalled his trust issues and how she'd felt him rise from the bed right before she fell asleep.

She should've tried harder to stay awake, not that it would've done any good. Ulrik still would've left, except she would've been awake to see it. At least this way, she'd been spared. Though she wasn't so sure it lessened the sting.

How could he touch her so tenderly, so passionately,

and not feel anything? A picture flashed in her head of him leaning over her as he thrust inside. His gold gaze had burned with desire.

He'd felt something, all right. Felt it so deeply that it blazed in his eyes.

No doubt if she confronted him, he'd say it was nothing but lust. But she knew what that looked like, what it felt like. Their attraction was deeper than mere desire. Or was she just deceiving herself?

Eilish lifted her chin. Perhaps she'd been the one played for a fool. Had Ulrik used her as he thought she did him? Had he betrayed her by awakening this yearning for him and forcing her to give in so he could leave her behind to deal with the aftermath?

She knew he was broken. Yet she'd thought while they were making love that he might not be as destroyed as she imagined. And that's where the betrayal came in. He'd made her believe he was something more, that *they* were something.

Even putting that possibility together didn't make her angry. It made her pity him. And it made her hurt even more because she'd felt something for him—still felt it.

From the moment Mikkel spoke of Ulrik, she'd been intrigued by the Dragon King. Mikkel's hatred for his own nephew only pushed her to learn more about Ulrik. Then she'd met him. And her heart had skipped a beat.

Not because a Dragon King had come to see her— the one she was supposed to kill—but because he was nothing like she'd expected. He was . . . more. So much more.

More gorgeous, more dangerous, more mysterious, and more mesmerizing. He was simply more of everything.

She'd reminded herself about her role in his life when

he first came to see her. Then he'd done the unexpected and brought Nikolai and Esther to her. That had thrown her for a complete loop. Just when she thought she had Ulrik figured out, he did something surprising.

Was that what kept her enthralled with him? Was it because he was unpredictable? Or was it because he was broken?

She'd never been one to want to fix people. She accepted them as they were, flaws and all. Yet with Ulrik, she felt an overwhelming urge to help him. Maybe she was the one going crazy.

Eilish blew out a breath and turned toward the bathroom. There was no use attempting to return to bed. The sun was up, though she couldn't see it behind the rain clouds. Besides, the sheets would smell like Ulrik, and she couldn't handle that right now.

After her shower, she returned to her bedroom and sat before her vanity to blow-dry her hair. The long, thick length always took forever, so she soon found herself reliving the night over and over again.

The joy, the pleasure, the unadulterated bliss.

She looked up after finishing her hair, and her eyes clashed with gold ones in the mirror. Her heart slammed against her chest at the excitement that swelled within her. She didn't care how long he'd stood there watching her, only that he was there.

Eilish turned on the stool to look at Ulrik. He was back. It didn't matter why he'd left, only that he returned. His unreadable expression gave her a moment of worry, but she pushed that aside and got to her feet.

Before she could utter a single word, he said, "Stop looking for your mother."

His statement took her aback. "Why?"

"The past is better left buried."

Well, that wasn't an answer. It was obvious that he

knew something, and now he wasn't going to tell her. "You have no right to say that since you've not let anything in your past stay buried. You keep it warm against you."

"I didna come to argue with you."

She raised a brow. "No, you came to order me about. This might come as a shock, but I don't have to listen to you."

He grabbed her, spinning her until she was pressed against the wall. It happened so fast, she couldn't stop it. His face was close, his eyes lit with some inner fire that caused her to hesitate.

"What do you know?" she demanded in a soft voice.

He gave a shake of his head and released her, stepping back. After a moment, he raked a hand through his hair and calmed. "Leave the past buried, Eilish."

"It's my family. I have a right to know."

"Sometimes, knowledge isna always good to have."

She pushed away from the wall and glared at him. "The more you say things like that, the more I realize you know something. And the more I'm determined to find out what it is."

His nostrils flared as he attempted to hold back his anger.

"I bet you wish you could wipe memories, don't you?" she asked saucily.

"I thought life was precious to you," he said. "Or was protecting the village just a way for them to ignore all the other mystical beings visiting."

She crossed her arms over her chest. "I do care about the village. I protect them to keep them from harm."

"Then think of them."

"You're not making any sense."

Ulrik looked away briefly, a muscle jumping in his jaw. "Did you ever think there was a reason you knew nothing of your mother? Did it enter your mind for even a moment that it was done to shield you from something?"

"What might that be?"

He didn't answer.

It made her roll her eyes. She dropped her arms to her sides. "You've made me more determined than ever to find answers. I've already begun. I went to visit Donal. We had a nice talk."

"What did he tell you?" Ulrik asked, his gaze narrowed.

She shrugged, shaking her head. "I know her full name now. I know she's from Dublin."

"If you want to live, drop this. All of it. Doona talk to Donal again. In fact, you should return home."

"This is my home."

His brows snapped together. "Did you no' hear me? You're in danger."

"I've been in danger since I came to Ireland. First from the Fae, then from Mikkel, and then the Dragon Kings. So who am I supposed to fear now?"

"Your family. Your mother's family to be precise."

That made her laugh. "If I can handle the Fae, I can fight and win against other Druids."

"The strength of your magic makes you a target. It's how Mikkel found you. It's how I found Darcy. If you doona want to return to America, then go to the Isle of Skye. The Skye Druids will help you."

"I don't need their help."

"Everyone needs help," he argued.

She smiled slightly. "Including you?"

"This isna about me."

"No, it's about me. My family, actually. You know I came here looking for my mother. I helped Mikkel because he has the information, and not once has he said anything about me being in danger."

Ulrik lifted one shoulder in a shrug. "That's because he didna speak to Patrick."

Her eyes widened as his words sank in. "You talked to my dad?"

"My people also found your mother's name and place of birth. They detailed her family, as well, but I knew there was one person who likely knew the story that had been so well hidden—Patrick Flanagan. So I paid him a visit."

"And he told you everything?"

"Aye."

She walked to her bed and sat. "I'm listening."

He shook his head. "I'm no' telling you to forget your mother just to rile you. I'm telling you to save your life."

"Is my mother dead?"

Ulrik shrugged and looked away. "That, I doona know."

"But you can find out, can't you?"

His head swung back to her, shock registering. "You want me to look for her soul?"

"That would tell us if she is living or not." And Eilish really hoped her mother was alive.

Ulrik blew out a breath. "You're like a dog with a bone."

"I'm going to find out about my mother one way or another. Mikkel has the information. So do you. Mikkel will only tell me after I've killed you and Con."

"Lass, you doona know what you'll be up against with either of us," he said in a low voice.

"I could call Patrick," she said. "But I'm sure he'll refuse to tell me anything. So that leaves you."

He closed the distance between them. His hand reached out to her face, but he stopped just short of touching her. "Druids are losing their magic. Every time they mix their blood with that of a mortal, their power decreases. At one time, Druids were the most feared and respected of the humans. Now, everyone believes you're a myth, just like dragons.

"The power I feel within you is verra rare. I know what it's like to watch my species leave. I know how it feels to know that I'm one of the last. So are you. Protect yourself as valiantly as you do this village."

She blinked up at him, his words touching her deeply. This was another new side of Ulrik, and she found she quite liked it. "I will protect myself, but I have to know what happened to my mother. Tell me."

His lips flattened briefly. "I fear if I do, it will only make things worse."

"You've no idea the thousands of different reasons I've thought of as to why my mother isn't with me. I know from Donal that he loved her, and she, him. I know she was powerful, and that she feared her family."

"Aye," Ulrik said. "She did. You should, as well."

She threw up her hands in defeat. "I have to know."

"And I'll tell you," he said. "Just no' now."

"When?"

"Soon. But I need something from you."

Eilish nodded eagerly. "Anything. What?"

"Stay away from Mikkel."

Her head bobbed up and down slowly as she got lost in his golden depths. His eyes were blazing with desire again, and it caused her belly to tighten and her sex to clench.

His knuckles caressed down her face. "I sense the darkness within you that matches my own. You keep it at bay, but one wrong move, and it will devour you."

"Did yours consume you?" she asked, her voice barely a whisper.

His gaze lowered to her mouth. "I sought it, welcomed it. And that darkness changed me. It'll do the same to you."

"Maybe not."

"It will," he pressed. "And . . . I doona want to see that." His arm dropped to her waist, and he pulled her against him, his lips hovering over hers.

Her heart was racing, her body eager to feel his once more. "Why?"

"Because you're perfect."

CHAPTER TWENTY-ONE

He knew it was a mistake. But Ulrik had to kiss Eilish. There wasn't any other option. His need to taste her, to feel her against him was as strong as his need to fly.

He savored the heady kiss, each seemingly relishing the fires of desire that roared to life. But he refused to let it overwhelm him again. Instead, he kept the embrace languid as he took delight in the way her breath fanned his cheek and how she dug her fingers into the backs of his arms.

She ended the kiss and leaned back. "So you no longer think I'm a spy then?"

Ulrik released her and took a step back. Why did she have to bring that up and remind him of his distrust? "I believe there is a significant threat to you."

"But do you still think I'm spying for Mikkel?" she persisted, a frown marring her forehead.

Apparently, he took too long to answer because her eyes widened and she gaped at him. "You do," she accused.

Ulrik wasn't going to apologize for what he'd been thinking. In all his dealings with humans and Fae, he'd been wrong exactly twice about someone betraying him. Twice out of eons of time.

The odds were stacked against her, but there was no use rubbing it in.

"How can you kiss me like that?" she demanded, hurt and anger in every syllable. "How can you touch me as if you've waited centuries to hold me, and still think I'm going to betray you?"

"Past experience."

Her green-gold eyes flashed with anger. "So you've kissed many women like that, huh?"

"No."

"As if I believe you."

He raised a brow at her flippant retort. "I've no reason to lie."

"Ha," she said loudly. "How does it feel to not be believed?"

"I—"

She held up a hand, stopping him. "I can't have you touching me as you did last night and kissing me like this morning while thinking I'm a spy. Get out."

Ulrik knew better than to try and argue with her. He'd give her time to cool down and return later—without kissing her—and convince her to give up looking for her mother.

And to forget Mikkel.

Ulrik touched his silver cuff and, with a nod to the Druid, teleported out.

Eilish was in turns furious and filled with pain. Damn Ulrik for kissing her in such a way. And damn her for forgetting who he really was.

Why did she have to fall for him?

Her knees buckled, and she sank onto the bed. No. Surely, she wouldn't have done something so idiotic, so reckless as to fall in love with the very Dragon King who was supposed to kill her.

Wasn't it bad enough that she'd let him into her bed? Her head dropped into her hands. My God, she was crazy. That was the only explanation. No one in their right mind would've taken the path she had.

But she'd run down it with a smile on her face.

Ulrik wanted her to stop working with Mikkel. Funny thing was, she'd already done that. Mikkel might not know it. But he would soon enough when he didn't become a Dragon King.

That made Eilish smile. She'd love to be there and see Mikkel's face when he realized Ulrik wasn't dead. As tempting as that was, she had other priorities—like finding her mother.

Ulrik's worry over her safety gave her some concern, but she was a Druid. She'd be able to handle anyone she encountered. Of that, she was certain. And he kept telling her how powerful she was. So why was he so troubled?

Because there was something he didn't want her to learn.

The same thing her dad, or rather Patrick, had kept from her.

It all came back to her mother. And it was time Eilish discovered the truth, no matter how awful it was.

She rose and put on the finger rings. Just as she was about to teleport to Dublin, pain exploded in her mind. She cried out and put her hands on either side of her head before she fell to her knees as the agony reverberated in her mind like the tolling of a bell.

Dimly, she heard what sounded like wood splintering. She tried to open her eyes, but it hurt to even breathe. Whatever was happening to her head magnified sound to the point where she could feel her ears bleeding.

Then she was lifted effortlessly from the floor and thrown against the wall. The pain in her head stopped, allowing her to open her eyes. When she did, she found herself dangling several feet off the floor. Her gaze scanned the room until she found the source.

Mikkel.

"I should've known better than to trust a Druid," he said as he removed his black overcoat that was soaked with rain and tossed it on her bed.

He raised his gold eyes to her, eyes that were so similar to Ulrik's. Where Ulrik's were filled with distrust and pain, Mikkel's were simply empty.

"I thought we had an agreement," he said as he put his hands into the pockets of his dress pants.

She clenched her teeth together as the agony in her head intensified. Had she really assumed she could *handle* Mikkel? The fact that he didn't have all of his magic was what had stupidly allowed her to think hers was stronger.

Instead of attacking him, she concentrated on her magic, letting it build inside her before she began to push against his. Just when she started making headway, the sound of Mikkel's obnoxious laughter reached her.

"Keep trying," he told her. "Every time you use your magic against mine, I'll double your pain."

A second later, the throbbing in her head returned, intensified so that her stomach rolled with nausea. She tried to hold back her scream, but it fell unheeded from her lips. She would've doubled over into a fetal position, but his dragon magic held her in place.

All Eilish could do was endure the debilitating agony. She had no idea how long it lasted. Time ceased to matter with such torment.

Then, to her shock, the pain lessened enough that she could once more breathe normally. Her throat hurt, and that's when she realized she'd been screaming continually.

"You've taken more than I expected."

She inwardly winced at how close Mikkel's voice was to her. If only she had the strength to lash out at him, to make him hurt as he'd hurt her. But she could barely even call her magic to her at this point.

"Your screams were deafening, but it was your tears I most enjoyed," he said with a chuckle.

Oh, yes, she hated him.

He put his hand over her boot-clad foot. "I'm not the monster here."

She would've snorted had she been able.

"I watched my father rule over the Silvers for what felt like an eternity. I was his eldest son. I did everything he asked of me, but it was never enough. He ridiculed me, beat me, and shamed me in front of everyone."

Eilish eyed him, not sure why he was telling her this.

Mikkel dropped his hand and turned away, walking around the bed to the vanity. He picked up a makeup brush and looked at it. "I endured all of it because I knew he was making me strong. He said his father had done the same to him, and it was why he became King after his dad. And so I would be King of the Silvers, as well."

He set the brush down and turned to her. "That was my life for hundreds of years. Occasionally, I'd do something right, and he would reward me. But it never lasted. I knew that I could bear it because he wouldn't live forever."

Knowing he'd been abused mentally, physically, and emotionally forced Eilish to look at Mikkel differently. And she didn't like that. He was an evil fiend who needed to die.

Mikkel released a long breath, his gaze turning distant. "Then Ualan was born. From the moment of his birth, my father treated him differently. He doted on my younger brother, and worse, he was kind. Father didn't beat him or shame him. All Ualan ever knew was love. Still, he was my sibling, and I loved him because of it.

"Dragons will wait for however long it takes to find their mates because we're together for eternity. I found mine in a dragon named Hefina. She was magnificent. The problem was, she'd fallen in love with Ualan, and he, her. Again, I kept my eye on the prize—the throne.

"Then the day finally came when I was ready to challenge my father for the right to rule. I issued my challenge, but we were invaded by another clan. We all gathered and went to help the Silvers that had been attacked by the Ivories. During the battle, the King of Ivories slew my father.

"I wanted to mourn. I tried hard, but I was waiting to become King. Except once more, Fate laughed in my face and gave the title to Ualan."

Eilish wanted to kick herself for feeling even a small thread of pity for Mikkel, especially after everything he'd done.

Mikkel laughed then and looked at her, anger tightening his face. "Ulrik was so young when I set up the Ivories to attack the Silvers again. I knew if Ualan fell, that I'd be King. But I wasn't." His nostrils flared as he stalked to her. "I sat by for eons and watched as my father, brother, and nephew made the wrong decisions. The only thing Ulrik ever did right was beginning the war with your kind. But he faltered and kept attacking the mortals when he should've taken out Con and ruled all the Dragon Kings. Now, it's up to me to set things right."

She wondered if Ulrik knew any of this, and Eilish was relatively certain he didn't. She couldn't wait to tell him. If she got the chance.

"It's a pity, really," Mikkel said, calm once more. "I

had the file on your mother ready to hand over to you. I had faith you'd actually kill Ulrik because you wanted to know where she was so desperately. Then I find out Ulrik came to see you."

He tsked, which made her want to kick Mikkel in the face. How dare he look at her like some judge ready to sentence her?

"What did Ulrik tell you?" he demanded.

Eilish refused to play his game, no matter how much torture he inflicted.

Mikkel's lips twisted as he shrugged with a helpless look on his face. She didn't have time to wonder what he was going to do before her thighbone was snapped in two.

Eilish threw back her head and screamed in anguish, all the while, she kept wishing Ulrik were still there. If only she hadn't sent him away. If only she'd let him keep kissing her. If only. . . .

"What did he tell you?" Mikkel bellowed.

She tried to pull away from the wall as she looked at him through the tears in her eyes. "I'll never tell."

No sooner were the words out of her mouth than he released his hold on her. Eilish attempted to shift her weight as she fell the few feet to the ground so that she landed on her good leg, but it didn't work.

She crumpled to the floor, her hands holding her right leg through the throbbing pain. All the while, she began directing her magic to her femur to heal it. She'd never used magic to heal herself before, but she knew some Druids were capable enough to do it. Because if there was even a chance for her to get away from Mikkel or to hurt him, she needed to be 100 percent. And she was far from that.

No matter how much magic she sent to her injured leg, it wouldn't heal. Then Mikkel was standing over her.

He bent, his mouth near her ear. "I'll break every bone in your body if you doona give me what I want."

She hid her smile. The Scots' brogue he fought so hard to hide slipped, which meant his temper had gotten the best of him. Now that was something she could use against him.

Eilish flung back her hair and turned her head to him. "Do you know why your father treated Ualan so kindly? It was because he knew your brother would be the next King. You've seen it pass you by several times. There's nothing you can do that will put you in the position to become King. Aren't there other Silvers trapped here? I bet one of them becomes King before you do."

"No' if I kill them first," Mikkel said before he broke her other leg.

CHAPTER TWENTY-TWO

"So you've kissed many women like that, huh?"

Eilish's question kept resounding in his head. Ulrik tried to shake it loose, to think of something—anything—else as he walked the perimeter of the lake, but it was no use.

Because of the answer. An answer he'd refused to tell her, and one that, even now, he was loath to speak aloud.

He hadn't kissed anyone like he'd kissed her. Not in a thousand years.

Not in a million years.

Not ever.

Why? What made the Druid so special? Was it her magic? No, it couldn't be. He'd felt absolutely nothing for Darcy or any of the other Druids he'd found and used through the years. Which brought him back to Eilish.

He glanced at the sky. Dark clouds were gathering. It was going to rain soon, not that it would send him indoors. He'd always loved the rain. From mists, to light showers, to thunderstorms. He'd seen them all and welcomed each one.

Ulrik stopped and turned back toward the cottage. He

couldn't shake the feeling that he shouldn't have left Eilish. But it had been the right thing to do. All that would've happened had he stayed was more arguing.

He couldn't start trusting people. It wasn't in his nature. Nor would he try to explain his reasoning after already telling her. If Eilish couldn't accept him, then. . . .

His steps slowed, then halted. Even before his banishment when he'd trusted nearly everyone, he'd read others well. It was little things his father had taught him to look for in others. Gestures, movements, eye contact—all could be used to determine if someone were telling the truth or not.

And Ulrik had grasped those lessons from his father eagerly, perfecting them until it was second nature to him. Once he was stuck in human form, Ulrik didn't bother listening to the human's speak because words were empty. He read body language instead.

Each time he'd seen Eilish, he'd done the same thing. Without a doubt, he knew she hadn't been faking with him the previous night.

He'd been so wrapped up in his uncle and Eilish's magic that he hadn't looked at *her*. Not really. He saw her beauty, her wit, her intelligence, and her courage. But he'd always connected her to Mikkel.

If he studied her without his uncle's connection, he would've believed her from the start. Yet he couldn't truly separate Eilish from Mikkel. After all, she had stood in Ulrik's antique shop and said she'd kill him and Con. There was no choice but to doubt her.

And for the first time, he wished he felt differently.

No doubt that's exactly what his uncle wanted, and it was the reason Ulrik would be extra cautious with the Druid. To do otherwise would jeopardize everything he'd planned and set in motion.

His thoughts shifted to his Silvers. When he woke

them and rid the world of the mortals, he would make sure all dragons returned. The Kings had lived long enough without their families. He wouldn't make the Silvers endure that, as well. But that was for another day.

It was his end goal, the thing he worked toward. His eye was never far from that, but he knew better than to forget about all the other moving pieces. Though, the majority of the work now rested on his shoulders.

And he was more than up for it.

That is if he didn't allow a dark-headed Druid with green-gold eyes to tempt him. Because she could be the one thing that set him off his course and cost him everything.

He really hoped she didn't realize that. In fact, if it had been anyone else, he would've already moved on and forgotten her once she didn't immediately accept his offer of help. But he very much wanted to help her remain a *mie,* as well as get far from Mikkel.

At first, Ulrik thought to use her to his benefit, but that had quickly changed. He could best Con on his own. He didn't need or want any outside help, be it from a Druid, a Fae, or even another Dragon King. This feud between him and Con ran too deeply for there to be anyone else involved.

Since Ulrik didn't need her to beat Con or unbind his magic as Darcy had, there was no reason for Eilish. Other than to have a Druid at his disposal. Even then, he had no need of her. His magic was greater than hers.

Why then couldn't he just forget about her? Why couldn't he walk away as he had a million times before? Why did he continue to meddle in her affairs?

And why the fuck was he worried about her?

Worried. Him!

That hadn't happened in . . . well, a damn long time. And he'd prefer if it weren't happening now.

Ulrik clenched his teeth and strode toward the cottage. Eilish had ruined his leisurely walk. She'd also wrecked his rest for the past several nights. Never mind that he didn't actually need sleep. The point was that the Druid was causing all kinds of havoc that had to stop.

By the time he entered the cottage, he'd decided never to visit Eilish again. He didn't need or want the trouble she caused.

If she was working with Mikkel, their plans had been foiled.

If she wasn't, well, she was a Druid. She could handle herself as she'd said countless times.

And if she attacked him, then Ulrik would be ready for her.

His head snapped around when there was a knock on the door. Ulrik stared at it a moment before he made his way over and opened it. He blinked in confusion when his gaze landed on Balladyn.

"I called out your name as you walked here," Balladyn said. "But by the look on your face, your ire was raised. I figured I'd better knock."

Ulrik stepped aside so the King of the Dark could enter. He closed the door behind Balladyn. "I didna hear you. What brings you here?"

"Something that's only going to make you even angrier."

Shite. Just what he needed. "What's that?"

"Word has spread through the Fae like lightning. Usaeil has banished Rhi from the Light."

"For what?" Ulrik demanded. He was furious on Rhi's behalf. At least when he was banished, there had been a reason. Rhi had done nothing to Usaeil.

But Ulrik suspected that was soon to change.

Balladyn blew out a breath, shrugging. "Usaeil didn't give a reason."

"Have you spoken to Rhi?"

"Nay."

Ulrik raised a brow. "You mean you came here instead of finding her? What the bloody hell is wrong with you?"

"I'm not sure she'll see me."

"You love her. You should've found out," he said angrily. "She's going to need you. Trust me."

Balladyn remained, his face impassive. "What if she won't see me?"

"What if she will?" When Balladyn didn't reply, Ulrik sighed loudly. "I know how she feels right now. She's been cast out of a place she always thought she'd be welcome. With the Fae Realm all but destroyed by your civil war, the Light Palace was her home."

"Then she'll have a place with us," Balladyn said. "I warned Usaeil that her time was coming to an end when I saw her. I'm going to start preparing my army."

Ulrik wasn't quite finished with Balladyn yet. "And my uncle? Did you leave him for me?"

"I did," Balladyn said with a smile. "But you should've seen his face. It was a moment you would've enjoyed."

"At least you got to enjoy it. Mikkel is going to pay for having Lily killed, for harming Rhys and Anson, and all his other deeds. I'm going to see to it."

"And who will make sure you pay for your deeds?"

Ulrik met Balladyn's red eyes. "I guess we'll know soon enough."

"I'll talk to Rhi in my own time. Until then, would you go to her? You're right. She's going to need a friend, and I'm not sure she still thinks of me that way."

Ulrik gave a nod. "I'll talk to her immediately."

Balladyn hesitated, and Ulrik knew they were thinking the same thing. That Rhi might very well be with the Dragon Kings. It was another reason Balladyn didn't want to go to her. It would confirm that Rhi was still very much in love.

"Thank you," Balladyn murmured before he vanished.

Ulrik's mind should've been on Rhi, but instead, he found it on Eilish. Then he recalled that he was going to forget about her. He was glad he had something else to focus on right now. Rhi would be hurting, or she was going to be so angry she might be glowing.

Either way, Ulrik would to be there for her.

He said her name, waiting for her to appear. Minutes passed. "Rhi, please."

More minutes ticked by. He used that time to think of all the ways he'd like to destroy Usaeil. A Dragon King had never gone against a Light. Usaeil's power had never come into question. Perhaps it was time that happened.

"What?"

He spun around at the sound of Rhi's voice. She stood stoically in her black pants and denim, button-down shirt, her chin lifted. At first glance, she looked as she always did. But then Ulrik saw the lines of tension around her mouth and the way her muscles were bunched.

"I'm sorry," he said.

Her silver eyes widened just a fraction before she asked, "How did you find out? Never mind. It doesn't matter. I'm fine."

"You're no'," he said and opened his arms.

She stood for another few seconds before her face crumbled and she walked into his embrace. Ulrik held her as she released the tears that she'd held back in order to remain strong. He'd always felt protective of her. It was ridiculous really. Rhi was more than capable of taking care of herself.

Perhaps that's why he offered her a shoulder to cry on. Because there were times even someone as strong as Rhi needed to lean on someone else. As loyal as she was to the Kings—and even him—it was no wonder that every Dragon King felt the way they did about her.

"Tell me you have a plan," he said when her crying finally subsided.

She sniffed and turned her head to the side, but she didn't pull away from him. "I'd like to knock her head off."

He smiled at the fury in her voice. "I'd pay to see that. But do you have a plan?"

"One is coming together."

"If you need me for anything, you simply have to ask."

She leaned back to look at him. "Even if it means you standing beside Con?"

"I'd be standing with you, and the answer is yes." Oddly, he wasn't as surprised by his reply as he would have been months ago. Rhi was the only person he never doubted. Mainly because, until recently, she had been unable to handle the pain that assaulted her when she lied. But also because Rhi didn't betray others.

Ever.

It was why his loyalty to her had never wavered. It was why he had gone into the Dark dungeons to free her. It was why he tried to help her with anything she needed.

There was a hint of a smile as she stepped back, wiping her face. "Thank you. I needed that."

"I know the anguish you're carrying. Along with the anger and distress. You'll survive until Usaeil is toppled."

Rhi sniffed loudly, her gaze lowering to the floor. "I knew she'd changed. I knew she'd begun to resent me, but I never thought she'd banish me."

"It was the one thing she knew would hurt you the most."

Silver eyes met his. "She succeeded."

"Doona let her know that."

"Oh, I won't," Rhi replied with a wink.

Ulrik paused before he said, "Balladyn was here."

"He told you."

"Aye. Usaeil banished you after she realized that Balladyn was King now and wouldna be helping her kill you."

Rhi nodded slowly. "What else did he say?"

"We're no' exactly friends. He didna come here to share his concerns with me. We spoke of you. He wanted to go to you, but he feared you'd either be with the Kings, or no' want to see him."

She looked down at her painted nails in a dark blue with silver tips. "I was with the Kings."

Ulrik almost asked if she was with *him*, but decided not to push things. "Then perhaps it's better he didna go to you."

"I'm sorry."

"For what?" he asked with a frown.

She lifted one shoulder in a shrug. "I never fully understood the ache you felt at being told you couldn't remain at Dreagan. How did you survive it?"

"One day at a time. Find something to focus on. For me, it was revenge."

"Usaeil hasn't given me any other options. Revenge will be mine, as well."

Ulrik smiled at Rhi. "Then that's the queen's ultimate mistake. She doesna know what you're capable of. Yet."

PART TWO

To trust is to be betrayed.

—ULRIK

CHAPTER TWENTY-THREE

There was nothing quite so defeating as discovering that magic wasn't the answer to everything. Unfortunately, Eilish learned that the hard way while trying to fight Mikkel.

And she had two broken legs to prove it.

She lay on the bed, uncaring that she was in a room fit for a queen. Wealth dripped from every surface, including the rug that not only predated her own but cost a million pounds more. But none of the beautiful finery mattered to her as it obviously did to Mikkel.

Her fingers drummed on the cream and pale pink comforter as she stared at her legs that throbbed with each beat of her heart. She had no idea where she was because she'd passed out. Or Mikkel had used his magic. Either way, she'd been unconscious.

Worse than being unable to move was finding out that she couldn't heal herself. She wanted to blame that on Mikkel because it was easier to believe that he was preventing her from healing than to realize she really couldn't do it.

It was then that her eyes snapped to her left hand. Her

finger rings were gone. Which meant she wasn't able to leave. She teetered between anger and shock. Those rings were everything to her.

The longer she lay there with her legs broken, the angrier she became. That ire was directed squarely at herself. She'd known better than to mix with Mikkel. It was the power of her magic that had allowed her to believe she could defend against anything he sent her way.

Her conceit, her arrogance were what landed her in this predicament.

Nothing more. Nothing less.

How could she kill a Dragon King if she couldn't fight against Mikkel? Granted, she'd never gone up against a King, but Mikkel had told her she had the power to do it.

Hell, even Ulrik had said she'd be able to touch dragon magic.

That, however, didn't mean she could kill one. Why in the world had she believed Mikkel? The only other beings she'd ever fought were Dark Fae. They had been relatively easy to kill, but it was difficult to compare since she'd never been in battle, much less a magical one.

Eilish turned her hands palms up. She felt the magic coursing through her. Based on what other Druids had told her, she knew the more a Druid could feel their magic, the stronger the individual.

So had she let her power go to her head? She feared the answer was a very loud *yes*.

Ulrik had warned her about her magic. He'd told her to be careful, and she'd ignored him simply because she'd had a few successes and magic came easily to her. Now she was paying a heavy price for such arrogance.

It was no wonder Ulrik hadn't feared her. She wouldn't have either in his place. He'd even told her, only a Dragon King can kill another Dragon King.

But Mikkel had been so sure. . . .

Eilish deduced by the way Mikkel spoke to her that he had truly believed she could kill a Dragon King. Now, he knew the truth.

And there was only one reason he was keeping her now—Ulrik.

Her heart hurt every time she thought of the King of Silvers. How different would things be now if she hadn't sent Ulrik away? There was a chance he could've defeated Mikkel when he arrived and ended whatever the bastard had planned for them both.

With Ulrik, she'd always felt invincible. It was an illusion Mikkel had begun, but it was Ulrik who brought it into focus. Now she knew the ugly truth of things.

She might be someone other Druids feared, and the Fae took seriously, but she had received nothing more than a brief glance from the Dragon Kings. Except she'd messed with the minds of two women who were destined to be their mates.

Which meant that Eilish had royally fucked herself.

The door to her bedroom opened, and Mikkel strode in wearing an Armani suit and a smug expression. How she wished she could scratch his eyes out, rip him bald, or do anything to wipe that shit-eating grin off his face.

"You look a bit peaked, my dear," he said as he strode to the foot of the four-poster bed. "Are you in pain?"

She didn't bother to answer. No matter what she said, he'd twist it to his own uses. With assholes like Mikkel, it was better to keep your mouth shut.

"Ah," he said, pinching his lips together. "I see. I could take away some of the pain."

Eilish held his gaze, once more refusing to take the bait.

He smiled suddenly. "As you can guess, I'll need something in exchange. Sadly, I overestimated the depths of your magic, but you're not a total waste."

Her stomach knotted because she knew that, somehow, he was going to use her against Ulrik. There was no way she'd willingly participate in such an endeavor.

"Or," Mikkel said, his voice lowering in a threatening tone. "I can make the pain worse."

To prove his point, he sent magic to her legs. Eilish squeezed her eyes closed and fisted her hands in the comforter as pain shot up and down her legs, making her stomach roil and causing her to break out in a cold sweat.

In the next second, that pain was removed. She was able to drag in a breath and relax.

"What happens is your decision, Druid," Mikkel said.

Eilish turned her head away. She liked it when Ulrik called her Druid, but she despised it when Mikkel did it. His tone made the title sound inferior.

While Ulrik's address made her shiver with excitement and eagerness.

She opened her eyes and looked at Mikkel. If she refused to kill Ulrik, then Mikkel would know that she cared for his nephew. That had the potential to make things so much worse. If she agreed to Mikkel's proposition, then there was a chance that she could heal herself as well as somehow warn Ulrik before things got out of hand.

No matter what decision she made, it would no doubt end in her death. She didn't want to die, but she had agreed to help a maniac. The only way to set things right was to fight Mikkel with everything she had, and that meant she had to be more cunning than he was.

Eilish was terrified of the prospect. She wasn't sure she was up to the task, but she wouldn't back down. She couldn't. Because she wasn't going to be another person who betrayed Ulrik.

Mikkel leaned his hand on a post at the corner of the bed. "Well?"

"Heal my legs."

One side of his mouth lifted in a grin. "The only one who has that ability is Constantine. And," he said, pressing his lips together in mock sorrow. "He isn't here."

"Then take away the pain."

His brows rose as he looked at her expectedly. "Does this mean you agree to help me?"

"Yes." As if she had any other choice.

"Brilliant." He straightened and clasped his hands behind his back. "I'm done waiting. The dragons will rule this realm once more, and it begins this night."

He turned on his heel and walked from the bedroom.

"The pain," she called out.

His reply was to shut the door.

Once he was gone, she closed her eyes and concentrated on her magic. She alone knew the depths of her powers, and she was the only one who had the ability to succeed or fail. So much of the magic had come easily to her, most without even trying. But she was more than willing to work for everything else.

And that meant she needed to go to the source of the Druids' power—the Ancients.

If only she knew how to contact them. Since she didn't, she would have to rely on herself until she somehow found a way to the Ancients.

Eilish steadied her breathing, concentrating on how the air moved in and out of her body. All the while, she pushed her magic to her legs and the broken femur bones. She visualized the bones knitting back together stronger than before. The movement of her breaths dulled the pain enough that she could focus on healing herself.

She had no idea how long she hovered in that in-between state of magic and meditation before she heard what sounded like distant drums beating a steady rhythm that matched her breaths.

Soon after, she picked up the sound of chanting. As the drums and voices grew louder, her magic swelled. And then she felt her bones begin the slow process of healing.

"*Be careful*," a thousand voices said into her mind.

"Who are you?" she whispered.

There was a brief pause before they said, "*You sought us. You know.*"

The Ancients? Had she really found them? She could barely contain her joy.

"*Keep your wits about you. You're going to need them for what's coming.*"

Before she could ask another question, the chanting faded away, and the drums soon followed.

Eilish felt bereft without the Ancients now. The brief interaction had been amazing, refreshing. Energizing. It renewed her strength, as well as her resolve.

It was several minutes later that she finally opened her eyes. Her femur bones had mended, and the only residual pain that remained was manageable. At least now, she could use her legs for running, or kicking. Yeah, she'd really like to kick Mikkel right in the balls. Hard.

She remained on the bed without moving so much as a finger. It was imperative that Mikkel believe she was still injured. He hadn't mentioned his plan to her, but it wasn't difficult to piece together. He was going to have her lure Ulrik there. That wouldn't be enough, however. No doubt Mikkel would want her to use magic to weaken Ulrik so Mikkel could strike the killing blow.

"Not gonna happen, wanker," she mumbled.

She'd lure Ulrik there, all right, but then she'd step back and watch as he annihilated Mikkel. And if Mikkel thought to have anyone or anything there to hinder Ulrik, then Eilish would stop them.

After a long exhale, she welcomed the peace that

came. Mikkel would be gone, and Ulrik could. . . . What? What could he do? Without his uncle as a distraction, Ulrik would get back on course with his revenge.

Some might push him to challenge Con and become the next King of Dragon Kings, but not her. Not only was there the danger that Con could win and kill Ulrik, there was also the fact that if Ulrik won, there would be no place for her. She and all the other Druids would be wiped from the Earth along with every other mortal out there.

Even recognizing that, she wasn't going to help Mikkel. There was nothing he could say or do that would change her mind.

Her head turned to the window, but the curtains were closed. She didn't know if it was day or night. Just as she was talking herself out of using her magic to part the drapes a crack, her door opened again.

She looked at the two women in confusion as they walked into the room, followed by Mikkel. Both women had dark hair. The eldest, who appeared to be in her early fifties, kept her locks cut very short. By the gray roots showing, it was time to color her hair again.

The other woman's hair hung just past her shoulders. And it was the way her hazel gaze watched Eilish with cold detachment that sent a warning through Eilish.

"As I told you," Mikkel said to the women, though his smile was directed at Eilish.

"She's the spitting image of Eireen," the younger woman said.

Eilish slid her gaze to Mikkel. She wanted to demand to know what was going on, but something told her to remain silent for the moment. It was no coincidence that her mother's name was mentioned.

It was then that she remembered Ulrik's warning. He'd wanted her to stop looking for her mother. He'd said she was in danger from her family. And Eilish suspected that threat had just found her—with Mikkel's help, of course.

The eldest turned her head to Mikkel. "You were right."

"This is going to be fun," the younger said with a smile.

They walked to either side of the bed. Eilish looked at each of them, unease rippling through her like the hands of death. "Lay one finger on me, and I'll shred the skin from your body."

The younger laughed and reached for her arm. Eilish jerked her hand up, sending out a wave of magic that had the woman flying backwards before slamming into the wall and knocking a picture from the hook. The woman crashed onto the floor unconscious a heartbeat later.

For a moment, there was shocked silence. Then Eilish turned to the other woman and sent her into a wall, as well. With both knocked out, she scooted from the bed and stood to face Mikkel.

"Nice try," he said as if he'd expected such a show.

She bared her teeth as her anger built. The force of her magic always frightened her when she allowed herself to become irate, but this time, she welcomed it, sought it.

Gathered it.

Then she unleashed it on Mikkel.

CHAPTER TWENTY-FOUR

Ulrik stumbled back a step when a shockwave of magic barreled through him. The force of it shook him almost as much as the fact that it was Druid magic.

But what made his heart race was that he recognized it as Eilish's.

"What the hell was that?" Balladyn demanded as he looked around as if expecting to see someone.

Ulrik rushed out of the cottage, looking for some sign of Eilish nearby. He recognized the tinge of darkness that clouded her magic. But she wasn't to be found anywhere.

Balladyn came to stand beside him. "That was a ripple of magic that came from some distance away. I've only ever known one who caused such a current."

"Rhi," Ulrik said, his eyes briefly closing.

"Aye. And this wasn't Rhi. You know who did this?" Balladyn asked, his gaze narrowed.

Ulrik gave a nod. Without another word, he touched his cuff, teleporting outside the door of Eilish's flat. He didn't hesitate to break through her spells and bust inside her place.

He expected her to come out, yelling at him. But there

was only silence. He glanced behind him at the stairs that led down to the pub, but she wasn't striding up them with anger in her green-gold eyes.

His head swung to her bedroom. Slowly, he made his way to the doorway. Nothing was out of place other than a small crack in the wall near the bed. It shouldn't be enough to cause him concern, but it did.

He hurried out of the flat, closing the door and using his own spells to keep others out, then he made his way to the pub. Just before he turned from the hidden doorway so that everyone could see him, he hesitated.

When the bartender got close, Ulrik whistled to catch his attention. Then he called Cody over.

"Have you seen Eilish?" Ulrik demanded.

Cody shook his head. "Not since last night when she rushed up the stairs."

The man returned to his duties, leaving Ulrik trying to think of where Eilish could be. He looked to the door of her flat. There was a chance Mikkel had come for her. The time limit his uncle had given her had run out.

And if Mikkel had her, she could be anywhere.

Ulrik returned to his cottage and yanked open the drawer in his desk for a mobile phone. He called one of Mikkel's workers who was spying for Ulrik.

"Where is he?" Ulrik asked as soon as the phone was answered.

"I don't know," came the reply in a thick cockney accent. "I've not heard from him in over a week."

Ulrik disconnected the call before repeating the same conversation with six others in Mikkel's employ that he'd convinced to spy for him.

And all had the same answer.

With one push of a button, he sent a message to everyone who worked for him to search their area for any sign of Mikkel. Then, he waited.

But he couldn't manage an ounce of patience. He tossed the phone onto the desk. Then he braced his hands on the wood and hung his head.

Of all the thousands of people that willingly—and not so willingly—worked for him, he realized that none of them could truly help. None of them had any idea who he was or what war they'd taken sides in. They didn't know about the Fae or Druids or dragons. The majority didn't even believe in magic.

This was one of those times he wished he were on Dreagan. All he would have had to do was go to Ryder.

Ulrik sighed and rubbed his eyes with his thumb and middle finger. None of this would be happening if he hadn't been banished. Mikkel wouldn't have caused his turmoil, Ulrik would never have met Eilish, and he wouldn't be worried about what his uncle was doing to her.

His head snapped up as he lowered his arm. Mikkel had believed Eilish's magic was powerful enough to kill a Dragon King. The scene in Ulrik's antique shop hadn't been faked. Mikkel truly thought Eilish could kill both him and Con. And while Ulrik had sensed the strength of her magic, he wasn't sure she could do significant damage to a King.

Unless she was hiding a secret.

No, he didn't think that was it. More likely, it was Mikkel who hid something.

Ulrik slammed his fist against the desk, smashing it in two. He straightened as the laptop and cell phones toppled to the floor. But he wasn't thinking about the electronics. His mind was on how to locate Eilish in a way that didn't involve the Kings. Because he really didn't want to go to Con and ask for help.

He hated the powerless feeling that continued to grow within him. It didn't matter that he ran countless businesses—some legal by mortal standards, some not. It didn't matter how many people he had investigating for him. It didn't matter how many spies he had.

No one could help.

It would take someone with magic to could locate Eilish or Mikkel.

As soon as that thought went through his head, he had an answer. Though it wasn't without risks. He accepted them, though. Then he touched his cuff and teleported to MacLeod Castle just outside the magical barrier.

He felt the pulse of magic in the air filled with the smell of salt from the sea. It was as strong here as it was on the Isle of Skye, though nothing could compare to the magic on Dreagan.

Ulrik listened to the sound of the waves far below the nearby cliffs. Then he took a deep breath and walked through the invisible barrier that kept the castle hidden and outsiders away. He hadn't gone three steps before a ball of fire the size of a soccer ball landed on the ground a few inches in front of him.

He stopped and looked at the flames before he raised his gaze to find a Warrior with red skin, claws, and eyes advancing toward him with two more balls of fire in his hands.

Instead of fighting Hayden, which was definitely appealing in his present state of mind, Ulrik held up his hands. "I've no' come to do battle."

"What if we want a fight?" asked Malcolm as he walked up and unleashed lightning from his hand, his skin shifting to maroon while claws extended from his fingers.

Ulrik looked at Malcolm before raising his gaze upward when he heard the leathery beat of Broc's wings. Soon, all fifteen Warriors stood around him in a semicircle, each with their skin colored by the primeval gods—or goddess in the case of Larena—inside them.

"I'm looking for a Druid," Ulrik began.

Ramsey, a Warrior who was also half-Druid, made a sound in the back of his throat. "I think you've found enough Druids."

Ulrik inwardly winced. He'd forgotten about all the Druids who had died while attempting to touch dragon magic and unbind what Con had done to him. It had been a *significant* number.

Ulrik's arms dropped to his sides. He felt as if his time were running out, and he didn't know why.

"Hate me all you want," he told them. "Hell, I'll fight any of you, and I'll remain in this form. But I have to find Eilish Flanagan."

It was Larena with her iridescent skin who asked, "Why do you want her?"

"No doubt to get her to help him instead of Mikkel," Galen stated.

Ulrik glanced at the green-skinned Warrior. "My uncle ordered her to kill me. He gave Eilish two days to do it. She decided no' to do as Mikkel asked. Now, I can no' find her."

"You felt the magic," Ramsey said, a frown marring his forehead.

Lucan, the middle MacLeod brother, shrugged his shoulders, the black skin of his god barely visible in the moonlight. "We all felt that small ripple."

"It originated in Ireland," Ulrik said. "I know because I was there. When it struck me, it was strong enough that it knocked me back a step."

"Why the hell are we even listening to him?" Hayden asked with a sneer.

Logan, with his silver skin, crossed his arms over his chest. "I'm in agreement with Hayden."

The earth rumbled beneath Ulrik's feet as Camdyn said, "Count my vote with Hayden, as well."

The youngest MacLeod, Quinn, looked at Fallon. "We know what Ulrik has done to the Kings. We shouldna be listening to him."

"Hang on." This came from the gold-skinned Warrior, Phelan, who was half-Fae and like a brother to Rhi. "I want to know why it's so important that Ulrik find this Druid."

Beside him, the copper Warrior, Charon, scratched his jaw. "We're no' going to get anywhere unless we let Ulrik talk. If he wanted to do us harm, he could've done it when he came into my pub years ago."

"Or anytime since," Ian stated before the light blue of his god faded away.

Arran shrugged, but the white skin of his god remained. "True enough."

"Answer Phelan's question," Broc said as he landed. He glared at Ulrik before folding his indigo wings behind him.

Ulrik looked at each of them, ending with Fallon, who had yet to say anything. There wasn't time to tell them everything, nor did he want to. But Ulrik would condense it.

"Eilish is looking for her mother. Mikkel used that in order to get her to do what he wanted. I'm no' making excuses for her. She did some bad things. We've all done such things."

"Some more than others," Charon interjected.

Ulrik glanced at the copper Warrior. "I was convincing Eilish to stop working with my uncle because if she continued, he would turn her into a *drough*."

"Why do you care what becomes of her?" Quinn asked.

Ulrik was answering questions he hadn't asked himself. And he wasn't comfortable with it. "The Druids are dying out. I know what it's like to be one of the last of my kind."

Malcolm laughed, the sound mirthless. "A *drough* is still a Druid."

"No' really, and you know that. Their power doubles, but they're no longer the holder of the sacred magic that once filled this entire realm. Now, there are only certain places you can detect such magic."

Larena tilted her head to the side as she regarded him. "You think Mikkel took Eilish?"

"I doona know. I can no' find her or my uncle."

"They could be working together," Phelan said. "It could all be a plan to betray you."

Ulrik blew out a breath. "I thought that. I even accused Eilish of it. But . . . I was wrong."

Damn, but that was hard to admit.

"How do you know?" Ian asked.

Ulrik looked up at the sky and the waxing moon. "I doona trust. I can no'. I learned to read people and detect the slightest inflection of their voice or movement of their bodies to indicate their lies." His gaze returned to Fallon. "Eilish is a Druid looking for her mother and was approached by the wrong man."

"You care about her," Lucan stated.

No way was Ulrik going to even acknowledge such a remark.

Quinn frowned as he widened his stance. "If the Druid thought she could kill you, then surely she can stand against Mikkel."

"The depth of her magic is amazing, but she's no' had proper training. She learned on her own," Ulrik stated.

"No' a good thing," Ramsey muttered "If that's the

case, she could have untapped magic that she doesna know how to use. And trust me when I say that could be fatal."

Ulrik swallowed. "There's more. It seems her mum was in the same predicament. She hid her magic from her family who didna have any. Eireen gave her daughter up, having a friend smuggle Eilish out of Ireland to Boston with the promise that Eilish would never return."

It was Galen's turn to frown. "Why?"

"Eireen disappeared shortly after giving birth. I believe her family did her harm because of her magic."

Camdyn shrugged as he looked at the others. "If they doona have magic, then Eilish isna with them. There's no way they could hold her."

But Ulrik wasn't so sure. "The man who raised Eilish, Patrick, is terrified of the Duffys. Eireen put that fear there. She would only have done that to make sure her daughter didna return."

"The question is why didna Eireen want Eilish in Ireland?" Phelan replied.

Fallon finally stepped forward. "Broc? Can you find the Druid?"

Ulrik's gaze swung to the winged Warrior as he waited expectantly.

"I've been trying since Ulrik asked about her." Broc's gaze turned to Ulrik. "I find no trace of her."

With six little words, Ulrik felt the last grains of time slip through his fingers.

CHAPTER TWENTY-FIVE

Dreagan

The time had come. The balls Con was juggling were about to wobble, and everything he'd worked so hard to keep together could very well fall apart.

He readily admitted that he could be stubborn, but a leader also had to realize when it was time to take action. And that time was now.

Con released a breath and pushed away from his desk, moving his chair back before rising. He buttoned his suit jacket and adjusted the cuffs of his shirt as he walked to the door.

As he made his way down the stairs, he spotted Asher and Kellan at the bottom waiting for him. Con halted once he reached them, looking from one to the other.

Kellan shrugged and met his gaze while leaning an elbow on the banister. "It's about damn time. And before you say anything, I'm coming with you."

"I doona need help," Con said.

Kellan pushed away from the banister and gave him a sour look. "I'm no' going for you. I'm going for me."

"We've all been anticipating this," Asher said.

Con should've known the other Kings would be waiting for a win—even a small one—after the heaps of trouble that had come their way of late. Besides, he'd charged Asher and Kellan with finding the spy. They should be there to see this through.

"Fine," he told them.

Asher grinned. "Ryder wanted me to let you know that he did another intensive background check on those employed at Dreagan. He can confirm that we doona have any other spies."

"All this time, I believed the person was working for Ulrik. I didna want there to be another enemy against us, but the truth about Mikkel has come to light," Con said.

Kellan crossed his arms over his chest. "It was easier to believe Ulrik was the culprit for everything."

"Aye," Con murmured. "Ulrik willna have a spy here. There's no need. No' when he's been coming onto Dreagan for some time now."

Asher's face went slack. "What? There's no way. He's banished. No' to mention Ryder's cameras would've picked him up." He then looked at Kellan. "Did you see this as Keeper of History?"

Kellan's frown deepened. "I have to record everything, as you know. Most of it I doona allow to register as I'm writing it. I can no' keep all that information in my brain."

Con shook his head, hoping the weariness assaulting him didn't show. "If Ulrik wanted to do any of us harm, Kellan, you would've known. Doona concern yourself with this. Besides, it seems Ulrik really does have a way of teleporting. He uses that to get in and out of his mountain, as well as to see the Silvers."

"Shite," Kellan stated.

Asher laughed as he shook his head. "That sounds exactly like something Ulrik would do."

It was just another strike against him, Con realized. He was trying to be everything for everyone, but he couldn't. It used to be simple. Before the spell that kept the Kings from feeling anything for the humans shattered. Before the mates.

There weren't just more women roaming Dreagan, there were more enemies against the Kings, as well. At least the Kings could fly once more.

Con realized the others were waiting for him as he'd been lost in his thoughts. The two fell into step beside him as they walked from the manor.

"Is everything all right?" Kellan asked.

Con glanced over and met Kellan's celadon gaze. "It hasna been for a long time."

"He meant with you," Asher said.

Constantine halted and sighed. "I take it you're both referring to Usaeil?"

"I'm talking about all of this," Kellan said. "You're shouldering everything, Con."

"It's my job."

Asher snorted. "It's going to be your death. You're no' in this alone, you know. This involves all of us."

Con looked out over Dreagan from the red-roofed buildings of the distillery to the mountains and glens where sheep and cattle roamed, then to the manor. It was a stunning place made more special by its magic.

This was the place all Kings gathered away from their lands and clan. It had called to them from the very beginning, beckoning the dragons with the magic that beat like a heart within the ground.

"There are only two other people who know just how badly I wanted to be King of Dragon Kings," Con said as he returned his gaze them. "Kellan, because he's Keeper of History, but can you guess the other?"

Asher nodded once. "Ulrik."

"We told each other everything once. He used to warn me that I didna know what I was getting into, that it should be enough that I was king of my Golds. But it wasna enough." Con smiled ruefully. "I hungered for this responsibility, and I made sure I got it. So now, when things are at their worst, I'm no' going to shirk my responsibilities."

"That never entered our minds," Kellan stated.

They continued toward the distillery buildings, but they didn't get very far before Asher spoke again.

"And Usaeil?"

Con couldn't help but grin. "I'll be taking care of that particular thorn in my side verra soon."

"But you willna be alone," Kellan stated.

"No," Con replied, the smile gone. "Rhi will be with me."

Asher blew out a long breath. "Things are escalating between those two."

Con nodded, unable to deny it. "Its Usaeil's doing. I never realized how jealous she was of Rhi."

"Usaeil is queen," Kellan said, his words tinged with frustration. "What else does she want?"

"She wants it all," Asher said as he shot Kellan a look.

"I believed Rhi left the Queen's Guard because of her own issues. I should've realized it was more than that," Con said.

Kellan grunted. "We all should have."

Their talk ceased as they approached the kilns. Con glanced at Kellan, who pivoted and walked toward the building where Con had an office for just such instances. Since he had to conduct business with mortals, he'd set up space in one of the back buildings long ago.

He glanced at Asher before they walked through the door. Con made his way to the back of the building where he spotted the short, blond waves he recognized as

Alice's. It still upset him that someone who was a fifth-generation worker and had been employed by Dreagan for nearly two decades would betray them.

Then again, it was human nature.

Alice's family had been good workers, so when she came to Dreagan for a job, Con hadn't hesitated to hire her. She'd proven she was an even better employee than her family. Soon, she was given more responsibility and was all over the distillery wherever there was a need.

Now, he would have to fire someone who they'd depended on because she was a spy.

"Hi," Alice said, flashing a big smile when she spotted him.

Con nodded, noting that her wedding band was missing. This was marriage number two. "I'd like to speak with you."

"Of course," she replied, turning her blue gaze on the man next to her.

They waited as Alice handed over the clipboard to another employee. Con then led her out of the building to his office.

The space gave all the appearances of a place that he used often. There was a beautiful antique desk, a chair that matched the one in his office in the manor, a sideboard with several decanters of whisky, chairs for visitors, and decorations that spoke of Dreagan's accomplishments and awards.

And while Dreagan did have the double dragon logo, Con kept the dragon decorations to a minimum in this office. There was also a token or two that reminded visitors of Dreagan's wealth—which always seemed important to mortals.

Con spotted Kellan standing in the corner when he walked into the office. He gave a nod to him before moving behind his desk and motioned for Alice to take a seat. Behind her, Asher quietly closed the door and set up sentry.

Con sank into his chair and leaned back as he watched Alice. She sat calmly with a smile on her face. There wasn't any indication that she suspected she'd been found out. And why would she? She'd possibly been a spy the entire time she'd been at Dreagan. Hell, Con had even sent her to help Cassie when she first arrived.

Because he'd trusted Alice.

Con couldn't help but see a correlation between him and Ulrik. It wasn't difficult to understand why Ulrik hated the mortals so. Or why his old friend trusted no one.

It wasn't by accident that he was relating to Ulrik. Had he felt even a shred of what consumed him now when Ulrik began the war, there was no doubt Con would've joined his friend.

But this was a different time. He had to keep that in mind.

And it wasn't easy.

With his focus back on Alice, Con studied her. She'd always been comely. Alice was cheerful as well as helpful. Few ever had anything negative to say about her.

"How long have you worked for us?" he asked.

She shrugged and crossed one jean-clad leg over the other. "It'll be twenty years come September."

"A long time."

"To be sure," she agreed. "But it's been amazing. I wouldn't want to work anywhere else. It is my family's legacy."

Con glanced at Asher before he continued. "You've worked your way up in the ranks."

"My daddy always preached that if I wanted something, I needed to work for it." She chuckled softly. "I knew after a month of being here that this was where I belonged."

"Aye. It's always nice to find a job that you enjoy."

She gave a nod of her blond head. "Exactly. Live to work, not work to live."

Con had thought long and hard about how he was going to fire her. He'd briefly toyed with the idea of letting her know he'd discovered her spying. Then he realized that it was better to leave it alone.

By not saying anything, it might push Mikkel to make another mistake. Like sending someone else to spy. It also helped that Con had a valid reason for dismissing Alice.

Con leaned forward and put his arms on the desk. "You've been a great asset to this company, Alice. That's why it's so hard to tell you that we're going to have to let you go."

Her smile dropped as her face went white. "What? I . . . I don't understand."

"For months now, we've caught you stealing whisky from the warehouse. I let that go since five generations of your family have worked for this company. I also turned a blind eye when you began taking other items from the store, but you got greedy and stole money from the register, as well."

She stared blankly at him, her mouth gaping open.

"I pay you well," Con continued. "I pay all of my employees well. I doona understand why you had to steal, but I'll no longer tolerate such actions." He rose to his feet. "Asher will walk with you to gather your things and see you off the property."

"I . . . I," she began, but couldn't finish.

Con walked around the desk as she stood and pulled out an envelope from an inside pocket of his jacket. "Here is your final paycheck."

He wanted to make sure there was no reason for Alice to ever return to Dreagan.

Asher opened the door and waited for Alice to walk numbly past him. He gave Con a smile and followed her out.

Con blew out a breath and strode to the doorway to watch them. It wasn't long before Kellan joined him.

"There's one problem out of the way," Kellan said.

"Aye. I allowed her to remain too long. I believed she worked for Ulrik, so I planned to use her. I realized that plan wouldna work once Ryder discovered payments to her from one of Mikkel's shell companies."

"Which meant there was no more need for Alice," Kellan stated and crossed his arms across his chest.

Con had to admit it felt pretty damn good to get a step ahead of Mikkel. Even if it was only a baby step, it was more than they'd had the day before.

"I feel like celebrating," Kellan said.

Con spun the gold dragon head cufflink on his wrist. "It's a small win, but we're going to celebrate."

Kellan slapped him on the back. "One down."

"A hundred other problems to go," Con said.

"Which one is next?"

Con shrugged. "We still have Stanley Upton in the dungeon."

"You should deal with Usaeil."

"Rhi is still reeling from the banishment. I need her head clear before we face the queen. My problem with Usaeil will come to a head soon enough. Let's focus on Upton."

CHAPTER TWENTY-SIX

No.

The word echoed in Ulrik's head with all the force of an exploding star. He stared at Broc, hoping the Warrior was joking about not being able to find Eilish.

"It's happened before."

The female voice jerked Ulrik out of his stupor. He looked at the flame-haired woman who'd walked up beside Broc. Sonya. A Druid who not only had special healing skills but was also able to communicate with trees.

Ulrik took a step back. For the first time, he wasn't sure what to do next. He'd counted on the Warriors helping him. He'd planned to beg, and if that didn't work, he'd make them. Now . . . well, neither option was available.

"Ulrik."

He blinked, his gaze focusing on a petite Druid with black hair and ice blue eyes. It took him a second to recall who she was. Isla. She belonged to the fire-happy Warrior who had yet to stop scowling.

Her hand lifted, and he watched as she went to touch his arm before hesitating. It made him want to laugh. Few mortals—or Fae for that matter—got near enough to touch him, and even fewer did it willingly.

Then her hand came to rest on him. "There's magic blocking Broc from finding Eilish. It's occurred a few times before."

So they were going to help him.

He turned his head to Broc. "Have you located her before this?"

"I never knew her full name before. I need it to be able to locate someone unless I know them," the Warrior replied.

Something squeezed Ulrik's arm. He was surprised to find that Isla still had hold of him. And by the anger contorting Hayden's face, the Warrior wasn't pleased by it.

"That magic blast we felt was hers," Isla said.

Ulrik nodded. "Aye. I'd know it anywhere. How do you know that?"

"The Ancients told me."

"Can you locate her like that?" he asked, hope burning in his gut.

Sonya said, "No."

Ulrik briefly closed his eyes. When he opened them, he spotted the rest of the Druids from the castle standing with their Warriors.

Was his attention so caught up with Eilish and not being able to find her that he wasn't noticing such things? He needed to get his head on straight in case Mikkel used this time to attack.

Isla dropped her hand from him. "I'm surprised to see you here. We all are."

"I have to find Eilish."

"So you said." Fallon tamped down his god.

Ulrik watched as the black eyes of Fallon's god that filled his entire eye faded and were replaced by dark green irises that pinned Ulrik.

"Now that we know the Druid's name," Fallon continued. "We can find her whenever we want. And we'll bring that information to Con."

Ulrik wasn't surprised by the statement. "I expected you to say that."

"And still, you came," Isla said, her eyes watching him with a mix of curiosity and unease.

Ulrik looked at the Warriors and Druids, recognizing the community, the family they'd established. He also knew there were children on the grounds.

"If I know of your existence, then so does my uncle. He's no' as strong as a Dragon King, nor does he have the favor of the Dark Fae anymore. But he could still bring about destruction here."

Hayden growled as he took a couple of steps closer. "Are you threatening us?"

"Warning you," Ulrik said, looking down at Isla. "I plan to stop Mikkel before anything happens."

Isla's head cocked to the side as she released him. "And you need Eilish for that?"

"No." In fact, she was more hindrance than help. But he still had to find her.

Fallon crossed his arms over his chest, the moonlight glinting off the torc at his neck that he and his brothers wore. "Then why do you seek the Druid?"

"Because I offered her my assistance."

It wasn't a complete lie.

"I—" Sonya began before her eyes took on a faraway look as she raised her gaze to the trees.

Ulrik turned at the sound behind him and saw the trees swaying back and forth, leaves rustling and branches bending. All with no wind.

"She's not here," Sonya said.

Ulrik looked back at her. "I didna think she was at the castle."

"No," Sonya said with a shake of her red head. "She's not on this realm."

Fear spiked through Ulrik. "The trees told you that?"

"Yes," she confirmed.

"Who took her? Was it a Fae?" he demanded, walking toward her.

Because if Balladyn were involved in any way, Ulrik would tear him limb from limb—their pact be damned.

Broc held up a hand, stopping Ulrik's advance. "Easy, Dragon King."

"Who took her?" Ulrik asked through clenched teeth, ignoring Broc.

Sonya shook her head. "No one. She left herself."

It was like a kick in the teeth. Each time Ulrik thought he had a way of finding Eilish, the rug was yanked out from under him.

"How?" he asked, more to himself than the others.

Eilish could teleport, but he didn't think her magic was strong enough to move her to other realms. Even the Dragon Kings needed a dragon bridge to do that. The Fae needed their doorways. So how the hell had she done it?

And then he wondered how he was going to find her. At least she was no longer in a place where Mikkel could hurt her. Or her family could find her. Perhaps he should leave her be.

But he knew he couldn't.

With no other reason to be at MacLeod Castle, he decided it was time he departed their company. No doubt the Warriors would contact Con immediately. Not that Ulrik cared.

"Wait," Isla hurried to say before he touched his cuff.

Hayden jerked his gaze to her, looking as if she'd sprouted a trunk.

That was enough to make Ulrik hesitate to see what Isla wanted. Because he really didn't like the Warrior.

"What is it?" Ulrik asked the Druid.

"If Eilish wants to return, she'll be able to."

He wasn't sure what that meant, and it did nothing to calm his need to locate her. But he recognized that Isla was attempting to help.

It was a curious feeling that swirled around him. He was used to manipulating others, forcing, or even paying for them to do his bidding. For someone like Isla to freely give him information was new. And unexpected.

"How do we know you willna send the Dark our way?" Hayden questioned as he still held the two balls of fire.

Ulrik looked at the fire and then back at the Warrior. "You do realize dragons are made of fire, right? If you're trying to scare me, you're no' doing a verra good job. However, I understand you're protecting your woman and your home."

The fire disappeared, and Hayden tamped down his god so that his red skin faded.

Only then did Ulrik say, "If I wanted to harm any of you, I could've done it anytime over the last several centuries."

"But we are human," Sonya said.

Ulrik looked at each of the Warriors and Druids. At one time, he'd considered Druids nothing more than mortals with a dash of magic. He wasn't sure when his thinking had changed, but it had.

"When the dragons were sent away, most of this realm's magic went with them. You want to know why Druids are losing their magic?" he asked. "It's no' just because they're diluting their blood, though that is a big reason. It's because they no longer believe in magic."

He jerked his chin to the castle. "There's power here. On this land. It's here because all of you are. It's a gift for humans, but to my kind, it was a way of life. Each of you has been chosen to keep magic alive, and it's that I protect. Because without it, I'm no' sure what will happen to this Earth."

With a nod to Isla, and then another to Fallon, Ulrik touched his cuff and returned to the cottage. He sank onto the bed and dropped his head into his hands.

His mind was wandering as he desperately tried to figure out where Eilish could've gone, when it suddenly hit him. He jerked his head up and got to his feet. If he couldn't locate Eilish, he could find where the ripple of her magic originated. That might help him determine where she was—and if she'd been forcibly taken.

He closed his eyes and thought about Eilish and her magic. The potency of it was strong, but instead, he thought about the tinge of darkness that made it distinct. It was that thread that set her apart. Because she could become *drough* with little effort, but she didn't give in to the darkness.

She didn't fight it either.

Eilish accepted it like someone would a missing limb. It was just a part of her. Thanks to that tinge of darkness, he was able to trail her magic over Ireland to a place about an hour from Dublin. As soon as Ulrik arrived at the estate, he hid behind some bushes to get a lay of the land.

He didn't need confirmation to know that this was Mikkel's place. It had all the markings of other properties that his uncle owned. Still, it wouldn't hurt to run into the weasel and end him.

Once Ulrik was sure the manor was abandoned, he walked closer to the building. That's when he noticed a room on the second floor where every window had been broken. Curtains billowed in the breeze, and shards of glass littered the ground at his feet.

He looked at the front door but decided on a quicker entry. Ulrik jumped, landing with bent knees on a windowsill. He glanced into the room before he put one foot and then the other on the floor.

The room looked as if a tornado had ripped through it. The large bed was broken in half, chairs were smashed, tables shattered. But it was the black spot in the middle of the vintage rug that caught his attention.

He squatted beside it, testing the spot. Magic sizzled up his arm. More importantly, it was Eilish's power he felt.

The black wasn't soot from a burn, but the remnants of a blast from a truly powerful Druid. What concerned him was that the darkness within it had grown significantly.

"What have you done, Uncle?" Ulrik murmured as he straightened. "And where have you gone, Druid?"

Eilish's was the only magic he felt, but he knew she hadn't been alone. Something must have set her off. Had it been Mikkel? Or someone else?

Someone like her family?

Ulrik was grasping at straws, but the facts were pointing him in a certain direction. What he needed was to find out the truth, and Mikkel would never tell him what happened. Which meant that Ulrik had to locate Eilish.

"Eilish, if you can hear me, I need you to come back. Come back to me."

He waited, hoping that she might appear. After several minutes, Ulrik left the room and walked through the estate, looking for anything that might tell him where his uncle had gone.

As he made his way to the front door, he spotted something on the floor that had slipped beneath a table. He picked it up, turning it over to see the address of the estate.

But it was the name at the top of the paper that caught his attention—Morna Duffy.

Now he knew Eilish's family had been there.

CHAPTER TWENTY-SEVEN

Something was very, very wrong. Eilish looked around in confusion. She was no longer in the bedroom, nor were Mikkel or the two women with her.

In fact, Eilish had no idea where she was. Everything was hazy, as if she'd stepped into the remnants of a fire. Or mist.

It clung to her, wrapping around her as if it were alive. She was able to breathe freely without choking, so maybe it wasn't smoke. But she'd never seen mist move like this. It made nary a sound, but it was so dense, she couldn't see through it. Which meant that anything could be out there waiting for her.

She slowly turned in a circle. The last thing she remembered was letting her anger rise up. Always before, she'd kept her rage in check because she could feel how it changed her magic. Ulrik had said he could sense the darkness around her edges. It was that darkness she let in.

Perhaps she should be worried about what she'd done to Mikkel and those women, but she couldn't drudge up even the tiniest thread of concern. They'd wanted to hurt her. Of that, she was certain.

She looked down, but the mist was wrapped around her legs, preventing her from seeing her feet, much less the ground. Unease began to grow, and soon, it festered into fear.

Her thoughts focused on Ulrik. No doubt he'd stalk through the mist, demanding that whatever was out there show itself. Then Ulrik would shift into his dragon.

What a glorious sight he'd been in his true form. When she followed Nikolai and Esther from the village, she'd never expected to see Ulrik as a dragon. But she hadn't been able to look away.

He'd swooped down from the night sky with a ferocity that had made her take a step back. Moonlight had reflected off his silver scales that were darker on the back of his neck. His sheer size had made her heart skip a beat. It didn't matter that Nikolai was just as large because she only had eyes for Ulrik.

He'd moved with such speed and grace that she forgot he was in the air. But his massive wings were never a hindrance. He used them as weapons, just as he did his body and long tail.

She couldn't remember what Nikolai looked like, but she could describe Ulrik down to the last detail. His large dragon head held big, obsidian eyes that saw everything. He had long, muscular limbs with four closely mounted digits on each foot that ended in extremely long talons. His body was elegant and powerful. There was a row of dark silver spikes that ran from the base of his skull down his back to the tip of his tail.

All in all, he was breathtaking. Utterly spectacular.

Alarmingly menacing.

And she wished he were with her. How silly she was to have fallen for Ulrik. Not just because he was broken or that he couldn't trust. But because he'd never be able to care about anything, which meant he could never return her love.

"Eilish."

She heard her name like a whisper, as if the mist tried to prevent the sound from reaching her. Yet there was no denying the voice. It was Ulrik.

Most likely, it was a figment of her imagination. Ulrik had other things to worry about than her. She was just a pawn he wanted to use in his bid to take down Constantine.

That train of thought brought a rush of anger that she tried to squash. But she was unsuccessful. It was Mikkel's fault. He'd made her lose control. And for what? Who were those women? What had they wanted with her?

Whatever they sought, it wasn't good. All she had to do was look in their eyes to know that. That had prompted her to defend herself. If only she knew what she'd done. Or was it Mikkel that had put her here?

She shook her head as she tried to look through the mist. Mikkel was giving her to the women. If he'd put her here, he would be her taunting her before handing her over. The fact that no one else was around meant either she was dreaming, or she'd done this to herself.

"Eilish . . . come back to me."

She stilled when she heard Ulrik's voice again. Her first thought was that it was some kind of trick. But what if it weren't? What if it really was Ulrik trying to find her?

Even if it wasn't, she didn't want to be in this place anymore. She was ready to return to her world, find Mikkel and those two women, and make sure none of them came after her again.

The darkness within her seemed to purr at her thoughts.

It urged her to kill them, to remove anyone who dared to stand in her way.

The power that darkness gave her was captivating. It enticed, it seduced. And she wanted to give in to it.

Then she recalled what Ulrik had said about her being strong enough to withstand the darkness. How she needed to cling to the pure Druid magic that was within her. Somehow, remembering those words was all she needed to resist the lure of the darkness.

But it wasn't finished with her yet. The mist began to move faster. It tightened its grip around her ankles and legs. She batted at it when it tried to wrap around her arms, but it did little good.

All too soon, it had her ensnared in its sturdy grip. No matter how hard she fought, she couldn't break free. Almost instantly, she began to get irate. There was so much for her to be angry about. Patrick lying to her, not being able to find her mother, Mikkel using her, and the women trying to take her.

Instead of letting her rage loose, she channeled her frustration into something else—Ulrik. Specifically, how she felt when she was with him.

The darkness was gradually pushed back to the fringes where it belonged, and her magic was able to rise. It filled every bone and muscle, every pore and fiber. Her body hummed with it.

And that's when she unleashed it.

She threw back her head and screamed. The mist's hold evaporated, and it shrank back from her as if in fear. But Eilish wasn't going to wait around to find out what its next move might be. She was leaving.

Her thoughts centered on Graves, but her mind kept conjuring Ulrik. All the while, she could feel the mist coming back for her.

She pulled up more magic. If she were going to get out, it was now or never.

Ulrik teleported back to his cottage with the new information on Eilish's family. If he were going to locate her, he had to plan out his next moves. It meant putting things on hold with Con, but once Ulrik found Eilish, he'd most likely find his uncle, as well.

And it was time to pull that particular spike in his side out once and for all.

Ulrik had played his part with Mikkel for too long. Since his uncle didn't know when to give up, Ulrik would have to show him.

He was walking toward his desk when he heard a crash from within his bedroom. Quickly changing course, Ulrik made his way to the closed door. He listened, his enhanced hearing picking up the sounds of ragged breathing.

With his magic at the ready, he threw open the door and spotted someone squatting on the floor. When wild green-gold eyes met his, he took a step toward Eilish, only to have her hurl magic at him.

He raised his arm to block it, but her magic fell short before even reaching him. She used her hands to help her turn in a circle, her eyes darting about in a crazed fashion. Blood ran from her nose, and he could feel her magic fading.

In two strides, he was before her, going down on his knees to come to eye level with her. He gently grasped her shoulders. "Eilish."

Her gaze jerked to him. She searched his face before the wildness faded and a frown formed. "Ulrik?"

"Aye, lass. It's me. I'm here."

"Am I back?" she asked, her voice cracking.

He pulled her against him, holding her tightly. "You're back. You're safe."

She sagged against him. When he looked down, he saw that she'd fallen unconscious. She needed her magic recharged. He didn't know why she'd come to him instead of a place that could give her strength, but he knew what he had to do.

Ulrik gathered her in his arms, shifting her so that he could touch his cuff as he thought of the Dooncarton standing stones. They were filled with magic and would help to recharge her.

Once inside the stone circle, he laid Eilish on the grass so that her palms were touching the ground. He knew he should leave, but he couldn't. He smoothed her hair away from her face that was turned toward him.

"What happened to you? Where did you go? And how did you get back?" he whispered before cleaning the blood off her face with the hem of his shirt.

He stayed sitting beside her as the minutes turned to hours while the magic pulsed around them before moving into Eilish. Her magic recharged, and she grew stronger, but she remained unconscious.

It wasn't until he felt how cold her skin was that he realized the temperatures had dropped. He lifted her, setting her on his lap to give her his warmth. He wasn't keen on leaving until she'd woken in case she needed more magic.

The quiet of the area soothed him, but it was the magic that eased his soul. It calmed him. Or perhaps it was knowing Eilish was safe.

Not that he wanted to go down that particular road and discover why he'd been so upset by her disappearance. That was a rocky path that would open old wounds he'd just as soon leave untouched.

The dark skies gradually turned gray. While sitting

amidst the stones with Eilish in his arms, Ulrik watched the sun rise. The clouds were a magnificent pink and red as the big, orange ball ascended into the sky, chasing away the night.

He pulled his gaze away from the sunrise and looked down to find Eilish's eyes open. Her green-gold orbs were softened by sleep. She reached up and touched his face, a grin lifting her lips.

"Ready to return home?" he asked.

She gave a nod.

Ulrik touched his cuff. In the next second, they were sitting on the floor of his cottage.

Though he longed to keep holding her, Ulrik knew he had to get her into clean clothes and get some food inside her. Still, he held her for a few more minutes.

"Hungry?" he asked.

"Starving."

He kissed her forehead and climbed to his feet with her in his arms. "How about a soak in the tub while I get food?"

"Yes, please."

As he walked toward the bathroom, he used his magic so that the tub was already filled with hot water. Once inside, he set her down, not fully releasing her until she was steady on her feet.

"Take your time," he told her.

A flash of concern appeared on her face. Ulrik put a finger beneath her chin and turned her head to him. "No one can harm you here."

"Mikkel got past my defenses."

Rage burned within Ulrik. It was just as he'd guessed. Mikkel had gotten to Eilish. He should've never left her. If he hadn't, he'd have been there to face his uncle.

"No one is getting through mine," Ulrik promised.

She nodded. "Thank you."

He released her and turned to give her privacy. At the door, he looked back after she'd removed her shirt and saw deep, red welts on her arms and back.

Whoever had hurt her was going to pay.

And painfully.

CHAPTER TWENTY-EIGHT

Ulrik. There wasn't a man—or dragon—alive who was more enigmatic or baffling. Eilish accepted this as she did the fact that the sky was blue.

She slipped into the water, sighing as she sat and let the heat surround her. As long as she'd been in his arms, she hadn't been cold.

Her eyes lifted to the window. It was morning now. How long had had they been at Dooncarton? And how did he know she loved that place? She remembered waking up and seeing the sun rising, but then she'd looked up and spotted Ulrik. Everything else had ceased to exist then.

She'd been mesmerized by the unfettered joy that she glimpsed. For those few moments, he'd let his mask slip. He'd been free to bask in the glory of the dawning of a new day.

In those seconds, she'd witnessed his wonder at the sunrise. She saw his delight when the first rays of the sun broke through the darkness. She watched him treasure every moment.

It was something she'd never forget because she knew

she'd seen the real Ulrik. The man he'd been before the horrors of life visited him. It made him more mysterious. And it made her love him even more.

Eilish remained in the tub until her fingers became pruney. That drove her out of the water to towel off. Since she didn't want to put her clothes back on, she searched for something else to wear. That's when she saw the hamper.

Curious, she walked to the wicker basket and opened it. Inside were Ulrik's clothes. She couldn't help but smile since she'd never imagined a Dragon King doing his own laundry. She'd just assumed that Ulrik used his magic and got new ones each time he wanted them.

This was just another layer to him. And one she quite liked. It made him more human, though she wouldn't tell him that. She knew how much he hated her species.

She grabbed a dark gray dress shirt from the top of the pile and put it on. As soon as it was around her, she smelled him. Power, woods, and darkness. She turned her head to the side and drew in a deep breath, letting his scent fill her more.

Now fortified, she opened the door and stepped out of the bathroom. Her stomach rumbled when she smelled the food.

"I got you some of your clothes," Ulrik said as he laid containers of food out on the table. "They're on the sofa."

She walked to him, smiling when she saw the assortment of food he'd gotten.

"I have some of everything." He looked up and stilled.

A shudder ran through Eilish as his gaze raked longingly over her. His eyes slowly roamed upward until their gazes tangled.

"Or you can wear that," he murmured.

She placed her hand on the back of a chair. "Thank you."

As if her words pulled him out of a stupor, he nodded. "Eat."

She didn't need to be told twice. Eilish pulled out the chair and reached for the container closest to her. It was a cheeseburger and fries.

Her eyes closed when she bit into the burger. It tasted so good. In between bites, she shoved fries into her mouth after dipping them in ketchup. She was halfway through the burger when she looked up to find Ulrik sitting across from her with a slight grin on his face.

She chuckled and swallowed her bite. Then she set the burger down and wiped her mouth. "I didn't realize how hungry I was."

"Doona let me stop you."

She licked her lips and sat back. "Something happened today—I mean, yesterday."

His face grew serious as he pushed a glass of water and a bottle of ale toward her. "Want to tell me?"

"Yes," she said and reached for the water. She downed the entire glass before she grabbed the ale. After a few swallows, she set the bottle aside and released a breath. "Mikkel came. He busted through my shields as if they were nothing more than the feeble locks people put on their doors."

Ulrik's brow furrowed as he leaned his arms on the table. "He shouldna have been able to get through them so easily."

"I think I underestimated his strength."

"Nay," Ulrik said with a shake of his head. "When you didna kill me, Mikkel found another way."

This made her frown. "Another way?"

"He'll stop at nothing to end me. He tried to use you.

When that didna work, he found someone or something else."

"What? Who?"

Ulrik shrugged, his gaze dropping to the floor as his mind worked. "That I doona know. Yet." He looked back up at her. "What did he say?"

"Your uncle was livid that I hadn't killed you. He kept asking me about what you told me, but I refused to tell him anything."

"That's all?"

She made herself hold his gaze. "He . . . hurt me, but I withstood it."

Ulrik's hand clenched into a fist, his knuckles white. "What did he do?" he demanded in a low, dangerous voice.

"It doesn't matter."

"It does to me."

She reached across the table and put her hand atop his. It was enough that he became angry on her behalf. "How much do you know about your uncle?"

"What do you mean?"

"His story? Do you know his background?"

Ulrik shook his head.

She took a deep breath and released it, sitting back. "Then let me tell you what he shared with me."

For the next thirty minutes, she told him everything Mikkel had divulged about his past while he held and tortured her, but Eilish left out the particulars of what Mikkel had done to her.

The entire time, Ulrik remained as still as stone, not uttering even a single sound. When she finished, he drew in a deep breath and released it. Only then did he unfurl his fisted hand and lay his fingers flat on the table.

"Did you believe him?" Ulrik asked.

Eilish gave a small shake of her head as she shrugged. "I suppose I did. Why would he make up such a story?"

"I never heard anything like that from anyone in my family. Ever."

"Perhaps it was something not spoken about."

Ulrik made a face that said he highly doubted it. "Mikkel usually kept to himself. I tried many times to make him part of the family, but he chose to live away from us."

"Maybe because of what his father, your grandfather, did."

"Even if what Mikkel said is true, that gives him no right to act the way he is."

Eilish tucked her damp hair behind her ear. "But it allows you to understand him better."

"You're comparing me to him."

She quickly shook her head. "I'm not. He was abused. You were betrayed. Those are two different things."

"Are they?" Ulrik asked in a soft voice.

She quirked a brow. "Yes."

"What did Mikkel do to you?"

"As I said—"

"Doona tell me you survived it one more time," he interrupted. "I want to know what my uncle did."

She discovered she was absently rubbing her hand along one thigh. The pain was gone, but the memory of the bone snapping in half would never fade.

"Eilish," Ulrik urged.

Swallowing hard, she said, "He got in my head first. The pain was . . . debilitating. I heard the door splinter, and then he was in my bedroom. He threw me against the wall and held me up by the ceiling, choking me. I couldn't use my magic to defend myself. It was like it couldn't hear me trying to gather it."

"And?" Ulrik said, his hand fisted once more.

She held his gaze for several tense seconds. "He broke my leg."

Ulrik's knuckles went white again. "And?"

"He dropped me to the floor and broke my other leg."

Without a word, without any movement, she felt Ulrik's wrath. His gold eyes burned with a fury that made her shiver—not in fear, but in anticipation.

She licked her lips before continuing. "When I woke, I was in a bedroom that I didn't recognize. The windows were covered, and I couldn't move because of the pain in my legs. I tried to heal myself, but I couldn't. Then Mikkel came in and said he could take away the pain if I helped him. I knew he meant that he wanted me to get to you."

"And you agreed."

It wasn't a question. She nodded. "With the knowledge that I had no intention of doing anything for Mikkel. When he left without helping me, I focused on my magic. Then, I felt the Ancients."

"They spoke to you?"

"They did," she replied with a smile. "They cautioned me to be careful."

"About?"

Eilish shrugged. "I assumed Mikkel."

"It could've been about anything."

That was true enough, not that it mattered now. "I was finally able to heal my legs. It wasn't long after that when Mikkel returned with two women. They said I was the spitting image of my mother."

"They were your aunts."

"I figured as much," she said in irritation. "They tried to take me, but I fought them off. They had no magic, but they didn't seem worried about that."

Ulrik blinked, his gold eyes locked on her. "Was there a fight?"

She thought back and slowly shook her head. "When I become angry, my magic . . . well, something changes within me as well as my magic."

"It's the darkness."

"Yes," she agreed. "I knocked my aunts out, and then I faced Mikkel. I didn't hold back my rage. I unleashed it and everything that came with it." She paused, her gaze lowering to the table as she recalled the power that had rolled through her like a tsunami. "I remember screaming my anger. I remember releasing the magic around me, directed at everyone."

Ulrik's voice penetrated her thoughts then. "Your magic busted windows and broke everything inside that bedroom."

"You went there?" she asked, her gaze jerking to his.

He gave a single nod. "When you unleashed your magic, it sent a boom across the land, causing a ripple of magic. It nearly knocked me off my feet. It was even felt in Scotland."

She wasn't quite sure what to say. Should she be glad she had such power? Or terrified that she could unleash such darkness?

"There were no bodies in the manor," Ulrik continued. "In fact, it was deserted. They left in a hurry. But I'm more interested in where you went."

"I don't know. I saw nothing but mist. It was thick and cloying. It surrounded me, and even tried to trap me there."

He nodded at her leg. "Is that what those marks are from?"

Frowning, Eilish turned her leg to look at it. She saw nothing on either limb. "What are you talking about?"

"The red marks. I saw them on your back when you undressed. I see them on your arms, as well. They were done with magic." He sat forward, his gaze penetrating. "Who did that to you?"

A shiver went through her as she recalled how tightly the mist had held her. "The mist."

"Doona ever go there again," he ordered.

"I don't want to."

His eyes narrowed slightly. "You have that power. You get to decide if it happens again. You got out once, you might no' get a second chance." His forehead furrowed slightly. "How did you get away?"

Her lips parted, thinking of some lie. Then she realized she wanted to tell him the truth. "You."

"Me?" he asked, surprised.

"I heard your voice tell me to return. I focused on you and let my magic build. Then I released it again."

CHAPTER TWENTY-NINE

Desire raged, burned within him. And Ulrik had no interest in ignoring it. Not when Eilish had been returned to him. Not when she'd heard him call to her. Not when the thought of him had brought her here.

He reached for her arm and pulled her up the same time he got to his feet. Her lips parted when their bodies collided. He wrapped an arm around her, holding her tight.

Or maybe he was holding onto her.

It didn't matter. Not as long as she was near.

Looking into her green-gold eyes, he didn't want to think of his uncle, Con, his revenge, or even his feelings for the Druid. All he wanted was her.

She placed a hand over his heart. It pounded erratically. Then again, that's what she did to him. From the very beginning.

She broke through his darkness, pushing past it as if it couldn't touch her. And she accepted him. All of him. His past, his present, and his future. She didn't demand he stop his vengeance, didn't tell him it was foolish.

In return, she silently—and continually—showed him

she was on his side. All the while, his desire smoldered and flamed.

For her.

Her pulse beat frantically in her throat. Her ragged breaths filled his ears. She'd been through hell and back, and came out stronger. But he was very aware of how easily he could've lost her.

He ran his fingertips from her cheek down to her throat. Her gaze briefly lowered to his mouth.

By the stars, this woman had him in such a state of need. He knew to give in to the desire that blazed would pull him deeper into the emotions he was trying to ignore.

But he couldn't seem to help himself when it came to Eilish.

His hunger, the unquenchable need to sink into her body, overruled everything else. When they were together, they were the only two people in the entire world.

The past hurts and grievances and present pain and anger couldn't touch them. They were wrapped in a thick blanket of desire that couldn't be penetrated by anything. Or anyone.

Her hand that rested on his waist slid around to his back as she rubbed her body against his arousal. Longing spiked through him. He sank his hands into her damp locks and gripped her head. With a seductive grin, she removed his clothes with her magic.

Her hands roamed over his shoulders and chest, a sound that resembled a purr falling from her lips. He didn't release his hold on her hair as her hands continued down his body until they wrapped around his cock.

His staff jumped and swelled at her touch. She met his gaze and slowly knelt before him. He couldn't take his eyes off her as she caressed his rod as if it were a prized possession. Then her lips parted and slipped over the head.

Ulrik's eyes slid closed as his head fell back. Absolute pleasure engulfed him with each soft pull of her mouth and lick of her tongue along his length. He moaned in delight when she cupped his balls.

He stood there as long as he could before tugging her hair back and looking down at her. There were no words needed. They understood each other on a cellular level.

She licked her lips and stood, her eyes darkening with longing. He grabbed the neck of his shirt she wore with both hands and ripped it open, sending buttons flying across the room before dinging slightly when they landed.

Eilish sucked in a breath. He seized her by the waist and lifted her as he turned. Holding her with one arm, he swiped the containers from the table before setting her atop it.

She pulled his head down for a kiss that made his heart catch. There were no soft caresses, no tender words. She'd gone to another place and almost got trapped. He didn't think he'd ever be able to let her out of his sight again. The near loss made them both crazy with the need for something solid, something real.

And the craving they felt was definitely that.

Her ankles locked behind him as their frantic kisses became even more heated. He leaned over her, one arm around her, the other on the table. She was the one who reached between them and guided him to her entrance.

As soon as he felt her slick heat, he thrust deep.

She tore her face away from him, gasping for air, her head thrown back. He couldn't look away from the pleasure that passed over her while he pumped his hips, sliding in and out of her tight body.

He was enraptured. Completely. Totally.

And he couldn't care less.

There was no stopping whatever it was that had overtaken him, and he was just fine with that. It felt too good, too . . . right.

She lifted her head, her gaze meeting his. Then she threw herself toward him. It sent him stumbling backwards while holding onto her. He slammed into a cabinet before he dropped to his knees and laid her down on the floor. She then shoved at his shoulder until he flipped onto his back with her straddling his hips.

As he looked up at her with her dark locks in disarray and need burning in her eyes, he was captivated. The beautiful, seductive Druid was his.

He caressed up her arm, loving the soft feel of her mocha skin beneath his palm. She braced her hands on his chest as her hips rocked back and forth.

His gaze landed on the red marks on her arm, and his chest tightened. Magic or not, Eilish was still very mortal. She could be killed by anyone. And if Mikkel discovered Ulrik's connection to her, then his uncle wouldn't stop until Eilish was dead.

She leaned down and kissed him as if sensing his thoughts had turned dark. Ulrik splayed one hand on her back, and the other over her bottom. She didn't stop moving. And now that she was leaning over him, her breasts rubbed against him, driving him wild.

With each move of her sensuous body, he was coming closer and closer to orgasm. He couldn't get enough of her. The more he tasted, the more he craved. She was like a drug, and after one dose, he was hooked.

He would never be free of the addiction that was Eilish Flanagan.

And that only gave him a brief flare of concern. Then she was kissing him again.

Ulrik sat them up, kissing down her neck. She gripped his shoulders and rode him hard as her soft moans filled the air. His lips wrapped around a pert nipple and began to tease the tiny bud.

Her cries grew louder, and her nails dug into him. He moved to her other breast and suckled until her body jerked and he felt her clamping around his cock.

He lifted his head, watching the climax sweep through her. Though he tried to hold off his orgasm, the feeling of her combined with observing Eilish was too much. He was quickly pushed over the precipice into the awaiting arms of ecstasy.

And just like the first time he'd made love to Eilish, he was transported, his worries wiped away like condensation on glass. Everything was in harmony. It was such an amazing experience that he never wanted it to end.

All too soon, the pleasure faded. He opened his eyes to find her staring at him with a slight smile. Then she rose to her feet and held out her palm. It never dawned on him to refuse. He took her hand and climbed to his feet. To his surprise, she released him and walked to his bedroom.

Curious, Ulrik followed. He grinned when he saw her climb into his bed and turn onto her side facing him, her gaze locked on him to see what he would do. He'd left her the first time. He wasn't going to repeat that mistake.

He made his way to the other side of the bed and lifted the sheets to climb beneath them. One of his rules was that he never spent an entire night with a woman. He hadn't shared a bed with anyone since Nala.

And yet, he wanted this. He curled his body around Eilish's and draped an arm over her waist. She snuggled back against him, sighing contentedly. Almost immediately, she fell asleep.

But he couldn't. Not when he could still see the red marks on her body. They were fading, but slowly.

He needed to know where she'd gone, so if it happened again, he could get to her. Though he hoped she never went there again. It was too dangerous. Especially since the mist she'd spoken of seemed to be sentient.

That threat was concerning, but there were other things he needed to focus on. Namely Mikkel and the Duffy family. Eilish's aunts wouldn't stop until they had her.

Which wasn't going to happen.

As he lay there planning the different ways he could approach them, it finally dawned on him that he couldn't help Eilish and take down Con.

Everything was primed for him to challenge the King of Kings. If he waited, he might have to start all over. Hadn't he waited long enough for his revenge? Hadn't he given enough?

With Eilish sleeping, he slowly extracted himself from her and rose from the bed. He walked out of the bedroom, summoning his clothes as he did. Just as he was about to touch his cuff, Eilish cleared her throat behind him.

Ulrik turned to her. "You're safe here. Rest."

"And what are you planning to do?"

"Find my uncle."

She smiled and walked to the stack of clothes he'd laid on the couch. "He took my finger rings. I want them back."

"Eilish," he began.

Her head snapped up from pulling on her jeans. "You'd better not be about to tell me to rest."

"You've been through a lot."

"And I'll go through a lot more, no doubt. Shall I do it with you beside me? Or should I do it on my own."

Ulrik clenched his teeth. Damn woman. She'd known he wouldn't let her do it on her own.

"That's what I thought," she replied with a grin and finished dressing.

Once the white tee shirt was in place, her black boots zipped, and the black leather jacket on, she turned to him.

Ulrik held out his hand. As soon as she took it, he touched the cuff and returned them to her flat. Though she said nothing, he felt her tense when she realized where they were.

"He used magic. I'll be able to trace him from it," Ulrik told her.

"Why didn't you do that before?"

He glanced her way. "Because I was looking for you."

"Oh," she said, but her smile said she was pleased.

Ulrik walked to the entryway and looked at the splintered wood. No foot kicked that in. It was magic. He squatted and ran his hand over the space near the door, waiting to feel dragon magic. He did, but it was so slight that he frowned. Almost immediately, he felt more—Druid magic.

Except this magic wasn't *mie* or *drough*. It was . . . wrong.

The combination of dragon and Druid magic perplexed him. Even someone like Mikkel would have more magic than a Druid. So why would he combine it with power that was so . . . off?

"What is it?" Eilish asked as she came up behind him.

Ulrik dropped his hand as he rose to his feet. "You said Mikkel was strong."

"He was. I couldn't use my magic at all."

"I think I know why."

Eilish raised her brows expectantly. "Care to share?"

"You wanted to know about your family. It looks like you're going to get your wish."

Lines of worry tightened on her face. "I'm not going to like what we find, am I?"

"Probably no'."

She squared her shoulders. Her green-gold eyes eagerly met his. "Then what are we waiting for?"

He took her hand and touched his cuff.

CHAPTER THIRTY

Paris, France

The world looked vastly different from a great height. Rhi lounged against the metal pillar at the very tip of the Eiffel Tower. It was no wonder the Dragon Kings loved to fly. Looking down upon Paris, it was easy to dismiss the trivial issues others faced.

But Rhi couldn't fly. Her feet would always be planted firmly on the ground. However, that ground could be anywhere. It didn't mean she had to remain in this realm. After all, what had Earth done for her?

Not a fucking thing.

It had given her a Dragon King, then took him away.

It had given her a best friend, then took Balladyn away.

It had given her purpose, then took that away.

It had given her a second home, then took that away.

It had given her hope, then took that away.

She had no home, no family, no function, and no people to call her own.

The only thing she had was the darkness that continued to grow within her. The hate and anger she felt toward Usaeil only made it spread.

She feared that. But how much longer would that anxiety hold? Because once it was gone, Rhi would be the very thing she'd sworn never to be—Dark Fae.

This was usually when she'd turn to Balladyn since she couldn't go to Dreagan. But Balladyn had become someone she didn't recognize. Perhaps he'd been like that all along and she just refused to see it.

Daire wasn't even following her anymore. The Reaper hadn't said anything to her. One day, he was just gone. She hadn't seen him since, and she'd become accustomed to him always being with her and listening to her.

She thought of Phelan but promptly nixed that idea. Every time she went to him and Aisley, she brought danger with her. So far, there were only a few who knew that Phelan was half-Fae. And if Usaeil ever discovered that there was an heir to her throne, Rhi knew the queen would kill Phelan. She had no proof, just a feeling that had been there from the very beginning.

Rhi had long kept Phelan's identity a secret. She wasn't going to waste everything she'd done to lose him now. Or ever, for that matter. Which meant that she couldn't turn to him.

There was Ulrik. As soon as she thought about him, she shoved the notion aside. Ulrik was too caught up in his quest for vengeance to do anything but use her for his own means. Although, he had been different the last time she'd spoken with him.

But talking with Ulrik was like navigating a maze of death. She had to consider everything she said, and study each word that came out of his mouth.

She briefly thought of Rhys. The Dragon King was a true friend, but anything she told Rhys would get back to *him*. Everything she did on Dreagan always got back to *him*.

Why then did she continue to return there? Apparently, she liked torturing herself. She should've cut whatever cord was keeping her connected to Dreagan long ago, but she couldn't then.

And she couldn't now.

Which put her exactly in her present predicament.

"What a fine mess I'm in this time," she murmured to herself.

She should be down on the streets of Paris, shopping and having fun. It was difficult to be so carefree after being banished. Though she'd tried.

Her gaze drifted down to her nails. She'd gone to see Jesse in Austin. Her amazing nail tech had done a spectacular marbleized effect using a prismatic glitter shimmer called *Desperately Seeking Sequins* and a fabulous deep sea indigo color called *Russian Navy*.

As much as she loved her nails, it did nothing to lessen the anger that kept building.

"This isna what I expected."

She jerked at the sound of the Scottish brogue, but more so because it was Constantine's voice. She gaped at the King of Dragon Kings. The wind ruffled his blond hair and caused the hem of his suit jacket to flap, but otherwise, he stood like a mountain—imposing and unmovable.

"What the hell? How did you find me? And how did you get up here?" she demanded.

He ignored her questions and said, "I knew if I called to you that you wouldna come. So I found you instead."

"I might've come," she retorted crossly.

At his raised brow, she rolled her eyes. How she loathed when he was right.

He came to stand beside her and looked down upon the city. "Doona do this alone."

"Alone?" She cocked an eyebrow as she looked askance at him. "You mean, the very way you made Ulrik do it?"

Con blew out a breath. "I expected you to bring him up."

"Because you know I'm right."

"Do you want me to say it would've been kinder if I had killed him?" Con asked, his head turned to her. "It would have. Immensely so. But I couldna do it."

She leaned her hip against the railing. "You might not have a choice now."

"I realize that."

There was a long stretch of silence while they looked over the city. Finally, Con said, "I've been told I'm handling too many things."

"Yep," she stated. "I told you that, as well."

"I took care of one earlier. Mikkel's spy has been removed from Dreagan."

She nodded, thinking it was a smart move. "That's good."

"Ulrik could challenge me at any moment."

Her gaze swung to him. "You've known that for some time."

"Aye. But that was before I said I'd help you with Usaeil."

Rhi laughed, though there was no mirth in it. "I don't need your help to face her."

"That's no' what I meant, and you know it. She dragged me into this."

"Oh, no," Rhi said with a shake of her head. "You became part of it the minute you jumped into her bed."

His lips compressed briefly, but his face remained impassive. "That's true. I'll add that I didna jump. But do you think she'll stop with me? If Ulrik defeats me, do you really believe Usaeil willna go after him or another King?"

"I really do hate when you're right." Because he was almost always right. Though she wouldn't tell him that.

Con didn't rub it in. He put a hand into his pants' pocket. "I planned to go after Mikkel. Then I thought about all the things you've done for the Kings and Dreagan. I put you off with Usaeil long enough."

"If you get tangled in a war with her—because we both know it's going to get very ugly—that leaves you vulnerable to Ulrik."

"I'm aware."

She shook her head and took a step back as she glared at him. "No. Don't put me in the middle. You know I care about the Kings, and that includes Ulrik. I don't want either of you to die."

"He willna stop, Rhi. You know this. And if I were in his place, I wouldna either."

She looked toward the sky before she turned her head away. Crossing her arms over her chest and said, "Ulrik isn't working with Mikkel. His uncle has made it so that Ulrik will have to kill him."

"You're telling me this, why?"

"Because I know you've figured it out, but you're second-guessing yourself." She looked at him. "And because you might want to think about teaming up with Ulrik to take out a mutual enemy."

The lights on the Eiffel Tower reflected in Con's gaze as he moved closer to her. "If I offered, Ulrik would think it a trap. And we both know he'll never come to me for help. Mainly because he doesna need it. Ulrik is strong enough to kill Mikkel without breaking a sweat."

"I know. It was wishful thinking on my part."

Con shrugged one shoulder. "Besides, Ryder will find Mikkel. When he does, I'm going after him."

"And the Dark?"

She hated to ask, but she wanted him to know she comprehended exactly what troubles hounded Dreagan and the Dragon Kings.

A blond brow rose. "Are you worried I'll kill Balladyn?"

"Yes. And no. I would've fought for him. I would've even fought you for him. Balladyn is my oldest friend, but he's shown me what he truly wants."

"What Balladyn has done isn't against you," Con said.

She forced a smile. "As Ulrik pointed out to me, it would've happened sooner or later. Knowing that's the truth doesn't make it hurt any less. If I hadn't asked you to save him—"

"I'd be fighting another Dark King," Con interrupted her.

"How do you choose who to fight when all of them can hurt you equally?"

He took his hand out of his pocket and turned the gold dragon head cufflink at his wrist. "The Dark hurt us through the mortals. We've vowed to protect the humans."

"But if you're gone, then there's no one to guard them," she replied.

He gave a nod of agreement. "Precisely. I've sat back, waiting for our enemies to strike, and that has put us in a precarious position. I've no choice but to attack now."

"Then attack them all," she said with a grin.

His wide lips softened into the barest smile. "All?"

"You said Ryder will find Mikkel soon. Send a few Kings to dispatch him. You and I will go to Usaeil."

"And Ulrik?"

She shrugged, making a face. "You'll be ready for him."

"That's all well and good, but you're assuming we win. And you've left out the Dark."

"We will win. When has a Dragon King lost?"

A full smile filled his face then. It was such a rare event that she almost conjured a camera to take a picture of it. "As for Balladyn, I'll take care of him."

And just like that, Con's smile vanished. "You'd face Balladyn alone?"

"He'll know anyone else is a trap."

"He's likely to think the same of you," Con cautioned.

Rhi drummed her nails on the railing. "Balladyn won't be cocky like Taraeth. He'll guard himself and the Dark with vigilance. No Dragon King will get close to him or drag him from the palace."

"You believe you can still get in?"

"Only way to find out is to try."

Con returned his gaze to the city for several quiet minutes before he spoke. "That isna attacking everyone at once."

"True. I could leave you to deal with Usaeil, and I could focus on Balladyn."

"No' after what Usaeil has done to you," Con said. "Although, there might be another way."

Rhi frowned at him. "What do you mean?"

"We have a Fae who's a mate. How much magic do you think it'd take to change Shara's appearance to look like you?"

"A Fae can change their hair and eye color, but not their face. Then again, there's never been a reason for a Fae to do that."

Con looked at her expectantly. "So there's a chance?"

"A slim one. But you forget that Kiril won't let Shara go in alone."

"She willna go anywhere. You're going to call Balladyn to her."

Rhi wasn't sure she liked that idea, but how was it any different than attacking Balladyn herself. "I'll be setting him up to face multiple Dragon Kings."

"As he and the Dark have done to the humans."

"I know, it's just . . . if I was the one fighting him, it'd just be me."

Con gave a loud snort. "If you really believe that, then you doona know what kind of friends you have."

"I have to face Balladyn. Just as I have to with Usaeil."

The King of Dragon Kings bowed his head. "Usaeil is going to expect you to come for her."

Rhi smiled. "And I plan to use that to my advantage."

CHAPTER THIRTY-ONE

Dublin, Ireland

The excitement and thrill of being with Ulrik easily shoved aside Eilish's unease about locating her family. The very people who intended to do her harm.

It made her wonder what those assholes had done to her mother.

"Easy," Ulrik said in response to her anger that welled up.

She looked away from his gold eyes to find them in an alley as a light mist fell. Dublin. She'd only visited a few times in her years living in Ireland, but this was a part she hadn't seen before.

"It isna too late to turn back."

Her head swiveled to Ulrik, who didn't seem to care that he was getting wet. "It was too late the moment my mother had to give me up."

One side of his lips lifted in a heart-stopping grin. "Good."

"Is this where my family is?" she asked, looking around at the buildings they were currently between.

He faced the street and pulled back his long, black hair

to fasten a strip of leather around the locks at the base of his neck. "They're no' far. It was the only place I knew of for us to arrive undetected."

"Since when do you care what mortals think?" she teased.

There wasn't a responding smile. "The Duffys have proven they'll go to any extremes to have you. Now that they're working with Mikkel, he'll be here, as well."

"Then I can take back my finger rings."

"Aye. Would you like the hand that's holding them also?"

Eilish smiled at him as she moved aside her damp hair. The fact that Ulrik would offer such a thing made her love him even more. Because if she said yes, she knew he'd deliver a hand to her—and it wouldn't matter whose it was.

"I'll take that as a yes," Ulrik said. Then he gave her a nod. "Ready?"

She looked out toward the street and the people and vehicles that went about their business. Jacket hoods covered bowed heads as they hurried through the misting rain. Was she ready to confront those responsible for separating her mother and father? Was she prepared to encounter those who caused her to be taken from her mother? Was she prepared to come face-to-face again with those of her blood who wanted to do her harm?

Ulrik's hand met her palm, his fingers sliding around hers. "I know what it's like to have those bound to you by blood. I'm fully prepared to do what I have to with regards to Mikkel, but you've no' been around such things."

"Patrick lied to me."

"He sheltered you, protected you. It was his promise to your mother."

Her gaze glanced at the gray sky. It was as if the sky was crying because she couldn't.

Ulrik turned her to face him, forcing her to meet his eyes. "If you go after them, you'll have to kill them. You willna have a choice, because they're going to come after you."

"Why exactly? I knew those women, my aunts you say, wanted to hurt me, but you're leaving something out. Something Patrick told you."

"Aye," Ulrik said. "I was hoping you'd heed my words and forget the past. I should've known Mikkel would get involved. It must've been how he found the information on Eireen."

She tightened her grip on his hand. "Tell me. All of it."

"What your biological father, Donal, told you is true. Your aunts didna have any magic. But your grandparents did."

Eilish jumped at the unexpected boom of thunder. "How is that possible?" she asked as Ulrik led her beneath an overhang to get out of the weather. "And I don't mind the rain."

"You're mortal," he replied matter-of-factly, as if that explained everything. "The Duffys are descendants of Druids. They were no' particularly powerful, but they held their own. Unfortunately, like most Druids, they discovered that each time they married someone without magic, it diluted their bloodline. Each child was born with less and less power."

She thought of the strength of the magic running in her veins. She wasn't weak at all.

He grinned as if reading her thoughts. "There were those in your family who searched for a way to keep the magic. They used what little they had and took it from other Druids, but that soon came to an end."

"The Druids fought back," she guessed.

"Aye. Your ancestors didna give up, however. They discovered that every generation, one of their own was born with power. They realized that one of them could have it, or they could share it."

She frowned, not liking his choice of words. "I have a sneaking suspicion that the option of *sharing* wasn't a choice given to the one with magic."

"They were given a choice. Freely share it, or it would be forcefully taken."

Her stomach clenched painfully. "My mother was the one with magic. They forced her, didn't they?"

"From what Patrick told me, Eireen was successful in keeping her magic hidden for most of her life. She slipped up when she met Donal."

"Because she fell in love and thought she was safe."

Ulrik nodded ruefully. "When your aunts came for her, your mother knew if she fought back, Donal would be dragged into it and killed by her parents. She didna want that."

"Donal might have been able to save her."

"At what cost to others? How many would've lost their lives?" Ulrik asked.

Eilish glanced away. She couldn't answer because she knew he was right, but she couldn't help but wish her mother might have fought so they could have been a family.

She drew in a shuddering breath and returned her gaze to him. "What happened?"

"Patrick got a message from Eireen. While she waited for the ceremony where she would share her magic with her family, she discovered she was pregnant with you."

Eilish turned and put her back against the building as she watched the rain drop from the overhang. "This *shar-*

ing you keep talking about, my family doesn't leave any magic for the one they take it from, do they?"

When Ulrik didn't answer, she turned her head to him. His gold eyes were hooded, a sadness there that made her breath catch.

"The one who has the magic is sacrificed in the ceremony," he finally replied.

Now, more than ever, she wanted to find her so-called family. "What kinds of monsters would do that?"

"The kind who want power above all else."

"That they can so easily kill one of their own?"

He touched her face, pulling her closer. "The allure of magic for those who doona have it is strong."

"So my mother is dead," she said, putting her forehead against his chest.

Ulrik lowered his chin atop her head. "You encountered your aunts. Did they have magic?"

"No." She looked up at Ulrik. "So, there's a chance my mother is alive?"

"Doona get your hopes up. Patrick remained with her, helping Eireen deliver you. After holding you for a wee bit and naming you, she handed you over to him and demanded that the two of you leave Ireland immediately. Patrick wanted to find Donal for her, but she refused because she knew her family would be watching him. Their argument was cut short when the Duffys found her."

Eilish frowned as she asked, "You said my aunts didn't have magic, but my grandparents did. So that means. . . ."

"Your grandfather stole it from one of his kin and shared it with his wife."

"Dear God. And I'm related to these people," she said, sick to her stomach.

He took her face between his hands. "But you're no' them."

Eilish rose up on her toes and kissed him. "Let's find these horrible people and make sure they can't harm anyone else ever again. Then, I want to find my mom."

"Doona let your guard down with them. They'll say and do anything."

"They went after my mother. They came after me." She raised a brow. "I dare them to do something so stupid."

Ulrik grinned. "We're going in separately. I will look for Mikkel and make sure my uncle doesna interfere."

Eilish started to balk at the plan, but she knew it was the smart thing to do. "He's strong."

"No' as strong as I am. Besides," Ulrik said, "I want him to attack me."

She listened as Ulrik told her the address for the house, but her mind was on something else. "If something happens to me, will you tell Donal everything? If my mother is still alive, I'd like them to be reunited."

"Nothing is going to happen to you. But I give you my vow to do as you've asked."

Eilish turned to walk away when he pulled her back. With one arm around her as his other hand cupped her cheek, he gazed at her a silent moment before slowly lowering his head to kiss her.

She sank into him, savoring the amazing, powerful taste of him. Unhurried and deliberate, the kiss inflamed her desires and made her ache for everything she could never have with him.

This tender, affectionate side of Ulrik was surprising. And incredible. Why couldn't she have met him before Mikkel? Why couldn't they have had more time together?

She ended the kiss, the emotions too much for her to handle without breaking down. When she tried to look away, he stopped her, a frown marring his brow.

"What is it?" he murmured.

"Thank you for helping me. I know you're after Mikkel, but it's nice not to have to do this alone."

His gaze narrowed a fraction. "Mikkel is a benefit. I'm here for you."

Her heart leapt at his confession. Whether it was the truth or not, his words made her incredibly happy. "If you find your uncle, don't hesitate to kill him."

"You willna be there alone. You may no' see me, but I will be there."

She gave a nod and stepped back. With one last smile directed at Ulrik, she walked into the rain and began the trek along the streets of Dublin.

With her thoughts fixed on the Duffys and what was awaiting her, she didn't see the cobblestone roads or the buildings and houses. The drizzle turned into a steady rain, but she didn't feel it soaking her hair or jeans. She didn't notice the drops falling from her collar down her shirt and traveling along her skin. Her fury at what her grandparents and aunts had planned to do to her mum kept her from feeling the cool air.

Block after block faded beneath her feet. She didn't slow until she found herself in the neighborhood. Before she knew it, she was standing in front of the house.

Its charming façade of the all white, two-story house with the bright red door hid the evil within. She tried to image her mother growing up in such a place, but all she saw was anger and violence.

All because of magic.

She clicked her left fingers together, realizing too late that her finger rings were still gone. She was going to get them back. They were her only link to her mother. She wondered where Ulrik was. He was out there. She knew it. Was he watching her now?

Eilish walked to the short, wooden gate and placed her hands on it. She felt old magic, spells to keep others out.

And no doubt ones that would alert the Duffys that a visitor approached.

Just as she expected, the front door opened, and an elderly woman bent with age stood, leaning on a cane. Her white hair was cut short and flattened on one side from where she'd been sleeping.

As decrepit as the woman appeared, her eyes told another story. There was still strength in the green depths as they locked on Eilish. She placed one gnarled hand atop the other and laughed, the sound like nails raking down a chalkboard.

Eilish hated her immediately. Without having to be told, she knew this woman was her grandmother. Whatever motherly instinct most females had for their children, it had bypassed this woman completely.

"I knew you'd come," she said.

Eilish shot her a hard look. "Lady, I'm here to find the bitches who tried to hurt me. Then I'm coming for you for wanting to kill my mother."

"Is that right?"

To show she meant business, Eilish sent a blast of magic toward the house. There was a second of silence before a boom sounded, and the windows shattered.

CHAPTER THIRTY-TWO

There should be backup. As strong as Ulrik knew himself to be, and as powerful as he knew Eilish was, it was the unknown of the Duffys that caused him concern.

The more he thought about the Druid magic Mikkel had, the more disturbed he became. He'd believed Eireen was alive, which was why he hadn't searched for her soul. Yet the more he thought of Mikkel, the more he began to doubt it.

If Mikkel took the magic the Duffys had gotten from Eireen, no doubt it was in exchange for him bringing them Eilish.

Ulrik was about to stop Eilish so they could reevaluate things when she blew out the windows of the house. There was no going back now. For better or worse, things would get resolved one way or another.

He remained hidden, watching the back of the dwelling through the rain. It wasn't long before he spotted movement in an upstairs window. A woman with short, dark hair looked outside, her gaze scanning the area. Then a suit-clad arm yanked the curtain closed.

"Hello, Uncle," Ulrik said.

He glanced at Eilish to find her shoving through the gate and stalking toward the house. Ulrik moved from his hiding spot and made his way to the fence. It took little effort to break through the old spells around the yard. Then he put a hand on the short fence and jumped over it.

A look at the windows showed that all the curtains were drawn. No one stopped him as he walked to the back door. He moved his hand to the doorknob and felt the wards there. They were new, but more importantly, it was dragon magic.

Ulrik took a few steps back before he launched himself into the air, landing softly on the roof. He moved to the edge and used his powers to bust open the back door.

Almost immediately a blast of magic barreled through the door where they had expected Ulrik to be. He waited until he saw a head appear. With a twist of his hand and magic, he broke the woman's neck.

His enhanced hearing picked up shouts from within the house. He heard Mikkel start to say something, but a rumble of thunder drowned it out.

Ulrik waited until he heard nothing more coming from upstairs, then he used magic to unlock and raise a window. He flipped through the air, grabbing hold of the windowsill with one hand before he pulled himself into the room.

Standing in the small bedroom, he smelled old age and approaching death. A little, yellow bird flung itself around its tiny cage, screeching to be free. Ulrik walked to it and unlatched its cage door. As soon as the gate swung open, the bird flew straight out the window and into the rain.

Ulrik's head jerked to the hallway when he heard a loud crash below. He strode to the doorway and listened for any sign of Mikkel. No doubt his uncle was staying just out of the way. Keeping close to the mortals but not close enough to be hurt if Eilish got the upper hand. This was one of the many reasons why Mikkel could never be a Dragon King.

"Where's my mother?" Eilish bellowed.

There was a loud bang followed by the sound of wood splintering. Ulrik checked every room upstairs before made his way down the stairs. When he reached the bottom, he found Mikkel, along with the grandmother and the younger aunt surrounding Eilish. She was holding them off for the moment, but she wouldn't last much longer. Their gazes met briefly, but she hastily looked away before anyone knew that he was there.

There was no sign of the grandfather, which meant he was the cause of the stench of death that filled the house. With everyone Ulrik needed to worry about before him, his mind quickly went to work on a plan.

Mikkel's eyes were alight with victory, his face a mask of cruelty and hatred as he held up his hands and battled his magic against Eilish's.

Ulrik was about to step in, but Eilish gave him a small shake of her head.

"Where is my mother?" Eilish demanded again.

The aunt laughed. "I can't believe you're still looking for her. Don't you know when you're defeated?"

"I can't believe I'm related to any of you," Eilish said. "The horrors you've inflicted on past generations won't be repeated in the future. My magic is mine. I'll never give it up."

"Your mother said the same thing," the grandmother stated.

Ulrik saw Eilish weakening under the onslaught of Mikkel's power. No longer could he stand there and put her in danger. He sent a blast at his uncle, knocking

Mikkel to his knees and disrupting the assault directed at Eilish.

Mikkel spun around, causing Ulrik to dive from the doorway and roll to his feet. He held up his hands, deflecting the magic Mikkel sent his way toward the two Duffy women. The youngest jumped out of the way, but the grandmother was too old to move.

Ulrik didn't waste another thought on the bitch as she crumpled dead to the floor. He glanced at Eilish, expecting her to use her magic. Instead, he found her on her knees, her face contorted in pain as her aunt stood beside her with some artifact that looked hundreds of years old.

"What's it going to be, Ulrik?" Mikkel asked with a laugh as he got to his feet, dusting off his suit. "You going to kill me or save the Druid?"

Ulrik watched his uncle stagger a bit before finding his balance. Instead of answering, Ulrik shot a short burst of magic at the aunt to knock her and the object away while he rushed Mikkel.

His uncle's eyes widened as he put up a weak defense that Ulrik quickly broke through. Mikkel then drew out Eilish's finger rings and used them to disappear. Furious at losing Mikkel once more, Ulrik spun around to see Eilish standing over her aunt.

"Where is my mother?" Eilish asked.

The woman rose up on an elbow and glared at Eilish. "How dare you and your mother think you don't have to do your duty?"

"Duty?" Ulrik repeated. "If it was your magic others were after, would you willingly give it up?"

"Aye," she spat.

Ulrik used magic to lift her and slam her back against a wall, keeping her dangling above the floor. "Is that so? Let's put it to the test, shall we. You can either tell me the pact you made with Mikkel, or I'll force it out of you."

"I'll tell you nothing," the woman stated angrily.

Eilish stepped forward. "Let me," she told him.

Ulrik gave a nod, stepping aside so that Eilish could do as she wished. He would keep a close eye on her, though because he could sense that the darkness always on the fringes of her magic was growing bolder, stronger.

Eilish stood before her aunt with her legs braced apart and her back straight. "Did you enjoy hurting my mother?"

"It's the right of our family to take magic," the aunt stated.

Ulrik watched as Eilish merely pointed to the woman's pinky finger, which broke at such a hard angle that the bone protruded from the skin, the aunt's scream echoing through the house.

Eilish smiled. "Does that hurt? I hope it does."

"I can take it," the woman said, her face pale and sweat covering her face.

Ulrik watched a second and third finger break. He stood beside Eilish, patiently waiting for the aunt to stop shouting her pain.

It was several minutes later before she calmed enough that Eilish could talk. "No one has the right to take another's magic."

The aunt laughed through her tears. "It's so easy for you to say that since you were born with magic, power that is rightfully ours."

"You willna get anything more from her," Ulrik said to Eilish.

Green-gold eyes met his. "I know."

He saw the pain in Eilish's eyes at the knowledge that her mother was forever out of her reach. He couldn't imagine the agony Eilish was in.

"Whatever deal you struck with Mikkel willna come to fruition," Ulrik told the woman.

Snot ran from the aunt's nose as blood dripped from her fingers onto the floor. "As long as I'm alive, there's a chance."

"All I have to do is end your life," Eilish stated.

Ulrik grabbed her hands, stopping her. "Doona," he warned.

His soul was blackened by taking lives. Hers didn't have to be—and wouldn't be if he had anything to say about it.

"She deserves to die," Eilish said.

He nodded in agreement. "That she does, but I doona want you to be the one to do it."

"Why?" she asked in confusion.

"You willna come back from it." He glanced down at her arm to see that the red stripes were turning black. "Let me do it."

She blinked up at him. "This isn't your burden."

"But I'm offering to take it."

"Why?"

He wasn't sure he could answer that. Mainly because he couldn't exactly name why he wanted to keep the darkness from growing within her. And also because he didn't want to confront his feelings for her.

"Does it matter?" he asked.

The aunt laughed. "Aww. Isn't this cute. Is my niece falling for a Dragon King?"

Ulrik stalked to stand before her. "Mikkel left you to die. You stupidly gave him your magic. Why?"

"Because Eilish has twice the magic my sister did."

"Did you even hesitate in killing Eireen?" he asked.

The aunt sniggered. "Will it make you happy to hear that I did? But then I thought of the magic I'd have."

"You bitch," Eilish said as she came closer.

Ulrik held out his hand to stop her. Then he returned

his attention to the aunt. "You deprived Eilish of her mother. You went after Eilish with the intent to kill her as you did your own sister."

"That's right," the woman replied. "Magic should be shared with the family. No one person should hoard it and have the ultimate power."

Eilish gave a loud snort. "You're batshit crazy."

"And you've no right to keep all of that magic!" her aunt screamed.

Ulrik had heard enough. With just a thought, he broke her neck, ending the tirade. When he faced Eilish, she was pale, and her lips were pinched in anger.

"It's over," he said.

Eilish slid her eyes to him. "No. It's just beginning."

"Your family will never hunt you again."

She swallowed and released a breath. "I thought my mother might still be alive."

"I'm sorry."

"Those responsible for her cruel death have been punished. Justice has been delivered for her, and every other Duffy who had their lives snatched away because they happened to be born with magic."

Ulrik wrapped an arm around her shoulder. "I saw that Mikkel had your finger rings. I'll return them to you."

She leaned away to gawk at him. A brow rose. "You sound like you plan to go after Mikkel without me."

"I do."

"No, you're not."

"Eilish," he began.

She held up a finger, challenging him with a look to continue that sentence. "Don't you dare. I'm in this just as you are. Have you forgotten I helped your uncle?"

"Of course no'."

"I'm going to fix my mistake."

He gave a shake of his head. "Doona do this. Return to Graves."

"And do what?" she asked in an outraged voice, cocking a hip and resting a hand on it. "Wait to hear from you? *If* you ever return."

"Aye."

If it were possible, her indignation grew. She dropped her arm and lifted her chin. "Let me be perfectly clear in this. Either you take me with you so I can rectify the wrongs I've done, or I'll go to Dreagan myself. I know the Dragon Kings are searching for me after what I did to Kinsey and Esther."

Ulrik looked away, raking a hand down his face. Eilish was infuriating. Worse, he knew without a doubt that she'd go to Con. And the Kings wouldn't be kind to her.

He turned his head to her. "You willna help your cause by being with me. There are those who think I'm as bad as my uncle."

"They can kiss my ass," she said. "What's your decision?"

As if he had any choice. And truth be told, he was happy to have her with him. It felt good to count on her, to trust her. Though he'd keep that to himself.

Ulrik held out his hand to her. "Let's go find Mikkel."

CHAPTER THIRTY-THREE

Empty. That's what Eilish felt after discovering that her mother was dead. She was so immersed in the sorrow that it took her a moment to realize she was now standing in a pub. She looked around, recognizing the décor of The Porterhouse. Her gaze jerked to Ulrik.

"You need Donal just as much as he needs you right now," Ulrik said.

Eilish wasn't sure she could tell Donal what she'd learned. "We don't have time for this."

"We make time," Ulrik insisted.

He turned her around. With his hand on her back, Ulrik guided her to the bar. Her gaze roamed the floor they were on, looking for some sign of Donal as Ulrik asked for him. There was an exchange of words between Ulrik and the bartender, but Eilish didn't pay attention. Her ears were ringing with her aunt's and grandmother's words. The lack of magic had turned them into the vilest of creatures. Would she have become that if she hadn't been born with any?

"What of their kids?"

Ulrik frowned at her. "What?"

"My aunts. Did they have any children? Did either of my grandparents have siblings?"

"It's over," Ulrik said.

She shook her head. "I have to know if anyone else will come for me."

He blew out a sharp breath. "My investigators discovered that Eireen's oldest sister had two children. One died from an illness before her second birthday. The other, a son, was killed by a drunk driver five years earlier, along with her husband."

"And the other aunt?" Eilish didn't even want to know their names.

"She never had any children. Whether she was barren or it was her husband, I doona know. The husband left her twenty years ago. She never remarried."

Eilish nodded, feeling a little better. "What of my grandparents."

"The magic came through your grandfather. Your grandmother, as well as anyone married to a Duffy, is able to take a wee bit of magic from the ceremony they perform."

"Enough to make her crazy for more."

"Aye. Your grandfather had two brothers. He killed the one with magic, and the other didna want anything to do with it. He changed his name and moved away. From the smell in the house, your grandfather died recently. I can no' tell if it was natural or no'."

She closed her eyes and sighed. So that part really was over.

"Eilish?" asked a male voice in a deep, Irish brogue.

She turned and smiled at Donal, truly happy to see him. "Hi."

Donal beamed at her as he reached for her hands. "I'm delighted to have you back so soon. And who is this?"

"You know exactly who I am," Ulrik stated.

Eilish looked between the two of them. "Do you?" she asked her father.

Donal shrugged, grinning as he did. "I make it my business to know the goings-on in the paranormal world." He then gave a nod to Ulrik. "You're welcome here, Ulrik, King of the Silvers."

She glanced at Ulrik to see him bow his head as she came to terms with just how *in the know* her father was. She couldn't wait to pick his brain. But that was for another day.

"You look weary," Donal said.

Eilish lowered her gaze. "Yes."

"She could use a drink," Ulrik interjected.

"By the looks of it, both of you could. Come," Donal said and pulled her after him through the diners toward the booth where she had sat with him during her earlier visit.

Eilish slid in first with Ulrik sitting beside her while Donal took the opposite side. Two bottles of whisky were brought to the table—one Irish, and one Dreagan.

Ulrik didn't hesitate to take the Dreagan whisky and pour it into his glass, downing it in one swallow. After Donal had filled her glass and his, Eilish quickly took a drink. The warmth that spread through her belly helped to dispel some of the chills that had overtaken her ever since she walked into the Duffy house.

"I'll be happy to sit here all day drinking in silence," Donal said as he looked between her and Ulrik. Then his gaze returned to her. "But I've learned it's better to get whatever it is you're holding off your chest."

She refilled her glass. "I don't know where to begin."

"The easiest part to tell," Donal urged.

Ulrik reached over and covered her hand with his. She looked his way. He was waiting for her to give him some sign that she wanted him to spill the news. It would be far easier that way, but Eilish knew the responsibility lay with her.

She squeezed Ulrik's fingers and gave him a quick smile to let him know she was fine. Then she turned back to Donal, who waited expectantly.

"You're my biological father," she said.

His bright blue eyes crinkled in the corners as he smiled. "Aye. I was hoping that would be the case. I've lost many years with you, but I hope I don't lose any more."

She couldn't quite return his elation. "I've made some mistakes."

"Everyone does, my girl," Donal replied. "It's what you do once you figure out they're mistakes that count."

"I'm trying to fix them."

He gave a nod, his gaze skating briefly to Ulrik. "That's good."

She opened her mouth to speak but reached for her glass with her free hand instead. After tossing back the whisky, she lowered the tumbler to the table.

It was Ulrik who said, "My uncle approached Eilish, offering to tell her about Eireen in exchange for her helping him."

"Ah," Donal said, his gaze moving to Eilish. "That's when you used your magic on the minds of those two Dragon King mates."

Eilish hated that Donal knew about that, but she wasn't going to run from her blunders. There was nothing for her to do but own up to it. "Yes."

Ulrik stiffened slightly. "How do you know that?"

"As I told Eilish, I make it my business to know these things." His eyes slid back to Eilish. "I also heard you helped Nikolai and Esther."

Eilish felt her lips soften into a smile. "I did. With Ulrik's urging."

Once more, Donal's blue eyes locked on Ulrik. "Why did you want her to help your enemy?"

"I found Nikolai when he was just a hatchling and raised him as my own, though he's more brother than son," Ulrik replied.

Donal lifted his white brows. "And your quest to destroy the Kings?"

"Is there anything you doona know?" Ulrik demanded.

Donal merely smiled and waited.

Ulrik let out a sigh. "I'm after Con."

"Hmm," Donal said and sat back, his arms still on the table.

Eilish cleared her throat. "Mikkel ordered me to kill for him in Venice. I couldn't, so I wiped the woman's memories of him instead. That's when I knew I'd made a terrible mistake, but I still didn't do anything. Not until he gave me a deadline to kill Ulrik."

"I see," Donal murmured. "Does Mikkel know there's something between you two?"

Ulrik said, "No doubt, he does. I think he figured it out when he attacked her."

Donal's gaze jerked to Eilish. "Attacked?"

"I'm fine," she told him.

Ulrik grunted. "She wasna. The bastard broke both of her legs and took her for Eireen's sisters."

Donal remained quiet, his face ashen. "Her sisters?" he asked softly.

"Mikkel made a deal with the Duffys," Eilish told him. "I don't know if it was before or after I decided not to kill Ulrik, but they gave him their magic to battle me, and in return, he promised to hand me over to them."

"I see." Donal ran a hand over his mouth and down his jaw. "Did you find Eireen? Did you locate your mum?"

Eilish looked away as tears gathered. And once more,

Ulrik stepped in, relaying the story Patrick told him, as well as everything that had happened at the Duffy house. When Ulrik finished, Donal poured himself another drink and tossed it back. His eyes were red-rimmed when he looked at her, and he brushed a tear from his cheek.

"I always knew if she were alive, she'd have found a way to me. I know she didn't tell me what her family planned to keep me from getting hurt, but I would've gladly traded my life for hers." Donal sniffed and blinked rapidly. "I'm glad those responsible for harming my Eireen are all dead, though I wish I would've gotten to exact some vengeance of my own."

Seeing how shattered her father was, Eilish lost her battle to keep from crying. First one tear escaped, and then a second. That's all it took for her will to crumble.

Ulrik wanted to kill the Duffys all over again when he looked over and saw Eilish silently crying beside him. There was no messy show of emotion, no loud wailing. The sound of two hearts breaking for a woman they loved and would never see again was done quietly.

He wrapped an arm around Eilish and pulled her against him. Ulrik didn't realize what he'd done until she rested her head on his shoulder.

But Donal's keen eyes saw it all.

Ulrik liked the mortal instantly. Though his white hair and beard made many mistake him for an old man, Ulrik saw much more. Donal was still fit, his mind sharp, and he would be around for many years to come. Which is exactly what Eilish needed.

"I need a moment," Eilish whispered.

Ulrik stood to let her out. He watched her walk to the restroom before he sat down and looked at Donal. The two stared at each other. There were few humans who Ulrik respected, but Donal was one of them.

Not just because he was Eilish's father but also because Donal had his hand in everything. He'd make a great ally.

"I will find my uncle," Ulrik said.

Donal clasped his hands together on the table. "I'm going to hold you to that."

"I was planning on it anyway. Then Mikkel made the mistake of going after Eilish."

"I realize I'm new to this father gig, but I believe I have every right to ask what you're doing with her."

Ulrik looked into the mortal's blue eyes. "You do have that right, and I'd do the same in your shoes. I wanted her to return to Graves, but she intends to go after Mikkel, as well. My uncle took her finger rings."

"I gave those to Eireen, and she made sure they ended up with Eilish."

"It's just one of a long list of mistakes Mikkel has made."

"I owe Patrick much for taking care of both Eireen and Eilish," Donal said as he turned the whisky glass around on the table. "I'd like to meet him. And I'm sure he would like to see Eilish again."

Ulrik nodded. "Eilish may have lost her mother, but she has two fathers. She's lucky."

"Aye," Donal said with a smile. It soon faded as he drew in a deep breath. "Why did you want Eilish to return to Graves?"

"To keep her safe. The Duffys willna bother her ever again."

"And you thought that was all she was fighting for?" the human asked with a raised white brow.

Ulrik hesitated before he gave a nod. "Aye. But she said if I doona take her with me, she'll go to Dreagan."

There was a hint of a smile on Donal's face when he said, "So she left you between a rock and a hard place."

"If she goes to Dreagan, the Kings will want their revenge for what she did to the mates."

"Perhaps."

"It's a chance I willna take," Ulrik declared.

Donal's head cocked to the side as shrewd eyes pinned him. "Why is that?"

His mind went blank. He couldn't form a thought, much less words. And the longer the silence stretched between them, the steelier Donal's gaze became.

"What's going on?" Eilish asked as she walked up.

Ulrik got to his feet, thankful for the reprieve. Though he knew it was a brief one.

Donal gave her a smile. "Are you hungry? Let me feed you."

"I could eat," she said, turning her gaze to Ulrik.

Ulrik briefly nodded. "Then we shall stay."

He slowly sank onto the bench as Donal broke into a story about his first date with Eireen. Ulrik couldn't take his gaze from Eilish, who stared, enraptured by the story.

But all he could think about was Donal's question—and his inability to answer it.

CHAPTER THIRTY-FOUR

Somewhere along the Great Wall of China

Beauty could be deadly. It was something Mikkel was counting on Ulrik discovering. Mikkel ran his fingers along the intricate design on the finger rings.

He'd always assumed the power he felt from Eilish was all hers. How excited he'd been when he took the jewelry from her after breaking her legs and discovered they held their own dose of magic.

Magic strong enough that it allowed him to teleport anywhere he wanted.

He lifted his head and looked out over the mountains. This deserted, derelict part of the Great Wall offered him privacy. No one would ever think to look for him here. But he'd needed the distance to figure out his next move.

Of course, he'd known Ulrik and Eilish would come for the Duffys. But he'd expected to easily defeat the Druid and use her to make Ulrik stand down.

Unfortunately, that's not how things worked out. To his shock, Eilish had gotten stronger. He'd caught a glimpse of what happened when she disappeared from the manor after the scream that busted his eardrums.

Just as he'd felt the first time he met Eilish, he experienced a wave of power. It was how he'd known she would be able to weaken Ulrik enough for Mikkel to kill him. Same with Con. He needed Eilish's magic.

But he'd sensed a change in her that began in Venice. After Ulrik had gone to Graves and he and Eilish had their little chat. So, Mikkel had begun to keep a closer eye on Eilish.

The fury he'd felt when she didn't kill Ulrik and he hadn't become a Dragon King exceeded anything he'd ever felt before. Thankfully, he had a backup plan—the Duffys. It was only by investigating Eilish that he'd learned of her search for her mother. That's what led him to the Duffys. The natural thing for him to do was to ally with them.

If only they'd died once they gave their magic to him, but since they were merely vessels and not the original owners, they were able to live through the ceremony. They were so magic-hungry that they'd consented to his plan without having to be talked into it. And after the two aunts had witnessed Eilish's power firsthand at the manor, they'd been giddy to lure her to the house and take what they felt was theirs.

Mikkel couldn't stand them. Magic hadn't chosen them so, in his mind, they had no right to it. The fact that they took it from others sickened him. Each of the Duffys got what they deserved when he left them behind with Ulrik and Eilish.

He looked down at his palm where the finger rings rested. His dragon magic easily surpassed a Druid's and matched most Fae. But now that he had the Duffys'—or rather what was left of Eireen's—power mixed with his, he was easily three-times as strong.

The Druid magic mixed with his, and they fed off

each other, making him more powerful. To the point that he was confident he could challenge Ulrik and win.

Underestimating Ulrik had nearly cost Mikkel everything. Taraeth's death, and Balladyn's ascension to the throne of the Dark had been another hit he hadn't seen coming. But Mikkel was nothing if not persistent.

All was not lost.

Mikkel smiled. Ulrik had made another fatal mistake because, apparently, he hadn't learned anything from Nala's betrayal.

Mikkel closed his fingers around the rings. Eilish would want these back. Since Ulrik cared for the Druid, he wouldn't allow her to search alone. No, Ulrik would be right beside her when they came looking for him.

Yet Mikkel knew how to strike to inflict the most damage. A simple call to one of his many assassins would take Donal Cleary's life. Learning her mother was dead and losing her father so soon would destroy Eilish.

And with her off-kilter, Ulrik would be reckless. That would lead to him making a mistake, one that Mikkel was counting on to put Ulrik at a disadvantage. That's when Mikkel would kill him.

But . . . there could be another use for Donal, as well.

It was all within reach. For too long, Mikkel had waited, biding his time for when he could become King. The fate of the dragons rested on his shoulders, and he was going to ensure they survived.

For too long, he'd watched helplessly as the humans devastated each other. But that was never enough. They made weapons that could destroy everyone and everything. And all the while, they ripped the Earth to shreds, polluting the air, soil, and water.

They cared nothing for the planet. So it was time they left.

The first step was becoming a Dragon King.

The second, removing Constantine.

The third, returning the dragons.

Then hell would be unleashed upon the humans.

If the Fae wanted to join in, he'd allow them. After all, they would be helping him rid the realm of pests that had overrun everything.

It was going to feel amazing to annihilate the mortals. Mikkel couldn't wait to hear the screams of agony and terror. It would be music to his ears. And while the humans begged for mercy, he and the other dragons would roar their victory and wipe the putrid cities clean with dragon fire.

Somewhere in Canada . . .

"That's a wrap!"

Usaeil smiled as the cheers from the cast and crew of the movie filled the air. She could destroy a section of filming again to keep the production going, but she had other pursuits to keep her occupied.

With a wink to Jason Statham, Usaeil made her way to her trailer before teleporting to Con's bedroom.

Except she was thrown right back to Canada.

She clenched her fists and tried once more, choosing Con's office. And again, she was returned to the trailer.

Usaeil threw back her head and screamed. This couldn't be happening.

If Con wanted to play that game, then she was more than willing. He might be able to keep her out of his bedroom and the office, but he couldn't keep her out of the little village he so loved.

She snapped her fingers, replacing her movie attire with that of a short denim skirt and a purple shirt that fit like a second skin. Over-the-knee black boots completed the ensemble. Shaking out her hair, she fluffed the midnight tresses so they framed her face in wavy disarray. Then she teleported to the village.

A smile formed as she walked the streets while the silly humans—both male and female—stopped to ogle her, their blatant desire obvious in the way they hungrily stared. She winked and waved at several on her way to The Fox and the Hound, owned by none other than the Dragon King, Laith. The question was, would the King of Blacks be working?

No wards kept her from entering the pub. Not that she was surprised. The Kings were too confident that no Fae would ever have a need to venture so close to Dreagan.

But they hadn't counted on her.

She made her way to the bar and sat on a stool. Linking her hands together, she placed her arms on the shellacked wood. Her gaze landed on a woman with wavy, blond hair just past her shoulders. The fact the human wasn't smiling and flirting with her meant that she was looking at a Dragon King's mate.

"Hello," Usaeil said.

The music still blared from the speakers, but the conversation around the pub had gone silent. Not that she cared. She knew everyone's attention was on her. And that was how she liked it.

The mate tossed down the towel she'd been holding and put her hands on her hips. "You aren't welcome here."

The hint of a Scottish accent made Usaeil smile. "Which one are you."

"None of your fucking business," Laith said as he came from the back of the pub, his gunmetal gaze trained on her, and his long, dark blond hair loose about his shoulders. "Get out, Usaeil."

She looked around at the mortals who were gawking at her. "I'm having too much fun to leave."

"I can make you," Laith threatened.

Her gaze skated to him as her smile dropped. "You really want to make an enemy of the Queen of Light? You might want to rethink that. While you do, send for Con."

"Out!" Laith bellowed to the occupants.

Without question or complaint, the patrons set down their drinks and food before departing.

Usaeil blew out a breath as she rolled her eyes. "That was rude. I expected more from you, but we'll deal with that later."

"We willna deal with a fucking thing," Laith said, his eyes sparking with anger.

She crossed one leg over the other, hooking her fingers together and holding onto her knee as she leaned back. "Con. Now."

"What's the matter?" Laith asked sarcastically. "Is he no' responding to your summons?"

Usaeil was fast losing patience. "We can do this the easy way. Or we can do it the hard way." She looked at the female as she said the last part.

A growl sounded from Laith as his woman put a hand on his chest to halt his advance.

The mate laughed. "I've heard an awful lot about you. Now, I totally get what everyone says."

"That I'm beautiful, powerful, and magnanimous?" Usaeil asked with a grin.

The woman laughed louder, her head shaking. "Nope."

"What do they say?" Usaeil demanded, her gaze narrowed on the mate.

There was movement toward the back of the pub, and then another form appeared. Usaeil grinned at Shara. "Ah. Finally, an ally."

The Fae slowly walked toward Laith and the female. "Usaeil, what are you doing here?"

"I'm your queen," she reminded Shara. "And let's not forget that I'm the one who helped you become Light and shed the confines of the Dark you once were in order to be with Kiril."

There was a snort behind Usaeil. "I always knew you'd hold that over her."

Usaeil turned her head to find Kiril with his shamrock green eyes trained on her. "I don't know why all of you are in a huff. Con and I are friends. We've long *been* friends. Actually, we're more than that. Now, please get him here."

"No," Laith replied, his hands clenched at his sides.

It was Shara who said, "This wasn't a good idea, Usaeil. You should leave."

"Why?" she demanded. "I'm a queen. I'm *your* queen."

"You sure the fuck are no' mine," Kiril said.

Usaeil unclasped her hands and slid from the stool. "Each of you will rue the day you stood against me. Con and I are in love. We're going to be mated."

As she spoke, she looked at each of them, but their reactions didn't change. Though she expected some opposition, she was surprised by the lack of emotion.

That's when it hit her.

"He's already told you about us," she said.

Shara's silver eyes widened as she looked askance at her. "What did you expect when you posted copies of that tabloid picture all over the Light Palace?"

"He didn't want to tell anyone," Usaeil said. "But I'm not one to be kept hidden. We're two of the most powerful rulers on this realm. It's obvious we should be together."

Laith's lips twisted in a sneer. "What about what Con wants?"

"He needs a push, is all."

"He needs to burn his prick for ever sticking it in you," Kiril stated.

Her anger spiked. "And to think, I helped you. I came in peace, but you want a war. Well then, I'll give you one. And after Con and I are mated, I'm going to make sure he kills all of you."

Usaeil turned and looked directly at Shara. "And I'll deal with you separately."

CHAPTER THIRTY-FIVE

Eilish had been on her own for so long that it had become a habit to do everything herself. But she was discovering that there were definitely more pros than cons to having someone like Ulrik around.

He'd known she needed Donal before it even crossed her mind. The time they spent in England with her father had done her a world of good. And it had helped to heal her, just as she hoped it aided Donal.

She stared at Ulrik's profile as they once more stood within the Duffy house, she comprehended the steps he'd taken so they could be where they were—searching for a thread of Mikkel's magic to follow to his location.

"You're staring," he said without looking at her.

She crossed her arms over her chest. "We didn't have to leave here earlier. We could've been searching for Mikkel for the past several hours."

Finally, Ulrik looked up from the last spot Mikkel was seen and speared her with his golden gaze. My God, he was something to behold—both as a man and a dragon.

He literally made her heart race.

He was cynical, devious, and shrewd. Qualities that

weren't exactly bonuses. But added to his intelligence, his commanding presence, and his ingenuity and imposing personality, he was perfection in her eyes.

"You needed Donal," Ulrik said in a soft voice.

"But it put us behind."

He waved away her words and returned his attention to the spot on the floor. "Doona worry."

There was no way for her to turn it off. How could she not concern herself? Mikkel now had Druid power added to his magic. "Should we do this alone?"

"Do you want to ask Con to come along?" Ulrik asked, glancing at her.

She shot him a look that he missed because he'd looked away. "Don't be an ass."

"I can no' help it. It's who I am."

"No, it isn't. It's who you want everyone to *think* you are."

He sighed and raised his head to her once more. "I'm no' a good man. I've no' been for a verra, verra long time. I wholly accept who I am and what that means for others."

"What does it mean?" Her curiosity was piqued, but she also needed to know the answer.

"It means that as long as you're seen with me, there are those who will believe I've corrupted you. Humans—and even sometimes dragons—need to fit others into neat little categories. In all the advances your species has made, they still doona understand that things are never black or white. That will extend to you."

"I know."

"Nay," he said and took a step toward her. "You doona. The Druids might verra well ostracize you. You found your place in Ireland. No' just a location, but somewhere your magic soars, and you're connected to the earth, the people, and the magic. Doona discount the importance of that."

She swallowed, the sound loud to her ears. "I've never cared what others think."

"You'll change your mind when the business at Graves eventually dries up. Then what will you do? Return to Boston?"

"Why are you trying to push me away?"

He glanced at the floor. "Because it's the best thing for you."

"I've seen this scene play out numerous times in movies. This is where I tell you that I'm the one who should decide what's best for me."

A ghost of a smile curved his lips. "Ah, lass. If only things were as simple as that. This is the real world with magic, dragons, Druids, and monsters who doona have a script."

"It's still my life."

"Aye. I can no' tell you what to do."

There was something in his tone that told her he'd expected just such an argument. And he had an answer for everything. With the way Ulrik's mind worked, no doubt he was six steps ahead of whatever she might say or do.

He drew in a deep breath and released it. "If you go with me to face my uncle, you'll die."

"Hopefully not without delivering a few magical punches myself," she said saucily.

"I'll no' be able to attack Mikkel and protect you."

She raised a brow, cocking her head at him. "I'm not asking you to, nor do I need it."

"We'll get your finger rings, and then I want you to leave."

"I—" she began.

Ulrik spoke over her. "Mikkel will resort to anything to hurt you. If he doesna know of Donal, it willna be long before he does."

That put a whole new perspective on things. She'd

only learned of Donal recently, but knowing who her biological father was helped to soothe the loss of her mother. She couldn't lose Donal, too.

"You need to help protect Donal," Ulrik continued. "He's smart and surrounded by magic, but he doesna have any himself."

She nodded woodenly. How stupid of her to assume that Mikkel would run and hide, knowing that Ulrik would chase him. No, Mikkel was smarter than that. She'd just forgotten.

"I've continually underestimated your uncle," she said.

Ulrik squatted and touched the wooden floor of the living room. "It's no' something you'll ever do again."

She wasn't so sure of that. "Do you know my first battle with magic was after I arrived in Ireland?"

"You mentioned that before," he said as he lifted his gaze to her. "A Dark Fae."

"I got lucky. He could've easily taken me if he'd been prepared."

Ulrik straightened and walked to her. "Take the win however it comes. Whether because you're stronger than your adversary or it's luck. For whatever reason, you came out on top. Accept it. Own it."

"Yeah," she murmured. He was right. She needed to own it.

"Tell me, how many other battles have you been in?"

She wrinkled her nose. "I didn't keep count. There've been several. I had to let the Fae and Druids know that I would enforce the rules at Graves and in the village."

"You obviously won each time."

"I did," she said with a frown. "Why?"

He lifted a shoulder in a shrug. "I saw you earlier at the Duffys'. I know why Mikkel thought you could kill a Dragon King."

"No, he thought I could kill *you*."

Ulrik leaned close, a grin curving his lips. "Sweetheart, I'm one of the strongest."

Why the hell did that turn her on so much? She fought not to grab his face and pull him down for a kiss.

"If you continue to look at me like you want nothing more than for me to push you up against a wall and take you, I'm going to do just that."

It wasn't just the words. It wasn't just the heat in his eyes. It was those things combined with his sexy-as-hell brogue that sent chills racing over her.

"Eilish," he murmured in a husky whisper.

Her stomach fluttered in response. She put her hand on his chest and felt the heat of him through the shirt. His muscles flexed beneath her palm. She thought about his tattoo, touching it, imagining it was him. Somehow, she found the willpower to step back.

She let her hand fall from him. "We've work to do. We'll play later."

Gold eyes sizzled. "Aye. We will."

When he pivoted and returned to his spot, Eilish closed her eyes and blew out a breath. That man was sex on a stick. He was power and fury, grace and retribution, all rolled into one.

And he made her knees weak.

"I've got it," Ulrik said.

Her eyes snapped open. "You know where Mikkel went?"

"No' yet. We'll have to follow the trail."

"How do you know it's him?"

Ulrik turned his head and smiled. "Because I feel the magic of the finger rings. Your residual magic."

"We could be walking into a trap."

"Without a doubt."

Her brows shot up on her forehead. "You say that as if you aren't worried."

"Mikkel knows we're coming. He'll definitely set a trap, just as I know he'll send someone to kill your father."

"I should warn Donal."

Ulrik shrugged. "I've taken care of that."

She stared at him wide-eyed. "Unless you can manipulate time, you've not left me. Nor have you been on a cell phone."

He tapped his temple. "Dragons communicate telepathically. It allows us to talk over great distances."

"You contacted Dreagan?"

"I contacted someone I knew would help."

She shook her head in confusion. "Who?"

"Nikolai."

Eilish grinned when she heard the name. "When?"

"A few minutes ago."

"Will he do it?"

"Aye."

"You hesitated," she stated.

Ulrik gave a slight lift of his shoulders. "He's no' at Dreagan at the moment, but he said he'd take care of it."

She looked down at her fingers, wishing she had her rings so she could check in on Donal. "You trust him?"

For long moments, Ulrik held her gaze. "I believe he'll keep his word."

"So you trust him."

"I believe him," Ulrik repeated.

Eilish smiled sadly. She'd thought perhaps Ulrik was getting past his distrust of everyone, but she was wrong.

"Doona worry. Donal will be safe."

If Nikolai reached him before Mikkel.

She changed the subject. "When do we go after your uncle?"

"Now."

"What are we waiting for then?"

He glanced down at the wrist with the silver cuff.

"This is your last chance to change your mind about coming with me."

"I'm going," she stated.

"I can no' change your mind?"

She walked to him and rose up to press her lips against his in a brief kiss. Then she looked into his eyes. "I'm going."

"Be ready," he cautioned as he took her hand in his and touched the cuff.

She needed to find out where he'd gotten the bracelet.

That thought had barely finished going through her mind when she found herself standing on the Great Wall of China in the middle of the night. She turned in a full circle, taking it all in, wishing the sun was up so she could see more than the small patch of mountains the moon made visible.

As she waited for an attack, her gaze landed on Ulrik. She knew without a doubt that he'd defeat Mikkel, but there was a possibility that these were the last hours of her life. After everything Ulrik had endured, he needed to know that someone loved him. She'd intended to keep quiet about her feelings, but something urged her to tell him now.

"He's no' here," Ulrik said as he stalked a few steps away from her. "He stood here for a long time, though. The residue of your magic is strong."

"I love you."

His head whipped to her. His nostrils flared, and his brows snapped together. "Stop."

"I didn't mean to fall for you."

He stalked to her, causing her to retreat until her back hit the wall. "I said to stop."

She licked her lips. The anger blazed in his gaze as bright as a torch, but she saw the pain there, as well. "I love you."

"Stop!" he bellowed and struck a fist against the rock.

Bits of the wall fell at her feet, but she never looked away from him. His breathing was labored, his teeth clenched. But she didn't fear him.

"You can yell all you want. Order me to be quiet. But it won't change how I feel. I'm not asking anything from you. I just wanted you to know that I love you."

He looked away without another word. Then he took her hand. And just like that, China faded. They bounced around several other countries—at least she assumed they were different countries. The terrain changed, as did the time of day, but there were no markers for her to use to identify their locations.

Finally, they stopped in a dense forest. With her magic at the ready, she looked around, trying to determine where they were. The sun was still up, so they were no longer in or around China.

"He's here," Ulrik whispered.

CHAPTER THIRTY-SIX

I love you.

Ulrik didn't want to think about Eilish's words, but his mind was locked on to them. The more he told her to stop, the more defiant and assertive she'd become. Then he'd made the mistake of looking into her green-gold eyes. He searched for the lie, but it wasn't there.

With an inward shake of his head, he looked around at the dense woodland. They were back in Ireland. Why had Mikkel traveled so far, only to return to Ireland? Ulrik scanned the area. The huge oak and pine trees meant that Mikkel could be hidden behind any of them. But Ulrik wasn't going to search for his uncle.

"I was beginning to wonder if you'd come," Mikkel stated, his voice bouncing through the woods.

Ulrik glanced at Eilish as soon as he heard his uncle's fake British accent. "There was never any question about me hunting you down. Your time here is finished, uncle."

Mikkel's laugh filled the air. "It's just getting started, lad."

"Why are you hiding? Afraid of facing me?" Ulrik taunted as he attempted to pinpoint Mikkel's location.

"We'll get to that in a moment."

Ulrik frowned. Just what was his uncle up to? Mind games, no doubt. Ulrik turned his gaze to Eilish. Mikkel would use her. It was the obvious move.

"Have you seen the Silvers?" Mikkel asked.

Ulrik knew he was speaking of the four dragons locked away on Dreagan. He kept searching the trees, trying to locate where Mikkel was. "I've been sneaking in to see them for some time."

"It's degrading what Con has done to them."

"At least they're here and no' in another realm."

Mikkel grunted. "All I need are those four dragons to wash away the filth of the humans."

"They will never be yours to command."

"It's not like you've done a bang-up job."

Ulrik widened his stance. "The magic chose *me* to be a Dragon King."

"You speak as if you're above the rest of us." Mikkel came out from behind a tree about a hundred yards in front of Ulrik. "I know all about how the most powerful, the dragon with the most magic becomes King. But I've also heard that whatever it is that chooses the Kings looks deep into the heart of a dragon. How is it that they missed the hatred in my father's?"

Ulrik shrugged, his gaze locked on his uncle. "I heard about the abuse you claim."

"I *claim* nothing! It's the truth!" Mikkel shouted, spittle flying from his mouth in his outrage.

Ulrik was ready to shift and end this. "I doona care. I'm here to fight."

Mikkel suddenly laughed. "Still making the same mistakes of the past, aye, nephew."

Ulrik wasn't going to get into any sort of discussion involving Eilish. Mikkel would twist words to suit his cause.

"Nothing to say?" Mikkel asked cheekily before looking at Eilish. "I didn't expect you to bring backup."

She snorted loudly. "You're so damn full of yourself. Ulrik doesn't need anyone's help to fight you. I'm here for what you took from me."

Ulrik clenched his teeth in dread. If only Eilish had kept quiet, then he could've made sure Mikkel's attention stayed on him.

"These?" Mikkel asked as he held up his hand and wiggled his fingers. "So, they're important to you, huh?"

"They're mine," Eilish stated.

Mikkel nodded, his lips twisting. "I gather extremely important since they were your mother's."

Ulrik frowned, unease rippling through him. He knew Eilish hadn't shared that tidbit with Mikkel, and he wasn't sure how much the Duffys had known, but he doubted Eireen would've flashed the finger rings around. Which meant . . . Donal.

There was no time to warn Eilish as Mikkel motioned to someone. A moment later, Donal walked into view.

"Fuck," Ulrik murmured. Then, to Mikkel, he said, "Why are you bringing a mortal into our fight?"

Mikkel gave him an innocent look. "I'm here to set right what you cocked up. That means I'll use anything and any*one* I have at my disposal."

"No," Ulrik said to Eilish when she went to take a step forward.

Without taking her eyes off Donal, she whispered, "He's my father."

Ulrik studied Donal, but the human didn't seem himself. His gaze was unfocused as if he were being controlled. With Donal incapacitated, Ulrik wouldn't be able to get him to help.

"You want to save this old man?" Mikkel asked with

a laugh. "For *her*. You're so pathetic, Ulrik. Did you learn nothing from Nala?"

"I learned plenty."

"Then you shouldn't care who gets hurt. They're just mortals. They're beneath us."

Ulrik wasn't going to get into a debate with Mikkel. Something out of the corner of his eye caught Ulrik's attention. He looked over at Eilish to find the winding stripes on her arms were now a darker black, the edges sparking as if on fire beneath her skin.

"Fine," Mikkel said with a smile. "I'll let Donal go. But you'll need to kill the Druid."

Ulrik shook his head. "Can you no' think of anything more creative than that? I'd think with the time you spent among the mortals, you could at least come up with something new and original."

"I quite like this, actually," Mikkel said. "Because, either way, you lose."

"You assume I care what happens to the Druid."

Mikkel's smile was snide, his eyes glittering with merriment. "Don't you?"

"You used her. So did I."

Ulrik winced when Eilish looked over at him, her mouth gaping in outrage. He refused to meet her gaze. There was too much hanging on the next few seconds for him to divert his attention.

"Then why tell me to let Donal go?" Mikkel asked.

"Because I'm tired of waiting for our battle. You'll drag it out, talking and boasting. I'd rather get to the part where my fist connects with your jaw."

Mikkel's gaze moved to Donal as if contemplating Ulrik's words. Ulrik could practically feel the rage rolling off Eilish in waves, but she was directing it at his uncle.

"Are you so ready to die?" Mikkel asked him

Ulrik felt the dragon within him growl, eager to be freed. "Perhaps you should be asking yourself that."

"The one thing I respected about you was that you didn't get overconfident. I'd advise you not to do so now. Things change."

"I know all about you taking the Duffys' magic. If that's what you believe you need to defeat me, then get on with it." Ulrik took a few steps closer. "But consider things, Uncle. Even if you overpower me, you've done it by cheating. You'll never be a Dragon King."

Mikkel's face contorted in fury. "Doona presume you know anything!"

It always amused Ulrik how he could set Mikkel off. With the rise of his uncle's anger, the British accent vanished.

"Did I make you mad?" Ulrik asked. "Is it because you know I speak the truth?"

Spittle flew from Mikkel's mouth when he said, "There has to be a King of Silvers!"

"It willna be you." He walked closer. "It'll *never* be you."

"We'll see about that."

Ulrik knew the attack was coming before Mikkel even twitched. Ulrik directed his magic toward Donal as well as Eilish to push them out of the line of fire, but he took the full hit of Mikkel's blast.

The magic crackled through Ulrik's skin with almost as much pain as a Dark Fae's. The initial sting of it was nothing compared to the throbbing that grew the longer it was inside him.

Ulrik bared his teeth as he remained standing. Now that Eilish and her father were out of the way, he didn't have to worry about Mikkel turning his wrath on them.

All he could hope for was that Eilish would take the hint and make her way to Donal.

"You've shown your true colors," Mikkel stated.

Ulrik smiled. "I'll show you my true colors."

And with that, he shifted. Ulrik shook out his head and slammed his tail on the ground, causing it to shake. Since Mikkel's magic was still bound, he wouldn't be able to shift.

Which meant the battle wouldn't last long at all.

Ulrik inhaled, ready to release dragon fire at Mikkel. But the son of a bitch moved too close to where Donal lay unmoving, and Ulrik couldn't chance it.

"If you didn't care about the humans so much, you would've killed me," Mikkel said with a laugh.

Ulrik didn't care about them. But Donal was different. He was Eilish's father, and that meant he was exempt from Ulrik's disgust.

With a growl, Ulrik rammed his head into the tree Mikkel hid behind, the same time he surrounded his uncle with magic that pressed in on him from all sides. Mikkel's screams were music to Ulrik's ears.

He grabbed the fallen tree, roots and all, and tossed it away so he could get to Mikkel. But his uncle scurried away again. Out of the corner of his eye, Ulrik saw Eilish hunched over to keep out of sight as she made her way to her father. Once she reached him, she grabbed his arms and began to pull him farther away.

Ulrik threw back his head and roared as he opened the mental link and said to his uncle, *"You will die. Stop hiding and face me."*

"I'm not hiding."

"You bloody well are. But you forget how keen a dragon's eyesight is."

Mikkel moved from behind a tree, his face twisted with contempt. "You fuckin' bastard! How dare you

throw that in my face! You were no' supposed to have
your magic unbound before me!" he bellowed.

*"Shall I cry for you? How about, instead, I tell you
what it feels like to take to the skies again?"*

His uncle released a battle cry and threw volley after
volley of magic. Try as Ulrik might, it eventually became
difficult to stand against it. He was able to deflect some
of the twisted, offensive magic, but not enough. To his
horror, he realized he was weakening.

Being in his true form gave him added strength, but
he wasn't able to move as quickly. Ulrik shifted back to
his human visage and dove to miss another round of
magic while sending his own at Mikkel.

When he got to his feet, he stilled as his gaze landed
on Mikkel, who had Eilish on her knees before him.
She held her head in both hands, doing her best not to
scream.

Ulrik didn't know what Mikkel was doing, but he
wouldn't be able to do it after Ulrik ripped his head from
his body. As he prepared to launch an attack on his uncle,
Ulrik noticed that the marks on Eilish's arms were blazing red now and twisting over her skin on their own.

"How does it feel to know you'll be responsible for
another mortal's death?" Mikkel asked gleefully. "Eilish
was mine. You should've left well enough alone."

"What the hell are you talking about?" Ulrik asked.

Before the words finished, Mikkel disappeared. Ulrik
spun, waiting for the attack. He had his magic up and
ready to deflect whatever his uncle had planned. The minutes passed while Eilish began to scream, tears coursing
down her face. His gut wrenched with the agony she
was enduring. And he could stop it. All he had to do was
go to her. It's what Mikkel wanted.

And this time, Ulrik would give it to him because he
could do nothing else. It was Eilish, after all.

He rushed to her and broke the hold of his uncle's magic with his own. Just as he was reaching to help Eilish up, Mikkel appeared and thrust the finger rings into Ulrik's chest, raking down his front.

CHAPTER THIRTY-SEVEN

Time froze. But Eilish's heart pounded so hard, she could actually feel it knocking against her ribs.

Her gaze was riveted on Ulrik. He looked down at his chest as Mikkel vanished. The pain that contorted Ulrik's face made her blood turn to ice. He dropped to his knees, and his eyes rolled back in his head.

"No," she whispered as she rushed to him.

She grabbed Ulrik before he fell forward. It took all of her strength and some of her magic to keep him from landing on his face. She managed to turn him onto his back. Then her eyes locked on the blood.

It rushed from him as if being forced out with a pump. She knew he was immortal, so she waited for his body to begin to heal. But as the minutes passed and nothing happened, she became frantic.

Eilish looked over her shoulder at Donal. She didn't have her finger rings, and she couldn't carry either of them, much less figure out how to get Ulrik and Donal out of the forest. With her hand over the gaping slashes on Ulrik's chest, she fought to staunch the blood, but it seeped through her fingers and pooled on either side of him.

She'd isolated herself upon arriving in Ireland. There were no friends or allies she could call. The two she had were lying unconscious beside her. Her mind was frantically trying to come up with a solution. She didn't know why Ulrik wasn't healing, but she knew it wasn't good.

"Ulrik," she said. "Open your eyes. I need you to look at me."

She felt her stomach tighten, fighting the wave of anguish that washed over her. But she only allowed herself a few seconds of it before she took a deep breath and fortified herself. She sniffed and looked around.

There had to be some way to get them out of there. She wasn't keen on remaining in case Mikkel returned. And whatever the bastard had done to Donal, it wouldn't go away anytime soon. She tried to use her magic to see if she could reverse what had been done, but Donal didn't even twitch.

Eilish swiveled her head back to Ulrik, her gaze landed on the silver cuff circling his wrist.

"Yes," she hissed before she took it off and put it on her own wrist.

Now, she just had to hope that it wasn't warded to only work for him. She jumped to her feet and grabbed Donal's arm to pull him closer to Ulrik.

By the time she returned, blood had soaked Ulrik's front. She covered his wounds again and moved his hand so that he and Donal were touching.

But where did she take them? Where was the one place they'd be safe?

The answer was simple: Dreagan.

Without a second's hesitation, Eilish thought of Dreagan and Constantine. Then she touched the cuff as she'd seen Ulrik do. She blinked and found herself in a darkened cave illuminated by lights with no electrical cords anywhere to be seen.

"What the hell," said a deep brogue behind her.

Eilish kept her hand on Ulrik's wounds and looked over her should. "Please. I need Constantine."

"Why?" the man asked as others gathered.

She twisted to better see him. Cobalt eyes pinned her. "Ulrik needs help." She jerked her chin to Donal. "My father needs help."

"How the hell did you get here?" another asked.

She briefly closed her eyes, fighting to remain calm. "I'll answer every damn question you have. But, please! Help them."

The group parted, and a man in a dark suit walked toward her. The neck of his white dress shirt was unbuttoned, and she saw gold dragon head cufflinks at his wrists. With the wavy, blond hair and emotionless, black eyes, she had a feeling she was looking at Constantine, King of Dragon Kings.

A moment later, Sebastian moved to stand beside Con. What had she expected, though? After all the various deeds she'd done for Mikkel, she would have to face the shitstorm. The way Sebastian's topaz eyes narrowed on her, she knew it would only be a matter of time before the memories she'd buried deep within his subconscious found their way forward.

"I know you," Sebastian said in a low voice.

She nodded and motioned him forward with one hand. He hesitated before coming to stand before her. Eilish then put a hand on his leg and removed the spell she'd used on him.

Sebastian took a step back, his brows locked together as he frowned at her. "You were with Mikkel in Venice."

Eilish leaned over Ulrik to put more pressure on his wounds. "Yes. And I'll endure whatever punishment you have for me, but please, help Ulrik."

"Why?" Con asked.

She gaped at him. "Ulrik isn't healing. He told me you could heal anything."

"So you know me?"

Eilish was on the verge of losing her cool. She was frantic for Ulrik as his blood continued to pour through her fingers, and frustrated that none of the Kings seemed to care.

"Yes!" she bellowed, letting her fury show. "At least, I know you from Ulrik's description. Don't you care at all that he's injured? Shouldn't you be concerned that Mikkel has something that can do this?"

A King with short, black hair, and green eyes stood with his arms crossed over his chest. "After what Ulrik tried to do to Rachel in Paris, perhaps we should let him die."

Another with chocolate eyes and long, blond hair pulled away from his face shrugged indifferently. "You wouldna have to worry about fighting him, Con."

"He'd do it to you," someone else said.

Toward the back, another said, "Ulrik wouldna."

"You're all a bunch of assholes," Eilish stated.

She felt her anger rising as it had when her aunts tried to take her. But she didn't stop it. She let it build, welcoming the darkness Ulrik had warned her about. Coming to Dreagan had been a mistake. She knew that now. She was silly to think that the Dragon Kings would help Ulrik.

And all this time, she'd hoped to change Ulrik's mind about attacking them. She moved her hand to touch the cuff. She didn't know where she'd go, but she wasn't going to leave Ulrik there to die among those who had banished him.

Then a hand closed around her wrist, stopping her.

Her gaze lifted to stare into inky orbs. Con had moved so swiftly, she hadn't seen him. Yet it was the strength she felt in his grip that gave her pause.

"Why?" he whispered.

She glanced down at Ulrik. "Because he warned me about Mikkel. Because he had opportunities to kill me and didn't. Because he looked for me when Mikkel took me. But, mostly, because I love him."

Without looking away from her, Con said, "Darius, you and Thorn take the mortal into a cavern. I'll be there shortly."

"You're helping Donal?" she asked.

Con gave a nod of his head. "But I want to know everything."

"And Ulrik? Will you heal him?" she pressed.

"Kings are immortal. He'll heal."

She shook her head as his words sank in. Then she lifted her hand so he could see the wounds on Ulrik's chest. "Does this look like it's healing?"

A frown formed on Con's brow as he looked at Ulrik. He released her other hand and spread his fingers, his palm hovering over the wounds. His frown deepened. Then his gaze returned to her.

"This isn't a trick," she said. "Ulrik may be a lot of things, but he's not a coward. He'd challenge you in front of all the others."

"I know," Con said in a soft voice.

Relief spread through her when he lowered his hand to Ulrik's wounds. Her gaze dropped to the stone floor where blood had pooled beneath her knees, soaking into her pants.

"Come," a man with short, dark brown hair and stormy, gray eyes said.

She looked up at him. "I'm not leaving Ulrik."

"Leave her, Banan," Con said.

Banan didn't move away, though. He walked around to the other side of Ulrik and lowered himself to one knee. No one said a word.

Eilish didn't know if Con was doing anything or not. She hated that she couldn't feel the magic in others. How could she sense it within a stone circle but not in someone? Was that the Druids' punishment for the humans betraying the Dragon Kings?

It wasn't until she noticed the length of Ulrik's wounds beginning to shrink that she bowed her head, sending out a prayer of thanks.

She didn't know how long she sat there, never taking her eyes off Ulrik. He was so still and pale that it was hard for her to look at him. She only knew him as vibrant and imposing.

This was her fault. Had she not gotten involved with Mikkel, then he wouldn't have her finger rings, and Ulrik wouldn't have gotten hurt. And all this to find a woman who had been dead for years.

"What is it?" she asked when Con lowered his hand. She glanced at the wounds that were closed but still puckered. "Why did you stop?"

Con met her gaze. "I've done all I can."

She stumbled to her feet when several Kings, including Con, lifted Ulrik and carried him down a tunnel. Eilish hurriedly followed them into a small cavern with dim lights. They gently laid Ulrik atop a flat rock held upright by a huge boulder a few feet off the floor.

"I'm going to tend to your father," Con told her. "When I return, I want to know everything."

She nodded and slowly walked to stand next to Ulrik

as the others moved away. With nothing to do, her focus turned to the sight of Ulrik's shirt slashed and soaked with blood.

First, Eilish tried to hold the shreds together. That's when she realized how silly that was. Next, she grabbed the edges and tried to tear them apart. While she might have been able to do it with a dry shirt, the material being drenched in blood made it difficult. She tried again, ready to use her magic when she felt a hand on her shoulder.

Her head jerked to the side to find Sebastian and Anson. She stared at the two Kings, wondering what they were going to do to her. A quick glance showed her the other Kings had left, leaving her alone with these two.

"You wiped my and Gianna's memories," Sebastian said.

She licked her lips. "Mikkel wanted me to kill Gianna to hurt you."

"What stopped you?" Anson asked.

"I'm not a killer. Gianna was innocent."

Sebastian dropped his hand. "Ulrik and I were close friends. I went to Venice because I knew there was someone else involved."

"Aye," Anson said. "I sided with Ulrik in the war with the mortals. I wanted them gone just as much as he did."

Eilish looked from the two Kings to Ulrik. "He pretends otherwise, but he's lonely."

"He willna appreciate you saying that," Anson said.

She shrugged, uncaring. "There's much he wouldn't want any of you knowing. He believes it makes him weak in your eyes."

"Weak was never something Ulrik was or ever will be." Sebastian moved to Ulrik's other side and ripped the bloodied shirt in two.

"Bloody hell," Anson murmured.

Eilish looked between them, worry causing her heart to race wildly. "What? What is it?"

"His tat moved," Sebastian mumbled. "It was once on his back."

She frowned. Since when did tattoos move from back to front? Then again, Ulrik was a Dragon King.

It was Anson who raised Ulrik's torso so Sebastian could remove the shirt. Anson then passed his hand over Ulrik, and the blood vanished.

If only his wounds would, as well. She waited for Ulrik to open his eyes and have them fill with anger that she'd brought him to Dreagan. She'd readily endure whatever he had to say if only he'd wake.

"Sit," Sebastian ordered her.

Eilish hadn't seen a chair before, but then again, this was Dreagan, and she was surrounded by Dragon Kings and magic so intense that it enveloped her like a warm blanket.

"Ulrik, come back to me," she whispered.

CHAPTER THIRTY-EIGHT

There was nothing simple about life. Con knew that all too well. And his former best friend lying unmoving on a slab of granite was proof of that. To see Ulrik wounded so had shaken him to his core. It didn't help that Mikkel was the cause.

Con's gaze swung to Eilish. The Druid hadn't moved from Ulrik's side. She was staring at her hands that were still covered in Ulrik's blood. But it was the winding tattoos on her arms that interested him, especially since the ink appeared to be the same mix of black and red of the Dragon Kings.

To say he'd been shocked when she appeared in Dreagan mountain with not just Ulrik but also her father was an understatement. But when she stated her love for Ulrik, it had made Con feel as if the rug had been snatched from beneath his feet.

He gave a nod to Sebastian and Anson, who'd both remained with Eilish and Ulrik.

The longer he watched the Druid, the more he believed her words. At first, he'd thought them a ploy to get him to help. But no longer.

He wondered what Ulrik thought of it, and if his old friend loved her in return. After so many millennia hating mortals while forced to live among them, could Ulrik's heart have healed enough to accept another?

Con feared that Eilish might be disappointed.

"Would you like to wash? Perhaps get some clean clothes?" he asked her.

Her head jerked to him as she clenched her hands into fists. "I don't want to leave him."

"We willna harm him," Sebastian said.

She lifted her chin. "I'm not leaving him."

"What about your father?" Con asked.

Her face crumpled. "Oh, God. How is he?"

The fact that she'd been so concerned about Ulrik that she'd forgotten her own father spoke of how deep her love for Ulrik went.

Con walked a few strides into the cavern. "He's resting. It appears Mikkel tried to gain control of Donal's mind, but he was unsuccessful. All Mikkel could do was put him in a trace that held Donal under his sway."

"But he's going to be all right?" Eilish asked, apprehension filling her face.

"Aye. He's being looked after. He should wake soon, and you're welcome to see him."

Her gaze slid to Ulrik. "I can't leave him."

"You willna be far," Anson said.

She shook her head, her long, dark locks shifting with the movement. "You don't understand."

"Then tell us," Con urged.

Eilish licked her lips as she gave a nod. "I promised I'd tell you everything. And so I shall."

Con stood listening as she spoke of how she'd grown up having magic but hid it from everyone. It wasn't until Patrick gave Eilish her mother's finger rings that she had bought a ticket to Ireland.

As she talked about venturing across Ireland in hopes of finding her mother without even knowing her name, Con felt his respect for Eilish grow. It took a lot of courage to take on such a task.

He exchanged a look with Sebastian and Anson when she detailed her first run-in with a Dark Fae and how she'd fought—and won—against him. Then she told them about finding the building where she opened Graves and how she protected the small town. His interest grew when Eilish's story turned to meeting Mikkel for the first time.

"So he approached you?" Con asked.

She nodded. "I'd never heard of him before he sought me out at Graves. He knew about my search for my mother. All those years of looking with nothing to show for it, and Mikkel said he knew who she was and where I could find her."

"Most anyone would've accepted his offer," Sebastian said.

Con had to agree. "What did he want with you?"

"To kill Ulrik." Her head turned to look at Ulrik. "Mikkel told me he was his nephew but didn't give me a name. Mikkel mentioned Dragon Kings, and it caught my attention since I'd overheard some Fae speaking about the Kings." Her gaze skated back to Con. "I only had to make a simple query to Mikkel, and he told me everything about you."

There was a loud snort from Anson. "Everything? I doubt that, lass."

"He revealed to me what had happened with Ulrik and his banishment," she continued. "Mikkel also told me he was the rightful King of Silvers. I honestly didn't care. I just wanted to find my mother."

Con walked to the foot of the slab. He stared at Ulrik a moment before nodding at Eilish to continue.

She cleared her throat and said, "It didn't take long for me to realize that Mikkel was ridiculously jealous of Ulrik. I watched Mikkel interact with others. I knew he was power-hungry. And I knew he wasn't a good man."

"And still you worked with him," Sebastian said.

She lifted her shoulders in a shrug. "I was desperate to find my mother. I'd used both Druid and human resources to try and locate her but there was nothing they do without a name or a location. I just wanted something. I figured then I could get away from Mikkel. I carried on the charade for a long while. Even to the point of him asking me to kill you."

Con raised a brow. "Me? Why did he believe you could kill a Dragon King when you'd never met one?"

"I've no idea," she said with wide eyes. "It was a mystery to me, but he was convinced of it."

"Ulrik wasna scared of you, was he?" Sebastian asked.

A quick smile pulled at her lips. "Never. He came to see me at Graves. Said he wanted to find the Druid who had agreed to kill him while standing in his shop."

That was exactly something his old friend would do. Con glanced at the wounds on Ulrik's abdomen that had yet to fully heal. "And?"

"We spoke for less than five minutes," Eilish said. "But in that time, I saw he was the opposite of Mikkel in every way. I tried to get Mikkel to tell me something about my mother, but then he summoned me to Venice to make sure Sebastian could remember nothing of their talk. And ordered me to kill Gianna."

"To strike at us," Anson.

Con put his hands into his pants' pockets. "Why did you no' take Gianna's life?"

"As I told Sebastian, I'm not a killer."

"By defying Mikkel's orders, you put your own life in danger."

Her lips twisted as she lifted a shoulder. "He needed me too much, so I took the chance."

"Thank you for that," Sebastian said.

Eilish accepted his acknowledgment with a bow of her head. "Mikkel asked me to unbind the rest of his magic. But I'd figured out what he overlooked in his haste to take over."

"That if you unbind his magic now, he'd be stuck in dragon form because he isna a King," Con said.

She wrinkled her nose as she nodded. "He was none too pleased about that, but I did get him to tell me my mother's first name. The next thing I knew, Ulrik came to me and asked me to help Nikolai and Esther."

Con slowly walked to stand near Ulrik's head. "Which you did. Why?"

"I could tell you it was the sadness I saw in Esther's eyes, or that I felt bad for messing with her mind as well as Kinsey's. Both are true. But it was Ulrik. I could sense that there was a bond between him and Nikolai that went deep. When faced with all three of those things, I couldn't say no. In the end, I learned about Donal."

Con had to admit, the Druid wasn't at all what he'd expected. "How did you and Ulrik come to be together?"

"Looking back, it's difficult to say. Mikkel demanded I kill Ulrik in two days. He no longer wanted to wait. I went to Ulrik and told him. He offered to give me all the information on my mother if I stopped helping his uncle."

Anson asked, "Did you?"

"I wanted to. And, yes, I contemplated it. While helping Mikkel, I did things I would never normally do. Ulrik said I was walking a fine edge of becoming a *drough*. He urged me not to go down that path."

Con was shocked, but he didn't show it to the others. "And?"

"Obviously, I didn't kill Ulrik. I did nothing."

It was the way her gaze returned to Ulrik that told Con that his and Eilish's relationship had solidified into something profound.

"Mikkel came for me," she continued. "His magic was so strong, I couldn't defend myself. He busted through my wards and held me immobile with his magic. He kept asking about Ulrik. When I told him nothing, he broke both of my legs and knocked me out. I woke in a strange house where he said he'd take away the pain if I promised to help him betray Ulrik. I knew that if I couldn't walk, I wouldn't be able to fight him, so I lied and agreed."

Sebastian then asked, "What happened?"

"I heard the Ancients for the first time. They helped me focus my magic on healing myself. Then Mikkel arrived with two women who tried to take me. I fought them and . . ."

She trailed off, causing Con to scowl. "And what?" he urged.

Eilish swallowed hard. "When I get angry, I feel my magic get out of control. That time, I didn't pull back. I unleashed it and it transported myself to another place full of mist."

"That must have been when Ulrik went to the Warriors," Anson said.

Con nodded in agreement. When Broc hadn't been able to locate Eilish, it was because she wasn't on Earth. Somehow, her magic had taken her to another realm. No wonder Mikkel had thought she could kill a Dragon King. The Druid was even more powerful than Isla.

"The mist attacked me," Eilish said as she rose from the chair and stood beside Ulrik. "It wrapped around me. I don't know how long I was there before I heard Ulrik's voice calling me back. I don't know how I got there, and I don't how I left. But, somehow, I ended up in Ulrik's cottage."

Con jerked his chin to her arms. "And the tats?"

"Tats?" she asked in confusion, her face twisting. "Ulrik said I had red marks, but I don't see anything," she said and looked at her arms, twisting them one way and then the other. Her mouth fell open when she caught sight of the tattoos.

So Ulrik had seen them before she did. Interesting.

"Do you see them now?" Con asked.

She nodded woodenly, looking from one arm to the other. Then she raised her shirt to reveal more tats on her torso. Her gaze lowered to her legs. "I don't understand."

"None of us do," Sebastian said, a frown furrowing his brow.

Eilish shook her head as she dropped her shirt. "My tats aren't important. What you need to know is that Mikkel stole my finger rings. They allowed me to teleport, so he now has that power. But he also used them to do this," she said, pointing to Ulrik's wounds.

"Where? How?" Con demanded.

"When I returned to Ulrik from the mist, he said he could feel the residue of my magic from the finger rings. We bounced all over the world trying to find Mikkel. We tracked him to my family in Dublin where we learned they had given Mikkel their magic in exchange for me. Those vile people killed my mother to take her magic because they didn't have any of their own. It's a tradition that began centuries earlier. And they wanted to do the same with me.

"With Ulrik's help, I made sure no other Duffy would ever be put in such a situation. But Mikkel escaped again. We finally found him in the middle of some woodland where he had Donal. He and Ulrik fought, but Ulrik tried to get Donal and me out. That's when Mikkel used my rings and vanished, only to surprise Ulrik." She drew in a shuddering breath. "Ulrik fell unconscious, and I tried to stop the bleeding. He should've healed, but he didn't. And I knew we couldn't remain there in case Mikkel returned."

"So you brought him here," Sebastian said.

Eilish turned her head to Con and said, "Ulrik told me his story. Every horrific, ghastly, appalling part of it. No one should have to endure that kind of pain, but he did. He went insane and dug himself out of that. And then he made a plan.

"I know he's done horrible things. I've seen glimpses of the real Ulrik. He hides his true self, though I can't blame him. But he searched for me when Mikkel took me and when I was in the mist. He called me back from that horrible place. He could've beat Mikkel in the fight. It would've cost my father and me our lives, but Ulrik chose not to do that."

Con lowered his gaze to Ulrik.

"That's everything," Eilish said.

In a short amount of time, Con had learned a great deal about the Druid as well as Ulrik. And it caused him to reevaluate everything.

CHAPTER THIRTY-NINE

Eilish. It was Ulrik's only thought as he pushed through the agony and obscurity to consciousness. Even before he opened his eyes, he felt her.

Knowing she was there calmed him. He could hear her voice, though the words were jumbled. Focusing on her, he clawed his way through the last bit of pain and cracked open his eyes. The first thing he saw was the marks on her arms that were definitely tattoos now—and in the same red and black ink as his own.

His gaze moved lower to her hand that rested near his. There was dried blood on her, and he prayed it wasn't hers. He reached for her, wrapping his fingers around her hand.

Her head swiveled to him. When their eyes met, she smiled. "It's about damn time you woke."

The relief on her face ruined the stern approach she tried to take. He began to smile until he noticed that they weren't alone. He and Con stared at each other for a long minute.

"Don't be angry," Eilish said. "You wouldn't stop bleeding, and I feared Mikkel would return."

Ulrik's body was healing, but slowly. He gritted his teeth through the ghastly pain and sat up. Immediately, he saw Anson and Sebastian in the cavern with them. He glanced around for Nikolai, but when Ulrik didn't see him, he realized Nikolai must still be with Esther on the Isle of Eigg.

Instead of speaking to them, he turned his head to Eilish. "Is that your blood?"

She glanced down at her hands and shook her head. "It's yours. Mikkel never touched Donal or me. Thanks to you."

"Where is Donal?" Ulrik asked.

It was Con who said, "Recovering. Your uncle couldn't quite muster the magic to control the mortal's mind, so he tranced him instead."

Ulrik swung his legs over the side of granite slab and took a deep breath, his determination set. "I have to finish this with Mikkel."

"I know," Con replied.

Ulrik had sworn to never ask Con for anything again, yet there was something he needed. And it was killing Ulrik to be in this position. "I've a favor I would ask."

"Name it."

The quick agreement from Con surprised Ulrik. He wasn't sure how to feel about it either. Elated that Con was willing to help. But years of mistrust made Ulrik worry that someone who was supposed to be his enemy wouldn't want to help him.

But this wasn't about him. It was about Eilish.

"Keep Eilish here, safe. Until I finish with my uncle."

Eilish gaped at him, outrage sparking in her green-gold eyes. "No. That's not what we agreed."

Ulrik swung his head to her and felt his chest tighten. The sound of her voice announcing that she loved him still had the ability to make his heart skip a beat. Didn't she realize that she was important? That she had to stay out of Mikkel's reach? "I can no' fight him if I'm worried about you."

She didn't argue. But some of the light went out of her eyes. She released his hand and turned to Sebastian. "I'd like to see my father now. And possibly wash up."

Ulrik watched her leave with Bast without another look his way. It stung, but he also realized she was hurt by his words.

As soon as she was out of earshot, Ulrik's mind turned to the matter at hand. Con. He braced his hands on the granite and dropped his chin to his chest. "How much did she tell you?"

"Everything," Con replied.

Anson shifted near his position against the wall. "Are you in pain?"

"It's manageable." Ulrik cut his gaze to Con. "I suppose I should thank you for healing me."

Con shrugged indifferently. "I couldna exactly refuse your woman."

"She isna mine," Ulrik stated.

Anson raised a black brow. "That's no' what it looked like to me."

Ulrik ran a hand over his face. It didn't matter what he felt for the Druid. This went beyond him. Beyond all of them. "Eilish's magic is powerful. Mikkel can no' get ahold of her."

"She's welcome to remain here," Con said.

Ulrik straightened and nodded once. "Thank you."

"You're no' seriously leaving," Anson said in dismay as he walked to him. "You're still healing."

"And my uncle willna wait."

Con said, "I have a proposition."

Ulrik wanted to leave, but something made him hesitate. He wasn't sure if being back at Dreagan surrounded by his brethren was the cause, or if it had something to do with Eilish's earlier declaration. Either way, he decided to hear Con out. What could it hurt? And it would give Ulrik more time near Eilish. "What might that be?"

"We both track down the bastard."

Ulrik was so taken aback that he couldn't respond immediately. "You want to fight Mikkel together?"

"I think it's an excellent idea," Anson said with a half-grin.

Sebastian walked in then. "I want in on it."

Con raised a brow, waiting for an answer.

The first thing Ulrik thought of was that it was a ploy by Con to kill him. Then he realized if Con wanted him dead, he'd had plenty of time to do it. Including the last couple of hours while Ulrik was unconscious.

Ulrik looked at each of the Kings. Then he thought about Mikkel and his devious ways. Ulrik took a deep breath and immediately regretted it with the pain that movement caused. "I can handle my uncle on my own."

"I've no doubt of that," Con said. "But after the things he's done, we'd like a little payback."

Ulrik held his old friend's gaze. "I've also done my share."

Con lowered his eyes to the floor for a moment. Then he looked at Anson and Sebastian. "Ulrik has been carrying a secret of mine for a verra long time. He's threatened to tell all of you. Now, I'm going to. First, to the two of you. Then later to the others."

Ulrik watched Con, waiting to see if there was some ulterior motive.

"You see," Con continued. "Ulrik was there when I fought to become King of Dragon Kings. I battled Tarel for days. It felt as if it would go on forever. But I wasna giving up, and neither was he. Once I issued the challenge, only one of us would be alive at the end."

Leaning back against the granite, Ulrik listened, Con's words reviving memories and taking him back to that time.

Con ran a hand over the back of his neck. "I was wounded, and Tarel went down. I thought he was dead. Instead of checking, I looked at my injury. That mistake nearly cost me my life. Tarel attacked, tearing open my wound. I lost track of time after that. I was suddenly on the defensive, and then he knocked me out."

Ulrik looked away, not wanting to hear any more. It was bad enough that he had witnessed the event.

"You see," Con said, "if Ulrik had no' been there, Tarel would've killed me."

"We doona do that," Anson said in consternation.

Sebastian wore a deep frown. "It's an unspoken law that challenges are met and carried out with honor. No one would accept a Dragon King who killed one of their own who was unconscious."

Ulrik pushed away from the granite and faced Con. "Stop."

Con shook his head. "It's time everyone knows the truth." He looked at the others, meeting their gazes for a long, quiet moment. "I woke to find Ulrik holding Tarel back. Ulrik's intervention allowed me to regroup. The fighting resumed for another few days. When Tarel fell again, I believed it was another trick. Ulrik saw the truth and tried to warn me, but it was too late. Tarel was merely unconscious. But I'd already killed him. While Tarel lay there, totally defenseless, I ripped out his heart."

The silence in the cavern was deafening. Ulrik closed his eyes. At one time, he'd dreamed of telling the Dragon Kings of Con's disgrace. He'd longed to see his brethren turn against their King of Kings.

Now, he wished Con had never spoken of the secret. Though Ulrik wasn't the only one who knew.

Kellan, who kept the history of the Kings, was aware, as well. But not once had Kellan's trust in Con ever wavered.

Ulrik opened his eyes and looked at his old friend. "Anyone in your shoes would've done the same. Tarel had already pretended to be dead to trick you."

"I should've checked. You would have," Con said.

Anson said, "I agree with Ulrik. I would've done just as you did."

"You're my King," Sebastian stated. "It was an honest mistake, witnessed by your best friend."

Ulrik grew uneasy with such talk. His time of being Con's brother was long gone. Nothing could change what had happened in the past.

"Let me come with you," Con said to Ulrik.

Ulrik wanted to refuse, but he couldn't get the words past his lips.

"We made a good team once," Con argued. "Unstoppable, they called us. Mikkel has been a thorn in both of our sides for long enough."

Anson nodded, a lopsided grin on his face. "You two were relentless. Join forces once more."

Ulrik's gaze looked past them to find Eilish at the opening to the cavern, listening. She gave him a nod, urging him to take the offer. Could he? Should he?

The others were right. When he and Con fought together, they never lost. Ever. Mikkel wouldn't stand a chance. And wasn't that the main goal?

"Challenge me when we're done with Mikkel," Con added.

"Fine," Ulrik said. "We'll go after my uncle."

Eilish lifted her chin. "With me."

He opened his mouth to reply when she talked over him.

"This isn't up for debate," she continued. "I'm going.

Mikkel took my finger rings. He was going to turn me over to my family. I'm going."

She turned on her heel and walked away. Ulrik ran a hand down his face and sighed heavily. The woman had a mind of her own.

"She's feisty," Bast said with a grin.

Anson grunted. "And strong. Not easily manipulated."

The look that passed between Con, Bast, and Anson spoke of some deeper meaning. Ulrik wanted to ask what it meant, but he decided to hold his tongue. Not long after, Sebastian and Anson strode out of the cavern.

Con released a long sigh. "There is something I have to tell you."

Ulrik wasn't sure he was up for much more. "Spit it out, then."

"Back then, your woman didna betray you on her own."

Ulrik blinked. "Nala? What do you mean?"

"No one told me she planned to betray you. I learned it on my own."

The old hurts and anger returned with a vengeance, but Ulrik held them back. It was time he learned the missing part of the night that changed the course of his life. "Tell me."

Con nodded, his lips flattened. "I was having dinner with you. You leaned over to kiss her, and when you looked away, she made a face, as if repulsed."

That was difficult for Ulrik to hear. And if it were coming from anyone else, he might call them a liar. But the one thing Con had never done was lie to Ulrik.

"Go on," he bade.

"It didna sit well with me, so I began following her. She would sneak off to visit someone in the village. I never saw who it was, but I overheard them. Whoever it was convinced her to betray you."

Ulrik gave a shake of his head, confused. "That doesna make sense. I told her I was immortal."

"She probably thought you were lying."

"Who would do that?"

Con slowly walked a few paces to the left. "All this time, it's still bothered me that someone would do that to you. You went above and beyond with those mortals. The entire village adored you."

"Apparently, no' everyone."

Con grunted as he came to a stop. "That's just it, they did. Including Nala. Until someone poisoned her thoughts. It wasna until quite recently that I began to consider who that person was."

Ulrik looked askance at him. "You can no' mean Mikkel? He couldna talk to a human because he couldna shift. Only Dragon Kings can."

"Around that time, I heard rumors that a dragon, though no' a King, found a way to communicate with mortals. At first, I didna pay attention, but the whispers grew. There was mention of Druid magic, and humans saying that someone was taking over their bodies for a time. Something wasna right about any of it. So I investigated. It's why I was at your village that night for dinner."

"If any dragon could find a way to talk to the humans, it would've been Mikkel."

"And the Druids were coming into their magic at that time."

"Mikkel was so crazed to be a Dragon King, he would've grasped for anything," Ulrik said, running a hand through hair. "He's been after my throne since his father died."

Con scratched his jaw. "It passed to your father."

"Aye. And then me. I always said the battle with that

neighboring clan who killed my father came out of no-where. We'd had peace."

"Unless Mikkel began the skirmish, thinking with your father gone, he'd be the next King."

Ulrik fisted his hands. "Everything makes sense now. But I'm going to get him to confess. Then, I'll kill him. He'll never interfere in my life again. Nor will he get the chance to hurt Eilish or any other innocents."

"I like the sound of that."

Ulrik stalked from the cavern. "Let's find Eilish."

CHAPTER FORTY

Eilish was within the confines of Dreagan. Smack dab in the middle, surrounded by Dragon Kings. It felt so surreal. And it hadn't truly hit her until Ulrik woke.

The relief she'd felt after he opened his eyes quickly turned to irritation when he wanted to leave her out of the fight with Mikkel. There was no way she was going to let that happen. And it wasn't just what Mikkel had done to her. She wanted to be there for Ulrik—not that he needed her.

She was returning to Donal when she realized she must have taken a wrong turn in the maze of tunnels. Eilish pivoted and began to retrace her steps when she heard a voice—one that she recognized.

"You can't keep me here!"

She stilled before slowly swiveling her head to look behind her. That British accent was almost as hated as Mikkel's. She turned and continued down the tunnel, passing several caverns until she found him.

Stanley Upton.

At first, she didn't recognize him. His graying blond hair was in disarray, and his eyes were wild. Though he was well cared for. His clothes were clean, and there was a tray of untouched food on the floor. Yet there were no bars or door at the opening of the cavern.

"You," he said and rushed toward the entrance.

Eilish took an instinctive step back, but she shouldn't have been worried because he bounced off an invisible barrier.

"How did you get here?" Upton asked in a hushed voice, his gaze darting around.

She shrugged. "I strolled in."

"You have to get me out before they return."

Unable to help herself, Eilish decided to mess with him. "Who?"

His eyes widened. "Don't you know where you are?"

"Yeah. An office building in London."

"No. We're in a cave."

Eilish looked around before pointing to her left. "The lift is that way. The water cooler is to my right, and there is a conference room behind me. Not to mention all the cubicles around us. Why don't you step out of the women's bathroom, Stanley? There's a line of people who need to use it. Me included."

His mouth moved as he frowned, looking at her as if she were completely off her rocker. "Y—you're wrong."

"Stan, people have been looking for you for days now. Don't tell me we called the authorities for nothing? If you've been hiding in the restroom, they're going to want to know why."

"A dragon took me," he said, a vein protruding in his forehead.

It was all Eilish could do not to laugh. "A dragon? You do know they don't exist, right?"

"That's not true. They do. They live on Dreagan, the place we're standing. And you're a Druid. You have magic." He nodded vigorously. "That's right! Mikkel brought you to us. We put you in a room, and you did some kind of mind thing with Kinsey and Esther so we could get to the Dragon Kings."

Eilish shook her head, twisting her lips. "Wow. Have you ever tipped into crazy town. It's too bad I don't have magic. Perhaps I could've made you give me that raise I asked for last month."

"But . . . no," Upton stated and took a step back, his face contorted in confusion.

She peered inside the cavern.. "Is Harriett with you? We long thought the two of you had something going on. We haven't seen her either."

"No!" he bellowed, anger finally pushing through. "She's not with me! She's probably with Mikkel. You need to find him. The plan was for us to fly to Ireland to meet up with him if anything went wrong."

"Impressive," someone said.

Eilish turned her head to find Ulrik and Con standing together. Ulrik wore a grin while Con bowed his head in salute to her. She shrugged. "Sorry. I couldn't resist."

Con came to stand beside her. "He's refused to tell us anything about Harriett or Mikkel. You got what we couldn't."

"Wait, what?" Stanley said as he looked between them. "What's going on?"

Ulrik walked to stand on Eilish's other side. When Upton saw him, he stumbled back so quickly, he nearly fell.

Stanley pointed at Ulrik, his hand shaking. "Get him away from me."

"Where in Ireland were you to meet Mikkel?" Eilish pressed.

Upton looked away and mumbled to himself, "This isn't happening. We were supposed to win."

"Come on, Stan," she pressed. "Tell me what we need to know, or I'll let Ulrik in there with you."

Stanley's head snapped to her. He hesitated, his chest moving up and down rapidly. "We were to send a special message, and Mikkel would arrange transportation from London."

"It'll be a private plane," Ulrik said to Con.

Con turned on his heel. "I'll get Ryder on it."

Ulrik put his hand on her back and guided her away while Upton shouted for them to return. Though Eilish wouldn't mention it, she was happy to see that Ulrik appeared to fit right back in with Con at Dreagan. Because it's where Ulrik belonged.

"You did good," he said.

She grinned and lifted a shoulder. "As I said, I wanted to have some fun. He's always been a jerk, thinking that his money and position made him better than anyone else. But why do you need Harriett? You can find Mikkel."

"Aye, I can. But while I'm looking, Ryder can search for Harriett, helping to narrow the field. If she went to my uncle, it was because he has plans for her."

"Or he could turn her over to the Dark Fae."

Ulrik walked her through more tunnels. "That's definitely a possibility. He will no doubt do that, but he'll use her first."

"For what? He's already attacked you and taken my finger rings."

They finally stopped, and Ulrik faced her. "By now, Mikkel will know that I'm no' dead. There will be another attack, and he'll use Harriet. She's mortal, so she's expendable in his eyes."

"But you don't care about her."

"That's right. But Con and the other Kings will if she's a threat to the humans."

Eilish sighed loudly. "Shit." She thought about that a moment. "But Mikkel wouldn't know I brought you here."

"He doesna. Mikkel believes I'll be weak enough for him to kill. Then he'll head straight for Dreagan. With the Kings focused elsewhere, there will be few here. He'll use that to get in and attack Con."

She cocked her head to the side as she crossed her arms over her chest. "How do you know this?"

"I'm a good strategist. And I know my uncle."

"But you haven't seen him in ages. You changed. He could've, too."

Ulrik shrugged indifferently. "He's no' changed enough. In the time I was with him, I learned how he thinks, as well as the moves he'll make to get ahead."

"Are you ever wrong?"

"Never," Con said as he walked up.

Eilish raised a brow at Ulrik. "Well, look at you. You are indeed all that and a bag of chips."

The grin Ulrik hurriedly wiped from his face made her smile. It was a vast improvement over him yelling at her to stop when she told him of her love. She'd said it in case she died. Instead, he'd almost been the one to lose his life.

"We need to plan," Ulrik said and walked into a brightly lit cavern.

Con motioned for Eilish to proceed. She dropped her arms and followed Ulrik, looking around to find more of the lights and no cords. Was it dragon magic or the power in the land that kept the lights working? As cool as it was, she couldn't get past the fact that they hadn't left the mountain.

"Why are we doing this here?" she asked.

Ulrik's gold gaze landed on her. "What do you mean?"

She looked at Con. "Why aren't we in the manor?"

"Eilish," Ulrik began.

She ignored him and stared at Con. "Everyone saw Ulrik. They know you helped him."

"That they do," Constantine said.

Ulrik spoke before she could. "This is as good a place as any."

She slid her gaze from Ulrik to Con. Though the King of Kings had allowed Ulrik to stay and even healed him, Ulrik was still banished. As she digested that, she remained quiet as Ulrik filled them in on what he believed Mikkel's plans would be.

"He could use Harriet in a lot of ways," Con said.

Ulrik nodded. "It could be in London to pull the Kings far from Dreagan."

"No," Eilish said. "It'll be in Scotland. Mikkel detests anything to do with this country. He even hides his accent. The Kings love Scotland, so he'll strike here."

Ulrik blew out a breath. "She's right, but Mikkel will no' send Harriett to a large city."

"It'll be the village," Con said and briefly closed his eyes.

"Close enough to Dreagan so that every King could pitch in to contain Harriett while he sneaks in and readies to fight you. The magic of Dreagan will strengthen him."

Eilish smacked her lips. "We can put a big crimp in Mikkel's plans by taking my rings."

"He'll expect you to be with me," Ulrik said.

She grinned. "Unless I'm not."

"Meaning?" Con asked.

"He needs to discover that I'm somewhere else. And by discover, I mean see."

Ulrik raised a black brow. "How do you intend to get him to you?"

"Oh, I don't think it'll take much to get his attention.

Especially if I do it at Graves with lots of people listening, including his spies."

Con turned his gaze to Ulrik. "I like her thinking."

"After he sees Eilish, I'll challenge him," Ulrik said.

Eilish kept her smile hidden. If the boys thought they could keep her out of the battle, they were mistaken. "Once Mikkel goes off to fight you, I'll follow."

"With what?" Ulrik asked.

She lifted her wrist to show him the cuff.

Con dropped his chin to his chest, but not before she saw the half-smile he attempted to hide from Ulrik.

"That way, Mikkel thinks he's only fighting you," she continued. "He won't see me coming until after I've already taken my rings back."

"Then you'll return to Dreagan," Ulrik said.

She wanted to argue, but it was actually a sound plan. Especially since she knew Mikkel didn't stand a chance with either Ulrik or Con. Though she wouldn't be in a big hurry to return to Dreagan. She was looking forward to seeing Mikkel get his ass kicked, even if she wasn't the one delivering the punishment.

"Deal. Just make him suffer," she said.

Violence glittered in Ulrik's gold depths. "You can count on it."

"Where do you want me?" Con asked.

She found it fascinating to watch the two Kings interacting. Despite the hatred Ulrik claimed he had for Con, they worked well together. There was no animosity from either of them. It gave her a glimpse of the friendship that had once existed between them, a bond that no one thought could break. And it hadn't. Not really. It had bent to such a degree that it cracked. But it hadn't fractured apart.

There was still hope there. She wasn't sure if Ulrik saw it, but Con's willingness to heal him and then help fight Mikkel said a lot in her eyes. Surely, Ulrik saw it, as well. She worried that Ulrik's centuries of hatred might blind him to it.

If she couldn't have his love, she might be able to help him bridge the chasm that separated him from his brethren.

For so long, she'd searched for the missing piece of her identity through her mother. It was only a thimble of what Ulrik felt after being banished from Dreagan. Because he'd always known where his missing piece was. Now, he had a chance to mend what had been broken, to retake his place.

She hadn't cared to develop relations with Druids—or anyone, for that matter—while she was searching for her mother. Seven years in Ireland, and she didn't have one friend. She had plenty of acquaintances, but no friends. Not until Ulrik. To have a Dragon King as a confidante and lover opened her eyes to things she hadn't wanted to see before.

Now, everything was laid out before her—yet just out of reach. She wouldn't change the fact that she'd fallen in love with Ulrik. He'd given her tenderness, hope, and love. He'd never lied to her or tried to use her. He'd only ever wanted to help her.

It was inevitable that she would fall for him. No doubt he had other women who were in love with him, as well. He tried to hide his good side, but in the end, he'd shown her his true colors. And they were glorious.

While she could, she would help him end Mikkel. She was partly to blame for the predicament so she'd do her share.

Because she wanted him to be happy.

Because he deserved peace.

Because she loved Ulrik with her entire heart and soul.

CHAPTER FORTY-ONE

Never had Ulrik second-guessed himself before. But he was now.

He'd gone over and over the plans against Mikkel for the last few hours, making sure that he'd looked at every angle while Eilish was with Donal, and Con was doing whatever it was the King of Kings did. But Ulrik knew in his gut that if Eilish went with them, something would happen to her.

"She's verra pretty," Con said as he walked into the cavern.

Ulrik didn't reply. Instead, he asked, "Did she finally eat?"

"Aye. A couple of the mates gave her some clothes after she ate and had a shower. She didna want to go into the manor at first. No' until I told her you were no longer banished."

Even though he had been able to come and go at will on Dreagan for several centuries, to have the banishment lifted was . . . freeing. It was something Ulrik had longed for so desperately, he'd never thought it would happen unless he killed Con. And yet, somehow, it had happened.

Just as he and Con were talking as if several millennia hadn't passed with them as enemies.

Bracing his hands against the wall, Ulrik sighed. "Eilish is as stubborn as they come. It's what helped her survive when others would've crumbled beneath the weight."

"You admire her."

"Aye."

"The others have mixed feelings about her."

Ulrik dropped his arms and faced Con. "If they have a problem with her, they can come to me."

The slow rise of Con's brow spoke volumes. "If no' for us, Kinsey and Esther would've killed each other. Eilish is the cause of that."

"You could say that Mikkel is. Or, really, I am. Because had I no' been banished, my uncle would've never come into power. Or we could say you're the cause of it. Had you stood with me instead of against me, none of this would've happened."

"And you'd never have known her."

Ulrik studied Con. "What's that suppose to mean?"

"Eilish is good for you."

"Doona go down that road."

Con shrugged. "Why no'? What are you afraid of? Caring?" He gave a lengthy pause. "Or loving?"

"I'll no' discuss Eilish with you," he stated and turned his back to Con.

"It's a pity. She was ready to fight like a she-devil for me to heal you."

Ulrik leaned his head back and looked at the shadows on the domed ceiling above him. He didn't want to hear this. It was hard enough to try and forget her saying that she loved him. It replayed in his head constantly.

He knew all of Eilish's strengths, her faults, and her weaknesses. He knew the stroke of her magic—and the darkness that tinged the edges. It called to him. Both her magic and the darkness, where he had toyed around the edges for eons.

The taste of her, the feel of her, was branded upon him, sunk deep into his psyche, just as his tattoo was. She was a part of him. Whether he liked it or not.

And he liked it. Very much.

Too much.

"You had every right to hate the mortals back then. As well as today. Doona think it's weak to care for one."

"I did care for one," Ulrik said and lowered his head. "I loved her, remember? And look where that got me."

Con walked farther into the cavern. "Eilish isna Nala. You know that, even if you willna admit it."

"I can admit that Eilish is different than anyone I've ever known—human, dragon, or Fae."

"She loves you."

Ulrik shook his head before he turned his head to Con. "Doona say more."

A look of surprise shot over Con's face. "She told you."

"Aye," he finally replied.

"You care for her. I can see that."

Ulrik tried to deny it, but the words lodged in his throat. Finally, he ran a hand down his face and turned to lean against the wall.

"You can ask any King or mate here, but I didna want any of my men attaching themselves to mortals," Con said. "No' just because they could go insane as you pointed out once, but because I've always feared someone else would betray another of you. Yet I find that despite what Eilish has done, she's partially redeemed herself by helping Nikolai and Esther. And you. She's fighting against Mikkel. She told me you shared your story with her. Did you tell her all of it?"

Ulrik nodded, bracing one foot against the wall behind him.

"You wouldna have done such a thing if you didna trust her," Con said.

Trust. Did he trust Eilish? To his surprise, he did. That put Ulrik in a precarious position—the kind he'd sworn never to be in again.

He looked to Con. His old friend was watching him carefully. Was Con looking for a weakness? Something to exploit? "You're verra curious about my life."

"No' for the reasons you imagine."

"Really?"

"Really." Con twisted the dragon head cufflink at his wrist. "Do you want to know why I banished you?"

Ulrik snorted. "I figured that out."

"I doubt it."

"Then, please. Enlighten me."

Con's black eyes held his. "It would've been kinder had I killed you."

"That we agree on."

"But I couldna."

Ulrik frowned at the unexpected admission. Unease ran through him as he watched his old friend.

Con lifted one shoulder, his lips twisting ruefully. "I sent you away the night we killed Nala because I wanted to spare you. You, of all the Kings, didna deserve such a betrayal by the woman you'd fallen in love with. I didna do it to be cruel. I did it as a kindness."

"It took me a while to come to terms with that, but I do know you didna order her death lightly."

Con looked at the ground. "I'd never seen such anger in you once you learned what we'd done. Even then, I think you knew we did it because you were our brother." He lifted his gaze to Ulrik. "So you turned your anger on the only ones you could—the mortals."

"Is that why you stood against me?"

"I wanted to join you. I fought that every day," Con confessed.

Ulrik was confused by his words. "Then why?"

"We made a vow. If I disregarded it, it would set a precedent. So as much as part of me agreed with you—and wanted to join you—I had to stand against you."

"Why did you no' tell me?"

"Would you have listened?"

Ulrik knew the answer.

Con shot him a half-smile. "You had the majority of the Kings on your side at that point. You could've challenged me right then."

"Why would I do that? I never wanted your position. I just wanted the humans gone. But you condemned me to walk as a mortal without any magic and banished me."

"Aye," Con said with a nod of his head. "You wouldna listen to me. You backed me into a corner and gave me no choice. If I could go back and change all of it, I would. If you want to challenge me, then we can fight."

This might not have been in his plans, but Ulrik knew it was folly to pass up such an opportunity. Yet he found himself saying, "My focus is Mikkel right now."

"I've already told the others, but as of the moment I healed you, your banishment was lifted. No matter the outcome of today, tomorrow, or next month. This is your home. I overstepped when I sent you away. I was angry that I had to take your magic, and then you were so defiant. And once it was done—"

"You couldna undo it," Ulrik finished.

Con blew out a breath. "I had many siblings, but you were my only true brother. I'm sorry."

Ulrik dropped his gaze to the ground. Over the past several hours, he'd learned a lot, and he wasn't sure how to digest it all yet. After hating Con for so long, he couldn't just put it aside. Could he?

Instead of thinking about it, he changed the subject. "I doona want Eilish with us when we face Mikkel."

Con looked away, a flash of hurt in his black eyes that was quickly masked. "From what I've learned, she's more than capable of handling herself."

"He'll harm her," Ulrik said and raised his eyes to Con. "I know it. And it could put her in a position where she goes to that other realm again."

That was one outcome Ulrik refused to allow to happen. No matter what he had to do or say, he wouldn't lose Eilish to the mist again.

Con ran a hand over his chin. "You're the strategist. Where will he do it? And how?"

"Mikkel will look for a weakness in all of us. Then he'll use it. While Eilish's magic is strong, she couldna hold him off the first time."

"Weakness, aye?" Con murmured.

Ulrik lowered his foot to the ground. "Aye."

"Then I know how Mikkel will do it, and I know how you've overlooked it."

Ulrik threw up his hands in aggravation. "Care to share?"

"You."

He cocked his head to the side, taken aback. "What?"

"Eilish is your weakness. That's how he got to you in the forest. It's how he'll get you this time. He'll go for her, just as he went for Nala."

Ulrik pushed away from the wall with his shoulder and began to pace the cavern with long strides. "I didna think it was possible to hate anyone more than I hated you or the mortals, but Mikkel has claimed that spot."

"Then use that."

He halted and jerked his head to Con. "The hate?"

"Mikkel thinks he's smarter than you, but he isna. We both know that. He believes he's gotten one over on you all these years by convincing Nala to betray you. He expects you to be furious and to make mistakes. But he doesna know you well enough to know that when you're that angry, it makes you more lethal, more dangerous. And before you forget, I'm going to be there to have your back."

Ulrik found himself in the uncomfortable position of having his so-called enemy giving him praise and encouragement. "Mikkel willna come alone."

"A coward like him never does."

"He'll bring his mercenaries."

Con smiled then. "Do you no' have your own?"

Ulrik found himself chuckling. Damn, he'd missed his friendship with Con. If only Mikkel hadn't interfered. If he hadn't, Ulrik would be mated to Nala.

His thoughts ground to a halt, the smile dropping. But then he never would have met Eilish. He wouldn't have known the taste of her kiss, the feeling of her body against his, or the pleasure to be found in her arms.

"Do you remember when I told you I was taking Nala as my mate?" Ulrik asked.

Con nodded. "I do."

"You told me it was a mistake. Why did you think that?"

"She wasna your match. Nala was pretty and sweet, but she didna challenge you, she didna push you. Nor was she in love with you. You saved her and her family from starvation. So while you might have loved her, she returned the affection out of gratitude. It's why Mikkel turned her so easily."

Ulrik raked a hand through his hair. "I would've been miserable with Nala."

"No' at first. It would've taken time, but she wouldna have adjusted to immortality."

"I killed her."

Con look askance at him. "Nay. We did that."

"You doona understand. I found her soul and obliterated her so that she could never come back."

There was a beat of silence as Con's gaze briefly narrowed in surprise. "I didna know you could do that."

He shrugged. "I wasna able to confront her in life, so I did it in death."

"You're going to win against Mikkel. Regardless, doona leave here without telling Eilish of your feelings."

Ulrik shot him a dark look. "You've nerve to give me such advice."

"Because we're discussing you right now. When we're talking about me, feel free to give me all the advice you want."

Ulrik pressed his lips together. "I'll no' make Eilish happy in the long run."

"There isna a Dragon King who deserves to find happiness more than you, my friend. You need to go to her. If you can no' find the words, show her. Eilish is the kind of woman who will be loyal forever."

That Ulrik knew. He wasn't sure how. He just did. Just as his trust in her had come upon him unexpectedly.

"I'll be ready to leave whenever you give the word," Con said. "I'll stand beside you as we fight Mikkel. And, when we return, I'll be ready when you challenge me."

Ulrik watched Con walk from the cavern, his thoughts no longer on killing the King of Kings—but on loving Eilish.

CHAPTER FORTY-TWO

Eilish stood in the giant cavern in awe of the four Silvers sleeping peacefully within their cage. Other than the Kings, these were the last dragons on Earth.

She walked slowly around the enclosure, noting the metallic silver scales just like Ulrik's. The dragons were as large as he was, but Ulrik still managed to set himself apart. It was the strength and the natural authority and leadership he exuded.

Stopping, she bit her lip as she thought about touching one of the dragons. She'd seen Ulrik twice now in dragon form and hadn't been able to get close to him yet. When he fought Mikkel, she'd been trying to protect Donal, but it had been thrilling to feel the ground tremble beneath her feet and bask in the power and might that rolled off him in waves.

"Touch them."

Her gaze jerked to the entrance to find the very man she couldn't stop thinking about. She shivered—and it had nothing to do with the cool temperature of the mountain and everything to do with Ulrik.

His inky hair was shoved back from his face and hung

loosely about his shoulders. His gold eyes were piercing, as if they glowed from within. He'd found clean clothes, and the white Henley hugged every mouthwatering muscle from his shoulders to his waist. He gave a nod, his lips tilted slightly at the corners.

Eilish put her hand through the bars and laid her palm on the dragon. The warmth of the scales seeped through her skin. Magic swirled around her, greater than she'd ever felt in the stone circles.

Her eyes slid closed as she heard the distant beat of drums and chanting. The Ancients. They were with her once more. She didn't know what was more exhilarating, hearing the Ancients again or touching a dragon.

Then a hand rested atop hers. She didn't need to look to know it was Ulrik. He molded his body against her back, cocooning her. She held her breath when his free hand swiped her hair to one side. His lips pressed against her neck, causing her lips to part as the air whooshed from her lungs. He then anchored her against him with his free arm as his warm breath rushed over her skin.

"Your magic is moving around me like a caress," he whispered huskily.

She couldn't catch her breath. "What's happening?"

"The Silvers feel you. Your magic touched theirs. And they like it."

"And you?"

"You know I like it."

Her heart skipped a beat. It wasn't a confession of love, but then again, she hadn't expected one. In many ways, this was so much better. "The Ancients are with me, as well."

"That's the kind of power you have," he said, nuzzling her neck.

He spun her so quickly, it didn't register until her back was against the bars, her wrists trapped in his grip near her head. She saw the desire in his eyes, and her body readily answered.

"I doona want you in this fight."

She nodded, not wanting to talk, but to kiss. "I know."

"You doona."

It took her a moment to push past the fog of need for her to grasp that he was trying to tell her something, but she would have read between the lines.

"Tell me then," she urged.

"Your darkness that called to me has grown. So has your magic." His chin jerked to her arms. "The tats are proof of that."

She shook her head, wanting him to stop.

In a blink, his shirt was gone. Ulrik brought her arm against his dragon tattoo. "Look, Eilish. Look at the coloring. They match. In all of my eons on this planet, nothing has ever had the black and red mix of our tattoos. Nothing."

"What does it mean?" She was happy her voice didn't quaver, because inside, she was a mess.

"I doona know. This is new territory, but Mikkel can no' use you."

She gave him a dark look. "I'll never help that bastard again."

"But I would."

His words shocked her so much that her mouth fell open. "What?"

"If he had you, I would do whatever he wanted. And he knows that."

Chills raced over her skin. She couldn't breathe, couldn't think. Had Ulrik just said what she thought he had? Could he actually mean . . . ?

Abruptly, he released her and stepped back. "Please stay out of this fight."

"You need those finger rings away from Mikkel. I'm your best chance for that."

"I was hoping you wouldn't realize that."

Her eyes lowered to his tattoo. Her stomach fell to her feet when she saw it move as if turning its head toward her. And the tats all over her body warmed in response.

"Get the finger rings and get out," Ulrik told her. "Promise me."

She nodded, lifting her gaze to his face. He'd opened up to her, but now he was shutting himself off again. Since this could be one of the last times she saw Ulrik, she was going to take advantage of it.

In two steps, she was before him. She brought his head down and kissed him. His arms immediately came around her, holding her tightly as he plundered her lips in a kiss that made her toes curl.

She was the one who ended it, though it took all her willpower. With her hand on his cheek, she looked into his eyes. "I've given you a promise, but I want one in return. If Mikkel happens to catch me with the intent to use me against you, don't agree to any of his terms. Kill him. Even if it means I die."

Ulrik jerked back as if struck. "I can no'."

"You have to. I know what I'm getting into. I need to do this for me and for the people I hurt. It's my redemption."

He stared at her a long moment before he grudgingly said, "All right."

"Good," she said and dropped her arms. "When does it begin?"

"Whenever you're ready."

That meant she had to leave Ulrik, and she wasn't sure she could. She started to reach toward the cuff when he yanked her back against him for another scorching kiss that promised unrestrained passion and ecstasy.

The force of their hunger and yearning raged so hot, it could've scorched anyone who got close. There was desperation there, as well—from both of them. They clung to each other, using their hands and mouths to convey what neither wanted to say.

She was gasping for breath when he pulled back. He cupped her face between his hands. Some of the time they'd had together had been wasted. If only she'd known then what she knew now, she wouldn't have fought her desire.

"Doona get hurt," Ulrik said as he lowered his forehead to hers. "And doona die."

"Don't hold back," she told him. "Your uncle has done enough damage. It's time he was dispersed . . . elsewhere."

Ulrik surprised her with a grin. It quickly faded as he grew serious. "Be safe."

"I will." After all, she had a reason to live—him.

When his hands fell from her, she took a step back and smiled through the wash of tears that filled her eyes. Then, right before she touched the cuff, she said, "I love you."

In the next second, she was standing in her flat above Graves. Her face crumpled, and she buried her head in her hands as she let the tears come. But there was too much to do for her to cry. She lifted her head and sniffed while wiping her face. Then she walked into her room and straight for her closet.

Tonight, she was dressing for battle. And she had just the outfit for it.

Eilish removed her borrowed clothes and tossed them onto the bed. Then she changed into a black lace and leather bra and matching panty set. She grabbed a pair of black leather pants as well as a black tank that laced up the front. Next, she slipped her feet into over-the-knee black boots.

She walked to her vanity and sat on the stool. Styling her long hair up and out of her face, she turned her head from side to side, examining her reflection. Satisfied with what she saw, she leaned to the right and opened the bottom drawer. After her first run-in with a Dark Fae, Eilish had wanted to make sure she'd be prepared if she ever walked into battle again.

After all, a knight didn't go in without armor.

She might not be a knight, but she was a Druid. And her armor would help deflect anything Mikkel used. In all honesty, she'd never thought to use them. But she was glad she'd prepared.

Eilish shrugged on the knit jacket that fell just below her breasts. She fastened the button that would hold it in place and held out her arms. From her shoulders down to her wrists was black chainmail made of titanium— light, but sturdy. She'd added her magic into the armor, as well.

She lowered her arms and looked at herself in the mirror. "I'm going to be quick—quicker than I've ever moved. I'll steal back my finger rings, and I'll help Ulrik. Mikkel will never harm me."

After a deep, calming breath, Eilish rose to her feet and walked from her flat. As soon as she was in the stairwell, the loud music assaulted her. She ignored it and made her way down to Graves. Slipping from the hidden doorway, she was happy to see that while she'd been otherwise engaged, the pub had continued on. But that was because she hired good employees.

Her gaze moved around the dance floor and the crush of people before she looked up to the railing where others gazed down upon the dancers. She leaned her arm against the bar and studied those that lingered there.

Something touched her arm. She jerked her head over to find Cody, the bartender. He gave her a nod and a smile before motioning to the glass next to her. Eilish downed the whisky and set aside the empty glass. Then she made her way through the people, hoping that any of Mikkel's spies would see her.

She stopped at tables with regular customers and made sure they had everything they needed. Then she walked up the stairs. She made the rounds on the second floor, but Graves no longer felt safe.

There were eyes on her, watching her. It made her feel as though everyone in the pub was a spy for Mikkel. For all she knew, they were. It was disconcerting and infuriating.

The more time passed without Mikkel showing, the antsier she became. Ulrik's silver cuff was hidden by the sleeves of her jacket. Knowing that small connection was there helped to keep her calm and focused.

The first hour was nerve-wracking as the hairs on the back of her neck rose from the caress of unknown eyes. The second strained her patience. The third hour brought her to the point of breaking. At the start of the fourth, while she was at the bar, she spotted Mikkel walking toward her.

Ulrik's plan was well and truly a go now.

Somewhere in the throng of people was someone who was there to watch for Mikkel's arrival so they could alert Ulrik. She didn't know who it was. Ulrik had refused to tell her. He didn't want her looking for them. It couldn't be a Dragon King or a mate because it would alert Mikkel, and for the life of her, she couldn't imagine who it could be.

But Eilish didn't back down when Mikkel approached. Nor when he smirked at her before thrusting his index finger down on the bar, demanding a drink.

"You're not welcome here," she stated over the music.

Mikkel laughed as he took the whisky and brought it

to his nose to smell. "Irish whisky was never my favorite, but it'll do."

"Get out."

He took a small sip before setting the glass down and facing her. "Where's Ulrik?"

"How the hell should I know? He left me in that forest."

"When did you make it back?"

She cocked an eyebrow. "You know, Mikkel, you're not the only one with connections."

"Ah," he said with a nod, his lips twisting. "I'm also not stupid."

"That's a matter of opinion. Now get out of my pub before I toss you out."

He threw back his head and laughed. "Oh, I almost want to see you try. Besides, I know you really want these," he said and lifted his left hand, showing off her finger rings.

"You look like an idiot wearing those. And they will be mine again."

Suddenly, he leaned close, putting his face near hers, his nostrils flaring in anger. "You're the one who has worn out her welcome. I'm taking over the pub. And I'll be the one throwing you out."

Eilish smiled. "Please try."

"I—" Mikkel suddenly stopped. He paused for a moment before he said, "I'll be back for you."

Then, with a touch of the finger rings, he was gone. Before she followed, Eilish walked all four corners of the building, inside and out, placing spells so Mikkel could never enter again.

CHAPTER FORTY-THREE

Caledonian Forest, Scotland

This wasn't how it was supposed to end. That didn't make Ulrik want to change things, however. Mikkel was never supposed to be a part of the problem. Yet when Ulrik discovered his uncle was not only still in the realm, but vying to become a Dragon King, he'd quickly altered his plans.

But Mikkel hadn't been the only surprise. There had been Eilish, as well.

Eilish.

Ulrik didn't notice the giant pinewoods of the ancient forest. His mind was on the Druid. He still didn't know what to do about her. He wasn't ready to say good-bye, but he also couldn't give her more. And she deserved it.

"Ulrik."

He felt Con's voice in his head. After so many eons, it felt strange to hear his old friend through the link. *"Did you hear from Fallon?"*

"Aye. Larena spotted Mikkel talking with Eilish."

Ulrik immediately called Mikkel's name via the telepathic connection to get him away from Eilish. *"I just summoned him. Mikkel willna ignore me. He wants me dead."*

"Then you need to act like you're still injured. It's a good thing Anson saved your shirt."

Ulrik wasn't used to having anyone with him when he battled. After so many years on his own, it felt . . . odd . . . to trust someone.

And whether he liked it or not, he was trusting. He nearly snorted aloud. So much for him vowing never to trust anyone again, especially Con. But this wasn't just about him. This was also about Eilish.

Ulrik shifted his shoulders against his ruined shirt that was now hardened by the blood that had dried. He hoped he was doing the right thing.

"Your plan is solid," Con said.

Ulrik made it appear as if his wounds were still open and bleeding. *"Is it? I've failed a lot recently."*

"I'm no' sure you have."

At this, he did release a snort. *"How do you figure that?"*

"I doona think you really wanted to hurt any of the Kings or their mates. Why else would you save Lily and ensure that Darcy didna die?"

"This isna the time for such talk," Ulrik stated. He didn't want to discuss any of his deeds—the bad, or the rare good.

Con blew out a long breath. *"I've done a lot of thinking since I saw you in the mountain. I sat down and tried to discern what Mikkel did and which transgressions were yours."*

"And?" Ulrik asked. Then kicked himself.

He didn't want to know. He didn't want to know. He didn—

"You had plenty of opportunities to kill mates. You

had even more chances to challenge Kings. Yet, you didna."

"Lest you forget, I nearly killed Rachel in Paris."

"Did you?" Con asked. *"I know you, Ulrik. I know you better than anyone else, and I know if you'd really wanted to kill Rachel, you would have. Nothing would've stopped you. Just as nothing will prevent you from ending Mikkel this night."*

Ulrik was glad he didn't know where Con was hiding because he just might go over there and beat the shit out of him. *"Stop trying to make me out to be good. We both know I'm no'. Nor am I redeemable."*

"Is that why you willna give your love to Eilish?"

"Leave her out of this," Ulrik stated in a low voice.

Con was silent for a moment. *"Such statements reveal your feelings, brother. You love her."*

"If you—"

Ulrik's thoughts ground to a halt when Mikkel appeared in the clearing. He was more than ready to face his uncle and put an end to the chaos that Mikkel brought with him everywhere he went.

"I can't believe you're still standing," Mikkel said with a shocked grin.

Ulrik fought not to shift and end this quickly "It's just us. Let's stop the pretending."

"Who's pretending?" Mikkel asked. "I've chosen to leave the guttural, vile sound of the Scots behind me."

"Ah, but you slip whenever you're angry. You can no' hide who you truly are."

Mikkel raised a brow. "And you haven't been hiding? All this time, you've had your magic. Why haven't you attacked Con? Why haven't you claimed the ultimate throne?"

"I wanted to hurt Con. I wanted to strip him of everything as I'd been stripped."

Those words weren't lies. They were what had made Ulrik plot out every detail of his plan to take the Kings from Con one by one until everyone turned their back on Con.

Mikkel made a sound that was half snort, half laugh. "Keep telling yourself that. I know it's because you didn't have the balls to take Con out."

"And you do?"

"Yep. Right after I dispatch you."

Ulrik held out his arms. "What are you waiting for?"

"Where's the Druid?"

He cocked his head to the side, wondering why Mikkel would bring her up now. "Eilish? How am I supposed to know?"

"You had sex with her."

"Just like I have sex with a lot of women. My goal was to woo her away from you. I'd say I was successful."

Mikkel's smile was tight. "That is going to be the last time you take something that's mine. Know that once you're dead, I'm going to make the Druid suffer."

"You say that as if I care what happens to her." Those words were harder to say than Ulrik had imagined.

The slow smile on his uncle's face was filled with confidence and a wealth of contempt. "You're going to die. Our battle will be over before it begins. You're not healing, which will slow you."

"If that's the case, then you will want to gloat over the things you've done. Like having my father killed."

Mikkel threw back his head and laughed. "Oh, dear boy. I didn't have him killed. It's not my fault that he went into that meeting thinking it was a peace talk. It's not my fault that he didn't prepare for a battle. It's not my fault that Ualan didn't make sure no one betrayed him."

Ulrik didn't feel any better now that his fears were

confirmed. It only made him want to inflict as much pain on Mikkel as he could.

"You thought you'd be King."

Mikkel rocked his head back and forth as he glanced at the sky. "That I did. After all, you were so young."

"It infuriated you that I became the next King of Silvers."

"You could say that."

Ulrik clutched his fake wounds. "That's why you tried to leave the family."

"You disgusted me. You still do. I couldn't set up your death so soon. It would look suspicious. So I had to get away."

"Why no' challenge me? Were you that much of a coward?"

Mikkel scratched at the side of his eye near his temple. "You call me a coward. I say I'm smart. I'm not going to put myself in a situation where I won't win."

"So you cheat."

"I do what has to be done. That's what will make me a great Dragon King. No one will remember you when I'm finished. And once I kill Con, I'll become the greatest King of Dragon Kings that has ever ruled."

Ulrik couldn't believe such a snake had been in his midst for so long, and he'd been blind to it. It would give him great joy to see the life drain from Mikkel, but he needed something first.

"Nala."

Mikkel sighed loudly. "Still holding onto that garbage, I see."

"You turned her against me."

"How could I do that? I was a dragon, remember."

Ulrik simply stared at him. If Mikkel had pulled it off, he wouldn't be able to hold back crowing over such a feat. And Ulrik didn't have long to wait.

Mikkel laughed and clapped his hands slowly. "I wondered if you'd ever figure it out. Yes, I instigated Nala's betrayal. You made it so easy. You didn't seem to care what your family thought as you spent more and more time with the humans. Then you asked one to be your mate. I knew then that you had no right to be a King.

"Back then, it was easy to find Druids. I was able to locate one who was a bit daft. It was his madness that convinced him to talk to me. With his magic and some willpower, he was able to allow me to take over a human's body for a time."

Ulrik shook his head. "That's no' possible. We would've known."

"I'd gone away. You didn't realize it because your prick was buried deep in that mortal," Mikkel said, his lips peeled back in a sneer. "But it happened. I wasn't sure how long it would last, so I told him of my plans. Though, to be fair, he thought it was only going to be a joke played upon you."

The more Ulrik heard, the sicker to his stomach he became.

"And I watched it all unfold," Mikkel said with a wide grin. "It was glorious."

"You knew she couldna kill me."

"Of course. But I knew it would destroy your happiness, and you'd have no choice but to make an example of her. Not to mention, you'd be reminded that your true loyalties lay with dragons, not the mortals."

Ulrik made sure to remain in the same spot instead of moving too much to keep Mikkel believing he was gravely injured. "I would still have been King."

"You would've been heartbroken, which would've made it easy for me to find a way to set you up as I did your father."

"You had everything figured out. Even going so far as

to remain behind after the dragons were called to cross the dragon bridge to another realm. Why wait so long to approach me?"

Mikkel twisted his lips as he shrugged. "I intended to kill you a few centuries ago, but then I realized you could help me. I knew you would keep Con's focus on you while I positioned myself close enough to take him out."

"Would you shut him up already?" Con said in Ulrik's head. *"Also, Mikkel's plot with Harriett was just as you said. Sebastian and the others stopped her before she reached the village."*

Ulrik spotted movement behind Mikkel. When his eyes caught a glimpse of Eilish, he wanted to rush to her side. By sheer will alone, he remained where he was. "I believe you overestimated."

"Which part?"

The fact his uncle seemed genuinely curious baffled Ulrik. "All of it."

"Look at you," Mikkel said with a chuckle. "I won't even be winded when I finish with you."

Ulrik dropped his arm and stood straight. With a wave of his hand, the magic making it appear as if he were still bleeding and wounded vanished.

Mikkel's brows snapped together. "That's no' possible."

"Is it no'? Oh, and by the way, Harriett willna be harming anyone in the village."

At his words, Con stepped out from behind a tree and came to stand beside him. Ulrik might not admit it aloud, but it felt great to have his old friend with him once more.

"No," Mikkel stated.

Con grinned. "Oh, aye."

"This ends tonight," Ulrik said. *"You* end tonight."

Mikkel widened his eyes and bent over as he began to laugh. "Did you really believe I'd come on my own?"

"Did you really believe *we* would?" Ulrik replied. He

then let out a shrill whistle. Immediately, there were eight replies from different locations around them.

Con raised a brow. "In case you were no' sure, that means all of the mortals you brought with you have been detained by Ulrik's men."

"You've no' thought of everything," Mikkel said, his anger showing in his brogue.

Eilish sent a blast of magic into Mikkel's back, knocking him forward.

Ulrik closed the distance between them and ripped the finger rings off Mikkel before tossing them to Eilish. "Go. Now."

"Oh, I doona think so," Mikkel said as he rolled over and launched a volley of magic into Eilish that sent her somersaulting backward into a tree before she fell unconscious to the ground.

That's all it took for the rage to explode inside Ulrik.

He swung his head toward Mikkel. "Prepare to die. Painfully."

CHAPTER FORTY-FOUR

There was no hesitation when Ulrik landed his first punch, accented with a heavy dose of magic, into Mikkel's face. Thankfully, Con didn't interfere.

Because Ulrik wanted every piece of Mikkel for himself.

He wasn't angry because his uncle had turned Nala against him. He didn't resent that her betrayal had turned into a war that eventually led to his banishment. He wasn't even mad at Mikkel for using him.

But he was enraged that Mikkel hurt Eilish. Again.

No one laid a hand on her without feeling Ulrik's wrath.

No one.

He looked down in disgust at his uncle. Ulrik reared back, ready to deliver another blow when Mikkel punched the inside of his knee.

Ulrik felt it snap. He rolled to the side and came up to his feet as his bones quickly mended. But the feeling of dragon and Druid magic left behind hinted at something else—Fae magic.

And not just any Fae magic, Light magic.

"Con!" Ulrik bellowed in warning without taking his eyes off Mikkel.

His uncle grinned, blood showing on his teeth and lips from the hit Ulrik had delivered. "You've no idea what's coming."

Ulrik deflected another strike of magic from Mikkel before kicking him in the face and stepping on his throat. "You could defeat every Dragon King on this realm, and you'd still never be a King."

Mikkel used more of his mixed magic to toss him away. It came at Ulrik so quickly, he didn't have time to dodge it. He landed near Eilish, but she hadn't moved. Ulrik fought not to touch her to see if she was still alive. But it was a battle he couldn't win.

He put his hand beneath her nose and felt her breath. Relief rushed through him at such a high speed that he grew dizzy. He grabbed the cuff from Eilish's wrist and glanced over at Con to see him staring intently at a spot before him. He gave a whistle and tossed the cuff to Con, who snatched it out of the air without looking at him. Ulrik frowned when the space before Con began to shimmer.

A moment later, Usaeil appeared.

A blast of magic hit Ulrik in the left shoulder. He rolled away, gritting his teeth at the pain. But there was no time to think about how his body recoiled from such a mix of magic, or why it felt as if something had wrapped around each individual bone and was crushing them all while pulling his muscles apart because Mikkel was preparing another assault.

Ulrik jumped to his feet with his teeth bared and a growl. He deflected blow after blow of magic that his uncle directed at him. He never took his eyes off Mikkel, never lost his focus.

And with each blast, Ulrik took a step closer to Mikkel.

It irked him that his uncle had managed to increase the power of his magic to the point where it wouldn't be easy to kill him. But it would make the celebration that much sweeter once the deed was done.

Mikkel didn't seem phased as his cocky grin grew. Ulrik couldn't wait to knock that smile away once and for all.

"I think I should've gone to Usaeil sooner," his uncle shouted over their magic and the clashing of swords.

Ulrik looked at Con to find him and Usaeil fighting. It wasn't for show either. It was a down and dirty sword fight that also included magic. At the moment, Usaeil appeared to be winning, but Ulrik knew Con's ploy. He'd helped Con perfect it. Soon, his friend would turn the tables and have Usaeil at his mercy.

"All the queen wanted was Rhi," Mikkel said with a laugh.

Ulrik swung his gaze back to his uncle. "You should learn when to keep your nose out of other people's business."

"Why aren't you fighting me?" Mikkel taunted. "I think it's because you know I'm going to win and you're prolonging the inevitable."

"Will you shut up?" Ulrik shouted.

He waited until Mikkel sent another volley of magic. This time, Ulrik didn't deflect it. He turned it back toward Mikkel and added his own punch to it. The blast barreled into his uncle, knocking him flat on his back.

Ulrik jumped the short distance that separated them, landing with a foot on either side of Mikkel's chest.

Getting knocked out sucked. Royally.

Eilish curled her fingers and felt them sink into decaying leaves and cold, damp earth. Her ears were ringing, and it took her a second to realize that it was sounds of battle that filled the air.

Then she heard a loud war cry. She grinned because she recognized it as Ulrik's.

She got her hands beneath her and pushed herself up onto her knees. Something else had been added to Mikkel's magic, and it left quite the aftershock. Her bones felt like rubber, and her muscles like Jell-O. Thankfully, her magic responded quickly to help push out whatever Mikkel's had done to her.

Her gaze caught on something near her hand. When her eyes finally focused, she spotted her finger rings. She quickly put them on, her mother's magic swirling around her, strengthening her own. God, how she'd missed the rings.

With effort, she raised her head. Her gaze landed on Ulrik, who stood over Mikkel, ready to deliver a killing strike. But the clang of swords drew her attention. Eilish turned her gaze to see Con fighting a woman. The sight of the female gave Eilish pause because she looked familiar.

"Your sword can't hurt me," the woman said.

Con didn't reply as he parried, then pivoted and delivered a crushing downward swing that knocked the blade from the female's hand.

Though it appeared that both Ulrik and Con had the upper hand, Eilish saw the female's gaze was on Mikkel, even as he glared at Ulrik. Those two were working together, which meant they had a plan.

Eilish used the tree behind her to help her get to her feet. All the while, she gathered her magic, letting it swirl and escalate until even each individual strand of her hair was infused with it. She didn't know how long she'd been out, but it didn't matter. She was awake now and ready to do whatever was needed.

She faced the two fighting pairs. Then she put her hands in front of her, palms down until her hands shook from the force of her magic. She flipped them over, palms facing outward until they were even with her chest. With her teeth gritted, she took a step back and flung the magic—not at Mikkel, but at the woman.

As soon as she released the blast, the female sent a ball of magic hurtling toward Ulrik. Eilish didn't wait to see if her strike hit its mark. She rushed toward Ulrik. While Eilish pushed the bubble of magic away, Mikkel maneuvered it toward Ulrik.

She saw Ulrik jerk when the blast slammed into his chest. Then, suddenly, everything was spinning. She didn't know which way was up. Eilish used her magic to try and find her feet again, but it took a second for her to right herself.

That's when she found Ulrik on the ground with Mikkel over him. She couldn't believe what she was seeing. Her head swiveled toward Con and the woman to find Con with a hand around the female's throat while she smirked at Eilish.

In the next second, the woman was standing before Eilish. It was instinct that had Eilish putting up a shield, which is the only thing that saved her from the knife aimed at her heart.

"Usaeil!" Con bellowed and squeezed his hand tighter.

Holy shit! Eilish couldn't believe she'd been fighting the Queen of the Light.

Usaeil spread her fingers wide as she pounded Eilish with Fae magic. "You're nothing, Druid. Just a stepping stone to get what I want."

No matter how hard she tried, Eilish couldn't withstand the force of the queen's magic. She felt something trickle from her ears and run down her neck right before her eardrums burst. Despite her efforts, she couldn't hold back the bellow of pain.

The crush of Fae magic sent her to her knees, but Eilish didn't back down. She kept up her shield. She couldn't win this battle, but she wouldn't go out easily.

"Enough!" Con yelled and tackled Usaeil.

Then they disappeared.

As soon as the Fae magic was gone, Eilish took in a breath and returned her focus to Mikkel and Ulrik. There was no sign of Mikkel, but Ulrik wasn't moving. She started toward him but only took one step before there was a hand around her throat.

Mikkel moved so fast she hadn't seen or heard him. And now he had the upper hand. Quite literally. It was around her throat. There was no one to help her, but she wasn't scared. Because Mikkel wasn't going to hurt her ever again.

"What a fool I was to believe you could help me," Mikkel said with a sneer.

Eilish merely smiled before she kneed him in the balls. He instantly released her, bending over from the excruciating pain. She couldn't help but laugh. Who would've thought that a simple kick to the balls would beat Mikkel?

Her laughter died a quick death when he straightened with the knife Usaeil had tried to use on her. Eilish raised her hands, magic at the ready, as the blade came toward her. Her shields did nothing to stop it either.

"NO!" came a loud roar.

Then Mikkel was flying backwards, and Ulrik was on his feet, running toward her. All she could see was his tattoo, and she knew this was the dream she'd been having. This was when she would die.

Ulrik wrapped his arms around her as something thunked loudly. Before she could react, he released her and turned around, a growl rumbling in his chest. That's when she saw the knife sticking out from his back.

In the next instant, Ulrik shifted, the blade falling to the ground. She smiled at the sight of him. Mikkel frantically threw magic, but it didn't seem to faze Ulrik in the least.

Eilish watched, mesmerized, as Ulrik drew in a deep breath. The silver scales on his chest grew bright. Mikkel touched his fingers together, forgetting that he no longer had the finger rings. Then he turned and ran.

But it was too late. Ulrik released the fire. The bright red and orange flames swallowed Mikkel, and his screams were quickly silenced. When Ulrik halted the fire, there was nothing left of his uncle but ash.

Ulrik turned his head around to her, staring at her with unblinking onyx eyes.

"I did intend to leave like we agreed," she told him. "You can't be mad at me."

He huffed loudly in response.

She walked to his front leg and put her hand on his scales. "It's over now. Mikkel is gone for good."

Ulrik shook his head before he returned to human form. He stood naked in the moonlight with his black hair free and his gold eyes intent. "It's no' quite over."

"Meaning?"

He held out his hand. Once she'd taken it, he said, "I can no' take you with me where I'm going, but I'd like you to hold onto me."

She nodded as understanding dawned. He was going to the afterlife to find Mikkel and kill his soul. Eilish took his hand and smiled until his eyes closed. She held his hand with both of hers and waited.

It was only a few moments later that Ulrik's eyes opened. They were clear, as if all the hell he'd endured for untold centuries had been wiped away. "He'll never bother us again."

She smiled. It was over for her, but what about Ulrik? Could a vendetta thousands of years in the making be put to rest? Regardless, she would stand beside him. Always. "What happens now?"

Ulrik shrugged. "I'm no' sure. I'm no longer banished."

"I know," she said and threw her arms around him. "It's about damn time."

"I didna expect it."

She leaned back, smiling. "You can return to Dreagan now."

"Can I?"

"What?" Surely, she'd misheard him.

"I've done terrible things."

She put a finger to his lips. "I'm no' saying it'll be easy, but you have friends there. Nikolai, Sebastian, Anson, and Con, just to name a few."

"I've wanted nothing more than to make Dreagan my home again. Now . . . I'm no' so sure I can."

"I see." She licked her lips and glanced away. "Do you still intend to challenge Con?"

Ulrik's gaze looked past her. Eilish's stomach fell to her feet when she turned and found Con behind her.

"I gather the ash is Mikkel," Con said.

Ulrik nodded once. "It is."

Eilish didn't want them to fight. She didn't want Ulrik to lose, but she didn't want him to win either. Because she knew if he did, he'd never forgive himself for killing his friend.

"Where's Usaeil?" she asked Con.

The King of Kings blew out a harsh breath. "I'm afraid things with her will need to be settled verra soon."

"She tried to kill me," Eilish said.

Ulrik's nostrils flared. "She'll pay for that."

"Usaeil has a lot to answer for," Con stated in a tight

voice. "We'll have to get in line to take our pound of flesh from the queen."

Eilish looked between the two men. "Behind who?"

"Rhi," Ulrik said, his lips flattening.

Con grunted. "I get to tell her about this. She's going to be pissed that she wasna here to fight."

"Maybe we doona tell her."

Eilish rolled her eyes. "That's a mistake. Tell her before she finds out and kicks both of your asses for keeping it from her."

There was a stretch of silence before Con said, "I'll be at Dreagan, waiting."

Eilish saw him touch Ulrik's cuff that was now on his wrist. After he'd vanished, she turned to Ulrik. "You gave it to him?"

"During the fight, in case he needed it."

"What about you?"

"I didna need it."

She drew in a deep breath and slowly released it. "So. Dreagan?"

"Dreagan."

Sadness gripped her, but she didn't waste any words trying to talk him out of it. All she could do now was pray. She took his hand in hers and touched her finger rings together.

CHAPTER FORTY-FIVE

A decision had to be made. Ulrik no longer had a reason not to challenge Con. He hadn't wanted to think about it. But he didn't have a choice.

In seconds, he stood in the glen between his mountain and Con's. He was inside his mountain with the Silvers recently, but he hadn't walked the grounds of Dreagan since . . . well, a long, long time ago.

Con stood across the glen about fifty feet away, waiting.

The memories that rose up were like a tsunami, yet they didn't cause as much pain as they once had. Ulrik could stand beneath the sky, once more welcome.

The moment Eilish released his hand, he missed her touch. He turned his head to her. Her green-gold eyes held his without an ounce of censor. She didn't want him to fight Con, but she was willing to stand beside him no matter what decision he made.

There were things he should say, things he wanted to say, but he didn't know how. Or if he could.

Eilish's lips lifted in a sad smile before she gave him a soft kiss on his cheek. Then she was gone.

He stared at the spot for several minutes. It hadn't taken him long to get used to having her near. At one time, it had unsettled him that he liked her company. Now, it didn't even stir so much as a hiccup.

Ulrik drew in a deep breath and faced Con. All the anger and hate that had kept him going for so long seemed to be tapped out. As if someone had removed the stopper and released everything.

"You have to actually say the words," Con said.

Ulrik instead took in the vista he hadn't seen in ages. Even in the darkness, it was spectacular. The sky was turning gray, signaling the approach of sunrise. When was the last time he'd seen the sun break the horizon on Dreagan?

Finally, Ulrik returned his gaze to Con. "Do you know how long I wanted you dead?"

"Since the moment I bound your magic."

"Nay. No' until you banished me."

"I did what I thought was best."

Ulrik glanced at the ground. "Aye."

"What are you waiting for, then? Issue your challenge," Con urged.

"I didna lie all those years ago when you tried to force me to challenge you. I never wanted your position. I didna then. I doona now."

Con's brows snapped together. "What are you saying?"

"So much has changed, and I didna even see it happening."

"You mean Eilish."

"I mean everything." Ulrik ran his hand through his hair as the weariness settled around him. "Mikkel is dead. I should be rejoicing."

"But?"

Ulrik shrugged as he shook his head. "He was my family. And I did some terrible things, as well."

"Doona compare yourself to him. Mikkel's actions were all for him to be King of Dragon Kings and wipe out humanity."

"I wanted that, as well."

"Do you still?"

Ulrik opened his mouth to reply, then paused.

"My point," Con continued. "You didna hurt innocents. And I still hold to my opinion that you didna truly wish to harm any of the Kings or their mates. Your actions were based on a betrayal—from humans and me."

Ulrik dug his bare toes into the earth. The smell of rain hung in the air. "Everything that drove me before no longer seems to matter. All the hate is gone."

"It's Eilish's love."

He shook his head, turning away. "Doona say that."

"Since when did you no' want to hear the truth?"

"She deserves better."

"She deserves you."

Ulrik swiveled his head to Con. "I willna challenge you. Maybe I got it all out of my system fighting Mikkel."

"Or maybe you began to love."

"What about you?"

Con crossed his arms over his chest. "We're discussing you right now, no' me."

"I'd like to change the subject."

"No' going to happen. Go find Eilish. I'd tell you to find some clothes, but you'll probably take them off as soon as you see her."

Ulrik couldn't smile at the jest. He felt sick to his stomach. "I doona know how to be what she needs."

"She needs you," Con said, his arms dropping to his

sides. "You're all she wants. She'll be there to help you—if you allow her."

"She was the first person I trusted," Ulrik admitted. "It's what allowed me to trust you."

Con grinned, the corners of his black eyes crinkling. "Then I should thank her."

Ulrik couldn't quite believe he was welcome at Dreagan once more. He wanted to go to Eilish, but he couldn't stop looking at the sky.

"Fly," Con urged. "You've more than earned it."

Ulrik didn't need to be told twice. He shifted and jumped as he spread his wings. It only took a few flaps before he was in the air. He flew around mountains, dipped down to touch the tips of his wings in the loch, and dropped low in the glen. The joy that blossomed quickly spread, surrounding him.

It felt so good to be flying that Ulrik didn't think he'd ever touch the ground again. Then he thought of Eilish. She was the reason he would not only return to human form but also do it gladly.

Movement came up on his right. Ulrik looked over when he spied gold scales. He met Con's gaze as they maneuvered through the mountains as they'd done eons ago and watched the sun crest the horizon.

To be flying with Con again was glorious. Somehow, despite everything, there had been forgiveness on both sides. Through sorrow and pain, their friendship, their brotherhood was stronger than ever.

Their family was stronger, as well.

"You do know we can be picked up by satellites," Ulrik said through their metal link.

Con laughed. *"That was taken care of long ago. Besides, we have a friend in MI5."*

"Ah. Henry." How could Ulrik have forgotten the mortal?

"He's been a great asset. It's something I never thought I'd say about a human."

Ulrik diverted and turned toward the manor and Dreagan mountain. They came in from the back, flying low. While Con flew into the cave opening, Ulrik took one more loop around. As he made his way to the entrance, he spotted Eilish. She wore a wide grin while watching him. But his heart ached for her because, while she wasn't the only one who was at the cave opening, she stood alone, apart from all the others.

There were many at Dreagan who wouldn't want either him or Eilish there. While he could endure the anger, he couldn't put Eilish through that.

Ulrik landed just outside the cave. He motioned for her to follow him inside as he walked past the others to where Con was tugging on a pair of jeans.

There was a part of Ulrik who still wanted to call to his Silvers and wake them. But he didn't. Not only wouldn't it be fair to the other Kings who didn't have their dragons, but the Silvers wouldn't be able to live freely. They'd be kept hidden, trapped in a world that could never know about them. It was far better for them to remain sleeping until another dragon bridge could be opened.

While the Kings and their mates gathered around, Ulrik looked at Eilish. Who would've known that a mortal Druid would be the one to pull him back from the precipice of war?

He shifted into his human form, ignoring the cheers from the others. Con tossed him a pair of jeans that he quickly donned. Out of the corner of his eye, Ulrik saw something coming at him. He raised his hand and snatched the object from the air.

As soon as his fingers wrapped around the metal, he knew it was the cuff. Ulrik returned it to his wrist and gave Con a nod of thanks. Then Con called the others to gather around him.

Ulrik made his way to Eilish. He slid his hands around her and pulled her close before kissing her deeply. Thoroughly.

She pulled back, giving him a look as if he had just saved the world. "You didn't challenge him."

"I couldna."

"I'm glad," she said, running her fingers through his hair.

Behind him, the conversation grew louder so that he maneuvered her to a secluded spot.

She laughed and raised a brow. "What's wrong? Shout your victory over Mikkel and the banishment being lifted long and loud, I say. Or you could fly around some more because that was hot."

"Is that so?" he asked with a grin.

"Oh, definitely."

Though he'd known it for a while, it wasn't until that moment that he knew he couldn't part from Eilish. Ever. She was his mate, the one who would hold his heart for eternity. The love of his life.

"You know, I've been lamenting everything Mikkel did," she said. "But we can also look at it as a blessing. Without his interference, you might have challenged Con."

"And I wouldna have met you."

She grinned up at him seductively. "There is that, as well."

He blinked and looked at her jacket again. "Is that chainmail?"

"Yep. My kind of armor," she said with a slight lift of one shoulder.

"You're an amazing woman."

A dark brow arched as she gave him a scathing look. "You're just now realizing that?"

He chuckled at her teasing tone. "I knew it from the first moment we spoke at Graves. But I like to keep such things to myself."

"I know." She spoke softly, all jesting gone.

Ulrik shifted uneasily, not quite sure what the emotion was that made him like he might be sick. Then it hit him—nervousness. Nothing and no one had made him feel anything close to that in so long. It surprised him.

"Your power intrigued me. Your beauty enthralled me. Your courage captivated me. I thought I knew all there was to know about mortals. Then I met you." He swallowed as his heart rate increased, and he was struck by another dose of anxiety. "You acknowledge the darkness within you, but it doesna frighten you. Nor does it tempt you."

"You told me not to let it." She cleared her throat and touched his tattoo when her gaze lowered to his chest. "I began having dreams about a man with a dragon tattoo—this exact tat—before I came to Ireland. I knew that man was going to end my life, though I didn't know his face, only the tattoo."

Ulrik jerked at her words. "Why did you no' mention this before?"

"I didn't know it was you until we had sex."

"And you didna push me away? I doona understand."

She licked her lips and looked up at him. "Because of the way you made me feel. I went in knowing that you could be the one to kill me, but I didn't care. I wanted to know you. All of you. Then, last night, my dream became a reality."

"How?" he asked, his heart thudding in his chest.

"You rushed me when Mikkel threw the knife that

was meant for me. So, while I thought that you would end my life all of these years, you were actually my savior."

He cupped her face with his hands, utterly amazed by the woman before him. "I should let you go. I should send you back to Ireland and tell you to get on with your life."

"But you won't." Though her words were fierce, there was doubt in her gaze.

"Nay, I won't. Because I can no'. I need you."

Her eyes filled with tears that she hastily blinked away.

To his shock, his throat clogged with emotion. "Doona be too happy. Our lives will be difficult. There will be some who doona want either us of here."

"I don't care, as long as I'm with you. I'll endure anything with you by my side."

"Hold your words until you're faced with it."

She smiled and shook her head as more tears gathered. "My heart doesn't change so easily. There isn't much about my life that has been easy, but the one thing I know above anything else is that I love you."

Hearing her say it again now that he could admit that he did have feelings for her was freeing, as if all the chains around his heart had been shattered in one fell swoop. He suspected her words and actions had been chipping away at them for some time, but that didn't matter. The important thing was that he was no longer dead inside.

Because a Druid with green-gold eyes and steely determination brought him back to life.

"I love you," he whispered.

The tears that she'd been holding back began to fall. But it was the joy on her face that had him smiling. He lowered his head for a kiss, sealing their words with desire.

Suddenly, there was a thunderous cheer behind them. Ulrik turned with Eilish still in his arms to see all of the

Dragon Kings and mates shouting and clapping. For them.

Con stood off to the side, smiling.

Ulrik knew then that he'd never been meant for Nala. His true mate was Eilish. It had taken death, banishment, madness, and countless centuries for him to finally have the happiness and peace he'd always wanted.

As the Kings and mates surrounded them, he exchanged a look with Eilish. When everyone began to talk at once, he started laughing and held onto her tighter. His brave, beautiful Druid was unwavering in her loyalty and steadfast in her courage. She might bend, but she would never break.

The life before them would have its bumps, but Ulrik knew without a doubt that their love would only grow stronger.

A Dragon King and a Druid.

And a love for the ages.

CHAPTER FORTY-SIX

It had been a long time since Ulrik wore a smile. And he couldn't seem to stop. He wasn't even irked that Con had taken him from Eilish's arms so early in the morning.

His steps were light as he walked the tunnels to Con's mountain. To say he'd been shocked to discover that Con had kept a room for him at the manor all these years was an understatement.

After the cheers, Ulrik had issued an apology to all those he'd harmed in his quest for vengeance. He told Lily how he'd saved her and, to his surprise, she rose up and gave him a kiss on the cheek. Darcy and Rachel and even Sophie weren't as forgiving. Though, they did accept his apology, which was a step in the right direction.

There was a homecoming with the other Kings, and it was easy for Ulrik to put his old hurts behind him and look to the future. He'd looked over at one point and saw Eilish returning Kinsey's memories, too.

Then Ulrik saw Nikolai, who had hurried back to Dreagan with Esther and Henry. That's when the celebration truly began. Barrels of whisky kept for special celebrations were taken out of storage.

Amidst laughter and smiles, new memories were being made to wipe away the past. It was a fresh start that Ulrik hadn't realized he needed or wanted. And it had all happened with Eilish by his side.

As soon as they were able, they'd slipped away and spent the rest of the day and night in Ulrik's chamber making love and talking. It had been a truly glorious day. One filled with wonder, contentment, love, and peace. He'd never had one like it before, but he knew there was more coming.

Because he had Eilish.

Ulrik had also searched out Eireen's soul. He let her know that her daughter was safe and loved, and that the Duffys would never harm anyone else. He'd spent a long time with Eireen, speaking about Patrick, Donal, and Eilish.

The tears Eilish had cried when he relayed the message of love from her mum were ones of love and peace. And closure.

As he reached Con's mountain, Ulrik began searching for him, going lower and lower beneath the ground until he finally found him in a small cavern. He sat staring at the weapon he kept hidden from all.

Ulrik stopped at the entrance to the cave and leaned against the wall. "I should remind you that it isna verra nice to drag a man from the comfort of his woman's arms so early in the morning."

Con didn't turn to look at him.

"If you wanted to show me the weapon, I already know about it. I found it years ago," Ulrik said.

Con had his hands in his pants' pockets when he slowly turned to face Ulrik. "I know. I called you down here to show you this."

When Con took a step to the side, Ulrik's gaze moved to where the weapon was supposed to be. Only, the spot was empty.

He pushed away from the wall in shock and hurried toward Con for a closer look. "When? How?"

"I was hoping you had it."

He shot Con a flat look. "I admit, I thought about it, but I didna take the weapon."

"Then who did?"

"We'll know soon enough."

Con raked a hand through his hair. "Just when I thought things would be better after taking one enemy off the list, it looks like we have another. And they have the weapon that can kill us."

"Notify the others. Everyone needs to be on high alert."

"I'd hoped to deal with Usaeil today. It looks like that will have to wait," Con said and walked out of the cavern.

Ulrik fell into step beside him. "Rhi willna be postponed much longer."

"I know."

"What happened after you and Usaeil vanished from the battle?"

Con blew out a frustrated breath. "She brought us somewhere in Ireland. Then she got naked. When I showed no interest, she fought me again."

"She's unhinged."

"She gave some of her magic to your uncle," Con stated. "She's more than unhinged. And you doona need to say it. I know it was a mistake to take her to my bed."

Ulrik glanced at his friend. "She's been a hassle while trying to get you to make her your mate. When she stops that and decides war is the answer, then you need to worry."

"Well, then I'm worried. She officially declared war on me when I refused her this last time."

Ulrik halted and jerked his head to Con. "Why did you no' say anything?"

"We were celebrating your return."

"Con—"

He hurriedly spoke over Ulrik. "You deserved the time. I just wish I had more to give you."

"I have eternity."

"So you've asked Eilish to be your mate?"

Ulrik grinned as he thought about his Druid. "That's my plan for today."

"Then get your arse to her and do it. Our enemies are no' going anywhere."

Ulrik didn't need to be told twice. Not wanting to take the time to walk back to Dreagan Manor, he touched his cuff and was once more inside his chamber.

"There you are," Eilish said as she stretched beneath the covers after briefly cracking open an eye.

He walked to the bed and climbed in. Pulling her into his arms, he couldn't stop staring at the sleepy look on her face. "Are you awake?"

"Uh-huh." She blinked up at him. "See."

"We talked about a lot of things yesterday."

She nodded, frowning. "Yep. Like the fact that you haven't watched *Guardians of the Galaxy*. We need to remedy that. Like today. Actually, I need to baptize you in the entire Marvel Universe."

"As you wish. But . . . there is something else."

"Oh, yeah?" she asked with a grin. She rolled so that she rested her arms on his chest. "What's that?"

He tugged at her hair. "You being my mate."

"Mate?" Her face grew serious.

"I want you with me for eternity, Eilish. I know it's a big step, and we can wait if that's what you want."

"No," she stated and shifted so she was sitting cross-legged, facing him. "I thought it was what you'd want. You know, to make sure I didn't change my mind or fall out of love with you."

Ulrik yanked her down atop him before rolling her onto her back. "I know what I feel. And I trust you."

"I love you so much."

"So, you'll be my mate? My wife?"

She nodded, her smile wide. "Gladly."

"Get ready, Druid, because now that I have you, I'm no' letting go."

Hooking her leg over him, she flipped him onto his back to straddle him. With her dark hair in disarray, she looked down at him with desire. "That's a good thing since I don't plan on ever letting you go either."

"I love you," he whispered. It felt wonderful to finally say the words.

And the smile on Eilish's face was even better.

She leaned down until their lips were nearly touching. "I love you."

He captured her lips and let the outside world fall away. Con was right, their enemies weren't going anywhere, and he had the most beautiful woman in the world in his arms.

His woman.

His Druid.

His love.

EPILOGUE

Two days later...

V stood with his arms crossed over his chest, his gaze locked on a golden eagle diving from the sky as it went in for a kill. At one time, the dragons had been so free. He'd never get used to how things were now, but he also knew there was very little hope of the dragons ever returning.

But there was something he wanted, something that the mortals had taken from him.

"V," Ulrik said as he strode up.

He dropped his arms and faced Ulrik. "How does it feel to be back?"

"It's no' fully sunk in yet."

It was odd to see that easy smile back on Ulrik's face. "I'm glad things have been mended. It was no' the same without you here."

"I want you to know that I'm going to help you."

V frowned. "With what?"

"Finding your sword. Con and I agree that it should've been seen to ages ago."

V glanced at the mountains, his hands fisted at his

sides. He'd been planning to leave Dreagan in the morning to begin his search again. Now, he wouldn't have to do it alone. His elation dimmed when he thought of the threats against Dreagan—especially the knowledge that someone had stolen the weapon that could kill them all.

"We can no'," he said.

Ulrik clapped a hand on V's shoulder. "We can, and we are. We may no' be able to go after it right away, but Ryder is already searching. Roman has begun using his power over metals to search for it, as well."

V felt his lips curl into a smile. "I'm no' complete without my sword."

"You willna have to wait much longer, my friend. You've suffered enough."

V nodded as Ulrik walked away. He had endured a lot since his sword was taken, and the humans responsible were long dead. But whoever was still hiding it would pay a heavy price.

Con watched Vaughn drive off with Harriett Smythe and Stanley Upton to meet up with Henry's connection in MI5 that would see the two prosecuted for the murders of those who spoke against Kyvor. It was a good feeling to have another enemy—even a mortal one—removed from the playing field.

He turned and made his way back into the manor before climbing the stairs to his office. He was still uneasy about his conversation with Rhi. The Light Fae hadn't taken the news about Usaeil well. Rhi didn't utter a word in response, but he'd felt her rage in the way her silver eyes glared at him.

The battle with Usaeil was coming quicker than he wanted. It wasn't that he feared fighting the queen. In fact, he was looking forward to it. What worried him was Rhi. Things could either go well. . . .

Or they could be disastrous.

If anything happened to Rhi, Con knew the other Kings would rise up. And so would the Warriors and Druids. Then the battle with Usaeil would turn into a war with the Light and even possibly the Dark.

Keeping that away from the mortals was a nightmare in the making.

He ran a hand down his face as he walked into his office. Then came to a halt when he found a petite woman with black hair standing near the window. She turned and pushed her glasses up her nose before straightening the jacket of her grey pantsuit.

"Ms. Engel," he said as he walked around his desk and sank into his chair. "I didna expect you. Please sit."

She clasped her hands before her. "I think I'd rather stand for this."

Blossom Engel had been in his employ for years. She'd been a dedicated assistant each time he attended the World Whisky Consortium, and she'd graciously extended those duties to Asher this last time. Prompt, intelligent, and always thinking ahead, Blossom wasn't exactly homely. She was simply someone who faded into the background as those in her position were supposed to do.

Still. There was something about her that ignited a spark of recognition, but no matter how hard he tried, Con could never figure out why. He'd even asked her once, but her replies had given him nothing to connect how he might know her.

"Is there a problem?" he asked.

She nodded slowly. "There is."

He shifted his head to try and see her eyes, but the way her glasses sat on her face made it tricky. "Perhaps you'd better tell me."

"It'll be easier to show you."

"Show?" he asked in confusion.

The word was barely out of his mouth before the dowdy Blossom Engel was gone, and in her place stood a striking woman with lavender eyes and long, thick black hair that fell to her waist. A black tulle gown accented with a pale green underskirt graced her amazing body.

He slowly got to his feet as his gaze ran up and down her. It was then he felt the magic. It was unlike anything he'd sensed in a very long time. There were hints of Fae in it, but also something different . . . something stronger.

This wasn't the first time he'd felt such power. In fact, he had experienced it on multiple occasions. How had he missed it? How had he not connected the dots that led right to her?

"I wanted to get to know you before I showed you who I am," she said. "I wanted to do it some time ago, but the longer I held off, the harder it became to tell you."

Con narrowed his eyes at her, a mixture of anger and worry filling him. "And just who *are* you?"

"My name is Erith, but most know me as Death."

"Death?" Reapers. Con should've known.

Her lips curved into a smile. "I've watched you for a long time, Constantine. A very long time. Even before I first came to you. That initial visit was more than I expected, and I tried to stay away, but you and the other Kings intrigue me."

"So you returned without bothering to tell me who you were?" He didn't care that his tone was full of indignation.

"It was never meant to be harmful or disrespectful in any way. I admire you. You've done well with what has happened to your brethren. I'm also pleased to see that you and Ulrik have set aside your differences."

"What do you want?" he demanded. The idea that another being had been watching him and pretending to be an employee grated on his already stretched nerves.

"I know you're angry," she said. "I'm sorry for that. I come to you now for a couple of reasons. One, I want to help you. And two, my Reapers have already visited you."

The Reapers again.

She sighed, her shoulders dropping slightly. "Cael."

Con raised a brow. A moment later, the Reaper appeared by Erith's side. Con glared at the two of them.

Cael looked between Death and Con before he told Con, "I did say I'd figure out a way to prove to you who we were."

Fuck. Con missed the days when there was nothing going on, when there weren't a dozen enemies coming for them, and the year stretched endlessly before him. "So you did."

"Cael is only here to prove who I am," Erith said. "Con, I—"

But Cael interrupted her. "Where have you been?"

She didn't answer him, refused to even look at him. Con looked between the two. It made him feel better knowing that he wasn't the only one who had problems with those he led.

Erith continued talking. "Con, people are starting to look hard at Dreagan. Everyone here is reclusive, but it's making the mortals uneasy. You need to have some of the Kings get out and move among the humans, especially in the village. I'm afraid if you don't, the mortals might become a bigger problem for you."

Though he was loath to admit it, Erith had a point. He watched how Cael stared at Death while she continued to ignore him. The tension between them was palpable, and Con was interested to know what the story was between the two. But it would have to wait.

"Why do the Kings interest you?" he asked.

It was Cael who answered, "Because we're battling an enemy that may very well find his way to you."

"Bran," Ulrik said from the doorway.

Con looked past Erith and Cael to Ulrik. "How do you know?"

"Balladyn," Ulrik said as he walked into the office and came to stand beside Con. "And from what Balladyn told me, Bran is building quite an army of Dark Fae."

Cael's lips pressed into a thin line while Erith's gaze lowered briefly.

"I'll warn the others," Cael said before he vanished.

Erith blew out a breath. Her gaze landed on Con's wrists before she smiled slightly. "I hope my problem doesn't become yours, but I thought you should be warned."

"Can we help?" Con asked as he touched his dragon head cufflinks that she had given him. It wasn't as if he wanted another enemy, but Death and the Reapers could be good allies, and right now, the Kings needed those. Especially now that Usaeil had declared war on him.

Death gave him a benevolent smile. "There may come a time we can help each other. If you ever need me, just say my name. Good luck, Constantine," she said before she disappeared.

"Well, hell," Ulrik said with wide eyes. "Reapers."

"You're stuck on that? I'm wrapping my head around Death."

Isle of Eigg

The wind whipped around them as if attempting to remove them from the isle. But Henry knew that wouldn't happen. He stood off to the side and watched as his sister, Esther, and her mate, Nikolai, spoke to an old man.

Henry wanted to ignore whatever prophecy had proclaimed him the JusticeBringer, but it was rather difficult when he'd seen firsthand that Esther was the Truth-Seeker. Not to mention the dreams he'd been having.

It looked as if he didn't have a choice now. Ever since he'd been brought into the Dragon King world, he'd encountered some horrifying beings, magic he could barely comprehend, and love that transcended time.

Esther had found her love. Now, Henry just needed to convince Rhi that she was his. But that had been put on hold while he figured out the JusticBringer thing.

In truth, he was terrified. Esther had readily accepted her role, but Henry wasn't quite so thrilled. He just hoped he didn't fuck anything up. So much seemed to ride upon his shoulders now.

This went way beyond tracking the Dark. At least now, maybe he could be a part of the war instead of standing on the sidelines. Perhaps then Rhi would see that he was worthy of her love.

Dreagan

The rusted length of metal warmed before it became malleable in his hands. Roman worked the strip of iron into a ball before laying it on the table. He shaped it into the form of a dragon that would replace one of those hanging on the outside of the manor.

In his workshop within his mountain, Roman could forget about the numerous enemies the Kings had. He could pour his worries and anxiety into the various works of art that were displayed around Dreagan, Laith's pub, and the village.

Next up was the sign he'd been asked to make for the village's Big Brother group. They'd tried to pay him, but

Roman didn't need money. Besides, the children needed it much more than he did.

He immersed himself in the metalwork, molding it this way and that until it formed exactly what he wanted. If he couldn't have his Light Blues with him, he had to have something to focus on.

The art was a poor substitute for his dragons, but it was better than going insane.

Fae Realm

The darkness was going swallow her whole. Rhi knew it and accepted it. It was the price she'd pay for fighting Usaeil—and it would be worth it.

The queen had been her friend. It made Rhi sick to her stomach to think of all the times she'd gone to Usaeil with her troubles and listened to the advice the queen had given her. Now, Rhi knew everything Usaeil had said and done was to hurt her.

And Usaeil had accomplished that perfectly.

Rhi walked among the debris and ruins of the destroyed Light Castle. She'd hoped to never see another Fae castle destroyed. But it was bound to happen.

And she was the one who would bring it down. Piece by piece.

Stone by stone.

And Rhi would be smiling when she killed Usaeil.

Coming soon. . . .

DRAGON FIRE
A Dark Kings novel

Available in November 2018